# The Keeping
# of Secrets

*Alice Graysharp*

Clink
Street

London | New York

*Published by Clink Street Publishing 2017*

*Copyright © 2017*

*First edition.*

*ISBN: 978-1-911110-91-0 paperback,*
*978-1-911110-92-7 ebook*

*For my sister*

# Prologue

There are always days in one's life that remain forever fixed in the memory. The first day at school, the birthday when the dream of a special toy came true, the day our dog Peggy arrived, the day my father learnt of his brother Barry's death in that evening's paper.

I am Patricia Adela Roberts and Saturday 2nd September 1939 was the day my war began.

# PART ONE
# WAR

*Extract from a letter to 'the parents of children who have been removed with their schools to places of greater safety'.*

*Dear Sir or Madam,*

*As you know, the Government have made arrangements under which a very large number of children have moved out of the crowded towns for their greater safety from air attack. The children are being provided with board and lodging, and arrangements have also been made for their medical attendance...*

*... a scheme has been drawn up by which parents will be asked to make a reasonable payment towards the cost of keeping their children who are away from home...*

*... the Government have decided to fix 6s a week for each child as a sum which would be accepted as full discharge of this liability...*

*... I am confident that in the great task which lies before us we can rely upon your co-operation and goodwill.*

*Yours sincerely*
*Walter E Elliot*
*Minister of Health*

# I

# Evacuation

'Good mo-or-ning, Pat, dear.' My mother's soft sing-song voice from the doorway woke me from a sleep disturbed by vague dreams of gas masks, suitcases and a ranting little man with a moustache. 'It's nearly a quarter to five and I've finished making your packed lunch, so hurry and get ready and we'll have time for a little breakfast before you go.'

I was suddenly awake and alert, tense like the spring in my wind-up toy, anxieties bubbling up like lava. I looked around my room. Laid out on the chair at the foot of my bed was my school uniform, carefully ironed to a crisp, crease-free finish by my mother the day before. My dressing table stood against the wall opposite my chair, devoid of its usual clutter which was swept up into the case standing open on the floor below the window, ready for my tooth-brush and other last minute items. Except for my gas mask case, crudely yet lovingly made by my mother a year ago, a solitary sentry on the dressing table mat. *Like me*, I thought, *alone*. To the left of my dressing table stood my wardrobe like a towering sentinel, dark wood casting a shadow from the landing light.

Reaching out, I switched on my bedside lamp as no discernible daylight edged the blackout curtains. The room sprang into focus and I hastened out of bed, grabbing my dressing gown, and tiptoeing along the landing and in through the kitchen door to the partitioned-off toilet.

Vacating the toilet, I moved into the tiny kitchen created from the remainder of the original bathroom of the house. A wooden grooved draining board, on which my mother had stacked last night's dishes, sloped from the toilet room wall into a deep stone rectangular sink, beneath which lay a freestanding cupboard for pots and pans; to its left, jammed in between the sink and the board-covered bath, stood a small square table on which sat my father's bread tins. The wall between the door and the foot of the bath boasted the gas cooker with low cabinets either side providing further storage space. At the foot of the bath itself a cabinet had been hung on the wall.

I loved this miniscule kitchen. It was a step up from our previous lodgings where we'd made do with a Kitchener set in the hearth of the living room. A real kitchen created the illusion of permanence. My childhood was constantly peppered with moves from one kind of temporary accommodation to another. *Maybe evacuation will give me a proper home with a front door that I won't have to share with other tenants,* I thought, *and somewhere to live until the coming war's over without being constantly uprooted. A cottage in the country with a white picket fence and roses around the door.*

Setting my fantasy aside, I smiled wanly at my tall, slim, brown-haired mother scrambling eggs vigorously behind me as I washed hands and face briefly in the kitchen sink. Returning to my room, dressing, brushing and shaping my shoulder-length wavy chestnut brown hair, I stopped as I was about to stoop to cram my hairbrush into my case.

My reflection looked solemnly back at me from the mirror on the wall above the dressing table. High cheekbones, my father's blue-grey eyes and my mother's beaklike nose. I pursed my lineal lips, the top one relieved by two tiny peaks. I wondered if anyone would ever find me attractive and whether I would ever believe them if they said I was. I remembered a girl, aware of my presence, mocking me loudly to her friends the other side of the protruding rows of coat hooks in the changing room. 'That Patricia Roberts, she's so stuck up and ugly, what boy would ever take a fancy to her, and with that nose…!'

*Trust no one and you won't be disappointed*, was my motto. Although acquainted with girls at school, I had no close friends there. I did not dare get too close to any, partly because I feared they would ultimately let me down (after all, my parents had let me down when I was a child and they were my *parents*) and partly because there were family secrets my mother was determined should not be shared with anyone, and so discouraged me from pursuing school friendships in case I inadvertently let the cat out of the bag. I felt isolated. I hated my face and I resented my mature figure with breasts that had filled out alarmingly by the age of thirteen, envying slender, fashionably willowy girls at school. *At least my waist is fairly small*, I conceded, *but that only makes my bust and my bottom look proportionately larger. Still, none of that matters either way as don't want to step out with a young man. Well, not until I'm, oh, at least twenty-five and in a teaching career and earning decent money so I'm not beholden to anyone. And on the shelf, far too old.*

My mother called from the doorway of the living room, 'Breakfast's on the table.' She returned to the kitchen. I shook my head clear of my thoughts, shoved my hairbrush into my case and moved towards the living room.

The door between my room and the living room opened and my grandmother's silvery topped head peered round.

'So this is it, my dear,' she said, her square, heavy-jawed face creased with concern. 'Nearly time to go.'

'So sorry, Nan,' I said, moving towards her and hugging her in a dance of good morning and good bye. 'I didn't mean you to be disturbed.'

As tall as me and solidly built, Nan enveloped me with her affection.

'D'you think I could sleep well, knowing you're off to God knows where?' she demanded. She paused. 'I'll share a cuppa with you before you go.'

Grabbing her dressing gown Nan followed me into the adjacent room which, with a shared function of sitting room and dining room, was something of an obstacle course when the drop down table was opened out in the centre of the arm-chair circle. Peggy, a brown cocker spaniel and dachshund mix, now an old lady in dog years, yawned and stretched her front legs, then trotted over from her basket near the fireplace to nuzzle me as I slid onto a dining chair on the far side, and Nan took one opposite me. My mother followed us in and settled a brimming teapot on its little stand, covering it with the green and pink crocheted tea cosy, last Christmas' present from Nan to my parents. The tea cosy was reasonably sympathetic to our best pink rose tea service, but clashed a little with the functional yellow dinner service set out for breakfast. As a budding artist, colour coordination mattered to me. A crocheted mat of the same two bright colours stood on my dressing table, Nan's last Christmas present to me, and I made a mental note to add it to my case to take a special token of my world away with me.

I felt a little nauseous at the sight of the scrambled eggs and bacon mounted on toast, my stomach churning at the day ahead. I thought of my only friend Bill, most likely also getting ready for evacuation with his school right now. *He* wouldn't be nervous but, rather, excited about it, his zest for life and his love of the dramatic feeding the adrenaline. Bill was the nearest I had to a brother. We grew up alongside each other and whenever our respective parents got together he and I were left to entertain ourselves. Only six months older than me, he was in the same school year and when I was younger I sometimes pretended to myself that we were long lost twins. I loved looking at his *Boys' Own* magazines and playing with his tin train set. Although I had a doll, I always thought that Bill's toys were far more interesting than mine. As a young child I was convinced that when I grew up I would be able to choose whether to be a woman or a man, and I wanted to be the same as Bill. I was eight years old when I learnt to my horror that I was stuck with being a girl forever. It seemed to me that the boys had all the fun and the girls were expected to cook and clean and stay at home, whereas I loved to play with mechanical gadgets and longed to travel and visit all the exotic countries revealed by the pages of Bill's *Boys' Own* and my own set of the *Children's Encyclopaedia*. And I was comfortable with Bill in ways I didn't trust girls or grownups. He didn't demand emotional commitment or a swapping of secrets and confidences. Despite the endless practical jokes he played on me, or perhaps because of them, I grew to feel safe in a boy's world, so much less complicated than girls' endless petty arguments and friendships that waxed and waned according to mood.

'Come along, eat up, dear,' urged my mother, cutting across my thoughts. 'It'll be a long time to lunch.'

Ever the dutiful daughter I forced down breakfast and sipped my tea, and made a fuss of Peggy. 'Goodbye, old girl,' I said, stroking her head, and I slipped away to finish packing. Just the toothbrush now, and the dressing table mat, and, kneeling on the case, I forced the lid down just enough for the locks to catch and strapped my thin blanket roll to its side.

It was a little after half past five and time to set off. Nan kissed me and pressed a small silver sixpence into my hand, forcing it back as I mutely tried to return it. 'Never look a gift horse in the mouth,' she ordered, adding, 'I'll say goodbye up here,' and, holding back Peggy, shooed me and my mother towards the stairs.

As I turned at the stair head I looked round towards the back room, my parent's bedroom, chosen when we moved into the upper floor of the house so that my father could sleep through the daytime at the rear undisturbed by the clatter of trams at the nearby junction of Brixton Water Lane and Effra Road. I said a mental goodbye to him, at that moment finishing up another gruelling night's work at Nevill's bakery in Herne Hill.

My mother accompanied me down the stairs and out to the front gate and I turned to hug her goodbye. In the dingy drab half-light of the forthcoming morning I shivered, the chill of the hour exacerbated by the parting from all I knew. I thought I would cry, my mother catching her breath too and we looked at each other like conspirators determined to defeat the enemy of fear. *Yes*, I told myself, *I will see Mummy and Daddy again soon and, no, we might not all be dead before then.* Hugging my mother in a last embrace as she smiled tremulously at me, her blue eyes glistening, I smiled back, picked up my case and stepped out in the cool pre-dawn morning air.

Turning right from the end of Brixton Water Lane towards the foot of Tulse Hill, I gave my mother one last wave, gripping my little suitcase more firmly, settling my gas mask case – hanging from its long shoulder strap across my body – against my right hip, checking my packed lunch in a bag hanging over my right shoulder, and setting my face to the future.

Halfway up the hill I saw my father in the distance returning from his night's work. I knew he would be exhausted from standing baking loaves for London's hungry mouths and he could have caught an early tram home, taking a different route along the side of Brockwell Park. But he'd chosen the more circuitous option, knowing this was his last opportunity to see me before I disappeared into the unknown, his last chance to say goodbye. Beneath his short dark brown slicked back hair his grey eyes seemed brighter and bluer with unuttered emotion.

'Well, my girl, chin up and good luck, I'll see you again soon.'

Yet we knew neither when nor where that would be. I patted my pocket in which resided a blank postcard for me to send home my new address – when I had one.

'I'll write straight away, I'll let you know where I've slung my hammock,' I said a little breathlessly.

Daddy smiled at this metaphorical reference to his adolescent seafaring days about which he had regaled me through my childhood. An inch shorter than me now, his wide smile gave him a larger presence.

'Off you go, don't be late,' he chivvied. We embraced briefly and parted, moving off in our different directions, and I paused further up watching his figure fading down the hill. I raised my hand in a last wave as he looked briefly back. Swallowing the lump in my throat and blinking back my tears I carried on up to school.

Travelling away from home on my own was not a new adventure. Only a week ago I had returned from a visit to my cousin Jane in Hythe on the Kent coast, a trip foreshortened by the threat of war, my father telephoning to say that schoolchildren were being recalled from the summer holidays early. Fighting my way through the pandemonium of Hythe bus station, journeying alone to a different London bus terminus than usual, I considered myself, at fifteen years of age, a seasoned traveller. But today, I felt, was different. Although I would be travelling with my classmates, I felt alone, facing a future devoid of shape and structure, looming menacingly, like a deep, dark cavern.

Reaching school, I joined the throng of girls making their way indoors.

'Line up, girls, into your new classes, then we'll sort you into groups of ten pupils each,' Miss Landing, the Headmistress, directed at the milling crowd of parents and offspring in the school's grand, elegant main hall left unlit as there was no blackout at the high windows. The girls moved into ranks like soldiers on parade, spectres in the gloom of the soft dawn light, and the parents retreated to the hall's perimeter. I felt envious of the girls whose parents were seeing them off, but this morning my father needed his meal and his sleep.

St Martin-in-the-Fields school, proud of its 1699 foundation, had relocated in 1928 from its Charing Cross Road location, near its mother church at the edge of Trafalgar Square, to the leafy and spacious acreage of Tulse Hill and was honoured by its official opening there by the Queen, at that time the Duchess of York. The school was fronted by an elegant Georgian mansion with the new classrooms and school hall bolted on behind, all now to be abandoned to the vagaries of war.

I looked around at the portraits of the bewigged founders hanging along the side wall, and up at the portrait above the entrance door of a young girl in the brown uniform decreed at the time, cuffed sleeves ending just below the elbow, bodice overlaid with a deep rectangular split white collar, floor length skirt protected by a white pinafore and head topped with a white lace cap. She was holding a book in her right hand, her other arm and forefinger extended, as if pointing to the future. I wondered what my future held. As I moved into line with my classmates I batted away unhappy memories of early years' antipathy from paying girls wearing older siblings' hand-me-downs who resented me for the shiny new uniform of a scholarship girl. Despite the down times this school was my second home and I would miss it. *This will be my last year,* I thought, *before School Certificate exams next summer. Four years here gone already.*

Distantly I heard Miss Landing reminding the class teachers to check all pupils had their gas masks and blank postcards before we could set off. Gas masks were issued to us all a year earlier by Government instructors who demonstrated how to put them on and breathe through them. Claustrophobic and smelling of new rubber, the eye glasses of mine misting over, I had felt a sense of rising panic within an enveloping darkness. I looked down at my homemade gas mask case. The school's notification required waterproof lining material, suggesting American cloth or Woolworth's waterproof sheeting, the case to be *light in weight, and be worn on a long strap over the shoulder, in order to leave the hands free.* My mother made it with the Woolworth's waterproof sheeting. For a year my gas mask had personified the threat of war, yet now that war was virtually upon us there was a sense of unreality, as if I was in caught in the grip of a dream from which I would suddenly awake and find myself lying in my comfortable bed breathing a sigh of relief.

Miss Landing's address to the assembled pupils jerked me from my musings.

'Girls,' she declared, her voice well practiced with the art of projection, her gnarled hands clasped dramatically in front of her, her grey, bun-topped head held defiantly high, 'today is probably the most momentous day for our school since we were honoured with the presence of Her Majesty. For today you will become ambassadors for St Martin-in-the-Fields in a new place and in new circumstances that will test every fibre of your being. Separation from home may not be easy for some but we must all play our part in the coming war. Your fellow pupils will be your family and our teachers will do their best to provide you with the parenting care and advice you may need. Be kind to those who miss their homes and encourage each other to apply yourselves to your work so that you may emerge stronger from the new life upon which you are about to embark. Be polite to those strangers who are taking upon themselves the daily task of caring for you in their homes. I am confident that you will all be a credit to our school. Live up to our school motto, *mind measures man*. Work hard to learn as much as you can but also use your common sense in caring for those around you.'

After a slight pause to ensure that we all reflected on her homily, Miss Landing continued. 'We will shortly make our way to West Norwood Station. From there we will travel to Leatherhead where we are to share the premises of St Birstan's School for Boys.'

A slight murmur rippled through the hall, quelled by Miss Landing's steely glare. 'I shall expect my girls to behave with due modesty and decorum. You will be co-travellers along the road of education and learning.

'In a few moments we will leave in our groups. First we shall sing our school song, the closing words of which have an extra special resonance for us today.

'*From here into the world we'll fare,*' Miss Landing, stepping forward a pace, extended an arm dramatically, '*The wrong to fight, the right to dare / Remembering whose cloak we wear / St. Martin-in-the-Fields.*'

Miss Landing nodded to Miss Matthews seated expectantly at the grand piano, who immediately struck up the introduction and we sang of the saint who had cut his cloak '*in twain*' and given half to a poor freezing beggar beside the road. *What happened to the Lord's exhortation to give both the whole cloak* and *the shirt off your back as well*? I wondered cynically.

After the scramble for the toilets that followed – for who knew when the next opportunity might arise – we formed up in our groups outside in the rosy glow of the rising morning sun which was steaming off the early misty wisps. We set off. The air was chill on my cheeks and my ungloved hands as we made our way south in a seemingly unending crocodile towards Tulse Hill station, beyond which lay West Norwood.

'What's your lunch?' asked my brown-eyed companion, Joyce, as we walked, her wiry brown hair flying at the turn of her head.

'Mine's meat paste sandwiches,' interjected Vera over her shoulder from in front. She was shorter than Janet beside her, round of face, excitable and bouncy.

'I've got *real* meat in mine,' responded Janet, of medium height, curvaceous and oval faced, her blond shoulder length hair caught back in a ponytail. I was just about to chime in with my Edam cheese and cucumber sandwiches when:

'No talking, girls, decorum, decorum,' boomed Miss Marchant beside the line just ahead.

'What's decorum?' asked Vera, turning her head further round and bumping against Janet. As they recovered their stride, Joyce, herself skipping lightly to avoid the heels in front, quipped, 'A little Roman town near Bath,' and we all snorted and tittered at this well-worn double act, until Miss Marchant turned and quieted us with her famous Look.

As we reached the junction of Tulse Hill and Christchurch Road the crocodile was brought to an abrupt halt, shuddering and shunting like wagons on a goods train.

'What's going on?' hissed Vera as we cannoned into her and Janet, the girls behind us cannoning into Joyce and me in turn.

I stood on tiptoe, peering over the heads beyond me, my natural height giving me an advantage. But it was the sound that met me first. Steady, inexorable, relentless, rhythmic. It sent a shiver down my spine and a churning to my stomach. Troop movements. Yesterday evening the wireless news reported Hitler's invasion of Poland. War between us and Germany, as yet still undeclared, was inevitable. Today, while the nation held its collective breath, troops were being moved to their units in readiness. Ahead of us was proof, had we needed it, that the whole country was standing on the edge of the precipice and about to plummet. I rocked back down onto my heels. There was no need for me to say anything and I stood silent, cowed by the enormity of the future, a hard lump in my throat and an overwhelming feeling of loss.

After a while the crocodile resumed its previous momentum and, passing by Tulse Hill Station, moved on south to West Norwood Station where we saw a train waiting for us, one, I learnt later, of one thousand five hundred special trains laid on that weekend to carry London's children away to places of greater safety.

At first the train trundled along slowly, then faster and faster as grey grimy buildings gave way to green gardens and wavy washing lines. Girls chattered beside me in our ten-person compartment, some diving into their food, but I felt distant and dislocated, my thoughts concentrated on the coming war. I recalled my childhood memories of maimed beggars at street corners, the flotsam of the Great War, for whom I went home and wept. Last year we had the mock evacuation day when gas masks became a part of our school uniform. In newspapers and in newsreels at cinemas the Germans depicted themselves as victims, needing more room to live than was available and claiming they were picked on when Germans moved out of Germany to settle in nearby countries. Hitler's injured innocence and ranting rhetoric stalked his speeches and we had all laughed at the films of him leaping up and down, a comic figure shouting and screaming, sweating and spitting. I was not laughing now.

Leaning forward, across from me in the carriage, Kitty, dark, slender, waif-like, cut across my reverie, asking, 'Aren't you hungry?', her narrow head tilting like a listening bird. I drew my thoughts back to the present, feeling a little nauseous as the world flashed by my window seat, and shook my head.

'I'm starving,' declared a cheerfully countenanced dark-haired Gwen, sitting to Kitty's left and already halfway through her first sandwich. She turned to Joyce, my partner in the crocodile, now seated on Gwen's other side. 'Here, would you like one of my rich teas for a piece of your short-bread?'

'I can swap cream crackers with anyone,' offered Nora at the far end, a long-faced girl whose straight, dark hair held back in an old-fashioned plait gave an impression of studiousness, belied by a lively personality and a laugh of loud guffaws.

'*Look*,' cried Vera, beside me, jogging my arm as she pointed across me. 'Cows, sheep, this is *such* an adventure!'

'It'll be dark in the country,' Kitty quavered. 'Do you think some of us'll end up on a farm?'

'It was dark already in London last night,' countered Gwen, yawning. 'My mother went to Brixton market weeks ago and found some really thick dark curtaining, but, typical of her, she left it until the last minute to run them up.'

'My Dad just bought black paint for half our windows,' said Vera.

'I'd like to stay on a farm.' Gwen continued her response to Kitty's question. 'I might get to ride horses. I've always wanted to ride one. This evacuation business could turn out to be the best thing ever.'

'Trust you to look on the bright side,' said Kitty, turning to her. 'I think evacuation's perfectly *horrid*.'

'How can you say that? We haven't even got there yet,' challenged Gwen.

Kitty burst into tears. Gwen, contrite, put a comforting arm round Kitty, while Vera leaned across the carriage and patted her arm.

Smiling sympathetically at Kitty, I thought, *part of me knows how you feel. I'll miss Mummy and Daddy and Nan and Peggy. But things might not be so bad. Maybe I'll get to live in just one place for the whole time, maybe right through to the end of the sixth form, if this war lasts as long as everyone thinks it will.*

The girls settled back and the chatting resumed around me while the sun blazed in through the window and sweat trickled down and tickled my back. Early September was in the grip of a heatwave but we were evacuated in our winter uniforms – a treble pleated brown tunic, a long sleeved blouse, fine cotton 'Lisle' stockings and a plaited belt of woven material tied in a slip knot around our waists, all topped by a dark, deep rich chestnut brown winter coat!

I shook myself from my musings and joined in the hubbub. Feeling more relaxed, I opened my packed lunch only to find the train drawing to a halt in Leatherhead station. Hastily I scrambled the food back into its bag.

'Crocodile, girls,' commanded Miss Marchant and we marched smartly off in a long column, two abreast, Joyce again beside me, away from the station and round to the left at the end of the approach road, and left again into Kingston Road. About a quarter of a mile along on the right stood a smart new building with a round-ended protruding multi-paned window lying above a wide front delivery area. We trudged up some stairs towards a hall on the first floor. A large handwritten sign beside the entrance declared it to be the Evacuee Distribution Centre. Several of us dived for the toilets in the entrance foyer.

Passing into the hall I was momentarily distracted by a booming, "Eere's yer rations,' from a jolly red-faced lady who handed out paper bags from a pile on a large table beyond her. I peered into mine as I made my way to my class line up and found a big tin of corned beef, a small tin of baked beans and a small tin of evaporated milk. I clutched the food bag in one hand and placed my half-sized case on the floor close beside me. Last year on the practice evacuation day everyone brought full-sized cases and many struggled to lift them, bumping into others' legs, hogging valuable space in cramped pretend railway carriages and generally being such a nuisance that for the real event we were ordered to bring half-sized cases only.

A gaggle of people, mainly women, stood to one side of the hall raking us with assessing eyes. *We're just parcels of goods in a factory*, I thought, *packed, labelled and ready for distribution.*

The Evacuation Centre was initially crowded, the adults walking round the classes, like overseers buying slaves at a slave market but, as the local people chose girls to stay with them and headed off, gradually the numbers thinned out and the cacophony died down. Younger girls seemed to be the preference, older ones less attractive. I was so hungry that the table at the end of the hall laden with cakes and steaming cups of tea was torture, but I was determined to stay in my place in case I was missed. Eventually there were only a few of us older ones left, with no one remaining to choose us.

I stood in the centre of the hall with one of my crocodile companions, blonde, busty Janet, and with Becky, a tall, slender black-haired and brown-eyed girl with whom I was only vaguely acquainted. My anxiety was rising. *Where will I sleep tonight? The grownups have let us down. There's nowhere to go.* Feeling bereft, lightheaded through lack of food, and thoroughly miserable, I was immensely relieved when one of the organisers came up to us and said, 'I've got an address for you three. Transport has just arrived.'

We were driven by car, a rare treat for a working class London girl, to a house in Givens Grove on the southern outskirts of Leatherhead. Turning into a road lined with trees, I welcomed the breeze through the lowered window. The car swept onto a smaller gravelled road followed by a short driveway running up to the house. I felt like royalty as the chauffeur hastened out of the car and round to my door to open it for me.

As we disembarked, the front door opened and a tall, thin grey-haired lady in a grey dress emerged. 'I'm Mrs Harris, the housekeeper,' she announced grandly. *Mrs Harris, the Housekeeper*, I thought. *Like someone in Happy Families. And is this man Monsieur Charabanc le Chauffeur?*

We followed Mrs Harris to the kitchen. I felt horrendously hot and hungry. The house seemed immense around me, and through the kitchen window I spied a swimming pool in the back garden. I thought of my parents, my grandmother and me being grateful to have rented rooms on the upper floor of a terraced house in crowded London.

Mrs Harris offered us some water which I quaffed greedily like Lawrence of Arabia at an oasis.

'Now you've drunk your water, follow me to your room,' ordered Mrs Harris. To my surprise we were not led upstairs to a bedroom but along the hallway to a rear sitting room with easels, some with paintings on them, set out along the far wall.

'I love art,' I ventured, whereupon Mrs Harris sniffed, 'Mr Briggs does his painting here. You are *not* to touch *anything.*'

I spied a painting of a naked woman. While I was unfazed as I was used to nude paintings owing to my passion for art, I wondered what my parents might think if they saw it there!

''Zare you are!'

In bustled a portly and heavily made-up lady in a tweed skirt and flamboyant lace-bedecked white blouse. I gathered she was French. 'I am Meesis Briggs.'

We hastily introduced ourselves. Mrs Briggs merely nodded at each of us in turn, not even a handshake, although I was relieved she also passed on the traditional French-style kissing of total strangers on both cheeks.

'Meesis 'Arree will see to you and find you some bread for your tea.' Mrs Briggs' strong perfume had preceded her and it lingered as she strode from the room.

At last I had the opportunity to consume my sandwiches. Sitting gingerly on a delicate spindly chair, I wolfed them down while my companions unpacked their meagre belongings. After I finished I was still hungry, and was now thirsty again.

We settled down to write our new address on our postcards. I was deputed to find Mrs Harris to check the correct address as we had not noticed a house number.

'There are no house numbers in this road,' she sniffed, tilting her head back and looking down her nose at me despite being a couple of inches shorter. 'It's Givens House.' *You could have been nicer about it*, I thought. *What a truly horrid welcome.*

After returning and completing my own unpacking I felt restless, and Janet must have too. 'Let's go for a walk into Leatherhead town and explore it a bit,' she suggested. 'It's not even six yet and we can check what time to be back for supper.'

We looked for Mrs Harris but it seemed she had gone home. There was no sign of supper being prepared, and Mrs Briggs was not in the offing either, so Janet scribbled a note which we left on the hall table. We let ourselves out and set off north into Leatherhead, the warm early evening sun streaming onto our left shoulders across the fields as we retraced the route the car had brought us. After a few minutes the church I had spotted earlier hoved into view and, turning right, we climbed up the longstepped path to its west door. I turned round at the top and stood with my eyes closed, the wide, square, chequer-board edged tower looming up behind me. Soaking in the late sun's rays, funnelled through the fir trees lining the steps, I breathed in slowly, conifer scents mingling with the perfume of the grasses and late summer flowers, laced with a distant edge that was a little unpleasant and sour. I opened my eyes and saw the fields beyond the houses ahead glowing golden like a sepia photograph and the seated cows lying like boulders deposited randomly by a retreating ice age. Brixton seemed a distant planet away.

Janet tried the west door but it was locked. 'I'll see if there are any notices outside about tomorrow's services,' she said, disappearing along the side of the church. Becky and I followed.

There was no one about to ask, but the side door was unlocked so we slipped inside and found a notice that said 8am Holy Communion and 11am Matins.

We meandered up a road running at right angles to the church's side door, past a Methodist church on our left, and on to what transpired to be the top end of the High Street, its entrance dominated by a grand, red-brick building with stone-edged windows and imposing wings at either end. The central arched doorway proudly declared the Leatherhead Institute to have been erected in 1892. Outside a couple of ladies stood chatting and, emboldened, I crossed the road to ask,

'Excuse me, we would be most grateful if you could point us in the direction of St Birstan's School.'

'You're from the girls' school sent here to keep those boys in order?' one of the ladies asked, smiling indulgently and giving us directions. 'Second along the main road, then left, then right again and just past the recreation ground.' She looked at us dubiously. 'It's a bit of a walk.'

We thanked her and crossed the junction. A car motored slowly by, but the road seemed deserted compared with the bustle of trams, cars, buses and delivery lorries which carved their way from the south through Brixton to central London's busy streets. A little way along the main road we turned right, weaving through side streets, and about ten minutes later reached our goal.

'Golly gaiters!' exclaimed Janet as a four-storeyed ornately gothic Victorian grey stone building came into view beyond an imposing closed railinged gateway. Our own gentle Georgian school frontage seemed modest in comparison. The drive ran up to the large double fronted door that lay partially open as boys were exiting in a crocodile towards the separate red brick chapel on our right. Heads turned in our direction as we were spotted gawping at a scene from Tom Brown's schooldays.

'It must be a boarding school,' whispered Becky.

Janet chuckled. 'Shall we join them, girls, for their service, and lighten up their evening?' and we sniggered slightly.

'Strange, on a Saturday,' I mused, 'to have a church service, perhaps they're Roman Catholics?'

'Or perhaps they have a Saturday evening assembly to keep them out of mischief in the town,' Becky chuckled.

A few of the stragglers, older boys perhaps our age, waved in our direction. Janet, even more generously endowed than me, pressing herself against the bars, her breasts extending through, waved back and blew them a few kisses through the gate. 'Janet!' I exclaimed, a little shocked at this forward behaviour; meanwhile the boys, responding, were being sharply admonished by a tall, thin master sporting a flowing black gown.

Spectacle over, we returned to the top end of the High Street which sloped down to an impressively grand multi-gabled mock Tudor building dominating the far end. We walked down past the King's Head on the left, Gregory's bakery and tearooms on the right, and numerous small shops. Grocer, butcher, ironmonger, haberdashery, shoe shop, boot repairer. All that was missing was the candlestick-maker.

We greeted the few other St Martin's girls like us out on an exploratory jaunt. At the bottom of the hill, set slightly back on the right and just short of the mock-Tudor building, there emerged a truly imposing modern edifice with single and double ionic columns stretching skywards between two storeys of office windows above the shops below. By now the sun was getting low, a slight evening chill descending. We hurried left past the newly built Crescent Cinema in Church Street bedecked with posters and completed the circle at the parish church, then on through the glooming back to Givens Grove.

Mrs Briggs was waiting for us in her front lounge.

"Zere you are, you *naughty* girls!' she scolded. 'Meesis 'Arree found your note when she return from zee kitchen garden but now 'as 'ad to go 'ome so I 'ave 'ad to wait for you, I 'ave better use for my time!'

We muttered our apologies.

Mrs Briggs sniffed and added, as she swept from the room, 'Your supperrr is in zee kitchen.'

We hastened off, to be met by a plate of stale bread, no butter and a pot of tepid tea. Retrieving our food bags from our room, we shared out some, saving the remainder for another time. Tired and still hungry, we settled ourselves for an early night. I shot the bolt on the inside of the door and climbed onto the Ottoman divan; it was narrow, hard and lumpy with no sheet, only a blanket provided that scratched my neck, barely augmented by my own thin blanket. Janet and Becky shared the four-foot-wide 'double' bed.

I lay awake for a while, the events of the day churning in my head. I felt let down by the sheer discomfort of my bed and the unfriendly welcome. I was also angry with myself. My fantasy of a kindly, motherly hostess doling out plentiful dollops of steaming food was sadly awry. *Trust no one and you won't be disappointed*, I reminded myself, swallowing an unbidden lump of self-pity.

The early start eventually caught up with me and I was

sound asleep when, just around dawn, we were woken by a loud knocking on the door to the room. We started up and I climbed off the Ottoman, and nervously unbolted and opened the door. It was Mrs Briggs, who exclaimed, 'Oh, you *naughty* girrls, what iz ze lock doing on ze door? Do you know zere was a storm in ze night?'

We were so exhausted we had all slept through it.

She carried on, 'One of you used ze barzroom for 'arf an 'our last night, my 'usband wanted to use ze barzroom but it was not available!'

I remained silent. That was me!

Drawing in a deep breath laden with disapproval, Mrs Briggs added, 'From zis morning, girls, you will use *my* room.'

Feeling chastised and deflated, I staggered back to bed for a couple more hours' sleep. Later, Mrs Briggs showed us her huge exotically decorated bedroom, hung with heavily-braided bright yellow damask, with a curtained-off area in the corner containing a bath where were required to wash. We hurriedly washed and dressed and found our way to a deserted kitchen. The table seemed to be laid out for breakfast but on drawing closer I saw there were only stale crusts, a jar of indeterminate jam and a teapot.

'Ugh, what kind of breakfast is this?' I exclaimed, smearing the hardened crust with a layer of reddish brown goo from the pot of homemade jam.

Becky held her crust up to the light and sniffed it. 'I think it's meant to be strawberry jam,' she ventured.

I tentatively licked the top of my crust and recoiled at the acrid taste. 'Burnt strawberry jam you mean.'

Janet said, 'My mother always gives me porridge and a boiled egg and toast for breakfast, there must be something else to come.'

But there wasn't.

'Will you come with Janet and me to church?' I asked Becky hesitantly, not wishing to offend her, but not wanting her to feel left out. I vaguely recollected that Becky was Jewish but I had seen her in school assemblies and I knew there were girls whose parents were of a liberal Jewish persuasion.

'Yes, I will,' decided Becky. 'My parents told me to do the same as everyone else. They said I have to eat everything I'm given,' she added confidingly, 'even if it's pork.'

We made our way to Leatherhead Parish Church for Matins, arriving early as we didn't know how full the church would be. It was as well we did. Already it was almost full and we squeezed in near the back.

It was Sunday 3rd September 1939.

We sat in the pew awaiting the introduction to the first hymn. The vicar stood up and turned on the wireless that was placed in pride of place on a low table at the head of the chancel steps. It crackled into life and we sat electrified as Neville Chamberlain, the prime minister, told us of his efforts to avoid war and how an ultimatum had been given to Germany to withdraw from Poland and how the deadline of eleven o'clock had passed. He ended with the words,

'This country is now at war with Germany.'

The charged silence was broken by a low moan from a woman in the row in front and about halfway up the church another exclaimed softly, 'God help us all!' Another sobbed, 'Not again.' I sat in the pew feeling a little nauseous, waiting for the introduction to the first hymn and wondering if German soldiers were about to rain down from the skies and surround the church.

A dreadful rising and falling wailing sound erupted. Janet beside me jumped and I leaned into Becky and murmured, 'There's something wrong with the organ.'

Becky heard me faintly over the banshee and, glancing at me and deciding I was not being facetious, shook her head. 'I think it's an air raid siren,' she mouthed back.

I looked back at her in horror, my heart suddenly thudding. 'Air raid! Already?'

The vicar and other dignitaries sat stock still while many of the congregation twisted around in their seats, exclaiming anxiously, and some started to rise. A man in air raid warden's uniform rushed in through the side entrance, gesturing to the congregation to stay put as the siren tailed off.

Moving to the chancel steps, the vicar announced the first hymn, *O God Our Help In Ages Past*. Beloved of Armistice Day services, it now seemed to mock the future. Trust God, it seemed to say. *But where will God be when the Germans come knocking at the door of our shores?* I felt ashamed at my lack of faith while others around were belting out the hymn, and slightly sick, the acrid taste of overcooked homemade strawberry jam burning at the back of my throat. During the service several people pushed their way outside, seemingly overcome by the emotion of the occasion and I was glad to escape at the end into the warm sunlight and reassure myself that no invasion had begun.

Returning to the house the smell of roasting meat and boiling vegetables cheered me a little. The meagre breakfast and the walk to church and back had left me ravenous. After toileting and hand-washing we thought it best to congregate in the kitchen where an aproned, harassed lady we had not met before clattered and banged the pots and pans on the huge cooking range. *A cook, a housekeeper and a chauffeur,* I thought. *What next, a maid?*

The square table at which we breakfasted earlier supported steaming bowls and sauce- and gravy-boats and was not laid out for us. I was about to suggest decamping straight to the dining room when the back door to the kitchen opened and Mrs Harris stepped in. 'Oh, good, you're ready for a prompt lunch,' she said, indicating a side table against the far wall boasting three decrepit wooden chairs and some cutlery. She crossed the kitchen to the pantry and emerged a moment later with a large plate, on which sat a few slices of cold ham, a jar of pickled onions and three small bread rolls, which she deposited on the table. I sat down, silenced by incredulity, while Becky busied herself with getting a jug of water and three glasses, and we sat and ate our repast, Janet observing to Becky, 'Good job your parents said to eat pork,' and escaped to our room as quickly as we could.

I felt choked with disappointment. 'Well, Mrs Briggs certainly knows how to keep us in our place. Perhaps I'll ask my parents to bring me some extra food at the weekend.'

That was the signal for us to dive for writing pens and paper. I wrote to my parents describing the past twenty-four hours in some detail and ended, *so if you can bring a little extra food when you come to see me you will have one extremely grateful daughter.*

Stale crusts augmented by some of my corned beef for supper did little to assuage my hunger and that night I slept fitfully. At some point I dreamt I was lost in a hay-field, lying down on a bed of straw, only to come to with my scratchy blanket wrapped around my neck. Janet and Becky's night was again punctuated with 'Oi's and 'Ouch'es, as they repeatedly encountered each other unexpectedly in the 'double' bed.

The new morning saw us entering the school grounds, which proved to be very extensive, laid out to the rear of the imposing frontage we had seen the previous Saturday evening. The Victorian building at the rear ran along three sides of a grassy quadrangle. A more modern two-storeyed section made up the left side of the quadrangle and contained classrooms and science laboratories on the ground floor with a large room on the top floor. Daily assembly was to be held by St Martin's School in this upper room. Girls chattered excitedly around me comparing their billets, and I heard Gwen exclaiming to Nora nearby, 'The most *extraordinary* thing! I'm staying on a *farm!*'

Following our first assembly of the new term, we handed in our address postcards to be posted by the school to our parents. I made a mental note to later post the letter I had written. We were dispersed around church halls and sports halls in the town for the morning lessons. My morning of Mathematics, Biology and Keep Fit spent in the Methodists' church hall seemed to last for ever.

Just after midday I sat with Becky and Janet eating my four-penny lunch at the Scout Hut feeling miserable and disorientated.

'It's English next, I think,' ventured Janet, scrabbling in her bag to find the new timetable.

Becky perused her copy. 'Yes, but that's not at the Methodists' hall. It says here that English is to be held in the Parish Hall, even though we were told that most afternoon lessons'll be held in the science block at St Birstan's.'

We studied the street map with which each of us had been issued.

'We must have passed it as we walked in this morning,' I said, 'but look at the time, we'll be late if we don't hurry,' and we downed the rest of our food quickly, and hastened away.

By late afternoon I was ravenously hungry again.

'I could eat a horse,' declared Becky as we trudged wearily back to our out-of-town billet.

'If you're not careful, we will!' snorted Janet and we all chuckled at the allusion to Mrs Briggs' French origins. The memory of the strong, sickly smell of horsemeat cooking in the poverty-stricken back streets of south London washed over me and I shuddered and breathed in deeply the fresh sweet-scented country air around me.

We were again fed only with the Briggs' leftovers and the stale crusts from their meals the day before, supplemented with some of the remains of the rations handed to us on our first day. After doing this for a couple more days the rations ran out.

'Now, girrrls' said Mrs Briggs, late on our first Friday afternoon, 'Eef you 'ave no 'omework ziz evening you can make yourselves useful around 'ere,' and produced a set of weeding tools which she presented to us. Clearly, when our heads were not in our schoolbooks we were expected to weed her garden, which mainly involved removing clover from the lawn. So instead of the honoured guest I had expected to be, I and my companions were relegated to the bottom of the skivvy pile. The only relief from the dreadful misery in which I felt plunged was the letter from my parents which arrived on the Saturday morning. They were coming to see me the very next day. I was relieved to see that that the nude painting had meanwhile been removed from our room.

'Mummy, Daddy,' I cried as I ran along the platform to greet them on Sunday morning. After a flurry of hugs and kisses, I linked my arms in theirs and we strolled through the town, past the parish church and on to my strange new home. My mother was only twenty years older than me and we were often taken for sisters. She wore a pretty floral print summer dress and a tailored beige jacket with a narrow brimmed beige hat tilted at a jaunty angle. My father, an inch shorter than my mother when in stockinged feet, walked smartly upright in his grey flannels and her-ringboned sports jacket, his head topped by a trilby. He carried a small bag of non-perishable food.

Daddy's quizzically raised eyebrow was his only reaction to our surroundings on arriving at the house but my mother was more forthright.

'And what are your arrangements for my daughter to do her washing?' she demanded of Mrs Briggs, who dramatically threw her arms up in the air and declared 'She iz *not* doing zat *'ere!*'

Feeling unwelcome, my parents elected to take me to a cafe in the town which was fortunately open for Sunday lunch; it was crowded with other evacuees and their families and expensive. With a bag of unplanned washing to transport, my parents decided to return home earlier than origi-nally intended. The sight of the receding train chuffing my parents and my washing back to our snug little home in the heart of London blurred as, fighting the threatened tears, I waved harder, murmuring, 'See you again soon,' but feeling as bereft as if 'soon' was next year.

The following Sunday morning, depositing a bag of freshly laundered clothes and linen in my room, my mother whirled away, a human tornado, to find Mrs Briggs and to 'Give her a piece of my mind, not letting my daughter do her own washing here and making your poor father lug all your dirty washing home and your clean washing down here, and him having to go straight back to tonight's work after all our journeying which we *hadn't* planned on this weekend, and we're even having to bring you food for your weekends and your suppers while *she* gets money from the government for having you, so where's *that* money going I'd like to know...'

My mother's voice faded into the distance and my father rolled his eyes and sat down on my divan to await the outcome. Becky and Janet had both gone out with their respective parents for the afternoon and Daddy and I enjoyed a few moments to ourselves, catching up on our week's news while simultaneously straining to hear the verbal battle engaged in the garden. Eventually my mother returned thin-lipped, and with a defiant toss of her head swept us off out of the house and back to the town to Gregory's tea rooms for a light lunch before seeking a train that would get my father to work in time.

The following Friday at the end of the school day Becky called to me in the corridor, 'Pat, Pat, wait.' I turned.

'Miss Greaves wants to see us,' Becky continued breathlessly, 'the three of us, I mean, you, me and Janet.' Anxious grooves marred Becky's high brow as she reached out to detain me.

'Why? Are we in trouble with Mrs Briggs?' I asked apprehensively.

'I don't know, only it must be something to do with her, mustn't it, with just the three of us called in?' replied Becky.

Janet was already waiting for us by the school gates, and

moments later we were standing before Miss Greaves, like
the Three Little Maids from School, except I was tall and
well built, and Becky, while slender, was tall too and her
head always seemed tilted up with a slight air of defiance or
perhaps just self-assurance, and, although shorter than us,
Janet's generous endowment made her seem no more like
a Little Maid either. Standing quietly we awaited our fate.

When Miss Greaves began, 'I understand you're billeted
with Mrs Briggs,' I expected her to berate me for unaccept-
able parental behaviour or produce a list of our wrongdo-
ings, but she went on, 'and I have received complaints about
her hospitality from all your parents including the fact that
she does not provide you with an adequate breakfast nor
food of an evening, nor,' looking in my direction, 'sheets for
your bed. Well, girls, I've made arrangements to move you
this very afternoon to other accommodation that might be a
little more suitable. I've already sent letters informing your
parents. Go back only to pack your things and I've arranged
for a car to collect you from there and take you to your new
homes.'

We were speechless. Managing a murmured 'Thank you,
Miss Greaves,' we hastened to do her bidding.

Janet was dropped off at her new home first in a road near
the station. As we waved Janet goodbye I turned to Becky
and said, 'I'm so sorry we won't be able to put up together
now as I have *so* enjoyed your company.'

Leaving the car a few minutes later Becky turned, hugging me and promising, 'We'll still remain friends and let's
have our lunches together like before.'

The car, with me sitting in the back in solitary splendour
like a princess in her Cinderella carriage, came to a white,
double-fronted house with a front garden path bordered
by a low, brilliant display of asters. The front door opened
and an attractive slim black-haired lady in her mid-thirties,
much my mother's age, stepped out. Climbing out of the car
I found myself enveloped in a warm, scented embrace.

'Welcome, my dear, to Pachesham Park. I'm Mrs Fox,' she declared graciously. 'It's delightful to meet you. Do come and greet your fellow guests,' and her smile was as welcoming as her words. Mounting the steps, I could only gape in awe at a mansion that quite dwarfed Mrs Briggs' house by comparison.

'I expect you know Fiona and Daisy,' my hostess continued, leading me into the drawing room, and I nodded at the fair-skinned auburn-haired Fiona sitting on a low sofa and to our dark-haired athletically built Form captain Daisy, seated in an elegant Queen Anne chair.

'And this is Helga,' Mrs Fox continued, beckoning over a younger girl with long dark hair in two plaits and huge nervous dark brown eyes, standing near the window. I smiled at her.

Mrs Fox turned to Daisy. 'Perhaps Daisy can show you to your room as you will be sharing with her. When you've settled yourself in, come down for supper.'

Later, lying on a camp bed in a first floor room which Mrs Fox had previously been using as an architect's office, my stomach uncomfortably full from a huge serving of stew and dumplings followed by apple pie and custard, I was starting to drift off to sleep when Daisy leaned over the side of her camp bed and whispered,

'Don't you think it strange that Mrs Fox is looking after a *German* girl?'

'Well, not necessarily,' I replied 'There are Germans living near me at home who've escaped from Hitler's thugs.'

'D'you want to know Helga's story?'

I had always been told by my parents not to be inquisitive, not to stare at people and not to give anything away, and my natural curiosity warred with habit. Curiosity won. I sat up in bed. 'Yes.'

'Helga's Jewish,' started Daisy. Out of politeness I refrained from telling her that I had already worked that out.

'She lived in a flat and one night about a year ago she was invited to visit friends in the flat below hers. She had a friend about the same age as her. She stayed with them overnight.'

Daisy leaned forward conspiratorially. 'During that night her parents disappeared. They were taken by the Nazis and haven't been heard of since. The friends from the flat where she stayed hid her until they could put her on the *Kindertransport*.' Daisy sat back. 'Do you know what the *Kindertransport* is?'

*Where on earth does she think I have been living this past year?* I thought, irritated, but replied evenly,

'It's what the train's called that's full of Jewish children fleeing to other countries from the Germans' oppression of the Jews. The parents have to put money in a bank to show they'll pay for the children to go back home when the troubles are over.'

'Yes. Helga's parents had disappeared and the money was sent by the family who hid her. They knew someone who finds families to take these poor children in.'

Daisy lowered her voice further so it was barely audible. 'Mrs Fox has tried to find out what's happened to Helga's parents, and Mr and Mrs Fox hope to adopt Helga if her parents can't ever be found.'

I lay on my bed later trying to sleep but all I could think of was how Helga had lost her parents and how lonely and angry and scared Helga must be feeling. I was missing Mummy and Daddy terribly. *But at least I know they're safe*, I reflected.

Fiona and Helga occupied another room which was femininely decorated with wall fabric of a pink feather-shaped design. The Fox's house was palatial; not only did Mr and Mrs Fox's bedroom have an en suite bathroom, but at the end of the landing there was an entrance to a domestic's flat containing bedroom, living room, bathroom and kitchen. Downstairs was an enormous lounge/diner with dividing doors. Later I realised that Pachesham Park was not so much the name of the house but the exclusive private estate in which it was situated.

Mrs Fox was a lovely lady and fed us well. She had a big-lidded glass jar full of golden syrup which she shared out on huge slices of fresh bread and butter. Sitting at the head of the table and looking round with a satisfied smile, she'd say, 'Eat up. My girls are growing girls and there's plenty here for you all.' She frequently said 'my girls' as if proud of us and I felt a warm sense of belonging. I thought I had truly landed on my feet, especially after the hunger pangs of my first billet.

But only ten days into my stay I discovered Mrs Fox in angry tears in the hall, clutching a letter. 'My husband's relatives are all moving in from London at the weekend,' she sobbed. 'I am so, so sorry, I'll have to house them here which means I'll no longer have room for my girls.' My heart sinking and my stomach lurching, I tried telling myself it wasn't her fault, but deep down I was angry and blamed her for not standing up to her relatives, or finding a corner for me to stay on in her mansion too. It was surely big enough. *She took us on and said she'll be responsible for us and I liked her and next she discards us when it doesn't suit. Another adult who's let me down.*

'Well, Patricia, it seems you have itchy feet,' joked Miss Greaves the following day, although I didn't find it particularly funny. 'So far two homes in barely four weeks. Let's hope it's third time lucky. I've arranged for you to go to a home in Cobham Road this afternoon.' I clearly looked puzzled for she added, 'On the way to Fetcham.'

'Well,' I said to Becky as we ate our lunch, 'it's the third point of the compass. I've already been south with you and north at Pachesham Park. Now I'm going west. Let's hope I am not truly going west!'

'Oh, Pat,' sympathised Becky, 'I hope it's the last time you have to move.'

'How're you finding your billet now?' I asked her.

'Well,' said Becky, 'if you don't mind being kept awake by old Mr Hibbard snoring the other side of the bedroom wall, or the cat bringing in a mouse a day and leaving it on my bed, or trying to do my homework with an eight-year-old boy playing noisy planes, trains or cars at your feet, I suppose it has worked out all right. It's just a shame we couldn't have moved somewhere together.'

'Next time I move,' I joked, 'I'll make it an absolute condition that you move in with me and I'll refuse to go there without you!' And we both laughed at the absurd idea of standing up to Miss Greaves and the equally absurd idea that I would be moved on a third time.

At lunch the next day Becky quizzed me about my latest abode. 'Oh, Becky, it's a disaster,' I said. 'I thought I'd grown another head when I arrived. First Mr Haye looked at me in horror, Mrs Haye did too, and then their daughter Janice just snorted and laughed when she came downstairs to greet me. They hustled me into the dining room for tea and kept looking at me most oddly. Their other daughter Jillian arrived back from the hair salon where she works and kept rolling her eyes at Janice.'

'But why? *Tell me*,' Becky demanded. My face crumpling, I took a deep breath to compose myself.

'The bed. They put me in to share with Janice, so I was looking around for the spare bed but the only extra one was a short child-sized bed. Janice said that they'd expected evacuees to be children, so her father built the bed for a *child*.'

'Oh, no,' exclaimed Becky. 'I'm so sorry. What did you say?'

'I lied. I said it wouldn't be a problem.' Tears smarted as I recalled retreating to the bathroom with my washbag and sitting on the toilet pressing my fist against my mouth to stifle the sobs threatening to wreck my composure. I had longed desperately for my home in Brixton and the comfort of my own bed. 'My choice of sleeping posture alternates between curled up on my side or stretched out on my back with the lower half of my legs dangling off the end.'

I sniffed and, trying to lighten the moment, added, 'I

almost felt nostalgic for Mrs Briggs' divan and scratchy blanket!'

The term rolled on towards Christmas. I looked forward to sleeping in my own comfortable bed and catching up with my childhood friend Bill. On the Wednesday morning before Christmas I packed to go home for the holidays, my first time home since before war was declared. Not even the angry, hissing swans standing like spectral wraiths across the fog-swathed millpond footpath deterred me from reaching my goal of the station, the train and the arms of my parents.

# 2
# Bill

I emerged from a long sleep punctuated with the distant rattle of tram, the honk of delivery truck horn, the clip clop, rumble, rumble of horse and cart and the undulating aural landscape of distant voices. Indoors all was silent. The contrast with my crowded, bustling billet and its silent sheep strewn surroundings could not have been greater.

'Pat, dear, are you awake?' My mother's head emerged around the opening door, and I remembered my last awakening here before evacuation. 'Daddy's asleep and I'm sorry to leave you to fend for yourself on your first day but I'm just popping down to Brixton market. Can you see to your breakfast? Nan's out this morning but'll be back by lunchtime. You were sleeping so soundly we didn't like to wake you earlier.'

I blinked myself fully awake and nodded. 'Not to worry, Mummy, I'll be fine.'

Mummy smiled, retreated and gently closed the door to my room. I yawned and stretched, hearing the soft closing of the front door downstairs just below. Pulling on my woollen cloth dressing gown and pushing into my knitted homemade slippers, I padded to the toilet.

I paused to wash my hands and part-filled the kettle, placing it on the hob of the cooker. Striking a match and turning one of the low gas taps, a childhood memory flashed of turned black taps emitting a soft hissing sound, and a suffocating, gut-wrenching smell, and my mother dashing in, turning the taps off, throwing open the window, dragging me screaming from the room and smacking my hand sharply several times. My mother protested over the intervening years, 'How can you possibly remember that, you were barely two!' She was even more amazed at my recollection of a burning bread board accidentally left on the top of a lit hob. 'You were only eighteen months old! You must have heard us talk about it.' But I knew I hadn't and I grew to resent her for never seeming to take my pronouncements seriously. Falling into the childish trap of wanting to trust her, I often felt let down. A mother who said to her six-year-old, 'Close your eyes and I'll pop in something nice,' only to place a lump of soda on my tongue and laugh uproariously at my disgusted reaction was not one to engender confidence and trust.

Shaking off my depressing recollections, I dived into the bread bin on the left side low cupboard and cut myself a slice of slightly stale white bread, deliberately left to dry out to make cutting thinner slices easier and the bread appear to go further, and placed it under the grill. Juggling a pot of tea, I rescued the toast just in time, retrieving a sliver of butter and a jar of marmalade from the little cabinet at the foot of the bath. Placing my breakfast on a tray I proceeded carefully to the living room. Munching my toast, Peggy whining as she slept, stretched out on the hearthrug, I decided that a brisk walk with Peggy that afternoon to Brockwell Park would be just the ticket.

The front door closing heralded Nan's return. I smiled as I recalled her warm embrace on my return the previous day. 'Well, I do declare,' she'd said on first sight of me for nearly four months, 'you've got thinner but made up for it by topping me!' My sharp-eyed, upright grandmother, whose brisk and purposeful demeanour disguised a life of underlying sadness and regrets. It was Nan who chose my name, Patricia, in memory of Patrick, the only man she truly loved but who she gave up because of the untimely return of her injured fiancé from the Boer War. She felt duty bound to nurse my grandfather, Huw Caddock, back to health, but his drinking and gambling and consequent aggressive behaviour led to her fleeing London ten years later with her two young children, only possible because they were never married, and hiding in Kingston upon Thames for eight years, returning to her London roots after his death. Born to her unmarried mother by an unknown father, hiding behind her mother's subsequent marriage to her stepfather, William Warner, she kept her own children's illegitimacy hidden behind the false title of Mrs Caddock. Secret family history we kept firmly under wraps.

Later, after returning and offloading her shopping, perched on a chair and sipping the cup of tea I made her, Mummy announced, 'I saw Maud Whitshere at the market. Bill's just arrived back from Reading, so I've suggested they all pop round early on Saturday afternoon for tea and a few hands of whist.'

The next morning, I got a letter from Becky. *Dear Pat*, she wrote. *I shall miss our lunches during the holidays. Shall we meet up on Christmas Eve morning?* I wrote back straight away suggesting a time and place and caught the mid-morning post.

Apart from the blackout blinds at the windows and the hot topic of conversation being the government's proposals to start rationing food the following month, it seemed unreal that Britain was at war. The newspapers had little to report and much was made of the Royal Navy's attack on the German pocket battleship *Graf Spee* on 13th December in the South Atlantic. In September people had daily expected to hear of aerial bombings but the Government's precautions now seemed excessive and an untroubled London settled down to enjoy the season's festivities.

The following afternoon Bill came with his parents. As Bill, following his parents upstairs, reached the top, he produced a book from his pocket with a 'Ta-da!' flourish and held it high where I could not see the title.

'What's that?' I asked, curious. Bill waved it triumphantly.

'Picked up a copy this morning,' he said. 'One guess.'

'Oh, I don't know,' I huffed, slightly exasperated. 'Cricket?' I knew he was not especially keen on rugger or football.

'No, no, much closer to home,' Bill replied. 'What's seen but not seen, what can you read but not read?'

'Stop talking in riddles,' I scolded. 'Show me.'

'*The Little Book of Blackout Fun* of course,' Bill replied and thrust it into my hands. I took it excitedly.

'I've heard of this,' I said, 'but I haven't had a chance to hunt one down. It was only published last month.'

I opened a page at random and, scanning quickly, picked out a paragraph. ' "The Senses Game. As the sense of sight is denied by the blackout, test your other senses instead. You need a blacked-out room, a tray pre-prepared by the games master containing a variety of items that test the senses, and a torch taped to show a thin beam of light for assisting the gamesmaster only. Examples of items can be a dish containing scraps of a variety of foodstuffs for tasting, sealed containers containing items such as tea leaves or lavender soap for smelling, obscure lines from famous poems read out for guessing the poem and everyday items for identifying by touch" .'

I grimaced and looked down to the final line. ' "To reduce the temptation to cheat, bindfolds may additionally be used".'

I looked up. 'Under *no* circumstances will I play such a game with you as gamesmaster,' I said sternly. 'I know you too well. I don't trust you to not put something truly horrid in my hand!'

Bill struck a pose and thumped his hand across his chest. 'Perish the thought!' he declaimed grandly.

'Perish the idea,' I retorted tartly. 'I don't mind most things but I am not going to risk you producing something squishy and squirmy and alive!'

Bill roared with laughter – no doubt, like me, recalling

incidents from our childhood, primarily him chasing me with all manner of creepy crawlies in his clenched fist, and me running away squealing and shrieking. I was not laughing now either, but I softened when he sobered a little, hung his head and said, 'I must have been truly horrid when I was younger, and now I repent.' Bill had a slightly dramatic way of speaking sometimes and I was not always sure whether he was entirely sincere, but it was nearly Christmas and I had not enjoyed his company for over four months, so I was prepared to forgive him.

A phrase struck me. 'Perish the thought?' I queried. 'That's a new phrase you've not used before, where did you read that?'

'Picked it up from a chap I've become friendly with at school just this term,' Bill replied. 'Found myself billeted with him. Jon's a very jolly sort. He's taught me quite a few new phrases.'

I put on my best schoolmistress look and said, 'You shall desist from repeating them as I am sure they are *quite* unsuitable to teach to a young lady!'

Our stair-top banter was interrupted by my mother who emerged from the kitchen juggling teapot and milk jug.

'Pat, dear,' she said with a slight edge in her voice, 'When you have *quite* finished I would appreciate help with the tea.'

Diving into the kitchen I grabbed and conveyed plates laden with sandwiches, Bill following me with the Victoria sponge.

We settled down for an afternoon of fun, much enlivened by the puzzles set in Bill's new book. As the afternoon progressed the adults turned to reminiscing while Bill and I trounced each other at cards. Later on, my mother called for me to accompany a singsong with my piano playing. I looked out of the window at the gathering gloom.

'It'll soon be dark,' I said, looking at Bill and his parents in turn. 'What about the blackout? Won't you want to get back safely before it's totally dark?'

Reginald Whitshere, a bluff, stocky, older balding man with a bushy moustache, leaned towards me from his armchair and said, 'Good of you to think that, but I think we'll take our chances, don't you, Maud?'

This last, turning to his wife, who nodded her agreement, which did not surprise me. I had never heard her raise her voice against her husband or make any objection to his pronouncements. Much my parents' age and a good ten years younger than her husband, she was the antithesis of a Bright Young Thing. Her colourless personality was matched by her colourless looks: short, mousy hair above a forehead marked with anxious frown lines, her clothes always drab in contrast to my mother's bright frocks, and a slightly stooped stance as if she was constantly rushing to do her men's bidding. I found her eagerness to please irritating, used as I was to a grandmother who called a spade a spade and bent others to her will, and to a mother who constantly argued with my father and who as a child had been nicknamed 'Miss Contrary' by her step-grandfather.

'I can probably dig out a spare torch,' my father offered, but Reginald waved him away.

'No, don't worry, I brought one myself, it's in my overcoat pocket. Thought we might want more than just the afternoon to catch up on all our news,' he said. 'So, Ted, after our singsong how about a tot or two along with a hand or two of crib? Eh? Unless,' he added as an afterthought, 'you're off to work tonight?'

Daddy shook his head. 'Not tonight. I'm just in the bakery tomorrow night as usual.'

'Through Christmas Eve night into Christmas Day?' Reginald was incredulous, raising and dropping his hands onto his knees. 'Even the bank will be closed on Christmas Eve. It's a Sunday, for crying out loud.'

Reginald started in the bank as a very junior office boy, rising through the ranks to the lofty position of Branch Manager. Which was how he had been able to afford the fees for Bill's attendance at Archbishop Tenison's school in Kennington as Bill, unlike me, was not a scholarship pupil. Despite his star rising since first taking my father under his wing at the Clapham Cricket Club when I was a baby, Reginald maintained his friendship with us lowly souls, although I sometimes wondered whether that was primarily to remind himself of how far he had travelled from his humble beginnings, but then I would feel uncharitable and shove away the cynical thought.

My father defended the bakery. 'London needs its bread. We've all had to work extra hours the past couple of nights to cover the bread needed for Christmas and tomorrow night we'll be baking the bread for Londoners to eat on Boxing Day. We're splitting tomorrow's shift with New Year's Eve so I can take you up on your invite.'

After a few rousing Christmas carols, the men got down to the serious business of card playing while the ladies fixed some supper and Bill entertained me with comic tales from his book and a load of new 'I say, I say, I say,' jokes, like, 'my dog's got no nose' and 'how did the human cannonball lose his job?' acquired from his new friend Jon, and which I found far funnier than they really were.

As his parents were getting ready to leave, Bill offered to come over the following Wednesday and help take Peggy out for a walk. Realising my grandmother was in the kitchen, my mother was with his mother collecting her coat from my parents' bedroom, his father was fussing with coat, scarf and hat just outside the living room and my father was facing away from us at the threshold, Bill stood up and, drawing me up also by my hand, leaned towards me and asked quietly,

'How about you and me going along to the new Odeon on Wednesday afternoon, there's *The Man in the Iron Mask* we could see together,' and he suddenly seemed a little bashful, looking at me earnestly from his grey-green eyes which had always seemed at odds with his dark brown hair. He had been a podgy child and his father was a blueprint for Bill in thirty years' time, but I suddenly realised that the hand that held mine was attached to a firm, muscular arm and that he was leaner than the stocky boy I remembered. 'Jon and I have taken to cycling home at the weekends,' he said earlier and I exclaimed, disbelieving, 'What, all the way from Reading?!' But now I saw the effects of four months of austerity and exercise. And that he was also moving on in the manner of his affection for me.

I thought, *You're not getting soppy on me,* and so, extracting my hand, with an *en garde!* I threw him a couple of pretend sword thrusts, hoping I was restoring the brotherly and sisterly friendship we enjoyed. Bill joined in good-humouredly, his wide lips curling as he feinted and dodged. We were interrupted by 'William, your coat!' from Reginald and moved out to the landing.

Putting on his school raincoat, Bill fished around in a pocket, drawing out a small wrapped package, green crayoned holly decorating the brown paper.

'Happy Christmas, Pat.'

The earnestness was back, and I blushed a little.

'Thank you. Yours is in the bag with the other presents,' I said, nodding towards the cloth bag Maud was clutching. *As usual*, I could have added. Bill changing the annual routine felt vaguely threatening, firm ground giving way to shifting sands. 'I'll save this for Christmas Day.'

On returning from seeing the Whitsheres to the front door, and while Mummy and Nan were busy in the kitchen, Daddy said, 'A good night's sleep is what we need before our walk tomorrow.'

I looked at him in consternation. 'Oh, Daddy,' I said, 'I've just realised. Tomorrow's Sunday *and* Christmas Eve rolled into one and I've double booked myself. I'm meeting Becky after the early church service.'

'Becky?'

'Yes, you must remember her. We were billeted together at Mrs Briggs' house. She was the tall dark one.'

'Ah, yes,' replied my father, although I was sure that remembering my contemporaries was the last thing on his mind. 'Never mind, I've been getting used to my Sunday morning walks on my own now for the last term. Another Sunday won't matter.'

But I could tell he was disappointed. I put my hand on his forearm reassuringly. 'Don't worry, Daddy, I'll be here Boxing Day morning.'

He brightened and patted my hand. 'Right-ho my girl, Boxing Day morning it is.'

The next day I was up early to get to an 8am Holy Communion service and a little after that I met Becky outside Brixton Town Hall as I had suggested in my letter. Looking across at the cinema I thought of Bill's earnestness in asking me to go with him to the coming Wednesday's performance. *I really don't think I feel that way about him*, I thought. *How can I tell him without hurting him?*

'Penny for them,' said Becky.

My instinct was to shrug and say, 'Oh, nothing,' but I caught myself. We had become more than just acquaintances through shared adversity in our first digs and Becky subsequently made the effort to seek me out at lunchtimes and at weekends, and she instigated our meeting today. *She needs me as a friend*, I thought, flattered as well as a little threatened. I decided to risk my vulnerability and started with, 'An old friend of mine wants me to go to the cinema on Wednesday,' pausing as Becky looked a little puzzled, continuing, 'with him,' and pausing again as a slow conspiratorial smile spread across Becky's face.

'Him?' Raising an eyebrow and cocking her head.

I decided to risk all. 'He's a friend I've known virtually all my life. He's like a brother to me, but when he asked me to the cinema it wasn't like when we used to go to Saturday morning children's showings, it was, well, it was...'

'Like he wanted a bit more out of it? A date? And I'm guessing that's not quite what you want?'

I nodded, relieved at her quick perception and warmed by her empathy.

'Has his mother set him up to it?'

'His mother? Oh no, his mother's far too self-effacing to do that. Why did you think that? Oh,' I said, comprehension dawning, 'is there someone in the offing for *you*?'

Becky nodded, her face falling.

'And I'm guessing he didn't ask you to the cinema? Theatre?'

Becky nodded again. 'Just a matinee so he can see me home afterwards. It's been set up by our mothers. They think we're a perfect match.' She raised her arms and dropped them sharply in despair. 'I was only sixteen in October, for God's sake.' Blinking at the profanity, I put a tentative hand on her arm.

'I'm sorry,' I said, feeling inadequate but also flattered at her confidence. *This is what girl friendship is all about*, I thought. *Sharing and supporting.* A novel experience for me.

Becky's good humour couldn't be repressed for long. 'Then Reuben will have to get himself home afterwards to North London in the blackout. So hopefully that will put him off for life!'

'*North* London?'

'Oh, his mother's a friend of my aunt who lives in Golders Green. So really it's been concocted by my aunt, with my mother as a willing accomplice.' Becky, rubbing cold hands together, grinned. 'Let's have a pact. I'm meeting Reuben on Wednesday too, so let's meet up again, say on Friday and compare notes?'

I laughed. 'It's a deal.'

'Come on,' said Becky. 'Don't think about it anymore now. Let's see if we can find a stall selling hot drinks instead, I'm quite chilled.'

Usually Brixton Market was deserted on a Sunday morning. Although the stallholders mostly observed the Day of Rest, whether it was in church or in sleeping off the strenuous long hours of the preceding week and the drink of the night before, I really would not have liked to bet. But, today being Christmas Eve, Brixton Market was bustling. We wandered around dodging turkeys strung up in ranks like feathered soldiers on parade and grimaced at glass tanks filled with black writhing eels, condemned prisoners awaiting their executions.

On Christmas Day I attended church with Mummy and Nan while Daddy caught up on sleep. He arose in time for our turkey dinner after which we exchanged presents. I gave my mother a deep blue rayon scarf on which I had embroidered her initials and my father a set of three handkerchiefs on which I had embroidered his, and Nan a patchwork shawl I had knitted from scraps of wool through the autumn evenings away from home.

My mother exclaimed over a pair of expensive gloves from the Whitsheres and similarly lavish presents for my father and grandmother.

'What did you get from Bill?'

'Oh, I haven't got round to opening it, I'll do that later.' Distraction was called for, and fortunately on hand. 'It's nearly three o'clock, don't you want to hear the King's speech?'

We settled ourselves into armchairs, and Mummy turned on the wireless and we listened to King George VI's special speech, a message for his subjects on their first Christmas Day of the war.

'A New Year is at hand,' he concluded. 'We cannot tell what it will bring. If it brings peace, how thankful we shall all be. If it brings us continued struggle, we shall remain undaunted.'

As the end of his speech faded my grandmother said, reverently, 'God bless him and all our Royal family.'

We whiled away the rest of the afternoon listening to classical music on the wireless, playing cards, cracking nuts and passing the port. Well, the grown ups did the last, but I was allowed a long glass of port and lemonade. Later I played the piano for Christmas carols.

Realising by bedtime I couldn't put off opening Bill's present much longer, I retreated to my room and slowly unwrapped the small bundle. A Collins Library of Classics edition of *Great Expectations* small enough to fit in my handbag emerged. *Oh, how thoughtful, he knows I love Dickens.* Eagerly I turned the outer cover and stopped, thrill and horror spreading rapidly in equal measure.

*To Pat, With all my love, Bill* he had written in neat copperplate on the first, unprinted, page. A small upward diagonal line stroked beneath his signature, emphasising the sentiment. I flicked over to the title page and thought of Bill's love of jokes with double meanings. *This present isn't really about Pip's great expectations of wealth. Bill has his own great expectations of me.* A Christmas gift with a double meaning shrieking loud and clear.

Boxing Day dawned and Daddy and I set off for our walk. Every Sunday morning through my childhood Daddy would take me off while Mummy and Nan prepared the dinner. We would walk miles and if I stumbled my father, who required even the exercise of walking to be shipshape and tidy, would say, without breaking pace, 'Pick your feet up! Pick your feet up!'

My father varied the walks. Sometimes we headed south and east to Dulwich Park where we would sit for a while watching people enjoying the boats on the boating lake, though never tempted ourselves; or perhaps we would head west to Clapham Common, or north west to Battersea Park and making a slight detour either there or back to walk past the house in St Philip Street where I was born. Or, more often than not, straight north to Vauxhall, turning sharp right as the bridge loomed and following the south bank of the River Thames up to Westminster Bridge while watching all manner of boats sailing up and down and my father stopping us to admire the boats berthed at piers on the way. Sometimes we would cross the river at Westminster to view the boats and small ships berthed at Westminster Pier and along the Embankment. Then Daddy would check his watch, declare our route march to be at an end, and we would hop on a tram and make our way home.

Today Daddy chose the river route. I was not surprised. After all, there was a war on and had he not been invalided out of the Navy in 1919 following his survival of the 'flu that had swept the nations, estimated to have killed over twenty-one million people in the 1920s, perhaps he would still be the sailor he had been sent in 1914 at the age of twelve to Naval Cadet College to become. We wrapped up warmly against the dissipating damp fog of the previous night as the weak, watery sun threatened to break through the cloud layer, and we walked briskly along quiet streets and past closed shop fronts. London had so far escaped the snow currently blanketing the more northerly parts of the country.

Often we walked silently until we reached the river and Daddy would tell me about the vessels bobbing before us and estimate their tonnage. But today we had not long started when he said, 'I understand young Bill will be taking you to the cinema tomorrow.'

'Er, yes,' I replied, wondering what had prompted this.

'A word of advice.' Daddy paused as if choosing his words carefully. 'You're both growing up and I noticed Bill looking at you in a certain way on Saturday. A young man's way.'

By now my cheeks were fiery red and I thought, *Daddy never talks to me about such matters. Has Mummy set him up to this? Was it that obvious?*

He went on, 'Decide on your response and be true to it. It's easy for a young man to misread a situation and be led on even if the girl doesn't mean him to. Watch your behaviour towards him and don't give him false hope if that's all it would be.'

'I won't, Daddy,' I tried to reassure him. 'Bill's my childhood friend, not my childhood sweetheart. I don't *want* complications like that.'

'Well, my girl, just watch your step,' Daddy concluded and we continued our walk in silence.

The day brightened as the sun finally emerged, the Houses of Parliament dancing upside down in the glittering water like a fairy tale palace trapped by a witch's spell. I looked up at the building and thought of the enormous responsibility facing the leaders of the nation and, remembering the King's Christmas message, wondered how undaunted we would all really be if the threat Hitler posed was ever realised.

The next morning I was awake early, unsettled by the looming unknowns of the day. Bill arrived before lunch and we took Peggy for a walk in Brockwell Park. I was nervous, afraid he would swear undying love or some similar romantic notion but he seemed his usual bantering self. I began to relax, and enjoyed hearing more of his evacuation experiences in Reading with his friend Jon and swapping them for some of my own.

Trusting Bill again in his reversion to a sense of brotherly friendship, he caught me unawares at the cinema when Philippe of Gascony asked Maria Therese, 'Do you love me?' and she replied that she had always loved him. Bill's arm shot out and he enveloped my hand in his paw, squeezing tightly as they kissed on screen. I sat frozen, heart pounding, horror rising, gently attempting to disentangle my hand. As the next few scenes played out on the screen and my hand remained trapped I slowly realised that Bill might be taking my gentle finger wriggling as encouragement. To my enormous relief, after a while Bill released his grip, but instead of returning his hand to his lap he leaned forward, shaking his arm vigorously up and down, rocking the line of seats in which we sat.

'What on earth are you doing that for?' I hissed. A few heads were turning in our direction.

'Pins and needles,' he hissed back, and, with a flourish worthy of the sword-swiping playing out before us, finally rested his arm by his side. Folding my hands under my arms, I sat waiting for a groping hand to reappear but Bill seemed caught up in the action and only towards the end, searching for my hand, he had to settle for patting my left thigh as Louis of France roared his anger and desolation from behind the mask.

My own anger towards Bill for betraying our friendship mingled with apprehension as we filed out of the cinema.

'I say, Pat, that was jolly good. I hope you weren't too frightened at the end.' I made a gesture of dismissal and turned away towards Effra Road, but he caught my arm and said, 'Let's stop for a cuppa in the café in Acre Lane,' nodding in that direction.

'Oh, I don't think so,' I replied, 'it's getting rather late,' pointing upwards to a sky luminous in contrast to the darkening street. 'But thank you for having the idea of seeing the film.' Turning southwards, I added, 'I'll see you sometime.'

Bill's route home lay west along Acre Lane, but he had not been brought up to be a gentleman for nothing. Grabbing my arm, he steered me across the road, saying, 'I'll see you safely home as it's nearly dark. Otherwise I couldn't face your parents on New Year's Eve. Let's go along Brixton Hill for a change.'

A brotherly Bill's company I would have enjoyed, but crossing behind St Matthew's church and turning south towards the open land of Rush Common I was feeling a little apprehensive. Trying to lighten the conversation by asking, 'Have you seen anything of your new friend during the holidays?', I thought I had succeeded as Bill nodded and promptly regaled me with another evacuation tale, this time of a fishing rod, a stream and an irate landowner, finishing with, 'Well, how were we to know you have to have a licence to fish?', but as the junction with Brixton Water Lane drew near Bill said,

'Here, we can cut off the corner,' and, steering me along an angled path through the wartime allotments, stopped beside a beech tree. Pulling me into its barely discernible shadow, he said abruptly, 'Pat, will you be my girl?'

Turning my head away towards the road to avoid eye contact, I was unprepared for his enthusiastic kiss connecting with my left ear simultaneous with his forehead connecting with my temple. A loud bang resonated around my head, my ears ringing with a high-pitched whistle. I staggered a little and he reached out, pulling me back towards him, and, as I turned to remonstrate, planted a wet, slobbery kiss firmly around the outside of my lips.

I stood frozen, revolted by the kiss and horrified by the transformation puberty had wrought in my childhood companion. As Bill drew back for air, I gasped,

'I don't want to be *anyone's* girl. I really must be getting home now. My parents will be quite worried.'

Forcibly pushing his arms down and fumbling in my bag for my torch, I sped off, with Bill trotting behind me.

'Pat, please, stop, I don't mean to upset you, it's just that we haven't got long now before we have to go back to school and I thought we might just have a bit more time together, and you've always kind of been my girl. I thought we could make it official.'

By now I was almost running, keeping up the pace until I skidded to a halt outside the front door.

'Bill, I'm flattered,' I lied, panting, 'but now is really not the time. I'm busy up to the new term. I've already arranged to meet a friend. You'll see me anyway on New Year's Eve when we're coming to your place, but please don't say anything to anyone, I'm really not ready to be an official girlfriend.'

Bill sighed. 'All right, Pat, I won't say anything. We can keep it a secret for now if you like.'

Feeling boxed into a corner and too weak to fight I did not protest at this last, but, muttering, 'See you on Sunday,' I let myself in, leaving him standing on the doorstep.

Two days later Becky and I caught the 33 tram into central London, swapping our experiences. Reuben, it turned out, had been the perfect gentleman and seemed to understand what Becky required of him, which was nothing beyond a polite meeting of strangers, and stuck to the script. 'But I'm a bit worried about what our mothers might get up to behind our backs,' she confided. 'How did you get on?'

Becky laughed uproariously at my description of Bill's blundering kiss that made my ear ring.

'It might seem funny to you,' I said, 'but the next one was simply *awful*. He couldn't even kiss my lips. His mouth's far too big. How do movie stars make kissing look so *nice*?'

'Because they're paid to.'

'Nothing you can pay me will induce me to repeat the experience,' I shuddered. Softening, I allowed myself a small smile, 'Though I suppose it was a bit comical.' Sighing, I added, 'But, stupidly, I didn't refute his last declaration that we would keep it secret. There's no "it" as far as *I'm* concerned.'

'But you didn't make it clear to him that there is no "it"?' Becky surmised.

I nodded. 'Becky, what shall I do? I have to face him on New Year's Eve. I'd been looking forward to New Year's Eve until he went and spoiled everything by making up to me.'

'You could either write to him and set the record straight before Sunday, or you could see how the evening goes. He might've had time to think about it and realised you're not keen and you can let the notion die a natural death.'

'Becky, you're so sensible, there's me been worrying myself silly. I think I'll leave it and see what happens on Sunday. I'll only write to him if he hasn't got the message by then. I'm sorry to put such a dampener on today.'

'Not at all, that's what friends are for. Here's our stop coming up, let's have a good time and forget our boy worries.'

We reached the National Gallery shortly after eleven-thirty. Already the queue for the concert for the one day between Christmas and New Year at which Myra Hess would be performing was stretching around the corner up

Charing Cross Road. We joined the queue. Becky stamped her feet.

'It's turned really cold since last week,' I sympathised. 'It would just be our luck for it to snow in time for our return next week.'

'I don't mind snow in London so much, everyone just sets to and shovels it out of the way,' said Becky. 'I can't imagine people doing that in the country, though.'

'Maybe Leatherhead town centre will be alright, but I don't fancy a long walk from Fetcham in the snow,' I said.

'Just have to get our galoshes out of their mothballs.'

The queue suddenly surged forward.

'They must have realised we're freezing out here,' I said.

'If we think *this* queue's long, I can't imagine what it'll be like for the New Year's Day concert,' said Becky. 'The paper had an article about it today, there are some photographs of a rehearsal yesterday and it looks as if some pretty famous people will be taking part.'

'I read they usually let all the children and their parents in first. Perhaps we should have borrowed a child for the day,' I joked. But the queue was moving smoothly and the wait was not too long. We paid our shilling each and, after a trip to the Ladies, settled ourselves into seats in the gallery adjacent to the octagonal room in which the concerts were held. The seats being fairly central gave us a good view of the centre of the concert platform, if rather distant. By one o'clock the concert room and adjacent rooms were packed and some people strolled in the rooms beyond or sat on the floor. A few one-sheet programmes were circulating and Becky borrowed one from a neighbour.

'Oh, good, some Chopin, next Handel's 'Water Music', a touch of Scarlatti and lastly a bit of Elgar to stir the soul,' said Becky. 'I heard that the opening concert in October included Beethoven's 'Appassionata' which some of the audience weren't happy with. Not sure about them playing works by German composers with a war on.'

'Don't forget Handel was German,' I pointed out.

'That doesn't count,' responded Becky, 'as he became English in, I think, 1727. I identify with him because my ancestors came to Britain and settled, like him.'

'Oh, I don't mind the older German composers myself,' I replied, 'but I'm biased as Beethoven's my favourite of all.'

The room suddenly hushed as Myra Hess climbed up onto the stage and approached the grand piano, followed by a cellist, three violinists, a double bassist and three brass instrumentalists.

The Chopin was electrifying. From our angle all I could see was Myra Hess' short dark-haired head bobbing up and down and every now and then she leant back slightly, eyes hooded, head nodding to the rhythms of the waltzes and polkas. I had a Chopin music book at home and recognised several of the pieces she was playing, mentally following the remembered manuscript.

'Handel coming up,' whispered Becky as Myra Hess took her bows. Almost as if on cue, Myra Hess stepped forward and spoke.

'Ladies and Gentlemen,' she began. 'Welcome to our lunchtime concert. My choice of composers today demonstrates that music crosses all barriers and that if all peoples work together in harmony we can make the world a better place. We have felt solidarity with Chopin's Polish compatriots and now we celebrate a composer who made England his home. Later we will stand firm with Italians seeking to throw off the yoke of oppression and I invite you all to join in singing to our country's favourite Elgar tune at the end.'

As Handel's light and airy 'Water Music' struck up, a deep voice somewhere ahead of us said '*Bloody Krauts*,' which drew a few gasps and admonitions, and the voice caused further disturbance when a growled '*Bloody Eyeties*' met the opening bars of a compilation of Scarlatti's sonatas. I breathed a sigh of relief when the more controversial parts of the concert were over and we could all enjoy standing and singing 'Land of Hope and Glory'.

After the concert finished we wandered the echoing halls with their walls mostly bare, carrying the ghostly outlines of the requisitioned paintings. Only a few works of art remained, mostly transferred to the concert rooms, which I therefore presumed were not considered to be of great value for posterity. Even before war was declared most of the treasures of the National Gallery had been spirited away to a secret location.

Towards the end of our brief tour I pointed out a painting of a nude lady to Becky, saying, 'D'you think we'll find a Mr Briggs masterpiece here one day?'

Giggling like the schoolgirls we were, we tumbled out into the crisp, chill air, our breath forming clouds as we puffed imaginary cigarettes. 'Lyons Corner House for a late luncheon,' I said decisively and strode out with a 'Come along, girls,' mimicking Miss Marchant's strident tone, 'keep in line, decorum, decorum', while Becky chimed 'Yes, Miss, no Miss, three bags full Miss' and we laughed until we held our sides.

On New Year's Eve I eyed Bill warily as my parents, my grandmother and I were welcomed in turn by Reginald Whitshere's hearty handshake, Maud hovering behind son and husband, her hands reaching out to clasp coats and hats and bags. My mother and grandmother disappeared with Maud into the kitchen as usual and Reginald and my father beat a path to the drinks' cabinet. In the past Bill and I would have scampered up to his room to play with his train set or pour over his collection of *Champion* and *Hotspur*, reading aloud or enacting their scenes of derring-do and adventure. Bill leaned forward; tilting my head, I managed to reduce his embrace to a peck on the cheek. Feeling very self-conscious, I followed our fathers into the front room and was gratified when my father suggested a game of whist between the four of us. *I just need to avoid finding myself on my own with Bill, maybe he'll get the message. Then I won't need to see him for another term. Oh, why did he have to go and spoil everything!*

Shortly before midnight Bill was ejected from the house clutching a piece of coal, a salt cellar and a chunk of bread, his hair being deemed the darkest of all. Midnight arrived with Maud hastening to open the back door to let the old year out and Reginald flinging open the front door to welcome in the new with the supposed stranger. Bill, shivering and beaming, extracted a kiss from the ladies and, not wanting to cause a scene by demurring, I presented the other cheek.

As the adults later sat around clinking glasses, toasting the New Year again and speculating on what it would bring, Bill caught me unawares on my return downstairs from a trip to the toilet; gently pulling the door to the front room almost closed, he held me back, hugging me and pointing upwards with an eyebrow to the strategically placed mistletoe which I suspected had only just been placed there; I certainly hadn't noticed it earlier.

'My girl,' he said, and swooped, but I was wise to this now, turning my head away again so his lips scraped my cheek and I ducked out of his embrace and escaped to the front room, throwing a falsely cheerful 'Happy New Year, Bill,' over my shoulder.

We stayed overnight rather than face the blackout, their three bedroomed Victorian house tucked behind Acre Lane providing more accommodation than our own rented rooms. My father slept on a board covering their bath (it was fortunate that the toilet was in its own little room!) while my mother and Nan shared a fold-out settee bed in the sitting room and I enjoyed the luxury of the little guest room. Before I settled I placed the chair firmly under the door knob as heroines had done for centuries to protect their honour. The next morning I was relieved to find the chair unmoved and no evidence of any attempt on my virtue.

Breakfast was a quiet affair and we took our leave, Bill

and I saying our goodbyes in front of everyone, only his grey-green eyes eloquent of an inner torment. I feared that something indefinable had shifted and that our carefree, bantering friendship, where nothing untoward had been read into a hand clasp or a friendly arm around the shoulder, was lost forever.

Later that day I wrote,

*Dear Bill,*

*This letter is not easy to write as I am very fond of you and I don't know where to begin. I want you to understand that I am fond of you as a brother or a favoured cousin. I meant it when I said I don't want to be anyone's girl, not yours or anyone else's.*

*I want to get on with my studies and do well in the matric exams and go on to the sixth form and teacher training college and get a teaching job and keep it, so I don't expect to get married, ever.*

*We have enjoyed a lifelong friendship and I hope that we can continue to do so. I release you from any other sense of commitment or obligation you may feel towards me. It would be unfair of me to give you hope or to let you feel in any way that there is a future beyond friendship. I hope you meet someone else and will be happy with her.*

*I am sorry if this upsets you and I wish to reassure you that I remain always,*

*Your good friend,*

*Pat.*

# 3

# The Phoney War

A week after the start of the new school term my hostess Mrs Haye scanned a letter briefly over breakfast, muttering,

'They're doing a routine inspection of premises, how awkward. It says here they want to come on the tenth, which is today. Really, they could have given me a little more notice.' She cast me a resentful glance.

I shrank into my chair. My hopes of finding another Mrs Fox coupled with a permanent, comfortable home had not come to fruition here. Not only was the bed a continuing major source of discomfort, Mrs Haye made it clear that, although a useful source of income, I was proving to be a drain on her time and physical resources.

The next day Miss Greaves called me in to see her, saying, 'Your parents wrote to me complaining about your bed in your present accommodation and I was inclined to consider them unduly fussy. But,' she continued, looking me up and down, 'I inspected your current abode yesterday and I must say they do have a point. I've found you somewhere with a bed more suitable to your size. Mrs Grice in Fetcham will be your new hostess. You can move in there this afternoon.'

Sands shifting beneath my feet again, I wanted to weep and rail at the constant churning of insecurity and uncertainty. Well trained by home and school, gritting my teeth and attempting a smile rather than a grimace, I thanked Miss Greaves. *Four new homes in four months*, I thought. *Now I have to get used to* another *new set of people*. Never had my motto to trust no one seemed so apt.

Mr and Mrs Grice lived in a flat above a shop at the far end of Fetcham, two miles out of Leatherhead on the road to Stoke D'Abernon and Cobham. My dream of a cottage and a corner of the world to call my own seemed as far away as ever.

'Oh, Pat,' said Becky when I saw her the day after my move. 'You're even further away from me now.'

'I know,' I replied, 'I've let you down. I promised I would *not* move a third time unless it was *with* you.'

A half smile flickered on Becky's face at my pathetic attempt to lighten the mood.

Grimacing, I continued, 'What's worse is they've only got a *tiny* second bedroom. I can almost touch the wall on both sides. There's no chance of you moving in with me.'

'I'll get hold of a bicycle and cycle over to see you.'

'I would get a bicycle too,' I said, 'but there's nowhere for me to keep one.'

'At least you'll be able to sleep lying straight,' consoled Becky. 'Every cloud has a silver lining.'

'Will Mrs Grice give me enough to eat with this new food rationing?' I continued, and Becky rolled her eyes, saying, 'At least we'll all get a fair share, better than the shortages because some people have been stockpiling, and nothing can be worse than Mrs Briggs!'

'Yes,' I agreed, '*Nothing* can be worse than Mrs Briggs. And although the weather's cold, at least it's not snowing.'

Which only goes to show I am the world's expert at speaking too soon. Snow came to Leatherhead the very next day. And as far as food was concerned, although Mrs Grice was the cashier at a butcher's shop, I didn't benefit from the extra meat the butcher slipped into her bag as a bonus from time to time. Mrs Grice was short and plump and could at times be quite motherly but there was a hard set to her thin lips and she scooped up her whispy light brown hair in a bun, I suspected, to save the cost of a trip to the hairdressers. I felt the penetrating cold and the edge of hunger most days.

Towards the end of the Spring Term the silent, beanpole Mr Grice was called up to join the armed forces. Shortly after, Mrs Grice said to me one day at dinner (well, snack time as that's all it was), 'I've decided to move,' at which my heart sank. *Here we go again,* I thought, but Mrs Grice continued, 'I've found a nice little bungalow in Warenne Road and I thought with Mr Grice away I could have the single room and so the double room could be given over to you and another girl. Is there anyone you would like to recommend?'

For a moment I was speechless, then, 'Oh, yes, how kind of you,' I gushed, 'I know just the person, she is a lovely girl and a very good friend of mine. It's been so difficult to see her out of school and I am sure she would love to come and stay with you, her name's Becky, it's short for Rebecca, and you'll really find her no trouble...' and I continued on in that vein until Mrs Grice held up her hand.

'You need convince me no further,' she said, 'I'll write to your school today.'

So, six months after I promised Becky I would make it possible for us to lodge together, fate had stepped in and shown me the way. I didn't care that Mrs Grice's motivation, renting the bungalow with two evacuees rather than the smaller flat with one, was purely mercenary. Already I felt the boat steadying and moving into calmer waters.

For the first six months of the war there had been no fighting except for Royal Navy skirmishes with German boats in the Atlantic. As spring progressed Becky and I explored the surrounding countryside on bicycles and talked about our longing to be back with our families in London as the threatened bombing had not happened. Everyone called it the Phoney War.

Easter came and, apart from the rationing and Mummy having got herself a job in the recently created Beaver Club in central London, a centre for Canadian servicemen, you would hardly have known there was a war on. London was its usual hustle and bustle and a number of theatres re-opened.

The Criterion Theatre had been taken over temporarily by the BBC as its layout was effectively underground and Mummy and I queued on her day off to sit in the audience for one of its live light entertainment broadcasts.

Bill and his parents came over to see us on Easter Saturday afternoon and he and I took Peggy for a walk in Brockwell Park. It had rained heavily in the morning; now the sun was easing a few beams through the clouds but I drew the collar of my coat up around my neck against the chill breeze. I felt awkward in Bill's presence and was relieved that Peggy gave us a focus and a distraction.

'Here, fetch,' called Bill, throwing my old tennis ball we had brought with us, and Peggy bounded off, only to slow and lose interest in the chase as she became distracted by other dogs. I was surprised how many dogs there were around as many people had had their pets destroyed or given their dogs up to the army for the war effort to save the cost of maintaining them on rations. The ball was picked up by a black labrador and dropped into a muddy puddle before the labrador made off with it again. Peggy didn't even notice as she recklessly sniffed around a fierce looking bulldog. Bill barked with laughter and, catching my eye, coaxed a smile from me although I was still annoyed at the loss of the ball. A few moments later a middle aged man approached us apologetically with his labrador now on a lead and offered back a manky, chewed and soggy ball. I thanked him politely and turned away, holding the ball gingerly between thumb and forefinger.

'That's a goner,' guffawed Bill. 'Only use for that is water polo.'

'Ha, ha, very funny,' I said, and the absurdity of trying to rescue the ball and relief that the bantering between us had resumed struck me and I allowed myself a smile, widening to a grin, and a chortle.

Dropping the ball in a nearby bin, I moved to a bench and sat down, watching Peggy all the while.

'How's Reading?' I asked as Bill plonked himself down beside me.

'Oh, much the same.' Bill shrugged. 'Only one more term to go. Who knows what will happen after that.' He sighed. 'I don't know if I'll matriculate. Been struggling a bit. No matriculation, no Higher School Cert, no university. And no happy parents. It's a shame Jon's set on leaving this summer and getting a job. He's a good egg and if I get to the sixth form he would've been a good mate to have there. He's very good at physics, chemistry and maths, and has been helping me with some of it.'

Keeping an eye on Peggy's antics from afar, and using that as an excuse to avoid looking at Bill, I asked, 'Could your Dad not get you a job in the bank? Doesn't he want you to follow him into banking?'

Out of the corner of my eye I saw Bill shake his head. 'He wants me ultimately to become an accountant. He says that's where the big money is. But he doesn't understand I'm not interested in looking after other people's money and I don't get on with figures, I never have and I can't see that changing.'

'If you had the choice, what would you do?' I asked, curious, because as we spoke I realised that we had never before discussed Bill's career hopes.

Bill was looking straight ahead in Peggy's direction too. 'I want to go through sixth form and university and who knows where that would take me. Maybe into the Civil Service, or even the Foreign Office. I like languages. I wouldn't mind a foreign posting. If we're still all here and not overrun by the Hun, that is.'

'Do your best, Bill, that's all you can ask of yourself, and leave it at that. If you matriculate, that's good. If you don't, well, there'll be another path for you to follow. You just can't find out which path it will be until the exam results are known. One step at a time.'

Bill said abruptly, 'You're a good sort, Pat. Look, I got

your letter and you were right. I'm sorry I complicated things around Christmas time.' He turned to me. 'Pax. Just friends, eh?'

*Can you really turn the clock back, just like that?* I wondered. *If I did find myself a young man eventually, how would you feel about it? Would you* really *just feel pleased for me, like a friend would?*

But I was tired of the tension between us, and, deciding to take his peace offering, held out my right hand. 'Pax, let's shake on it like gentlemen. And now,' I added as he reciprocated, shaking my hand vigorously, 'I think it is time to extricate Peggy and head back.'

'Aye, aye captain,' Bill said, following up with a mock salute. He rose and strode off in Peggy's direction.

Our country's differences with Germany were not so easily resolved. The world was holding its breath. Everyone wondered when the Phoney War would end.

It ended with a suddenness that May that was shocking. While we girls sweated in a sudden heat wave over our exam preparation, the Nazis commenced their swift and devastating invasion of Norway, Holland, Belgium and France. On 22nd May 1940 the weather broke and the sky wept as if it knew we were only weeks away from the first bombs to rain down on London.

The same day I received a letter from my mother. 'Dear Pat,' I read, 'this letter may come as a bit of a surprise for you – as you will see from the address, we have moved to West Norwood, so when you come home for your half term break next weekend you will need to get the train to West Norwood and come straight here.'

The ground shifting sideways, I looked at the address from which my mother wrote, from Idmiston Road, West Norwood.

*What on earth induced them to move to West Norwood? Brixton is so much more convenient for everything, West Norwood is a backwater. And that's* another *home to get used to. When will I have the chance to ever settle in one place? I hate thinking, this is it, then off we go again.*

I read on,

'I am sure you will want to know how this has come about.'

*You bet.*

'Nanny had a disagreement with our landlady over the rent despite the rent book being in your father's name, and she was determined to find somewhere similar but cheaper. Of course, you know what a whirlwind your grandmother can be when she sets her mind to something and so in less than a week from your grandmother's row with Mrs Sterne we have found ourselves moved out yesterday and are now settling into our new home.

'Unfortunately the rooms are a little smaller, there's only a kitchenette on the landing, and you might find your room a little cramped,' *the old one was hardly palatial,* I thought, 'but at least the rent is less, so Nanny was quite right as usual. Unfortunately there is a young family on the ground floor and the baby doesn't seem to have stopped crying since we moved in yesterday and the sound travels up to our bedroom, which is a little worrying as Daddy will so need his sleep during the day. As you may imagine Daddy is not too happy at the move as the journey to Milkwood Road will be a little awkward and longer. Apart from all that it is a pleasant quiet road and not too far from the shops.' *What a disaster.*

Becky bounced into the living room.

'Post already?' she said. I pointed abstractly to the sideboard on which lay a letter for her. She grabbed it. 'Maybe my sister-in-law's baby's arrived,' she speculated, opening it excitedly. Her face fell. 'No, it's still not arrived. Well, not as of yesterday.'

'Perhaps someone will telephone Mr Parker and leave a message,' I ventured, returning to my mother's letter. Mr Parker, the butcher for whom Mrs Grice worked, had agreed for his telephone number to act as an emergency number for our families should urgent contact prove necessary.

Becky looked up.

'Pat, what's the matter, you look upset.'

'Upset!' I exploded. 'Yes, you could say that. My grand-mother's only gone and uprooted us *again* and now we're stuck out in the sticks of West Norwood!'

'Uprooted you *again*?'

'We lived in Branksome Road until about a year ago. My grandmother took umbrage at the cooking arrangements as we didn't have a kitchen, we used a Kitchener in the living room fireplace, and that meant getting food ready in the living room, and washing up in the bathroom. It *was* a little cramped. So Nanny decided she wanted somewhere with a proper kitchen and a bigger room for herself to entertain guests, and I think that was only because she wanted to entertain old Mr Torston, he lives in a house that backs on to the one we had in Branksome Road, so we moved round the corner to Water Lane, and now she's gone and moved us *again*, and to *West Norwood*. And what have my parents done to stop her? *Nothing*!'

I gasped for breath at the end of my diatribe, feeling angry and abandoned, a piece of flotsam flung around on the tide of my relatives' whims.

'Oh, Pat, I'm sorry, I really don't know what to say. You had so many different places in Leatherhead when we first arrived and to be moving your own home too must be *so* unsettling.'

Becky's sympathy was too much for me and I burst into tears.

'We have,' I corrected, '*had* a lovely place in Water Lane and my room, even though it was at the front, was quiet and so easy to study in. And we even had a proper little kitchen there. Now I am going to a strange home for the half term before matric exams where everyone will be at daggers over the move and apparently a baby cries constantly in the flat below.'

Mrs Grice, hearing the commotion, popped her head round the door.

'All right, dearie?'

To which the answer was patently 'No,' but I took a couple of shaky breaths and, wiping my dripping nose with my hanky, assured Mrs Grice that while I had been upset that I would be going to a new home on Friday, all was now well.

'Don't you worry, in a few days you'll wonder that you ever lived anywhere else,' soothed Mrs Grice. 'I'll bring in the teapot and you can have a nice cup of tea.'

I turned back to Becky.

'I'm sorry to be such a misery-guts,' I apologised. 'Families in Holland and Belgium are being murdered by the Germans and here I am worrying about a silly house move. Let's think about nicer things. Perhaps your brother's baby will come next week while we're all on half term.'

Becky brightened. 'Oh, I'm so looking forward to being an auntie.' She bent her head down back to her letter while Mrs Grice returned with the tea tray and we settled to our breakfast.

I returned to my letter while I chewed, swallowing painfully in my distressed state. 'West Norwood,' continued my mother, 'is, as you know, the start of the 33 tram run, so it will hardly add to my journey to the Beaver Club. I'll just have to allow a little more time at each end. I can get off in Brixton for shopping on my way home and get another tram and pick up more bits and pieces at the shops by West Norwood station. Well, dear, I'll sign off now as it is rather late and I want to post this on my way in to work tomorrow. Do write straight back so that I will know that you've received this letter safely and know to come to our new home and not back to Brixton on Friday.'

I looked at the date. Mummy wrote on Monday evening. Today was Wednesday. No time now to write before leaving for school. I sighed.

Becky said, her mouthful of toast, 'A big sigh. It'll turn out alright, I'm sure.'

I glanced at the clock. 'We'd better run,' I said, scooting out of the room and upstairs to grab my bag and my writing things for later. Becky followed in my wake.

The Whitsun Bank Holiday on 13th May having been cancelled by the government, our school deferred its half term break to the last week of May. That Friday Becky and I stood at the bus stop for the late afternoon bus into Leatherhead and the train home, our little cases by our sides and our heavy exercise book-laden satchels slung over our bodies. 'I'll come to West Norwood with you,' Becky said, 'and I can get a tram into Brixton and go home that way.'

On the train we talked about our plans for the coming week. 'I'll concentrate on schoolwork for the first few days,' I said, 'then maybe we can meet up?'

'Let's make it Thursday,' suggested Becky.

Emerging from West Norwood station I looked around, recalling our departure from here last September and our journey into the unknown. *All those hopes of having a settled second home, a cottage with a picket fence and roses around the door. Ha bloody ha. Five places in Leatherhead already, four hostesses. To crown it all, coming back to a new home in London. One day when I'm a teacher and in charge of my own life I'll get a little place of my own with my own front door and my own picket fence and my own roses round the door and I'll stay there for ever.*

'Here's my tram,' said Becky, bringing me back to the present. 'See you next week.'

# 4
# Encounter

I listened to the Doppler-descending wail of the baby retreating along the street and breathed a sigh of relief. Now I really could get to grips with my French translation exercise. The building was quiet and still, my father sleeping off the effects of his Monday night's work, my grandmother out visiting Mr Torston and my mother at work at the Beaver Club where I was due to call in to see her later. I wanted to catch up with events at the National Gallery and give myself a little jaunt out, a break from the studying. The first three weeks or so back at school from half term were to be taken up with internal tests and revision classes, our final preparation for the matriculation exams due late June and early July. *Shall I call in to the Beaver Club on my way* to *the Nash Gal or on my way* back *from the Nash Gal?* I pondered.

As an early lunch I heated up some of the soup made by my grandmother from the remains of the previous evening's meal, a casserole of braised steak, carrots and swede, now sieved into a beefy broth. On Saturday we had sausages and on Sunday we ate a half leg of lamb. The mystery of how my mother obtained so much meat on our ration cards was a stone I preferred to leave unturned, but still I worried at possible answers. Other treats appeared, especially two eggs each for Sunday breakfast and a cake made with real eggs for Sunday tea. Our rations books allowed us only one egg each a week. *What was going on?*

The day was turning brighter, the sun threatening to break through lowered brows of grey-lined clouds. At least the deluge of the previous week was now reduced to inter-mittent showers, but I shrugged on a rain mac to cover my pale yellow cotton frock and navy blue cardigan just in case. The tram wound its way into Brixton. I turned and looked fondly towards the further end of Brixton Water Lane as the tram jerked a little on its right turn into Effra Road. Past Brixton Town Hall and the cinema across the road, *I wonder if Bill's back for half term and if he knows I've moved?*, up through Kennington and a gradual westwards turn to cross the Thames over Westminster Bridge. Pride swelled as I saw the familiar sights, Big Ben and the Houses of Par-liament on the left and Westminster Abbey beyond. The tram swung suddenly right and we were speeding along the Embankment with the river sparkling like precious stones in the early afternoon sun. Mesmerised by the scene I nearly missed my stop, scrambling out at the last minute.

A brisk walk up Northumberland Avenue brought me to the southern side of Trafalgar Square and I paused to view Nelson's Column, thinking, *he scuppered Napoleon's inva-sion plans, who will do that for us against Hitler?* I transposed the vision from cinema newsreels of German paratroop-ers spread out around the Square with German troops goose-stepping across it. And a little shiver of fear ran down my spine.

Shaking off my gloomy thoughts, I now had a decision to make, whether to go across to the National Gallery now or to detour via the Beaver Club to greet my mother.

As if the gods were replying, the sun went behind a cloud that cast the Square in chill shadow. *That decides it,* I thought, *I'll warm up with a cup of tea at the Beaver Club first.*

Passing along the side of the Square, I turned towards the Mall, looking for the junction with Spring Gardens. Facing me there was an imposing four-storey colonnaded mid-nineteenth century building. My mother told me to ask at the main door for directions to find her in one of the can-teens. 'The main canteen's in the old Council chamber, but sometimes if it's a bit crowded at lunchtimes we use part of the basement as an overflow.' I moved towards the imposing main entrance.

As I hesitated outside, the right hand of double doors opened, the handle on the inside held by a man in door-man's uniform, a waft of music and conversation weaving out of the building, and three men emerged, two in army uniform and an older one in an air force uniform. I over-heard one of the army men say to the airman, 'Group Captain Bonar not coming with us?' and the other say, 'No, he wants to fit in some sightseeing,' their voices fading as they moved along the street. I stepped forward as the doorman moved to close the door, asking hurriedly, 'Excuse me, is this the Beaver Club?'

Eying me suspiciously, the doorman sniffed, 'It might be. It's a private club for Canadian servicemen. What do *you* want with it?'

'My mother works here and I said I'd call in to see her.'

'And your mother would be?'

'Adela Roberts. She works in the canteen.'

The doorman's severe expression softened into a smile.

'Of course, now I can see you're her daughter. I think she's in the basement this lunchtime. Come on in. Just had to be sure. Don't want any old riff-raff in here you know!' he added jocularly.

The doorman closed the door behind me and beckoned me to follow him. I moved through the imposing entrance lobby, with tall narrow windows either side of the front door and entrances to a couple of side rooms, and on through a large open doorway to a grand hall with an elliptical stair-case leading upwards to the first floor from where I could hear the chink and murmur of the main canteen customers and distant music, the staircase itself swarming with service-men of every description.

The head of the basement stairs was tucked under the sweep of its grand relation, and on the wall to my right in the alcove created by the staircase, and above a table, hung a set of lettered pigeonholes. Seeing the direction of my glance as we stopped momentarily at the top of the basement stairs, the doorman said, with a quirk of his eyebrow, 'Our own private mail service for the military gentlemen.'

I said, descending, the doorman watching, 'I'm only here to meet my mother,' and towards the bottom of the flight I turned my head back to add, 'and *not* the military gentlemen,' thinking myself a little risqué, but my words were cut short as I cannoned into a body in airman's uniform that was turning the corner at the foot of the stairs, his head turned towards the room lying beyond the lobby, saying to a man who stood on the threshold, 'No, I'm fine, thanks, I'll do little exploring on my own,' and the force of two objects meeting at speed meant that one of them was bound to come off worse, and, being the lighter object, that was me. I found myself bouncing downwards as my foot slipped, my backside fell heavily onto the stone step, and my head jerked and cracked on the side wall. My bag went flying and I flailed an arm for the handrail, but it was caught in a strong grip and I found myself hauled back up onto my feet, an arm encircling my waist to steady my balance.

To my mortification tears of pain overflowed as I looked up at the idiot who had bowled into me.

'Hey there, I'm sorry. I guess I wasn't looking where I was going. So, *so* sorry, hey, let me help you over here,' he added, half leading and half carrying me to a nearby chair in the basement entrance lobby. My bottom objected to the pressure on its fresh bruise so I half stood back up, but he pressed me down on to the chair again and called into the room,

'Hey fellas, lady down, could someone bring us a glass of water?'

My mother suddenly crossed my line of vision that had been hitherto blocked by the idiot.

'Pat dear, are you alright? What happened? Did you

knock your head?' This last as I was rubbing the side of my head where it had connected with the wall.

'I'm alright, I'm fine,' I lied, putting my other hand out for the glass of water that now appeared along with the doorman, who, rushing down, restored my handbag to me, and with several uniformed gentlemen all tutting and fussing around me.

'Hey, boy, you wanna keep a better lookout when Jerry's on the horizon!' chortled the one who had been standing on the threshold. It may have been an attempt to lighten the occasion but I shot him a venomous look. I realised my hand was trembling a little as I held the glass and a larger hand gently enveloped mine and held it steady. After a few sips the owner of the hand took and set the glass down on a nearby table.

'Okay fellas, thanks, but show's over,' the idiot said, flapping his hands and the audience melted away leaving just him and my mother ministering to me. Inside the canteen near the door, at the cash till, a soldier holding a tray called 'Shop!' and my mother squeezed my arm gently and said, 'I'm sorry, Pat, I'll be back in a minute, I have to see to my customers,' and sped off.

The idiot pulled up another chair and sat down and I looked across at him. He was certainly not a 'boy'. Below the short, fair, sandy hair and the faint tramlines betraying his forehead, crow's feet around his blue eyes and lines around his neat mouth deepened with his quizzical smile, and I noticed veins standing up a little on the hand resting on the table. Judging him to be perhaps ten to fifteen years older than me, probably nearer my father's age than mine, I found myself relaxing a little in his presence. He was nice looking, but no one I equated with my father could be someone to swoon over. Laughing inwardly at myself, for who was my current pin-up but Ronald Coleman, nearly ten years older than my father, I must have shown some expression of amusement, for my companion leaned back, his smile widening.

'Feeling better?'

I nodded.

'Can I get you anything? A cup of tea perhaps? I hear the English cure all ills with a cup of tea.'

I smiled back. 'Well, yes please, if you don't mind too much. That's really what I came in here for.' I indicated my smudged mascara and looked around. 'I think I need to fix this first.'

'At the far end of the canteen.' He nodded towards the door, indicating direction. I smiled, collected my handbag and retired to the Ladies, mouthing, 'I'm fine now,' as I passed my mother who glanced up from her busy till. She smiled and nodded, returning to her task.

The Ladies proved to be singular, with a basin in the tiny room. Lowering myself gingerly onto the toilet seat I managed to position myself reasonably comfortably. I was feeling a strong sense of embarrassment reliving the encounter. *Perhaps he'll be gone when I emerge and won't really stop to get me a cup of tea*, I half hoped. I felt a little mortified that he had been so profuse in his apologies whereas I had been at least partly at fault and said nothing. The rest of me was curious to see if he was still there.

Make-up restored, I returned to the basement room. It was larger than my first impression, taking up one side of the building, with a dado running at about waist height. Much of the room was occupied with an assortment of rectangular and square wooden tables around which were gathered a variety of service uniforms. At the end of the long serving tables, behind which hovered a couple of serving ladies, and nearest to the main entrance, stood my mother's till, beside which I noticed a table made ready for the clearers with three bins, one clearly a food bin and the next a receptacle for cutlery. The third, closest to the door, had a large notice attached in my mother's elegant handwriting, *Used ration cards and other papers please.*

The idiot was now inside the canteen room sitting

patiently at a table near the entrance with two cups of tea in front of him. Smiling, he rose, helping me to my seat and sitting down again.

'I hope I haven't interfered too much with your plans for this afternoon,' he said.

'Oh, no,' I assured him. 'I intended stopping here for a cup of tea before going on to the Nash Gal.'

He cocked his head half questioningly.

'You're not a member of staff here?'

'No,' interjected my mother, having followed me over upon my reappearance, 'Pat's with me.'

The idiot looked up at her, then across to me and smiled again. 'I can see you're related. Don't let me interfere with your afternoon, ladies,' and he half rose, but my mother placed a hand on his shoulder and pressed him down.

'I'm on duty and, as you can see, it's a busy afternoon,' she said. 'Enjoy your cup of tea. I'll see you later, Pat. Do you want to travel home with me? I'm finishing at five today.'

I checked my watch. 'I want to go to the Nash Gal first, and after that I could go on to do a bit of window shopping. Yes, I'll meet you back here at five.'

My mother nodded and returned to her till.

The idiot leaned forward. 'Pat? Is that short for Patricia?'

I nodded.

'A pretty name, from Patrick,' he continued. *Stating the obvious.* 'Ironically, *the* Saint Patrick was born British but became an Irishman. *My* family originated from Scotland but we're now Canadians. Have your family always lived in London?'

I was a little nonplussed at the turn of the conversation, but did my best. 'My family name is Roberts,' I said, and paused, sipping my tea. 'Originally from a farm in north Wales. That would be two or three generations back, I think. I know my two older uncles went back to the farm when they were in their teens and it was run by a great uncle of theirs so I suppose he would have been the brother of my great-grandfather who came to London.'

I thought further. 'And my other grandfather Caddock's family originated in the southern part of Wales, adding the extra "d" and the "k" on moving to London, at least that's the family legend. So I suppose that makes me similar to you,' I concluded. 'We *were* Welsh but emigrated to England.'

The idiot smiled.

'Allow me to introduce myself. I'm James Bonar. My family are linked to the Clan Graham of Montrose. Call me James.'

He held out a hand and I shook it formally, adding a little mischievously, '*Group Captain* James Bonar, I presume.' He looked a little startled, glancing down at the four stripes on his sleeve, seemingly impressed with my apparent knowledge.

'I'm kinda getting used to them, only just got the promotion before I was sent over here. They kinda missed out the Wing Commander stage as my duties will be administrative as much as flying.'

Fascinated by his alien, melodious, yet precise accent, I confessed that I had overhead an army man exiting the building speak his name.

'Ah, well, as long as it was a good report of me I won't be worried.'

'He said you wanted to do a bit of sightseeing.'

'It would be a shame to waste the opportunity. From this evening I'll be tied up with my duties and I don't know when I'll have any leave. So it's now or never.'

'Well, I really shouldn't hold you up,' I said, a little reluctantly.

'I heard you say "the Nash Gal",' James said. 'Would that be the National Gallery by any chance? The loveliest building in Trafalgar Square?'

I smiled. 'Yes, I want to find out what concerts and events are planned there for the summer.'

'Could I walk you there?' James suggested. 'It might be wise to be accompanied, at least for a little while, to be quite sure that you're not suffering any ill effects, say concussion, from our earlier encounter.'

*I think I'm suffering some effects from our encounter*, I thought, *but I wouldn't call them* ill *effects.*

Aloud I said, 'Well, that would be very kind of you, if it's no trouble.'

At the National Gallery I took down details of a War Artists' Exhibition scheduled for July and of the summer concerts timetable. James was interested that there were still a few paintings left hanging and he proved to be knowledgeable and cultured as we wandered the echoing galleries sharing our mutual interest in art. I thought back to the day Becky and I spent here, an antidote to my disastrous trip to the cinema with Bill. *Now look at me*, I thought, *walking the galleries with this handsome airman*!

As I stood on the steps outside, attempting, but quite failing, to summon up the right parting words, James asked, 'Is Buckingham Palace far? I'm a little disorientated now. Could you point me in the right direction?'

Breathlessly I replied, 'I could show you,' and wondered at my temerity.

James nodded and smiled, relief lighting his chiselled features. Leaning conspiratorially towards me he said, 'I would've asked if you hadn't offered,' and we laughed.

I announced, 'This way, Sir,' flourishing my hand and he chuckled at my mock subservience.

'I was told the Beaver Club provides tour guides, I guess you're the unofficial one.'

Moving into an easy, companionable stride, his long legs adjusting, we conversed about London's history and the places he wanted to see. In St James' Park we paused briefly to watch the ducks on the lake, moving on to the Queen Victoria Monument and the Palace Gates. We turned back east along Birdcage Walk and, cutting through side streets, reached Westminster, where James admired the Mother of Parliaments and Big Ben. We slipped into Westminster

Abbey, gloomy with the boarding up of the removed west window glass, and cavernous, denuded of its removable treasures. Later, Trafalgar Square loomed at the end of Whitehall and at our impending parting I felt a rising panic, curtailed by James' suggestion that we find some refreshment. 'Back to the Beaver Club?' he asked, but it was only a little after four and I didn't want the afternoon to end so abruptly. I thought swiftly.

'No tour guide worth her salt could allow a tour to end without a cup of tea at a Lyons Corner House,' I declared grandly, and James inclined his head for me to lead on. I took him to the one on the opposite corner to Charing Cross Station and we were placed at a table at one side of the room towards the back. James extracted a cigarette packet as we waited for our tea, a quirk of an eyebrow as I refused the proffered cigarette, but he made no comment, dragging deeply before blowing the smoke out of his flared nostrils. He said, 'It's been a very pleasant afternoon. You've been kind to a stranger in a foreign land and made me feel at home. Could I ask one more thing of you?'

At that moment the waitress arrived and we were busy for a few minutes with the flurry of activity. Once cups of tea were in front of us, unable to contain my curiosity, I asked, 'What's the one more thing you'd like me to do?'

James was in no hurry to reply, sipping his tea and helping himself to a small gingerbread cake, which he ate slowly, his even white teeth flashing as he bit into its soft brown depths, his lips meeting firmly, a slight lift to the side of his mouth as he chewed and watched me watching him. I blushed a little as if I had caught him in some kind of personal ritual and he swallowed and nodded slightly, as if coming to a decision, smiling more broadly now, the crow's feet crinkling, and I felt a melting inside me, and I thought, *I'd like to draw him*, and, blushing again, busied myself with cutting up my scone and butter.

James leaned forward and spoke quietly so as to not be overheard.

'Will you write to me? Become a kind of pen pal? Send your letters to me at the Beaver Club? When I was shown around this morning I was told letters can be sent to me there using the pigeonholes on the entrance floor. In the B pigeonhole in my case, or they can send it on to an address I give them when I know where I'll be for a few days. It's easier than trying to write direct. I'll be at Croydon for a coupla days then off to meet up with some of our fellas already over here. We have an RAF squadron of Canadians fighting in France, and other fellas in other RAF squadrons, as well as one of our own squadrons that came over in February. I'll also be checking things out in advance for RCAF squadron No. 1 which'll be coming over soon. And I hope to fit in a little flying where I'm needed. So I won't have a fixed address for a while. I don't know anyone else in England yet and it would be nice to have a pen pal a little closer than Canada.'

Thinking of girls at school corresponding with friends and relatives in the forces to boost morale and that now I would have one such of my own, I smiled up at him, saying, 'I'd be delighted.'

James nodded, smiling back. After a few more moments of companionable tea consumption, looking at his watch, James grimaced. 'The witching hour is here,' he said. 'I have to call in to my digs on my way, so I can't stop any longer. And you have your own appointment across the way there,' he added, tipping his head in the direction of the Square.

'*With my mother,*' I was about to say, but the words were unspoken as James called a waitress over and paid the bill, insisting that he wanted no contribution from me. 'A small price to pay for an afternoon of such pleasant company,' he smiled.

Outside the Corner House, shaking my hand, James leaned forward slightly, checked himself and drew back with a smile. 'So long, Pat. Please write.'

He turned, his wide shouldered, slender-waisted back

disappearing into the crowd milling at the entrance to Charing Cross Station. For a moment it seemed that he raised his right arm and waved before he was lost from my sight.

# 5

# Birthday

The following Saturday I celebrated my birthday a week early at home. With tests and internal exams coming up, my mother decreed that I should stay in Leatherhead over my birthday weekend to concentrate on my revision rather than lose the entire time to a trip to London. I couldn't see how a journey of less than two hours each way door to door could really make all the difference. After all, these were not the actual external matriculation exams. I protested that I could do my revision as easily alone in my little room at home, but my mother retorted, 'If you hole yourself up working in your room we won't see you anyway. You might as well make the most of the extra time there. Besides, I'm on the duty rota for next weekend at the Beaver Club so I wouldn't see you myself much even if you did come home. There *is* a war on, you know.'

I thought the weekend duty rota at the Beaver Club was the more likely explanation for her obduracy, jealous of my father and grandmother having time with me that she wouldn't.

'We've enjoyed having you here this past week,' Mummy added with a finality ending the conversation.

On my sixteenth birthday I awoke early and listened to Becky breathing evenly in the opposite bed. The early sunshine outlined the dark curtains and the birds sang as they swooped and fluttered outside the open window.

I stifled a sob, recalling my birthday with my family last year, my father bringing home a warm roll from his night's baking for my breakfast, my mother and Nan hugging me and wishing me a happy birthday and bearing gifts in their arms and love in their hearts. Today I felt like a poorly roped boat loosened from its moorings by the drifting tide.

Boats. My sob turned to silent tears as I thought of those poor souls who didn't make it off the coast of France, machined down by the Germans as they desperately sought the safety of the flotilla of boats sent to evacuate the retreating men. I heard the wireless pleas and saw the newspaper headlines begging the ordinary and extraordinary boat-owning people of Britain to play their part. The evacuation of the men fleeing for their lives began ten days earlier and lasted into early June. Small boats transported some troops from the beaches to the large troop ships lying off the coast in deeper waters owing to the lack of suitable harbour in the area, and boats of all sizes carried other troops all the way across the Channel.

I was astonished as the reports of the numbers rescued grew. It was said that the prayers of the nation, example-led by the King himself on the last Thursday in May, had been instrumental in saving so many. For during the next day a great storm arose, sinking German boats patrolling the waters and downing many of their planes not already beaten off by the RAF. As the little boats arrived in the storm's wake a great calm fell, the English channel like a mill-pond. The latest estimate was of more than three hundred thousand men having made it back to Britain. But still too many had died there, and many thousands taken prisoners of war, and I thought of the brave airmen fighting off the remaining German warplanes buzzing and harrying the fleeing men on the dunes and beaches. An estimated one hundred British planes were lost along with eighty pilots dead before their time. James had talked about Canadian airmen in France. *Had James fought with them?* I wondered. *And died?* I might never know. The uncertainty was unsettling.

The defeat of Holland, Belgium and now most likely

France, although I had yet to hear of a formal French sur-
render, was shockingly quick and now it was our turn to face
the threat of invasion. *Some Happy Birthday,* I thought bitterly.

After a trip to the toilet, an attempt to catch a little more
sleep came to nothing. Getting up and dressing quietly, I
heard the chime of Mrs Grice's mantelpiece clock. Seven
o'clock. Still an hour to go before Saturday breakfast. I stole
out into the hallway and let myself quietly out of the front
door, putting the key in the lock and turning it backwards
to bring the door closed without a sound, a technique I per-
fected over the years to avoid a slamming door waking my
father prematurely from his daytime sleep.

Warenne Road was still and silent, my footsteps bouncing off the path as I stepped briskly along, breathing in the
mayflower and cowslip scented air, the sun burning onto
the fields lining the road beyond the run of bungalows. I
climbed the gate. The track across the field led to a clump
of trees beside a further gate separating that field from the
next, and I rested on a fallen log beneath the trees, the dew
still glistening here and there in the shade. I stayed a while,
gradually calming my churning thoughts and nauseous
stomach.

*Why does everyone talk about a victory at Dunkirk?* I wondered. We lost, we were overrun, the French gave in and we
couldn't fight for them. Our boys retreated, we left the big
guns and tanks and just ran for it. *How can that be a victory?*
Another part of me reasoned, *well, they thought maybe only a few
would make it back to England, but instead almost the whole of the
army did. So that was something, I suppose.* My thoughts turned
full circle. *What about the tens of thousands who didn't make it?
Dead or prisoners of war. There will be plenty of wives and children
weeping today.*

In my mind I heard my father say – when he taught me,
aged five and starting school, how to fight – 'Chin up, my girl,
back to the wall and bring those fists up,' and now I imagined I was about to face an invading German. I looked up at

the sky, already a brilliant blue, picturing German soldiers parachuting down disguised as nuns (or so the newspapers warned), and what I would do, armed with perhaps more than my fists, maybe a carving knife, to one if he dared to land in the field before me. I would disable him and snatch his gun and cry, *'Hände hoch oder ich schieße!'*, this last courtesy of the Teach Yourself German I acquired from Brixton Library during the half term week. *Hands up or I'll shoot.*

*I'll definitely do German in the sixth form,* I decided, *so I can spy on them if their invasion succeeds.*

The absurdity of these thoughts brought a wry smile to my face and I stood, ready to retrace my steps back to my billet and thinking about the day ahead. Asking around my year if anyone fancied going on a picnic on my birthday, I had been pleasantly surprised when several girls eagerly assented.

Becky was awake when I returned, already half-dressed and planning to look for me.

'Did you guess where I might be?' I asked.

'Well, as those trees are where you always seem to head when you want to get away from it all, I don't think it would have taken me long to find you,' Becky replied with a warm smile. 'What is it, that you're sixteen at last but you wish you could stay fifteen forever, or you're feeling sad to be away from home, or,' and she leaned forward conspiratorially, raising an eyebrow, 'you have a beau with whom you were keeping a secret assignation? You're old enough to get married now.'

'Only with my parents' consent,' I laughed. An image of James' smiling, chiselled face rose before me.

Becky chuckled. 'A secret beau called James, perhaps, the one you told me about at half term? Aha, you're positively beetroot! Or your friend Bill? Or,' she added hastily, seeing my sudden frown, 'perhaps you'll have a chance at the dance with a St Birstan's boy. Hey, I like that, it rhymes. Chance at the dance,' she repeated to herself.

'*No* chance at the dance,' I retorted, although I was looking forward to the opportunity the forthcoming end of exams dance would give me to use my ballroom dancing skills acquired over many terms' dancing lessons partnered by various fellow St Martin's girls. Only problem was that, being tall, I tended to have to dance the man's role so I would have to think twice as hard to translate the steps into the lady's moves.

'Well, anyway,' said Becky, 'I was coming to look for you to wish you a happy birthday, and,' she continued, diving into her suitcase beneath her bed, 'to give this to you.'

I took the small package from her. It was wrapped in decorated brown paper and tied with a thin pink ribbon.

'What pretty paper,' I said. 'Did you decorate it yourself?' The paper sported little butterfly motifs randomly drawn and coloured in. 'How sweet of you.' I opened the package and found a small book entitled *The Impressionist Series: Monet*.

'Oh,' I squealed, 'what a lovely book, how kind of you. Where *did* you get it?'

'Charing Cross Road. I got it last week during half term break. It's second hand,' she added a little abashed, 'I'm sorry, that's all I could afford.'

'It's *perfect*,' I breathed, flicking through the pages and stopping to admire the black and white reproductions of some of Monet's most famous works, the 'Water Lily Pond' and 'The Woman in the Green Dress'.

'And here's your card,' added Becky, handing over an envelope which I opened and found a home made card with a butterfly theme too.

'You've really made my birthday special,' I told her, giving her a quick thank you hug.

Halfway through our toast a rat-tat-tat sounded on the front door knocker. 'The milkman?' speculated Mrs Grice with a frown as it was still rather early for someone to come visiting, and she made her way to the hall, closing the living room door behind her.

Straining our ears to the low murmurings at the front door, we jumped a little as Mrs Grice burst into the living room with a flustered,

'Oh, Becky dear, I am so sorry, your father's been taken very ill and your mother's asking for you to go to her straight away.'

Mr Parker hovered in the hall behind her. Becky and I looked at each other in alarm. For Becky's mother to have rung the one contact number she had other than St Birstan's School, and so early in the morning, the situation must be very serious indeed.

Becky rose quickly from the table and moved to the door.

'Mr Parker,' she said, 'did my mother say what's wrong?'

'No, Miss,' Mr Parker replied, clearly uncomfortable at being the bearer of bad news. He was slightly breathless, as if he had run here. 'Just that your father has been rushed to St Thomas' Hospital and your mother wants you to meet her there as soon as possible.'

'Goodness, it must be serious,' said Becky.

'How terrible for you, especially after the happy news of your brother's baby,' I sympathised.

Becky turned to me. 'Oh, Pat, what if I have to miss the revision tests next week.'

We looked at each other in horror.

'If it's *really* serious you'd not be able to concentrate anyway,' I said, a proper Job's comforter I realised as I said the words, and hastened to make amends. 'I'll walk with you to the station.'

'Oh, you don't have to do that,' Becky protested but I thought how I would feel if summoned by my mother under such circumstances and insisted.

Becky hastily crammed a few belongings into the little case unpacked only six days earlier and we hastened to the station. We took the short cut along the millpond footpath and made it in little over thirty-five minutes.

'I'm so sorry to miss your birthday picnic,' said Becky as we waited for the train.

'Don't worry about it, you've enough on your plate,' I replied. 'We can have a picnic any day. Your father's more important now.'

I waved her goodbye, remonstrating silently with myself for selfishly resenting the intrusion of her father's illness into my birthday plans. Becky had a naturally happy and bubbly personality and made a good companion. I was going to miss my best friend on my birthday.

The sun beat hard on my back as I returned. I stood awhile beside the millpond, marvelling at the stillness of the air and the quietness of my surroundings broken only by the humming of the bees in the wildflower-strewn hedgerows and the cawing of the crows on their treetop perches. Swans and geese swam towards me like a mini flotilla with ducks their pilot boats and I apologised to them for the absence of bread. A couple of geese mounted the bank ahead of me honking loudly and I thrust through them and hurried on.

Janet also missed my birthday picnic, away at a family wedding. The remaining nine of us gathered with our bikes outside the Evacuation Distribution Centre at the pre-arranged time of one o'clock. A ragged chorus of 'Happy Birthday, Pat,' accompanied the girls' arrivals and by one fifteen we were all ready. We sped off northwards towards Oxshott Heath, a long straggly ribbon of pumping legs and billowing skirts, our bicycle baskets laden with bread and tinned spam and a few luxuries such as cake, boiled eggs and early tomatoes contributed by the farmer's wife with whom Gwen was billeted.

Swinging off the road near the War Memorial at Oxshott Heath we pushed our bikes up the slope and stopped a while at the Memorial to admire the view south west across the Surrey hills. I originally intended us to picnic there, but the sun was beating down, the air still and heavy with the sweet scents of summer and the stickiness of another very hot day, so I brought out a sketch I had made for this very contingency from Mr Grice's old ordnance survey map of the locality. A lake lay perhaps a mile or so to the northwest. 'I think I've found somewhere to cool off,' I said. 'We'll eat our picnic there. Follow me, girls.'

A short way along the track northwards, before it plummeted downhill again, I remembered the smart second hand Box Brownie, an early birthday present from my parents the week before, resting under the food in my bicycle basket. Drawing to a halt, I ushered the girls together. As the sun beat down, Gwen, Kitty, Daisy, Nora, Vera and Joyce lined up in a clearing, some with arms around others' waists, to form a standing back row, while Muriel and Fiona knelt in the grasses in front of them. A solemn moment and made only the more poignant by Becky's unexpected absence, Muriel and Fiona instinctively sitting to the centre and one side, leaving a space in the cameo where Becky should have been.

'Now a photo of the birthday girl,' said Fiona, taking the camera and I obligingly stood still, squinting a little under the sun's brilliance.

Retrieving our bicycles, we bumped steeply downhill and cycled along a wide track to Sandy Lane. Mistaking a driveway entrance for the staggered trackway continuation shown on the map, I took us along the drive and past a silent, apparently unoccupied property. We pushed through a gap in the rear shrubbery to undulating forest slopes, aiming to rejoin the trackway proper from an oblique angle. Silver birches and oaks gave way to pine trees which stretched high above us creating a cool canopy, the unadorned trunks standing like paraded soldiers as we headed on northwestwards, pushing our bicycles around the trees. Worrying that we had missed the lake altogether, I was relieved to encounter the narrow but defined trackway that continued northwest and we sped on our bicycles over undulating ground, brushing ferns with our ankles as we skirted further deciduous foliage with sprouting bushes cloaking oaks, elms and more silver birches. Pressing on through ranks of pines again, I gave a cry of triumph as I spotted tall reeds grow-ing in the distance. Reaching the Black Pond's embanked western shore we discarded our bicycles and sank onto fallen tree trunks and hastily thrown picnic blankets, a pair of old curtains lent to Gwen by the farmer's wife. Old, gnarled oak trees shaded us while the sunlight sparkled and danced on the waters, the lake's surface broken into V shapes in the wake of ducks advancing on us like miniature battleship convoys.

'Sorry, duckies, we're too hungry to spare you much,' apologised Nora, as we dived into our baskets and retrieved our packages. I also laid out a tablecloth, brought from home the previous weekend, on the bare black soil that I presumed gave the lake its name. We set out our shared con-tributions to the picnic on the tablecloth and settled down, at first feasting silently apart from murmurings of 'Mmm, I love this *real* egg,' and 'This cake's *delicious*, who made it?' Hunger and thirst assuaged, cards and little birthday gifts were presented to me, a couple of small bars of soap, hand-kerchiefs, a lipstick, a costume jewellery broach and other trinkets. We swapped stories of our Whitsun break adven-tures, or, in some cases, the lack of them.

'It was really boring at home,' moaned Muriel, running her hands through her curly auburn hair, a self-deprecating grimace on her freckled face. 'My mother wouldn't let me go out much in case Jerry decided to pop over the Channel, as if he was interested in anything except bombing the hell out of our boys over there.'

'You poor thing,' sympathised Kitty. 'I had to do the rounds of relatives. Frankly, I'd rather sit at home watching paint dry.'

'Oh, that's just what I *did*,' laughed Nora, tossing her dark plait over her shoulder. 'My mother decided to have our downstairs redecorated. I ask you, just when I got home for the hols! A good job the weather improved as the week went on, as the smell of the paint was overwhelming. We had so many windows open at night with no lights on we might as well as bivouacked down in the garden!'

We all chuckled and Gwen, who had spread herself out flat on the ground like a star, drew her legs and arms back to her slender body and sat up, hugging her knees, asking me, 'So, Pat, what did *you* get up to last week?'

'Ah ha,' pounced Vera, 'she's blushing! Go on, Pat, who is he?'

The girls crowded in, chins in hands, and I thought, *I've already hidden enough family secrets to last a lifetime, I'm going to have to be better at keeping my own cards close to my chest.*

'Really,' I protested, 'it's nothing. An airman was just being friendly, that's all.'

'*Friendly!*' Vera pounced again. '*How* friendly? Who is he? How did you meet him?'

I hesitated, not knowing whether my mother would be happy for me to tell anyone about her latest employment. Throughout my childhood and youth I was sworn to secrecy that my mother worked as a cleaner, sometimes doing two jobs in the same day, one early morning and the other late into the evening after she'd given my father his breakfast and Nan and I our tea, and seen my father off to his night work. Nan, working at a laundry during the day until she retired, kept me company in the evenings. It simply was not the done thing for a housewife to work because she had to, not if you wanted to rise in society and claim a place at a middle class table. None of my contemporaries whose fathers were bankers or doctors or solicitors or accountants had mothers who worked. In some professions a woman even lost her job when she got married; there were no married women teachers in schools. But with the 1929 Wall Street crash, my father had been forced to take a one third cut in wages just to keep his job and my mother had been forced into menial work. Our family fortunes, little as they had been, never recovered.

*But there's a war on, and lots of women are now working, and some are even doing men's jobs.*

'We-ell,' I began slowly, choosing my words carefully, 'my mother's decided to do something to help the war effort, and helps out,' I hesitated to say *works*, 'at the Beaver Club just off Trafalgar Square. It's for Canadian servicemen when they're in London on leave.'

'You mean Canadian soldiers?' queried Fiona.

I nodded. 'And airmen. And presumably sailors too.'

Fiona continued, 'We have Canadian *soldiers* staying near Leatherhead. I know there are Polish and Czech airmen over here but that's because Hitler invaded their countries.'

'Canadians have recently been joining the RAF and some have formed their own RAF squadron apparently, and one Royal Canadian Air Force squadron's here already and now a second will be coming over too,' I explained. '*I* wouldn't have known that if my mother wasn't,' I hesitated again and jettisoned *working* for 'attending the Beaver Club. James says he's meeting Canadian airmen already over here and preparing for more to come.'

Vera pounced a third time, 'So, *James*, is it? You're on first name terms?'

'Well, not really, only it seemed polite.'

'So tell us,' persisted Vera, 'how did you get talking to him. Did he give you the eye? Or did you throw yourself at him?'

'Of *course* not,' I protested vigorously, to an echo of my father's admonitions the previous Christmas holidays about not leading young men on. 'I went to the Club to meet my mother and I bumped into him. Well, he bumped into me. Well, we bumped into each other.'

'*Bumped into each other*?' shrieked Vera, her stubby arms flailing, while Nora chortled, 'So you *did* throw yourself at him.'

Vera persisted, 'How do you just *happen* to bump into each other?'

I flushed. 'We-ell, he was looking one way and going another and I was looking back and he came round the corner of the steps just as I got there and we collided and I fell down and he helped me up...'

'*Helped you up*?!!'

I thought, *good job Vera's not near any glass*.

'Then I said I was going to the Nash Gal to check on the concert timetable for the summer, and he said he had just arrived in London on his way to Croydon that evening and had just a few hours spare for sightseeing and if I was going to the Nash Gal would I allow him to accompany me and, well, one thing led to another...'

Daisy leapt in with, 'One thing led to *what*?'

'Oh,' I recovered, 'I don't mean *that* sort of thing. I mean, I took him to the Nash Gal, and he wanted to see the Palace, and after that Westminster, and we went back to the Square and stopped off at the Lyons opposite Charing Cross station for afternoon tea. Then he had to go...'

'So,' breathed Daisy, 'when will you see him again?'

'Goodness, I've no idea, probably never,' I shrugged, looking across the lake and not meeting anyone's eye and certainly not mentioning the promise he had extracted from me to correspond with him via the Club.

I turned to Daisy. 'I was just being polite to an overseas visitor.'

'*Polite?*' shrieked Vera, bouncing on the spot. 'Polite is saying, "Good bye, sir, nice to have met you", not *walking the streets with him*.'

'It wasn't *that* sort of walking the streets,' I snorted indignantly. 'Besides, my mother knew he was accompanying me to the Nash Gal. It's not as if we were anywhere other than in public at all times.'

'How old is he?' This was Vera again.

'Oh, *ancient*,' I replied. 'Must be, I don't know, maybe somewhere between twenty-five and thirty, I'd guess.'

'But what was he *like*?' persisted Vera.

'Well, he was very polite and personable, I suppose.'

'*No*,' Vera's voice squeaked off the end of the scale, 'I

mean, what did he *look* like. Is he handsome? A Clark Gable, or an Errol Flynn, or a Tyrone Power?'

I hesitated, picturing the straight nose, the square jaw with its central dimple, the deep blue eyes and the almost blond, with a hint of auburn, short back and sides looking down from a near six-foot height. And the quirky tilt to his lips when he smiled and the laughter creases at the side of his eyes.

'More Wayne Morris,' I decided. 'We-ell, somewhere between Wayne Morris and a sandy-haired Cary Grant.'

'Now *there's* a combination,' said Nora dreamily.

'Wayne Morris?' asked Kitty.

'Oh,' interjected Gwen, 'I know who he is too. I read about him in an old copy of *Movie Mirror* my American cousin Penny sent me. I passed it on to Pat. Hey, Pat, have you still got it?'

I nodded.

'Well,' continued Gwen, 'Wayne Morris is tall and blond and kind of cute. *Movie Mirror* said he's up and coming and going to blow the whole Hollywood scene away.' As she said this she flung her arm up in the air in a dramatic arc.

'I'd rather have a tall, dark and handsome Tyrone Power,' said Muriel.

'Instead of which, all *we'll* get stuck with at the dance is a whole load of pimply, gawky boys, not muscly, handsome men,' laughed Nora.

'Oh, they're not so bad,' Joyce volunteered. 'I'll bet the muscly, handsome men were pimply and gawky once. And Peregrine Brake is really rather awfully sweet and he says he'll dance with me.'

'How do you get to even *talk* to the boys at St Birstan's?' Nora asked her. 'The whole school day seems especially designed to keep us separate as if St Martin's was invisible. And you know we'll get into trouble if we're seen talking to them in the street.'

'Oh, I met him in Woolworths one Saturday afternoon

and we got chatting. So now we have secret signs so that if we see each other across the quadrangle, for example, he'll signal, see you Saturday three o'clock in Woolworths and I'll signal yes, and then we just *happen* to both be near the hardware section at the back at that time the following Saturday and no one would know it was a set up.'

'Well, *we* know *now*,' chortled Nora.

'Oh, but you won't tell anyone, will you?' asked Joyce anxiously.

The conversation moved on and away from my own romantic interlude. Well, it had hardly been that. James had been the model of decorum and, anyway, how could an afternoon stroll around the tourist spots of London in the company of a stranger, who at a rough estimate had to be at least ten years older than me, amount to a romantic interlude? *He's probably nearer my mother's age than mine,* I thought. *Romantic? What a daft idea, I'm getting soppy in my ripe old age of sixteen. Bearing in mind I'll probably never see him again.*

Gradually our circle split up, some going in search of wild strawberries and early blackberries, though mostly unsuccessfully, others removing shoes and socks and dipping hands and toes into the water to cool off, and some picking wild flowers to take back to their hostesses. I bagged up my presents and cards with the Box Brownie and returned the bag to my bicycle basket. We regrouped and played hide and seek amongst the tall reeds and the line of deciduous trees to the north of the lake, squealing as we were found, regressing to early childhood in our eagerness to shake off the oppression of war. Beyond these trees a swathe of ground the size of two or three football pitches had been levelled, the trees chopped down, the bushes cleared, surprising evidence of human activity in an otherwise unspoiled landscape. At one point I thought I heard lorries on a distant main road but they stopped some way to the north. We were in a magic kingdom, cocooned from the real world.

We reconvened beside the lake to finish the rest of the

drinks we had brought with us, cooling ourselves in the trees' shade. I was thinking of gathering up the remains of the picnic when I heard distant aeroplanes buzzing closer. We looked around and up and three aeroplanes hoved into view from the east across the lake in a V formation, disgorging parachutists who first floated high like flying insects, growing larger and larger like birds of prey as they descended towards the bare ground beyond the trees bordering the lake to the north.

'It's an invasion!' squeaked Joyce, scrambling up.

'Nonsense, there are no church bells ringing,' Nora tried to reassure us, but, 'Only because we can't hear them from here,' said Gwen.

'Run, girls,' I cried, springing up from the picnic remains, grabbing my bicycle and running with it into the southern tall pine tree cover to retrace our route in. The other girls did likewise as the first of the parachutists dipped down beyond the northern tree fringe, others following, and suddenly Vera, who, like Lot's wife, was looking back, emitted a loud shriek,

'*Soldiers!*'

And, as we all turned to look, it was as if the foliage on the north side of the lake had erupted and a wave of soldiers burst through the trees and the reeds and ran onto the western embankment, yelling and screaming and firing towards the parachutists' landing area.

'Leave the bikes, just *run*,' I screeched, throwing mine to the ground and running as fast as I could. We sped on through the pine forest to the deciduous treeline ridge beyond, hastening back along the track, bracken and ferns swiping our legs as we stumbled ungainly, the commotion behind us growing a little distant. Suddenly, to our horror, a line of twig-behelmeted soldiers emerged from the foliage alongside the track ahead of us, weapons out and shouting, 'Stop, don't move, hands up, stand still!'

*Thank God they're English.* I thought, my heart thudding

and my legs trembling as I skidded to a halt. *No, not English. American accent. No, not American, no Americans over here. Maybe like James. Canadian?*

By now we were surrounded, and I realised Joyce was not the only one openly crying with fear.

'*We're English,*' Nora yelled. '*We're on the same...*' She didn't finish as one of them, a sergeant, stepped forward and thrust his hand over her mouth.

'Quiet, all of you,' he hissed. 'Get down, over here.' He indicated the line of shrubbery behind him and we were thrust through it and down a slight incline beyond. 'Sit down and keep quiet now, don't move.' He turned back to the track.

'I need the toilet,' whimpered Joyce. 'Me too,' muttered several others of us, but there was nothing we could do but hold on and cower behind the screen of bushes while a long line of soldiers silently passed our hiding place, leaving two behind to guard us, or perhaps to prevent any further accidental military encounters.

We heard spasmodic firing in the distance now, a lot of shouting and after perhaps fifteen or twenty minutes all seemed to go quiet. One of the soldiers on guard duty shifted uneasily and the other hissed at him, 'Wait up.'

'I can't wait any longer,' gasped Joyce and, scrambling in a crouched stance down the slight incline beyond us, disappeared behind a further clump of bushes beside a large oak. The soldiers shrugged at each other and waited and Joyce shortly emerged looking happier, her place being taken by others of us for whom the stress of the event was proving too much to bear.

Not wishing to catch the soldiers' eyes, who seemed amused by the turn of events, we gradually resumed our places and waited for events to unfold.

We waited for what seemed a lifetime.

Suddenly the soldiers stood to attention and a gruff voice called out, 'You can come out, girls, and *not* with your hands up.'

We scrambled out of our hiding place onto the track and met with an older, clearly higher ranking officer than the sergeant who had 'captured' us.

'Ladies,' he addressed us, his accent both clipped and melodious, like James'. 'You will give your names and addresses to the sergeant here before you go. You will all be aware of the Official Secrets Act. Not one word of this afternoon's exercise is to be spoken to anyone. *Anyone.* Do you hear me?'

'Yes, sir,' we chorused.

'Not to your parents, not to your friends, not to your young men, and you are not even to discuss this event with each other. Ever. *Do you hear me?*'

'Yes sir,' we parroted again.

'Now go home and remember Esher Common is given over to the Canadian army for training exercises and is *off limits to all of you in future.*'

The sergeant stepped forward, reaching into his pocket for notepad and pencil, as his superior officer turned to go.

'Sir,' I called to the officer, petrified, but feeling responsible for the girls' frightening experience and for their belongings, as it was, after all, *my* birthday party and the jaunt to the lake had been my idea, 'please may we retrieve our bicycles, otherwise we won't have transport, and our parents will want to know what we did with them.'

I saw the officer take in the unassailable logic of my request. He appeared to mentally count our number and turned to the sergeant. 'Get nine of your men to find these girls' bicycles and bring them here and two of your men can escort them off the common.'

We left behind my mother's tablecloth, the farmer's wife's curtains and the remains of the picnic for the ducks' pleasure. I found with relief that my presents and camera bag had remained safely stowed in my bicycle basket and set off southwards to Sandy Lane. There our escort, with a mock salute, turned back while we sped on to Leatherhead.

We stopped briefly outside the Evacuation Distribution Centre and I said, 'Before you all go, I just want to say sorry, girls, I had no idea I was leading you into danger,' but they all shushed me with,

'But not your fault, Pat.'

'My, what an adventure!'

'Easy to say it's an adventure when it's all over.'

'Shush, we mustn't talk about it or they'll shoot us!'

'What about your curtains, Gwen?'

Gwen shrugged. 'They were old and patched and she said she didn't want them. I'll say I gave them to jumble.'

'What I want to know is,' this from Kitty, 'why no signs? We saw no signs warning us off.'

'Or sentries,' said Vera.

Muriel suggested, 'There probably *are* signs on the main roads, on the Esher and Cobham roads, and we would have missed any sentries at the Sandy Lane track entrance when we cut down that driveway. We were just unlucky with the route we took.'

'All's well that ends well,' said Nora. 'Something to tell the grandchildren when we're in our dotage.'

And we laughed with nervous relief and peeled off in our different directions.

# 6

# Midsummer

Just before the end of the half-term week I had sneaked a letter to James into the B pigeonhole in the Beaver Club entrance hall. Not wishing to burden him with the trivia of exam preparation while he was setting off to engage in a life and death struggle, I recounted an amusing incident during a trip to the park at half term with Peggy, told him about a concert attended on the Thursday of that week with Becky and ended with my hopes that his duties would go well for him and that he would have plenty of opportunities to enjoy a good English cup of tea. *And thus think of me*, was the unspoken other half of that sentence.

Let out of school the Friday following my birthday earlier than I intended admitting to my parents, I came home via central London. With my heart in my mouth I entered the front door to the Club. I checked the R pigeonhole and found a letter addressed to P. Roberts c/o the Beaver Club. I offered a whole sixpence to the doorman for his silence. Pressing it back into my hand with a shake of his head, a wink and a finger to his lips, he shooed me outside. Trembling, I thrust the letter into my pocket and, lugging my suitcase, raced back down Northumberland Avenue for the tram. My mother's shift was due to end at four o'clock and so she would not be long behind me.

I climbed onto the tram, paid my fare and took James' letter out.

*Dear Pat,* he wrote, *Thank you for agreeing to be my pen pal and thank you for your letter and your news. I liked your story about your dog. I would like to go with you to a concert one day.*

*I can't believe I have been here a week already.* I checked the date. Written just over a week earlier, it had probably been waiting for me the previous weekend when I was being chased over Esher Common by Canadian soldiers. I smiled wryly at the irony.

I returned to his letter. *I have been busy learning the British ropes, not so different from our own but your airplanes have their own idiosyncrasies* (I thought he must be pretty well educated to spell that word correctly first off) *and it's important I get to grips with everything. I have flown a couple of sorties this week to get my hand in, nothing to write home about (so I am writing to you instead!). I was only in France briefly, and now back in England following the retreat to English shores. Next week I'll be off to other aerodromes. I think you'll understand why I can't go into any more detail here.*

*Thank you for showing me your beautiful capital city. I am sure there is plenty else I have yet to see and if you would be willing to show me around London some more when I get my next leave, your kindness towards this stranger from another land would be much appreciated. I will see what leave I can wangle. Possibly the weekend of 15th June.* (That's this weekend, I realised.) *All leave is officially suspended while we wait to see what the Hun will get up to next. However, as I am only an honorary member of the RAF while awaiting our own squadron, my arrangements are a little more flexible. I will aim to be at the Beaver Club around two-thirty to three o'clock in the afternoon of 15th June. I can't promise, of course, but if you happen to be there too perhaps we could have another chinwag over a cup of tea. Yes, I've been drinking plenty of those in the past week! If you can pass your reply letter to the doorkeeper (or do you call him the concierge? Doorman?) it can be sent on to me here.*

*With all good wishes,*
*James.*

I read the letter twice more on the journey and hid it in my pocket. I needed to work out how I might manage to see him the next day without my parents knowing.

Before my father left for work I fished out a form to be completed asking about my sixth form choices. Definitely *not* A Good Thing.

'Commercial subjects, most definitely,' said my mother.

'But Mummy,' I protested, 'I don't *want* to become a secretary. You know I want to teach.'

'Teaching's all very well until you get married and then you'll be out of a job,' my mother replied tartly. 'If you get called up at eighteen you can avoid doing anything dangerous by offering secretarial skills. Besides, secretaries can earn good money if they land in the right place and it's respectable for a secretary to work after they're married if they want to earn a little pin money.'

'But you didn't want anyone to know *you* were working when I was younger.'

'Cleaning work's not the same. Besides, I worked because I *had* to work. As a secretary you'll meet all kinds of well-off men who can offer you a better future than your father and I can.'

My father, buried behind the Friday evening paper in the corner armchair, shook the paper slightly and cleared his throat. The implication that his baker's wage was not enough to keep the family without recourse to other income was clear. I felt a pang of sympathy for him. *It's not his fault,* I thought, *I'm the lucky generation that has the opportunity of a proper education.* Both of my parents were intelligent, cultured people who just happened to be born into a stratum of society where education required money, and money was the one thing they had lacked. I had been so lucky to win a Junior County Scholarship and I knew that my parents went short of essentials, as well as luxuries, to provide for my uniform and school books and other expenses that went with being a high school girl. My contemporaries who had gone at eleven to the local central school had left school at fourteen and were now contributing much needed family income. This point did not elude my mother.

'And another thing...'

From my seat near the window I leaned back gently, and oh, so slowly, so that Mummy would not discern the movement, and caught my father's *here she goes again* roll of the eyes. I suppressed a snort of laughter as my mother's haranguing continued unabated.

'...your father and I are sacrificing *everything* to keep you at school into the sixth form while half your class are leaving school this summer and getting a job and paying their way. Not that I am saying *you* should do *that*,' she added, having noticed me open my mouth and take a deep breath as a prelude to speaking. 'We're prepared to see you through to eighteen when it will be high time you pulled your weight, and,' she continued triumphantly, her logic unassailable, 'with secretarial qualifications behind you, you'll walk straight into a good, steady job.'

My father lowered his paper a fraction and, knowing that from where she was sitting facing me and away from him, my mother was unlikely to see him clearly, raised one eyebrow while frowning slightly, an expression I knew only too well from the many years he had ridden my mother's carping, and which meant, *Say no more now, we'll speak later when the coast is clear.*

So I swallowed my retort and rose to clear away the tea cups.

As I reached the little kitchenette area on the landing with the tea tray my mother, who just did not know when to stop, caught up with me.

'I'm prepared to indulge your desire to learn German, as that *might* come in useful one day, though, as God knows, the reason why is the *last* thing anyone wants, but we have to be prepared for the worst. And I *am* willing to indulge your enthusiasm for art, although I can't imagine anyone respectable actually earning a living from it, so you'll have to do something practical with the rest of your time and get yourself a good foundation for earning a living when you've finished there.'

By the end of her speech I was vigorously scouring the tea china in the tiny sink and dumping the pieces with a clatter on the wooden draining board, my anger having risen like an enveloping tide.

'Be careful with those, that was my grandmother's precious china,' admonished my mother as she grabbed a tea towel and started drying the pieces up.

'I *will* be doing something practical if I go into teaching,' I growled. 'I'm sure you were grateful for what you were taught at school.'

'Your temper and snide comments will get you nowhere,' my mother retorted. 'I stand by what I say, and,' she added in a raised voice as I finished my task and fled back into the living room, 'don't go back to school without getting Daddy to sign the form and *giving it to me to check.*'

My father raised an eyebrow.

'I'll walk a little of the way with you, Daddy,' I said, as my father got up and started to gather himself ready for his journey to the bakery, signing the school form on his way from the room.

We both shrugged on rain macs as the hot weather of the previous weekend had given way to cool, rainy days and, although at the moment of our departure it was dry, the low clouds were threatening and a chill dampness permeated the air. For a few moments we walked contemplatively together.

Daddy said, 'Let her have her way for now. Don't fight it. Enjoy your art lessons and put up with the rest. She'll come round. I think this war is changing things. I remember after the Great War life was never quite the same. Ladies now do things undreamt of before then, and I think this one will change things around again. In a year's time, who knows where we'll all be.'

*Why does he always give in to her?* I thought. As I opened my mouth to object, Daddy held up his hand to shush me.

'If you give the commercial training a go this year, this time next year I'll see if you can switch to something more of your liking.' He turned his head towards me. 'Your mother has a point. Commercial training will give you skills that will give you an option. Give yourself a year to learn some commercial skills. If you're still as set on teaching this time next year then I'll support you applying for teacher training. That would mean you won't be called up and so the issue of what you do if called up won't arise. But for the moment see your mother's wishes as keeping your options open.'

We walked westwards along Idmiston Road and onto Chatsworth Way, and now we were crossing the Norwood Road for the tram stop and I knew my time with my father was up. It would only leave a bad taste in my mouth if I argued with him, so close to parting. Besides, perhaps his wait and see policy would pay off in the long run.

'Very well, Daddy. I'll do as you say.' The tram stopped beside us.

'Chin up, my girl, TTFN.' *Ta ta for now.* The tram swooped him up, my handsome, dapper father who always tried to say something sensible even if he were powerless to follow through. *He can only be about ten years older than James,* I thought.

Clasping the letter concealed in my pocket, not risking leaving my mother alone in the flat with a letter vulnerable to discovery, I turned towards West Norwood station, diving into a general grocers that was still open, buying writing paper, pen and envelopes. I sat on the station entrance kerb, oblivious to the passengers stepping around me and wrote hurriedly,

*Dear James, Thank you for your letter. I am sorry I have not replied sooner. I live in Leatherhead during the week where the school is evac-uated and I was not home last weekend for my birthday so I have only just picked up your letter this afternoon. I am glad you are settling in*

well. *I hope the weather this past week has not proven adverse to your progress. Everything here is much the same. I will be pleased to show you more of London when you have the opportunity and I will do my best to be at the Beaver Club between 2.30pm and 3pm tomorrow, but if I can't perhaps we will meet again some other time. See you later, alligator.* And agonised as to whether with the last I was being too familiar.

I addressed the letter to him care of the Beaver Club and dashed to West Norwood Post Office. They were closing, but I just caught that evening's post. *At least he'll get the letter tomorrow,* I thought, *or if he can't be there it will be sent on to him.*

Satisfied that I had done all I could, I set off home, realising as I sped along Idmiston Road that the sprightly figure ahead of me was my grandmother.

'Nanny,' I called and she turned, waiting for me to catch up and giving me a kiss and a hug.

'Lovely to see you again, my dear,' she said. We linked arms for the last hundred yards or so to the house.

'How's your love life going, Nanny?' I asked, a little cheekily. 'How's your Mr Torston?'

'He's doing very well, thank you my dear,' she replied. 'And how's *your* Mister Whoever?'

'I don't have a love life,' I responded. 'I'm far too much of a swot for that.'

'Nonsense, my dear,' she retorted, pulling back and turning to me. 'You've a sparkle in your eye and I don't suppose it was young Bill who put it there.'

I laughed, throwing my head back. 'Ah, well, there are *any* number of young men at St Birstan's to choose from. And when I'm walking out with one of them all nice and proper you'll be the first to know.'

'That means it's not one of them either,' observed Nanny, and I laughed again, tapping my nose with my forefinger and steering her towards the front door.

That evening I mentioned in passing that I had in mind to seek out Becky the next day, from whom I had received a brief missive on Wednesday telling me her father had died and she would not be returning to Leatherhead that week. 'I want to buy her some flowers from the market and maybe spend a little time with her.'

'Oh,' said my mother, 'I have plans for this weekend, but in the circumstances, they can wait.'

'I'll give you the morning,' I offered, 'and head off at lunchtime.'

'Well, why don't we get the tram to the market and you can choose some material for a new summer frock as I've been saving clothing coupons, and we'll pick up some food for the weekend.'

The next morning I solved the mystery of the plentiful supply of food in our ration-strapped household. Not content with concentrating on two or three shops in total, my mother darted in and out of three different butchers, four different grocers and two delicatessens, mostly in and around Brixton and the remainder in West Norwood as we arrived back from our outing. We filled a couple of capacious bags she had chosen with fastenings and cloths to cover the food as it was plunged into the depths of the bags.

Away from the busy main road with no one to overhear, I demanded in a low voice, 'How can we be buying all this food on our ration cards? Where have all the ration stamps come from?'

My mother turned and, putting her finger to her lips, tapped the side of her nose and actually winked.

'Be thankful for small mercies,' she murmured. By now we had moved from Chatsworth Way into Idmiston Road and my arms felt as if they had grown several inches with the weight of the bags.

I persisted, 'Please don't tell me you've got them off the black market. They could be stolen and there would be hell to pay if you're discovered.'

'Don't use such language,' scolded my mother, 'and they're not stolen, merely discarded.'

I stopped as a memory assailed me. 'The Beaver Club. There's a bin near the tills. It says ration cards and other things.'

'I can't fault your powers of observation,' said my mother acidly as she carried on and I hurried to catch up. She sighed. 'I might be one of the few paid staff there, but it's no more than cleaning would pay. I *do* get a free lunch thrown in, I suppose. Anyway, one day I realised the boys were throwing their week's rations cards away with unused ration stamps as they left at the end of their leave.'

By now we were at the front door and she turned to me as she extracted her key from her bag. Speaking low, she said defensively, 'It's not stealing, you know. Those cards would just be thrown away. I could find a buyer, I suppose, who would make me a penny or two on the black market, but I don't want to get embroiled in something so underhand. I still have to pay for the food, of course, but as part of the regular ration arrangements. It's not like I'm having to buy the food at sky high prices like off some of those dodgy market stalls.'

As she turned to the door and inserted the key, she hissed over her shoulder, 'Don't tell Daddy. I'm sure he's worked it out but he doesn't want to *know*, if you understand what I mean.'

Leaving me speechless on the doorstep she marched inside. Following her up, I reflected, *well, it's not as if I can honestly say that everything I've done is straight down the line. What does writing to James without my parents' knowledge count as? Or not telling them I'm meeting him again today? I'm not sure they would approve, which is why I'm not telling them.*

I left again as quickly as I could after a hastily prepared cold lunch, pleading Becky as priority, and saying I wasn't sure when I would be back as I might take Becky into town to cheer her up. I grabbed the small bunch of flowers I had bought earlier and hastened back towards Brixton. Becky was in and delighted to see me. The home above the tailor's shop was packed with relatives and after a short while I made my excuses. Becky came down with me to the front door.

'Thank you for coming and for the flowers. I know how difficult it is to find some now. I'm sorry I won't be back for another week or so. Miss Greaves sent me some test papers to work through in my own time. The school's been very supportive. I'll be back maybe a few days before the exams.'

'If there's anything I can do, let me know. I can send you some of the revision notes. I'm sorry I didn't think to bring any with me. I didn't know how you'd be bearing up.' I turned my head towards the Effra Road and Water Lane junction, cocking it slightly, listening for the clatter of advancing trams.

Becky looked me up and down, raising an eyebrow. 'You're looking *especially* smart for a Saturday afternoon trip to see me. Going on into town?'

I hesitated. She was my best friend. I could trust her.

'James. The airman I met at half term. I heard from him yesterday. Just a bit of sightseeing.'

'And I'm guessing I make a good excuse to be out this afternoon?'

I blushed, and Becky laughed. 'Don't worry, your secret's safe with me. I appreciate you coming to see me first. Just don't do anything you wouldn't want to tell me about. Now go, don't miss this one.'

The tram could be heard rounding the corner from the Brockwell Park direction into Water Lane. A quick hug for Becky and I hastened to the tram stop. It was a little past two now and, boarding the tram, I was panicking that I would be too late for James.

I hared along Northumberland Avenue and into the Square, round to the Beaver Club, but was brought up short with the thought, *What if one of Mummy's co-workers sees me and tells her, oh my goodness, I didn't think of that*, and as I stood outside dithering, the front door opened and James stepped out.

'I saw you from inside,' he said, smiling, and I felt as if the sun had burst from behind a dark cloud and my cheek muscles hurt from my own wide, idiotic smile. He put out his right hand and I shook it a little more vigorously than etiquette demanded, and, keeping hold of my hand, he moved to my side tucking my arm in his. Patting my hand, with a quirk of his mouth, he said,

'Thanks for your letter. I've just read it so I knew you were coming. Ready for that second whistle-stop tour you promised me?'

And I threw my head back laughing as we stepped out towards the Square.

'Where would you like to go today?' I asked him.

'Oh, you're the tour guide,' he answered. 'Take me anywhere you can with a bit of history.'

'*History*,' I repeated, and dramatically swept a wide circle with my free arm while clutching at my bag before it flew off the end. 'It's all around you. Take your pick. Roll up, roll up, join Patricia's magical mystery history tour.'

He laughed as one or two passers-by glanced at us with bemusement.

'Let's hop on a bus and go as far as St Paul's,' I suggested. 'I'll show you the City of London and we'll see if the Monument's open and if we're fit enough to climb all three hundred and eleven steps.'

And so St Paul's and the City is what we did, although we were unable to climb the monument to the start of the Great Fire of London as it was closed owing to there being a war on.

'A pity,' I said, standing beside its base. 'The view over London is breathtaking.'

I looked at him and laughed, at myself. 'Listen to me, as if you don't see a spectacular view every time you go up in that aeroplane of yours.'

James smiled, fishing out a packet of cigarettes and a box of matches from a top pocket. 'Well, you know, it can be cloudy sometimes.' He offered me a cigarette. I hesitated, not wishing to seem gauche, but I had seen contemporaries choke and gag on their first cigarette and I chose the lesser of the two evils, declining with an apologetic shake of the head and a downward flutter of my right hand.

In an attempt to cover my social ineptitude, I asked, 'Have you ever seen London? I mean, from the air?'

James nodded and lit up.

'It must be the most wonderful thing,' I said. 'Is it true everything looks like dollshouses from the air?'

'Have you never flown yourself?' James asked.

I shook my head.

'When this awful war's over I'll take you up and fly you so high even the clouds will look like dollshouses,' he declared, emitting his own miniature clouds and raising his cigarette hand in an upwards motion.

*When this awful war's over. That rather implies a long term friendship*, I thought, and felt momentarily uneasy. *We hardly know each other and I'm just keeping him company while he's over here. I'm not ready for anything more.*

As if he sensed the serious turn of the conversation, James turned away slightly, indicating the direction of the main road with his other hand. 'Time for tea, as you English say,' he said in a lighter tone. 'Is there a suitable venue you can recommend? The Savoy, I hear, is good for tea.'

'*The Savoy?*' I squeaked.

'Or a Lyons Corner House?' he suggested, smiling.

Riding in the bus along Upper Thames Street and on to the Embankment, walking round to the front of Charing Cross Station and crossing the road, James kept the conversation light and humorous. We both laughed as by chance we were shown to the same table we had occupied before. Later, as we sipped a second cup and I dusted the crumbs of the shortbread off my fingers, the waitress finished clearing empty tables and started to upend chairs as a preliminary to sweeping the floor. Realising it was six o'clock, I felt like Cinderella, my lovely day slipping away. James looked around.

'Time to move, I guess. It's been a great afternoon.' He hesitated. 'Pat, would you like to go to a dance next Saturday?'

I blinked. 'Where?'

'At the Beaver Club. I'm told they regularly clear the canteen in the old Council Chamber on the first floor and set it up as a dance hall. There's a midsummer dance planned for next Saturday from around six. I think I can wangle leave for that. My squadron isn't due to reach Liverpool for another ten days or so. It'd be nice to go back to my duties after the weekend with a happy time to remember. Meet me there a little before six?'

What else could I say to that but 'Yes, of course, I'd love to'? Such men and boys were risking their lives daily for us and we owed them a little light relief in return. I shelved the worry for later how to wangle the time, especially an evening, away from home without my parents' approval.

James shook my hand as we parted, again hesitating as if about to offer more, stepping back and moving off, and I was not sure whether I was relieved or disappointed that his Canadian background seemed firmly British stiff upper lip and not more flamboyantly French.

Three days later a newspaper headline in Leatherhead screamed,

### FIRST BOMB ON LONDON

A high explosive bomb landed the day before in a ploughed field in Addington, which counted as London because Addington was in the London Borough of Croydon. But I read the report avidly, worried by its proximity to Croydon and Biggin Hill aerodromes, and hence to James if he was at one of them.

The following Friday my mother, seeing me arrive at the top of the stairs, relayed an invitation she had received earlier in the week from Maud Whitshere inviting us to a

Midsummer party from five o'clock onwards at the Whit-shere's home.

*The perfect cover,* I thought. *I'll feign illness at the last minute. How ironic I've spent the past week worrying how to wangle time tomorrow evening to myself so I can get to the Midsummer Dance! Wait, what about Nanny?*

'Your grandmother's invited too,' added my mother, almost as if she had read my mind, 'although my guess is that she'll want to spend the evening with her Mr Torston. Still, we can call in to Mr Torston's on our way back and accompany her home.'

'Is she there now?'

'Where else? I don't wonder that she moves in with him, she spends more time there than here. Why she wanted to drag us off to live in West Norwood and then grumble about the trouble she now has to see Mr Torston, I really don't know!

'Unfortunately Bill will be in Reading this weekend studying for matric,' my mother added, turning back to the kitchenette to rescue a boiling kettle. 'I've arranged to finish early at the Club tomorrow and I should be home around three.'

I put my case in my room and moved into the living room to find Peggy. I had noticed on visits home recently that Peggy had no longer been running out to greet me enthusi-astically. Instead she would wait until I found her curled up in her basket and stretch out a paw in greeting.

I stopped short. There was no basket and no dog. My stomach lurched.

'Mummy, where's Peggy?'

'Oh, my dear, she's gone.'

'Gone, gone where?'

My mother's silence answered. Grief swept over me like a tidal wave and I sank down onto a chair. My little compan-ion of childhood, and I hadn't been with her at the last. As if in answer to my silent question, my mother, following me and placing the tea tray on the table, said, 'This morning. I was going to take her out for an early walk when Daddy got home and before I left for the Club, but when I went to call her she didn't respond and I realised she was dead in the basket. She must have died early in the night. She was quite stiff and cold.' She sat down and put a hand on mine. 'There wasn't much room in the garden what with most of it being taken up by the Anderson and the rest vegetables, but Daddy managed to dig a hole in the far corner and replanted some carrots and so there she rests, God bless her. Nanny took the basket and the collar and lead to old Mr Paine's shop, you know, the second hand shop near the station, to get a few pennies for them. The rug's had to be thrown out as it was a little soiled.'

At this last I wept uncontrollably. There was nothing left of Peggy for me to mourn.

My mother rose and, bending a little, wrapped her arms around me.

Gradually the storm of weeping subsided and I scrabbled my handkerchief from my sleeve.

'Have a nice cup of tea,' said Mummy, a little inanely.

*I hear the English cure all ills with a cup of tea.* Somehow meeting James didn't now seem quite so important.

By the following afternoon I was definitely thinking of standing James up. I felt desperately miserable about Peggy and my family had been so understanding and sympathetic that I felt guilty over my planned deception.

When my mother got home she was brimming with excitement.

'Pat, dear, you'll *never* guess who I bumped into at the Club today. Well, not bumped into literally, not like *you* did! Yes,' she added, with a little laugh at my astonished and slowly comprehending look, 'that nice young airman James Whatshisname. He asked after you and I told him your sadness about Peggy and he said, a midsummer dance would be just the cure, and I said, what a splendid idea and did he have a girl yet and he said he'd be delighted to escort you, and, well, to cut a long story short, I've arranged for him to meet you off the tram at the Northumberland Avenue stop at around five-thirty, and he has promised to return you to the tram safely later, it's light until nearly eleven now, so you'll have plenty of time to enjoy yourself, and, oh, how I wish I could come with you but Daddy and I have already accepted Maud and Reggie's invitation, never mind, I am sure he's the perfect gentleman and you're sixteen now and when I think at sixteen I'd been out at work for two years.

'No,' she added, drawing breath and cutting off my half-hearted protest with a raised hand, 'you're going to have an evening to enjoy yourself and that's all there is to it. You'd better get a move on and get yourself ready.'

A little over two hours later, bathed, hair-washed, made up, powdered, perfumed and decked in my finest lace-edged and embroidered frock, I stepped off the tram to a hand-shake and a brief grip of the upper part of my other arm. James offered me his arm and I tucked mine in his and we walked along together as if we did this every day. Beyond a brief, 'Hello, Pat, good to see you again,' and a 'It's good to see you again, too,' from me, we walked in companionable silence for several minutes and when Trafalgar Square came into view James led me across to the centre. We perched on the side of the silent fountain base.

'Before we go in,' James said, turning to me, 'I just want to say how sorry I am about your dog. I grew up with plenty of dogs on our farm and I was very fond of them all. I've been sad to lose some while in the air force and I understand you were especially close to yours.'

I blinked back my sudden tears, afraid my makeup would smear, and replied, 'Thank you, that's very kind. She was my lifeline. We got her as a youngster when I was recovering from a childhood illness and she helped me through a difficult time. I suppose with being away at Leatherhead during the week I got used to not seeing her every day but it's different knowing I'll never see her again.'

My voice broke a little as I spoke and James slid along the fountain's rim and his arm went round me. We sat silently for a moment and then I roused myself.

'But as the song says, I have to "pick myself up, dust myself off and start all over again",' I smiled tremulously up at him, for a man on leave needed a happy face, not a sad one, to remember.

He leant in and kissed me, a gentle, tentative kiss, just enough to place his lips on mine for a few seconds, not demanding, but comforting. We drew back, smiling simultaneously at each other. *His mouth fits mine perfectly*, I thought.

'You're a brave girl,' he said. 'Thank you for coming this evening. When I heard the news I thought you might feel too upset to come.'

'Not at all,' I lied. 'Anyway,' I added, to deflect attention from my woes, 'I'm intrigued, what's this about a farm? I thought you were a career flyer.'

'I am,' he replied. 'My father's greatest disappointment, but I told him it was his fault anyway as he wanted me to learn to fly when I was younger so I could cover the huge distances we need to travel to get anywhere in Canada fast. The main farm's right out in the middle of the prairies and it can take days to get anywhere by road. I learnt to fly in the school holidays when I was fifteen. My father said he'd started to learn the business from his father when he was fifteen, so it was time for me to start too. He thought he would in time have his own private pilot *and* representative at stock and supplier's meetings and the ability to move fast on business deals, instead of which three years later he got a son in the Royal Canadian Air Force he doesn't see from one year to the next. Still, at least he has my younger brothers, Duncan and David, to take my place.' James looked down at his feet then turned his head back towards me.

'Do you feel ready to dance? I've been practising you

know.' He smiled a little sheepishly. 'I arrived on leave on Thursday in time for Miss Mee's evening lesson. The Club even supplies dancing shoes for us uncivilised clodhoppers.'

I laughed and felt that my life could go on. Sending a silent apology to Peggy that I was enjoying myself less than two days after she had left us, I rose with James and we made our way to the dance.

There was no time for maudlin thoughts or even romantic interludes as we foxtrotted, quick stepped, waltzed, swung and even jitterbugged our way through the evening. I had heard from our school dance teacher that shorter men tended to make better dancers, witness Fred Astaire, but although James was almost six feet tall, at five foot eight and in heeled shoes I felt well matched and his slenderness lent dexterity to his movements. We glided like swans crossing the Thames and I was lost in the music and rhythm. The more traditional dance music gave way to big band swing rhythm and James lifted me several times, turning me round at one point and holding me under my arms to swing me in a circle above the ground. I drew a line at being turned completely upside down, unlike some of the girls there, and he seemed to sense my reticence for he didn't throw me around more than I cared for, or perhaps it was just that he'd worked out I wasn't the lightest of girls he'd ever danced with.

Later, laughing and breathless, we retreated to the basement for refreshments, pausing and smiling at each other at the foot of the stairs where we had met so abruptly a month ago, and returning fortified in time for the finale, a breakneck compilation which abruptly slowed at the last song, 'A Nightingale Sang in Berkeley Square', during which James held me tight and crooned the words softly into my ear. I closed my eyes and thought, *I'll capture this moment for ever in my memory, and when things are tough I'll recall it.*

Afterwards, walking to the tram stop, James was preoccupied and we spoke little. Shaking his hand, saying,

'Goodbye and thank you for a lovely evening,' I boarded the tram. As it started moving away James leapt up and on, landing beside me on the hard wooden bench.

'What...?'

'Time for my tour of South London,' he said, smiling. 'I'll see you to your front door.' He looked out of the window. 'Dusk now, can't have you walking the streets on your own in the dark.' Insisting on paying, he also insisted on my giving him a running commentary of the districts we passed through on the 33.

'So here is Brixton,' I said, as the tram glided past the Town Hall. 'Where I have spent most of my life until the school moved out to Leatherhead last September. And just beyond here, to the right, is where I used to I live, and soon we'll be going past Brockwell Park where I take, I mean *used* to take, Peggy...'

James put a sympathetic hand on mine. We rode in silence the rest of the way. As we alighted and set off along Chatsworth Way and into Idmiston Road, James said, 'I shouldn't tell you this, but I'll trust you to keep it to yourself. Our squadron arrived in Liverpool two days ago and should be in Hampshire around now. Group captains have responsibility for a group of squadrons; there's no set number and,' he added, ironic amusement tinging his cadence, 'I'm going to be responsible for just the coupla RCAF ones over here. But I'll also be keeping my liaison role for Canadian pilots in the RAF and with the bombings and the increasing threat of invasion I'll be slotting in a fair amount of flying where I can help out. I was lucky to wangle this leave, but I have to report to our squadron's base in Hampshire tomorrow.'

James looked down towards me, reaching out to draw me into his side as we slowed, the end of the road in sight, the end of our journey together. 'I'm telling you so you'll understand I'm not expecting to have any leave now for a very long time and I'm not expecting to be able to collect post from the Club easily. I'll make sure arrangements are in place to send on anything for me. If you don't hear back from me for a while, it won't mean I'm not thinking of you.'

'Of course, I more than understand. Don't worry about writing to me. I'm sure you'll have plenty of company now your squadron's here. I'll be busy anyway...'

I was going to continue, '...*with my matriculation exams,*' but he cut in,

'No, I *will* write to you, I'm just not sure how busy I'll be while we're settling in and getting everyone up and running.'

The houses loomed in the dusk like silent watchers, their blacked-out windows mournful eyes. We reached the end of the terrace and I stopped, realising that the night was gathering pace.

'James, I'm so sorry, I think the last tram will have gone.'

He shook his head. 'It's no trouble. I'll pick up what transport I can, if not I really don't mind the walk, I'll just follow the tram lines north.'

'But it's miles,' I protested.

James smiled, and the crow's feet crinkled. 'Don't forget, I'm a man from Canada, the world's second largest country. Distances in this tiny island are nothing compared to home.'

He looked first up and down the silent street, then, gently placing his hands around my upper arms, he leant forward and kissed me, slowly at first, increasingly urgent, his right arm, and next his left, sliding round my back. His tongue flicked my teeth, parting them, exploring my mouth, his encircling arms holding me tightly, his body pressed against mine.

Just as I thought I would have to take a breath, my head spinning and my legs suddenly weak, he let go of me, nodding slightly, saying, 'So long, Pat,' and he stepped back, indicating the front door for me, turning and walking away down the road. I watched him go, shrinking as perspective kicked in. Some way down he slowed, there was a sudden flare and I realised he had fished out a cigarette and lit it and

I saw the soft red glow of the cigarette end rise and fall as he lifted that hand and waved, and he turned back and was swallowed into the night.

# 7
# The Battle of Britain

I found myself reliving James' last kiss and the sense of passion behind it. And I was only just sixteen and flattered at the attention and I enjoyed hugging the secret of his affection to myself. Outwardly I was casual, dismissive even, to my parents and grandmother, and spoke no more about him to my school friends, not even to Becky on her return later in the week. Not that we had much time for small talk, or for anyone to tease me about the revelations of my birthday picnic. The following Friday we sat the first of the public exams, English. I turned the page of part II and almost wept. Question 3 was,

'Write a letter (not exceeding 150 words) to a friend *either* serving in one of the fighting forces *or* living in the town from which you have been evacuated, giving some of your recent news.'

*What shall I write*, I thought, *to someone serving in the fighting forces? That I lie awake at night waiting for Becky to fall asleep, then I lie awake longer wrapping my arms around myself as you did, thinking of your warm smile, your crinkly laughter lines, your hands about my body, your lips on mine, your tongue…?* My sense of the absurd reasserted itself and I smiled wryly. Well, it might liven up an otherwise dull and uninteresting narrative for an examiner but it was unlikely to curry me any marks.

With the weekend sandwiched between the Friday afternoon's Arithmetic paper and the following Monday's Geometry and English Literature papers, followed swiftly by Algebra, History, Biology, Geography, French, three Art papers and two Latin papers, I had no time to even write to James, let alone dwell further on our last meeting.

I listened with mounting horror to news on Mrs Grice's wireless of German bombing raids on the ports of the Bristol Channel, and on Hull and Wick on 1st July. Raids on Swansea and South Wales followed. *So the invasion's really going to happen*, I thought. *All those poor people dead or injured and families torn apart. And London will be next.* In the afternoons in Leatherhead, despite our teachers urging us to remain indoors during break, we spilled out onto the playing fields of St Birstan's lying north of the quadrangle along with the boys, watching vapour trails and specks in the sky growing larger and smaller. Once a parachutist was spotted in the distance and we followed his line of descent to the horizon while we heard the rumble of trucks on the distant main road, presumably to chase him down and either arrest him if a German or ensure there was no misunderstanding by the local populace if he were on our side.

Joyce was very worried. 'Do you think they'll cancel the Summer Dance on Saturday?' she speculated. 'Peregrine thinks they might.'

'Well, the fighting seems to be during the day and the chances of a stray German landing on the school field of an evening is pretty remote,' I smiled. 'So Peregrine is still your beau for the evening?'

'Oh yes,' said Joyce. 'Who's yours?'

'I don't have one. I don't feel much in a party mood.'

'Oh, Pat, it'll be fun. I'll ask Peregrine on Saturday if he'll ask a friend to partner you.'

'Still meeting in Woolworths, eh?'

'Don't avoid the subject, Pat,' Becky interjected, mock severely. 'Joyce, do your best.'

Joyce did her best and I found myself partnered by a stocky, ruddy-faced boy who introduced himself as Alexander, 'but my friends call me Alex,' with dark hair and earnest brown eyes and much the same height as me. He concentrated on the dance manoeuvres as if his life depended on it, holding my hand tentatively with one hand while barely touching my back at waist level with the other. If it were not for his clear determination to undertake the assignment with as much precision as possible, which I thought rather sweet, I might have become impatient with him. But the contrast with James' lively and spontaneous dancing could not have been greater and the only emotion I felt towards Alex was pity. He freely admitted that he had no sisters and wasn't 'great shakes' around girls, and knew only what he did of dancing from the lessons at the school, which he further admitted he had done much to avoid. The contrast with the Beaver Club's midsummer dance was unbearable. I longed for James in the midst of the festivities, a hunger and taut- ness in my very core. I suggested that we sit some dances out and we sneaked outside to beyond the science block where the school land met the recreation ground, concealing our- selves in the lee of outbuildings, as the sun dropped over the western horizon spreading pink and golden fingers of cloud above us and I made desultory conversation all the while watching the sky and wondering what James might be doing right now.

The following weekend I returned home for the holidays and to constant daily air raid sirens. My father had given up on the Anderson shelter, preferring his own bed for the day's sleep and after a while he could even sleep through the siren. My mother seemed to spend even longer at the Beaver Club, while my grandmother had more or less moved in with Mr Torston, only coming home as dusk fell. So that left me cooped up indoors trying to do some holiday reading ready for the sixth form with the most exquisite form of torture from below in the form of the screaming baby.

After a few days my mother said, 'I'll get you a volun- teer duty or two at the Club for the holidays and you can come down to the basement when the sirens go off in the Square,' and within a couple of days I was travelling in with her, doing four hours' volunteer duty, everything from table clearing to cleaning the library to helping with a bingo session, wherever the need was greatest.

I looked daily for a letter from James and felt both relieved and desolate at the same time that there was none. Each week I dropped letter marked 'Please Forward' into the B pigeonhole, a short letter as I didn't know what to say. I didn't want to burden him with my worries about my forthcoming exam results so I kept it light, sticking to such topics as my journeys, the weather, books I was reading, the occasional concert I attended, the War Artists' exhibition at the National Gallery and events being put on at the Beaver Club.

One day in early August the doorman gave me a wink, saying 'There might be something waiting for you,' and I found a letter addressed simply, as usual, to 'P. Roberts c/o The Beaver Club', and I put it in my pocket for reading in private later.

*Dear Pat,* he wrote, *Thank you for your letters. I can now tell you that I am serving again with our squadron, No.1 RCAF, stationed at Croydon. So the wheel turns full circle and I am back where I started in England.*

*We moved here a couple of weeks or so ago and it seems as if I have never left. Except that now I am flying mostly with my compatriots. However, we are all working towards the same end, the removal of the threat from across the Channel, so I am happy with whomever I fly. We are but part of a larger whole. I am flying Hurricanes which I prefer as although they may not climb or fly as fast as the Spitfire they are resilient, manoeuvrable creatures and provide a better chance of survival in combat. I have heard of losses of other Canadians serving with RAF squadrons. So far my squadron has not lost anyone although I guess that is just a game of chance.*

*I am sorry I may be a little maudlin. I would rather write to you about happier times and so thank you again for accompanying me to the midsummer dance and for your companionship over the past couple of months.*

*Looking forward to meeting again,*
*Please keep writing,*
*With all good wishes from*
*Your friend in the skies*
*James.*

I was a little nonplussed by his signing off. *Good wishes. Your friend in the skies.* I wondered what these words signified. They hardly smacked of passion. Perhaps he was regretting his parting kiss. Or perhaps he kissed all the girls. Or perhaps he signed off ironically, meaning in reality he regarded himself as more than just a friend.

Still, any letter, I decided, was better than none and I would write back tonight and bring my letter in for onward posting the next day.

A table had been placed next to the one below the pigeon-holes and above it a small noticeboard erected. A small vase of flowers sat on the table and the noticeboard carried the words 'In Memoriam' across the top, below which were pinned small pieces of paper. I read of two Pilot Officers downed in July. Some servicemen drew up behind me and stopped, silent, for a moment as I stepped aside, then they turned back up to the next floor, their bantering resuming as they mounted the stairs.

*Please God*, I prayed, *may I never see James' name here.*

Still daily the air raid sirens went off and still daily I ignored them and spent my mornings volunteering at the Beaver Club as increasing numbers of the names on the In Memoriam notice board were pinned up. One day I saw that a Pilot Officer was lost in a Hurricane over the Thames and his resting place was not known. I thought, *Hurricanes might be* resilient, manoeuvrable creatures and provide a better chance of survival in combat *but they're not infallible.*

Some afternoons I curled up at home with my holiday reading, but I was restless and felt constantly on the edge of nausea. On a couple of occasions I met up with Becky at Brockwell Park, much of its land now requisitioned for anti-aircraft gun batteries and allotment use. On other afternoons I watched the skies from vantage points across the hills of South London: Norwood Hill, Tulse Hill, Beulah Hill, Gypsy Hill, and even as far as the site of the former Crystal Palace that had burned down in 1936 and not been replaced before the war started. Many people would be gathered too, perhaps stopping for only a few minutes, some for an hour or more, to watch the dogfights in the skies over the North Surrey and North Kent suburbs and countryside, vapour trails weaving ethereal baskets.

To the north above London the air was a sea of barrage balloons and sometimes aeroplanes overshot and got caught up amongst them and came down. People cheered when they saw a plane downed that they thought was German; there was anxious murmuring or even crying out when they saw it was one of ours. Spent rounds and cartridges clattered down from the skies and children darted about collecting them as souvenirs.

Following notification of my matriculation success in the summer exams, my mother decreed that my parents would take me to the theatre in celebration. On Saturday 24th August, sitting in the Criterion Theatre watching Noel Coward's *Private Lives*, towards the end of the performance we heard the air raid sirens. As the theatre was in the basement of the building, notices in the foyer indicated that the play would continue in the event of an air raid. We remained in our seats despite the distant muffled explosions and unending sirens. The tense, dramatic scenes of the play were ruined by the intermittent rumblings and wailings and towards the end, in response to one of the character's lines, 'Where are you going?' the other exasperated actor ad-libbed, 'I'm going to tell Mr Hitler to stop making those blasted bangs!' This brought the house down, fortunately only figuratively, with much clapping and cheering.

The few air raid sirens up until this night had tended to

sound for only an hour or two's duration with perhaps a wait of up to another hour before the All Clear. However, that night, no soon as there seemed to be a lull, the distant bangs resumed, the sirens wailing all the while. The performance having finished, cigarettes were lit and packs of playing cards appeared from pockets with some of the men setting up small groups of card games to while the time away. There was community singing and eventually the manager called for quiet and announced that the bar would re-open for refreshments.

While the bar had plenty of drink it unfortunately had no food. Mummy, sipping a port and lemon, another of which had been commandeered for me, said, 'I'm hungry. I keep thinking of the cold supper I prepared for our return and now we'll be lucky to have it for breakfast. Ted, dear, do you think you could find us something to eat?'

My father demurred, pointing out that once the All Clear sounded we could go home and that could happen any minute.

'But what if it doesn't?' countered my mother. 'We could end up here all night. And we've not had a proper meal since lunchtime. Go and see if there's anything upstairs to eat.'

If there had been any food upstairs my father would have returned sooner but we waited quite a while and Mummy was getting twitchy when he eventually reappeared carrying a bulging paper bag, a bemused smile below dancing eyes.

'Whatever took you so long?' grumbled Mummy. 'I suppose there were long queues.'

'Oh, there was no food upstairs so I took myself off up Shaftsbury Avenue to see what I could find.'

'What?' cried my mother, her hand flying to her mouth. 'You went outside? How dangerous! Ted, you shouldn't have.'

'A lot less dangerous than nights at a bakery next to a railway line,' he retorted. 'Besides, the bombs that are being dropped are some way off, east and west, but none nearby. And,' he added, 'I got these,' handing the bag to my mother with a flourish.

My mother gasped at the sandwiches and their exotic fillings.

'Where ever did you get *these*?'

My father's bemused smile grew wider. 'Oh,' he said, casually, 'at a nearby theatre.'

'Which one's going to be open this late, let alone with sandwiches and let alone with sandwiches like *these*?'

By now I was getting impatient and my afternoon cup of tea with a slice of bread seemed a long time ago. I took the bag from my mother and dived into the bag myself and brought out a smoked salmon sandwich.

'It's even got a creamy cheese,' I said, amazed, and bit into it.

'Ted, you didn't *steal* them from somewhere?' whispered my mother hoarsely.

'No, of course not,' protested my father. 'I saw some other people being offered some at the back door which was very slightly ajar and I asked if I could take a couple for you and Pat and they insisted on taking me inside so they could close the door and observe the blackout, and they took a little while finding me a bag, then, well, hey presto!' He flourished his hand at the bag as he said this. 'I let them think my daughter was a little girl and they took pity on us,' he added apologetically to me.

'Te-ed,' said my mother warningly, suspicion narrowing her eyes. 'Did you happen to turn off Shaftsbury Avenue into Great Windmill Street?'

'Ah,' said my father. Caught out. As a Londoner and a theatregoer, despite my young age and sheltered upbringing even I had heard of the Windmill Theatre and the 'Tableaus' of naked or near naked women, as I knew it was against the law for a nude to move on stage.

'And did '*they*' happen to be young ladies?'

127

*Oh Mummy,* I thought, *just let him be. He's risked London bombs to get you what you wanted and all you can do is castigate him for the source of it.*

'I'm sure they were quite decently clad at a partly open back door,' I interjected, 'weren't they, Daddy?'

'Oh yes, oh yes, ah, quite so,' responded my father, a little flustered, and I made a fuss of my mother, finding a clean hanky for a makeshift plate, while my father regained his composure. We had more than enough food and I offered the remainder to our near neighbours who I was sure had heard my parents' exchange but who tactfully said nothing.

Sometime after midnight the manager, who had been clutching a tin box which I suspected contained the night's takings, disappeared upstairs and returned a few minutes later with an air raid warden in tow, who announced that owing to the presence of a few planes still dropping the odd bomb around London as well as the suburbs, the authorities were taking no chances and it would be a little while yet before the All Clear.

Grumblings and mutterings met this pronouncement but gradually people settled themselves down for what was left of the night. My mother commandeered a section of side wall near the back of the theatre beside which I was required to lie. She set herself down next to me and on the outside, on guard, was placed my father. 'We're protecting your virtue against strange men,' sniffed my mother. I thought I could not possibly sleep but I must have drifted off as next I knew the All Clear was sounding and it was getting on for four o'clock. Carefully making our way home through the blackout, we arrived safely in the early pre-dawn gloom.

That morning at a late breakfast my grandmother announced, 'I have something very important to tell you all. I would have told you yesterday on your return from the theatre but Mr Hitler had other ideas.' She took a deep breath. 'Albert and I are getting married next Saturday at the Register Office,' adding diffidently, 'You're all welcome to come if you like.'

I leapt up and hugged her. 'Nanny, I'm delighted for you, though,' I added mischievously, 'I'm not surprised. I thought you'd moved in already. I'm glad he's making an honest woman of you at last.'

'Go on with you,' she said half-laughing, but sobered quickly as she hastened to complete her announcement. Looking a little challengingly at my parents, she added, 'And my father will be named on my marriage certificate as William Warner and I'll be using my surname of Caddock.' Neither 'father' to be left blank, as was on her birth certificate, nor her true surname to be recorded, that of her illegitimate birth, Garey.

'And why wouldn't you?' responded my father after only a momentary pause. 'Your step-father was the only father you knew and I've only ever known you as Mrs Caddock.' So that settled it and family skeletons retreated and locked themselves firmly back in their dusty cupboard.

I could hear my mother's mind whirring with, *she drags us all out to West Norwood and three months later she's off back to Brixton leaving us stuck here. And now we're short of her pension.*

But my mother forced a smile, for once making the best of it, and said, 'Congratulations, dear, or rather I should be saying, best wishes, but, either way, we'll be there.'

The night of the theatre trip the course of the war changed. The previous bombing of London had been peripheral, but that night one of the German bombers unleashed his cargo on its heart. Other bombs were dropped in West Ham, Stepney and Bethnal Green, and also as far west as Esher and Staines. However, it was the attack on the City of London itself which proved to be the ultimate affront that could not go unchallenged. Two days later the newspapers were full of reprisal raids on Berlin. We all feared that German retaliation would be inevitable.

The following Saturday, a lump in my throat, bursting with affection, I watched my sixty-six-year-old grand-mother marry seventy-three-year-old Mr Torston in a short, simple ceremony and become for the first time in her life a respectable married woman. I was saddened that her son, my uncle Dennis, dead of a heart attack five years before, was not with us to share in the family occasion. My grandmother wore a grey suit and Mr Torston's sons helped him in and out of the Register Office and stood forward to sign the register as the witnesses. My parents and I were just bystanders. My grandmother had not even asked my mother to be matron of honour. I knew my mother was upset but for once she gritted her teeth all through the ceremony and the wedding breakfast, a cold compilation back at the marital home, and bore it. We did not stay late, fear of what might fall from the skies before we could reach our shelter hastening our steps.

Daily overhead the fighting in the skies continued and men died, all because of one nasty little man called Hitler.

Becky, despite her terrible bereavement, achieved matriculation and we returned to Mrs Grice at the beginning of September. Having managed to meet up on only a couple of occasions through the summer holidays, I was pleased to be with Becky again.

'Don't apologise for not seeing much of me in the summer,' Becky said the first evening of the new term. 'We had a nice couple of afternoons together in the park and I know you were doing your bit for the war effort at the Beaver Club. I was so tied up visiting or being visited by yet *more* relatives. I'm glad to be back, if only for a rest! My oldest brother's taking over the business now. I can't believe it's only three months since my father died. I miss him terribly when I'm home, so maybe it's good that we're back and can get on with the new courses.'

The new courses. I sat back on the bed, momentarily miserable again.

'Oh, Pat,' said Becky, seeing my shoulders slump, 'chin up, Shorthand and Typewriting aren't that bad, I'm sure.'

'Sorry to be a wet blanket,' I said. 'I found out today that my mother has me signed up for the full *two* years' Short-hand and Typewriting courses, not just one year.'

'But you *are* doing Art as well, aren't you?'

I sighed apologetically. 'Yes, I'm sorry, it seems petty, I know, when there's a war on. At least we'll be starting German tomorrow.'

'So what exactly *are* you doing?'

I enumerated with my fingers as I recounted each subject. 'English, French, German, Biology, Shorthand, Typewriting and Art. Oh and, of course, I still have PE, they won't let us off lightly on that one. What about you?'

'I'm doing the whole gamut of commercial subjects: Commercial Arithmetic, Shorthand, Typewriting, Book-keeping and Commercial Practice plus English, Economics, and of course, PE.'

'Well, we'll be together for,' I calculated rapidly, 'three subjects. Oh, and, of course, PE.' This last parroting together, and falling back laughing.

As we recovered, Becky asked, 'Did you hear about Janet?' Blonde, busty Janet of our billet with Mrs Briggs this time last year.

'What about her? I didn't see her today, but maybe she's coming back late?'

'She's not coming back at all. Gwen told me. She got married last weekend.'

'What, *married*? Why would she go and do something so *stupid*?'

'She's got herself in the family way.'

'*What?*'

'You remember she couldn't make it to your birthday picnic either, because of a family wedding? Well, she played fast and loose with a cousin there. Gwen's sister, who got it from Janet's sister, says they sneaked off in the middle of the dancing.'

'But Janet was here in the summer and took her matric.'

'Did you notice she wasn't well at the dance in July? Oh,

no, you went outside with that Alex boy. Janet came over sick and faint towards the end and had to go home early. Everyone thought it was a touch of summer flu. Janet only owned up a couple of weeks ago and I gather it was a bit of a shotgun wedding.'

I was stunned. 'How can anyone be so *idiotic* as to throw away a good education and the chance to have a career, a proper job? For *what*? Well, obviously I don't know *what* exactly, but all that's needed is a bit of self-control. I always thought she was a bit forward, like she was with the St Birstan's boys on our first evening, but to give in to a young man just like that, well, words quite fail me!'

Becky's generous mouth curled in amusement. 'I hardly think words failed you there.'

Humour overcoming outrage, we chuckled together.

It might have been a relief to be back at a school truly evacuated to the depths of the countryside, but the north Surrey downs and towns seemed to me to be just as dangerous as London with the shift in the Germans' tactics, no longer primarily attacking airfields and aircraft factories, but targeting roads and railway lines as well. Over the next few days I heard stories of trains, cars, lorries and even cyclists being machine gunned down in towns and cities all over the southeast, including someone's dog in a bicycle basket, and at first if I was out and heard an aeroplane approaching I would leap off my bicycle, running for the nearest form of shelter, if only a doorway or low wall. After a couple of days, though, despite planes swooping overhead, I kept my nerve, continuing on to my lesson or to the library or wherever I was going and made it in one piece.

We travelled back to London for the weekend. Having worked to the last bell on the Friday, I couldn't get back early enough to include a detour via central London. Any letter from James would have to wait until the morning.

Saturday 7th September 1940 dawned dry and warm. As usual, the latter part of August had been cold and miserable and as soon as the schools went back we enjoyed an Indian summer. I made my way into central London after lunch alone. To my immense disappointment no letter awaited me. I checked the In Memoriam board, breathing a sigh of relief, and I wandered round to Trafalgar Square. Fantasising a scenario of James suddenly appearing through the crowd and sweeping me off my feet, reason reasserted itself and I felt as down as ever. I stopped a while at St Martin's church, saying prayers for James and all the airmen defending our shores, sipped a nostalgic cup of tea at the Corner House and boarded a tram homewards.

As the tram trundled through Brixton air raid sirens started wailing in earnest and as usual no one took any notice. By now it was around five o'clock. Round Brockwell Park and towards West Norwood the sounds of the anti-aircraft guns, the aircrafts' own guns and the bombing hit us. It went on and on, my fellow passengers looking at each other increasingly alarmed. The tram stopped abruptly just short of my own stop, the electricity supply affected, and I leapt off and ran fast along Chatsworth Way and Idmiston Road. Diving through the house's ground floor and out to the shelter I found only the downstairs family. Rushing upstairs I cried, 'Mummy, Daddy,' only to be hushed by my mother.

'Leave your father to finish his sleep,' she scolded.

'Mummy, there's something really wrong, the guns and the bombing seem much worse than before. We really should take shelter. *Now*.'

My father was already emerging and we hurried down into the shelter. The raid itself lasted about an hour and we waited for the All Clear, but the sirens kept wailing. The next bombing wave hit a little after eight o'clock and we could hear the ack-ack sound of the anti-anticraft guns firing a mile away in Brockwell Park. It felt as if the ground was reverberating beneath our feet. The baby screamed itself into an exhausted sleep in its mother's arms. I wondered why she was still in London with her children. Although not evacuated in the first wave of September 1939, she could have been with the second wave of evacuations in the summer of 1940. But Leatherhead, which was still taking such evacuees, was hardly proving to be a place of greater safety, I thought, having heard from Mrs Grice that an estimated twenty high explosive bombs had fallen around the Ashtead–Leatherhead border on 27th August, even before our return, killing one person and damaging several houses. More bombs had landed three days later in Ashtead, killing five people.

I smiled reassuringly at the older children, a boy of about eight and a girl of about five. 'It won't be long now,' I said, 'these sort of raids never last long.'

I could not have been more wrong. Later I was to read that an estimated eight hundred to a thousand German aircraft arrived over the southeast that afternoon and night and, despite the RAF and RCAF fighters, the enemy planes kept on coming. I also learned that the bombs first started falling as near as Woolwich, Millwall, Rotherhithe and Surrey Docks, this last little over five miles away, then the bombing moved to the north side of the river, devastating the East End. It felt much nearer.

After a couple of hours or so the children started to whinge that they needed the toilet. 'Use the bucket,' their mother ordered, and the dank, stale smell of the shelter was overlayed with the sweet, acrid stench of urine. We fished out emergency rations and shared them out, and still the barrage continued.

By now the night was moving on and when in desperation I hared indoors for the toilet myself, I was astonished how light it was. I thought I must have misread the time and that it was early evening still with a distant sunset, but the glow was in the wrong direction. Perhaps dawn had arrived while we cowered in the ground. Realising that the orange glow of the sky was neither sunset nor sunrise, *where's the fire?* I thought, a little panicky, but the houses around were all intact. I heard some neighbours in another garden, who had also become curious about the strangely lit sky, exclaiming about it.

And still the bombing continued. Although the centre of the action was clearly some miles away, no one could anticipate what would happen next or whether the tactics would change and that we would suddenly find high explosive bombs and incendiary bombs raining down on us. So we passed a virtually sleepless night in cramped, smelly, claustrophobic conditions. Around four o'clock in the morning the sounds of the bombing seemed to lessen, becoming a trickle and eventually stopping altogether. About an hour later the All Clear sounded. We emerged from our primitive cave and staggered back to the house. I vaguely wondered where the neighbour's husband had been all this time, but most of me didn't care, just to get to my bed was all that I wanted.

'You'd better get yourself back to Leatherhead as soon as you can,' said my father at our later than usual breakfast following a few hours' snatched sleep. 'We don't know when they'll be back and you need to be in your billet safe and sound before that happens.' So lunchtime was spent travelling with a packed lunch balanced on my knee, a year and six days on from my first ever journey to Leatherhead station. This time I ate my lunch before I arrived.

The bombers were back that night. Becky and I, exhausted from the previous night's London raids, retired to bed early, listening to distant droning and muffled, far away rumbles. Suddenly the air raid warning started up. For a few moments we remained in situ, too tired to move, but Mrs Grice was banging on our door calling,

'Pat, Becky! We have to go to the shelter.'

We dragged ourselves out of bed, shoving feet into shoes, grabbing a bag each that we had put together just in case, and wrapping ourselves in dressing gowns and overcoats. Mr Grice while on leave during the summer holidays had finally built an Anderson shelter in the back garden. We descended the few steps hewn into the soil overlaid with runners of wood (*need to watch out for these getting slippery in wet weather*) and settled ourselves on the benches built into the inside of the corrugated iron shelter. *Please God, not another whole night in one of these*, I thought. On further reflection, *but at least no screaming baby*.

At first it seemed a false alarm as we sat dozing the hours away, then we heard the distant droning drawing nearer and explosions occurring only a few miles away. The newspaper a couple of days later told us that on the Sunday night attacks had been made on railway lines running south out of London.

'Fat lot of good us being here,' said Becky as we wheeled our bikes away from the newsagent in the town centre. 'Don't know why anyone thought Leatherhead might be safe.'

I mounted my bike and, as I set off, said to Becky over my shoulder, 'Well at least they're mostly coming over at night now and giving us a chance to get back safely from school.'

I was a bit of an expert at famous last words. As we passed the field entrance, at the southern end of Warenne Road, the roar of a high revving engine and the descending flight of a falling bomb assailed our ears. Instinctively we threw ourselves off our bikes onto the side of the road, covering our heads with our hands. Just beyond the gate the bomb detonated. My head seemed to implode with the pressure of the shockwave, my body bucking at the earth tremor and a shower of earth, stones and splinters of wood descended, pummelling my back and protective hands. My face felt fiery where it scraped the ground as I landed. I heard only a high-pitched ringing tone and the pain in my ears was beyond any I had ever experienced before. I lay stunned and unmoving, feeling my heart thudding in my rib cage and an unbearable tightness in my throat. I realised I was not breathing and felt a rising panic. *Is this how I die?*

As the screeching in my ears subsided a little, footsteps

came running in my direction. A hand was laid on my shoulder and a male voice said urgently, 'Are you alright?' Which was probably the best thing he could have said, for the absurdity of the question made me half laugh and I drew breath and realised I had only been winded. *Well, apart from my body feeling it's just been ground into powder, my knees shrieking from taking the brunt of my fall, my face aflame, knitting needles forced in my ears and blood now seeping from the sharp flints that assailed me, I'M FINE! Of course, what you really mean is, 'Are you dead?'*

I stirred and sensed the man's relief. I turned my head and looked for Becky. She was beginning to sit up at a lady's prompting. A few more neighbours came running along the road, some to gawk, others more practical. Another lady appeared with a bowl of water and a ragged sheet off which she tore a square, dipped it in the water and started to wash away some of the mud and grit adorning my face.

I realised that my father's instructions had probably saved my eardrums for, even in that extreme moment, I remembered his words, 'and if a bomb goes off near you don't put your fingers in your ears but instead open your mouth.' As a navel cadet literally learning the ropes on the HMS *Impregnable*, a 121-gun sailing ship built in 1860 and rigged out as a training ship, he had had plenty of experience of loud bangs from the canonry on board.

Shock was setting in for Becky too. Blood ran down her neck from her ears. Shivering and shaking she was slowly helped to her feet and my ministering angel moved over to wipe off the worst of the field debris that had landed on her.

'Where do you live?' the man asked, and another lady answered for us, 'They're the girls with the Grices, about halfway down the road.'

Two of the neighbours retrieved our bicycles and our little procession made its way slowly along the road to be greeted by Mrs Grice hurrying down the road from the opposite direction wringing her hands and looking anxiously up and around, saying, 'Oh my goodness, oh my goodness, where *did* he come from? Are there any more to come? Why no warning?' To our rescuers, 'Thank you for bringing them back safe. I heard the bang at the shop and thought, our road's been hit. You'd all better come in for a cup of tea, I suppose,' but fortunately for Mrs Grice's larder the house-holders all had more important things to do like sort out their shattered windows. Mrs Grice's bungalow was just far enough away to have survived unscathed.

The news continued to mount of the night time raids mostly, but not exclusively, to the east side of London. We also read that Kingston, Malden and Surbiton, all London suburbs less than ten miles away, were badly hit.

The daytime battles in the air were still continuing with daily reports of downed planes, mostly German fighters. I worried about James and was anxious to get back to London the following Friday and see if he had written, but again, when I did, still no letter.

My father and I decided to resume our Sunday morning walks which had become somewhat disjointed recently, promising my mother that I would be back in time to head off to Leatherhead sooner than usual. We left early that morning, 15th September, around nine o'clock, thinking to beat the air raids, and walked to Dulwich Park. As we arrived waves of Spitfires and Hurricanes in formation flew overhead and shortly after, not only to the distant south-east, but all around and above us we heard the fighting and the bombing and the sounds of planes falling out of the sky, criss-cross patterns of vapour trails in their wake. Later that afternoon, having sped back to Leatherhead in what proved to be a lunchtime lull, there was a second wave of fighting and the skies of London and all over the south east were again filled with swooping, swerving, spiralling winged creatures that belched bullets, smoke and death.

The following Thursday I found a letter from my mother waiting for me when I got back from school. 'Don't come home this coming weekend, dear, it's so dangerous. I have spent every night so far this week stuck in that dreadful shelter with that dreadful family. I've offered to spend the nights with your grandmother but she said she didn't marry her Albert only to spend her nights cooped up with a load of other people. I am not a load of other people! I'm her daughter and they may be newlyweds but they're not exactly spring chickens.'

I chuckled at this and Becky looked enquiringly at me from her homework.

'My mother's suffering over my grandmother's marriage,' I explained. I glanced back down. 'Oh my goodness, we're moving *again!*'

I read on, aloud, 'I've managed to get accommodation for us back in Water Lane a few doors further from Effra Road from where we were before, it's the next but one house up from the junction with St Matthews Road. It's one of those three-storeyed houses and I'm afraid we're on the top floor with two flights of stairs but at least we're back in Brixton and I am sure we'll get used to it. We'll have a living room, a bedroom and a kitchen in the little front room and we will share the bathroom on the middle floor with the middle-aged couple living there. There's an attic room above which you can use as a bedroom. An elderly couple live on the ground floor.'

*That's three flights of stairs for me*, I thought.

I continued reading. 'The family that was there have had their boy called up and they're moving to relatives in Hampshire. I've told your father I can't put up with being here any longer on my own at night and I've arranged to put in extra hours at the Beaver Club. I'll stay overnight between shifts in the Club's basement shelter, so I'll be quite safe, don't you worry. Your father can have his meal at the café on his way home. We'll be moving on Sunday so while an extra pair of hands might have been useful we would have been sending you back early anyway because of the dreadful bombing. Mrs Grice gets money for a full week's food so you shouldn't starve.'

I looked back up at Becky. 'She drives me *mad!*'

# 8

# James

The glow of the early autumn days seemed to mock the infernos raging in the East End. My mood was more reflective of the wet and cloudy days later in the month and only Becky's ready smile and optimistic outlook helped keep me from retreating into a permanent state of misery. I kept my regular letters to James – apart from recounting the night in the theatre and the bomb in the field – short and light. I didn't want to seem so insensitive as to chat inanely about everyday school life nor be too serious about the wartime conditions. I heard nothing from him and anxiously scoured the In Memoriam board at the Club.

The mainly night time raids continued virtually unabated and I thought how *terribly* badly parts of London must be suffering to now be sending yet another wave of evacuees to bomb-ridden Leatherhead for their safety. Every evening we checked that the shelter's buckets of sand and water were stood ready and that we had a bag of essentials ready to grab on hearing the siren.

On the last Saturday in September when I had quite despaired and was scolding myself for being so obstinate and not accepting that James had just been a pleasant summer's interlude, I found a package in the R pigeonhole addressed to P. Roberts and my legs suddenly felt weak and my hand trembled slightly as I clutched the package tightly to my side. Escaping the conspiratorial eyebrow of the doorman, I fled into the Square and, despite the chilly day, sat outside on the edge of the fountain where James had kissed me for the first time a little over three months before. Hastily I tore the package open and out spilled several letters wrapped around with a larger sheet of paper. *He's dead and they've sent me back my letters,* my mind shrieked. *No, please God, no.* Then I caught sight of his handwriting on the larger sheet.

*Dear Pat*

*Thank you for your weekly letters which have been reaching me and so cheering me up, I really can't tell you how much. Forgive my tardiness in writing. I have written back to every letter you've sent but have been rather worn out with all the flying and have not had the strength to even get them to the post until now. One day I was so tired I landed the plane and promptly fell asleep at the controls and had to be woken by the ground staff who thought I had been wounded and had conked out!*

*Here are all the letters I've written and if you read them in order I hope they make a decent narrative.*

*I hope you haven't given up on your friend in the skies. Your weekly writings give me hope that you haven't.*

*We are told the threat of invasion continues, though in a few more weeks the weather will make it impossible for an invasion to happen before next Spring. As Mr Hitler seems to want to keep us fellows in the RCAF and RAF fully occupied fighting off his raiders, I won't be able to get into London on leave for a while yet. Also, I and a couple of my compatriots are about to be seconded elsewhere, in fact anywhere that the need for extra hands with Hurricanes arises, and I could find myself anywhere around the country in the next few weeks.*

*Chin up old girl, as my RAF colleagues say. Please keep writing to me, as you have been, of the things that keep civilisation going – art, books you are reading, of plays and musical performances – anything to help lift me from the everyday routine. I laughed out loud at the funny side of your story of your night at the theatre and I hope you don't mind that I read it to some of my buddies.*

*I hope this finds you well and looking forward to seeing you again one day.*

*Yours*
*James.*

By the end the page was a blur and I blinked back the tears to save my mascara and to save face, as it was just not the done thing to show such emotion in public.

*He's alive, he's just tired, he hasn't forgotten me!* I wanted to dance around the fountain and yell and scream with happiness. Of course, I did none of those things and instead took myself off to my favourite seat in the Corner House and caught up with the missing weeks there. While my father and I had been about to flee from Dulwich Park two Sunday mornings previously, James had been taking off at Croydon *to rendezvous at 20,000 feet, but as we climbed we saw what I estimated were about a hundred enemy planes in our sector: Heinkels, ME 109s and No 110s, so we got behind them and lined ourselves up in a semi-circle with the sun on our backs and, extraordinarily, the Heinkels broke away and engaged us – right into the sun. It was their mistake. We gave them everything we had.*

My blood ran cold as I read in another letter that he had been downed by *rounds from an ME 109 which took me out, but I managed to crash land at a nearby aerodrome and the erks, as the British so quaintly call the ground staff, had my airplane repaired so quickly I didn't even have time to hear back about leave I'd applied for while she was being mended. I thought I might sneak a few days to see you while she was out but no such luck. Within a couple of days she was back in the air.*

As I re-folded the last of his letters I thought what an amazing narrative they made and how vividly immediate they were, just the sort of stuff he could turn into an autobiography on his retirement from the airforce or, using my second favourite subject, English, I could write up as a biographical novel about him one day. I would keep them forever.

Four weeks later his letter said simply, *I will at last have a week's leave, from 1st November. I can fly down to Croydon and get a billet sorted, then I'll be free to meet up with you on the 2nd. Can you come back from Leatherhead for that weekend? I suggest we make the most of it especially with the darker evenings and the blackout, perhaps meet at around eleven in the morning at the Beaver Club? Please write back and say you can. The Club will know where in the country I am. I'm so very much looking forward to seeing you again.*

I was up early on the morning of the 2nd November. My mother was working that day and I wanted to catch her before she left, having decided that the benefit of telling her about my plans outweighed the danger of her not knowing them and spotting me and James together later in the day. I casually dropped into the conversation, 'I've heard from the airman who was kind to me in the summer after Peggy died and took me to the midsummer dance. He'll be on leave this weekend and has asked me to provide him with a further guided tour of London.'

'He can get guided tours from volunteers at the Beaver Club,' said my mother.

'Well, mine's a sort of individually tailored tour,' I said.

'Well,' responded my mother, 'just make sure you don't guide him off the beaten track by mistake. Stay in public at all times.'

'Oh Mummy, he's just an acquaintance really, just someone I was friendly with.'

'Young men starved of female company can get a little out of hand when they're back in it,' my mother countered darkly.

'He behaved with complete propriety,' I protested, 'and he even made sure I got home safely to the front door after the dance. You're being unfair to him and reading too much into it all!'

By now I was seething and resented my mother's implications. But I wanted her blessing and was afraid that she would pull the plug on the while idea, so I let her have the last word, 'While I agree he is a most pleasant young man, be careful. You never know what someone else is thinking.'

I spent an hour or so bathing, dressing, undressing, spreading my clothes out and agonising over what to wear, finally choosing my knee length mid blue worsted skirt and jacket and my sky blue rayon blouse, topped with a silky blue and white paisley patterned scarf below my navy blue overcoat. A sky blue beret perched at a jaunty angle completed the picture. A conscious tribute to the blue in James' uniform.

When I arrived in the Club's foyer I found James chatting to some fellow airmen. He detached himself from the group to greet me with a brief hug and a kiss on my cheek. I smiled up at him, thinking, *he's thinner than I remember, a little gaunt, maybe.* His uniform hung a little on his frame and he seemed to have aged more than the intervening four months since our last meeting. *He's been to hell and back, though I bet he'll never admit it.*

'Come and meet some friends,' he said, leading me over and introducing me to Tony, Stuart and Douglas. Tony, tall, dark and cadaverous leaned down and shook my hand enthusiastically.

'So this here's my friend's tour guide for the day,' he joked. 'Where do I sign up? Does this Club have any more like you?'

I blushed a little, acknowledging the compliment with a slight nod, and turned to greet the others. Stuart was the youngest of the trio, fresh faced and seemingly barely older than me, beaming as he shook in turn. Douglas, older, I thought, than even James, stepped forward.

'Hie there, lassie,' he said in a broad Scottish accent which to my soft southern ears made his next sentence mostly incomprehensible; I took from it only an oblique reference to James being busy the previous day, but an answer did not appear to be required so I nodded and smiled vaguely. I was used to hearing a variety of accents at the Beaver Club as it prided itself on welcoming any serviceman from any background who happened upon it, but was curious as to the Highlander's comradeship with the Canadian airmen and, as we left the Club and James turned me towards St James' Park, he told me that Douglas had emigrated to Canada only ten years before and so had brought his 'hieland' accent with him.

As we walked in the Park, warming ourselves in the weak late autumn sunshine, distant Lowry figures tending their Digging for Victory plots of brussel sprouts, broad beans, hardy peas and other autumn vegetables, James regaled me with pen pictures of some of his colleagues and re-enacted incidents they had experienced.

'And one morning after a particularly busy night of sorties,' he concluded, 'Douglas keeled over forwards into his porridge and we tried to shake him awake, but he gave us a string of words in his comatose state not suitable for *your* ears and fell back deep asleep. When he finally woke, the porridge was solid and came up out of the bowl like a brick attached to his forehead. He then complained that we hadn't wakened him earlier!'

I laughed at the image James conjured but put my hand on his arm in concern. 'You told me about falling asleep on landing,' I said, 'what if it happens when you're in the air?'

'Oh, don't worry on that score,' he replied, patting my hand as it rested on his arm and smiling down at me. He reached into a pocket and extracted a cigarette packet and a lighter. We stopped while he offered me a cigarette out of politeness, smiling at my refusal, lighting up one for himself. 'The adrenaline rush when the Hun's taking pot shots at you keeps you wide awake, I promise you. It's only when it's all over and you're down safely you'll fall asleep anywhere.'

'Pot shots hardly reflect the danger you're in,' I said, my voice rising, momentarily forgetting the First Rule of War: only talk about positives, keep it light, keep it bright. 'You mentioned in a letter that you were shot at and had to crash land. You made little of it but I think you were lucky to escape with your life.'

James shook his head. 'Perhaps I shouldn't have written to you about that. I was perfectly fine, just the odd scrape and Jerry only holed the webbing, he didn't hit any of the vital parts. Though I had to make a bit of a crash-landing, I'd made it to the aerodrome and my Patty was mended and back in the air in a coupla days.'

'Patty?'

He grinned. 'I re-named her after you.'

I felt both flattered and alarmed. *He hardly knows me, I'm just a friend* (I lied to myself), *is he reading more into our friendship than I am?*

And I was curious. 'How can an aircraft that's just been downed and crash-landed be up and running again in just a couple of days? How can you rely on the repair? Isn't that very dangerous?'

'Hurricanes are built like biplanes,' he explained. 'The fuselage is held together with steel tubes and wooden frames are fixed to these,' he demonstrated, loosely layering one hand over the other, then lifting his lower hand above and gesturing with it in a widening, circular motion, the cigarette smoke mimicking the vapour trail from an aeroplane, 'over which a linen covering is laid. So when the rounds hit me all they really did was go through this covering and out the other side, taking some of the wood and steel framing, enough to make her unstable but not enough to bring me right down. The only thing to *really* worry about are the second and third fuel tanks which you'll find one each side of the cockpit. If they get hit you're probably a goner.' At this point I felt a little faint. 'I brought her mostly under control and headed back to base, but she was a bit of a devil to land with a chunk taken out of her. Hurricanes are easier to repair than Spitfires because Spitfires' bodies are completely metal but, hey, *my* girl's a fighter, in more ways than one. Like you,' he added, drawing deeply on his cigarette and exhaling, his left arm circling my shoulders and hugging me a little.

'Me, a fighter? *You're* the one on the front line.'

'So are *you*,' he said, dropping the cigarette stub and grinding it with his heel. 'My brave girl, with a bomb

146

blasting off right next to you in the field. Remember, you wrote to me about it? Your Leatherhead doesn't sound any safer. And London's constantly under attack. It's not called the home front for nothing. But at least I can fight back. Here on the ground you're all sitting ducks.'

'We have the anti-aircraft guns.'

'It's just pot luck if they get an airplane flying by. I know they fire saturation shots in the direction they *think* they're going, but you need a better way to predict these things than the predictors they use at the moment. You need the anti-aircraft guns and searchlights to be as accurate as possible because us fliers can't stop Jerry at night. Without some form of night radar we're flying blind. I'm sure in time with proper research and development things will improve. It just isn't out there right now.' He paused, tightening his grip further. 'I hate to think of you so vulnerable.'

Swinging me round, he kissed me, gently at first, then harder, his arm moving down to my waist, the other somewhere between us, nestled, I realised as his tongue probed my mouth, against my right breast. I was a little stiff in his embrace at first, then melting, kissing him back, my arms around him, my head swimming, my body warring with my accusing mind, *you flibbertigibbet, you like this, don't you, you shouldn't let him but you like it...*

James drew back smiling, breathed in deep and tugged at my hand. 'Come on, I want to see if those ducks we saw last May haven't been sitting targets and requisitioned for someone's dinner table.'

We half-trotted to the lake, holding hands, laughing, while I recovered my poise, grateful for his deft turn of the conversation. There, having satisfied himself of the ducks' wellbeing, James looked at his watch.

'Not far off lunchtime. I have a table arranged at a place near Piccadilly Circus. Can my tour guide take me there? In return for your tour guide services the meal's on me.'

The 'place' turned out to be the Regent Palace Hotel, an

imposing immediate post-Edwardian building that boasted the greatest number of rooms in any hotel in Europe at its opening. I had passed it many times but would never have had the means to pass over the threshold, let alone eat there. I hung back, daunted, but James urged me in.

Excusing myself to the Ladies room, promising to meet him back at the restaurant entrance, I welcomed the few quiet moments to draw breath and say to myself in the mirror (fortunately there was no one else there!), *stop being ridiculous, he's just being friendly the only way he obviously knows how. I've shown him Lyons Corner House and now he's showing me his version, that's all,* but a slight sense of panic still rumbled.

My suspicion that James was not just a simple farm boy but part of a prosperous business-owning family was confirmed when, rejoining him at the restaurant entrance, his confident manner had waiters bowing subserviently at us and one led us away from the restaurant area to a private dining room on the first floor.

A waiter took my coat, scarf and beret and hung them on a hanger on the hook on the back of the door. James asked formally for my permission to remove his jacket as he was plenty warm, he said. *Yet another example of his gentlemanly manners,* I thought, feeling flattered at being treated like a real grown up. He laid his jacket and cap on the chaise longue and resumed his seat.

The food was exquisite, each of the five courses delicately arranged on the plate and the variety was nectar to a ration starved girl. I declined the red wine and stuck to the white despite the move from fish to beef bourguignon, failing in my attempt to appear sophisticated, feeling ignorant and gauche, but afraid of the effect any stronger wine would have on me. Already my head was swimming a little with the unusual amount of alcohol. *Thank God for the whisky in my hot milk and for port and lemon, at least I have some experience of it.*

Relaxing a little and curious, as we ate I peppered James with questions about his family and his flying career.

'My mother? Not much to tell really. She died five years ago. I'd been doing my usual selfish stuff and hadn't bothered to take leave when it was due. Flying was everything to me. All I'd get from my father when I went home was, when was I going to give up on prancing about in the air and get some honest to goodness work done in the family firm instead. So that year I took my leave as a secondment to a training school instead of going home. I fancied working as an instructor and was asked to stay there for a while. We knew that war was likely and needed to prepare for it. We like our fighter pilots not too inexperienced but not too old. In flying terms I was getting on a bit, even at twenty-two. I'd worked my way up to Flight Lieutenant.' He pronounced 'Lieutenant' like the British 'lef-tenant', not the American 'loo-tenant'.

In answer to my further question, James added, 'There are two Flights to a squadron, usually six airplanes which are in turn divided into two sections identified by a colour name: red, blue and so on. Promotion within the squadron occurs maybe because someone is moved elsewhere or simply because someone has gone and got themselves killed accidentally.'

James paused, his mouth turning down, seemingly recalling colleagues lost to momentary inattention.

I put my hand on his arm sympathetically. He patted my hand and, rousing himself, continued.

'After that I went onto bombers for a spell and back to flying with fighter squadrons shortly before war was declared, where I moved up to Squadron Leader. That was my favourite role. There's something magnificent and humbling at the same time to see your squadron up there alongside you, high up where you're above everyday life, with vast tracts of Canada laid out before you.'

James' eyes were focused beyond me, as if he was flying high, searching the skies. I asked, 'What do you like most about flying?'

'When I first flew an airplane I felt as if a missing part of me had been put back. Up there I feel whole. Complete. When I'm on the ground part of me is always wanting to be up there. Down here I feel I'm missing a layer. In my plane I feel properly clothed. Fulfilled.

'I can't expect anyone who hasn't been there to really understand.' He looked at me, refocusing, smiling. 'But I appreciate your trying.'

'The nearest for me I suppose is art,' I said. 'I can be lost in a painting for hours. And I often have an urge to draw things and people, to translate what I see.'

'Would you like to draw me?'

Our first meeting, his teeth sinking into the gingerbread, my secret *I'd like to draw you* thought. I smiled. 'Of course. I wanted to the first day I met you.'

James chuckled. 'At the Corner House? I thought you wanted to *eat* me.'

'Was I that obvious?'

After a few moments of shared amusement and sipping wine, I persisted. 'You were telling me about your mother. She died young.'

'She was forty-four. Cancer. She didn't deserve to die. I'd last seen her about a year earlier. No one told me she had it, that she was dying. My father expected me to come home for leave as usual and so be there in time and was angry when I didn't come, so didn't tell me until it was all over. He forbad my brothers to contact me. My mother was deeply upset that I chose not to come home. She didn't know that no one had told me. Right up to the end she was asking for me. I only know *that* because I went to the hospital after the funeral to thank the nurses for their care and they told me.' He was silent for a moment, head bowed, lips pressing together, emotions simmering. He took a shaky breath.

'James, I'm so sorry. I didn't mean to churn up old feelings. I was being intrusive. Forgive me.'

James looked up at me. 'Not at all. I'm glad you asked.

I'm not used to anyone being interested. It took me a long time to find some peace over it.' He paused. 'The person we find hardest to forgive is ourselves. For a while I even hated flying and thought about throwing in the towel. Then one day when I took a youngster up he was doing fine with a spin until he sent us into a stall. You're supposed to pull out of a spin in time but he delayed too long and there we were hurtling towards the ground at an ever-increasing speed and the young pilot blacked out and it was just my instruction sticks, my experience and a large slice of luck between life and death. I pulled us out of the stall as the belly of the airplane brushed the treetops and if the ground had been rising, even a fraction, we'd have been a goner. Fortunately the ground was falling away and I got her on a level course and we made it home. All I could hear in my mind on that flight back to base were my mother's parting words the year before, *Forget your father's views. Go and enjoy your flying wherever it takes you. There'll be plenty of time to do other things later. I love you, my son.*'

After a moment James continued softly, 'It seemed as if she was there with me, next to me in the airplane, as if she was protecting me. Fanciful, I know.' His face relaxed and I smiled tentatively, in sympathy. He continued, 'But strangely, I've enjoyed my flying again after that.'

After we finished dessert and a coffee pot and cups were provided, James offered me a cigarette, smiling indulgently when I refused, and said, 'Come on, Pat, it's really nothing to worry about you know. I can't believe you've never tried, but if you haven't, hey, there's a first time for everything. Here,' and he lit one and passed it to me, nodding. 'Go on, try it.'

I breathed in hesitantly, not wishing to seem unsophisticated, but also not wishing to look like a good-time girl, and gagged as the smoke caught me at the back of my throat. James laughed, though not unkindly, and said, 'It gets better as you go on. Try again, give it a good drag then exhale slowly,' so I tried again and after a few fish-like gasps I found a rhythm and felt an all-pervading sense of sweet ease spread slowly through my body to the very end of my fingertips.

We finished our cigarettes and James poured more coffee. I stood up a little unsteadily, saying, 'I think a trip to the Ladies is called for,' turning towards the door through which I had entered. 'Through here,' said James, swiftly steering me to another door in the side wall. Puzzled, I stepped through into a bedroom with a further door beyond. James nodded in its direction.

*This is like Alice in Wonderland*, I thought as I sank onto the en suite's toilet pedestal. *I was expecting another private dining room but, hey presto, it's a bedroom with its own bathroom.* I giggled. *Whatever will James conjure up next?* Leaning my head against the cool tiles the slight tilt to the room gradually righted itself and I felt as if I was returning to earth. *I wonder if that's what flying's like.*

'Pat, are you alright?' James, knocking gently on the door.

'Yes, I'm fine,' I called back, wondering how long I was sitting in my reverie.

Emerging from the bathroom I found James standing by the net curtained, tape-strewn bedroom window overlooking the street. I joined him at the window and said,

'Thank you for a lovely meal. Where would you like to go now? We still have a couple of hours of daylight before I have to be getting back.'

James emitted a low groan and, clasping my waist, span me around to the wall beside the window and kissed me long and hard, his tongue darting between my teeth, catching me unawares. The wall against my back allowed no retreat and already my body was betraying my intention, rising on tiptoe to meet his, pressing breast to chest, hip to hip, thigh to thigh, pubic bone to hardness. The now familiar melting, longing, aching, and I kissed him back, exploring his mouth with my tongue, eyes closed, his cigarette scented nasal breath warming my face, lost in the moment.

His hand moved up from my waist to my left breast underneath my blouse (*how did that come adrift?*), moving my nipple between finger and thumb through the cloth of my petticoat and brassiere. The other hand firmly in the centre of my back, steadying me, then moving down to my right buttock, squeezing gently, and a sticky wetness in my knickers (*but I've just been to the toilet and anyway it's not coming from there*), and I was lost in the desire to melt and mould to him and never let go.

Pulling back a little James said, smiling tenderly down at me, 'Pat, there's something I want to ask you.'

But it was sensation, not conversation, I wanted, aware that the afternoon was retreating and not knowing when I would see him again, or whether he would even come back from his next dog fight. I reached up, pulling his head down, and kissed him again, hard, demanding, revelling in the moment, his tongue and lips sending waves of sensation to the pit of my stomach, my arms entwining around his neck, my fingers furrowing through the stubble of his hair. James groaned again, and, with a swiftness and strength that caught me unawares, lifted me up, deposited me on the bed, unbuttoned my blouse and, pulling my breasts over the top of my petticoat and brassiere, buried his face in them, his mouth closing on my right nipple, his right hand working my left breast.

I stiffened, shocked, looking down at the top of his head, a small voice at the back of my mind saying, *stop this, stop this, you mustn't, you mustn't,* another voice saying, *he's done this before, he knows what to do, my God, what's happening to me,* more flooding wetness, floating sweetness enveloping me, and when his other hand fumbled at the buttons of my skirt, mine moved against my will to assist. Knickers followed and he raised his head, shrugging off his shirt, scrambling out of his clothes, kissing me while freeing me from the tangle of jacket, blouse, petticoat and brassiere, leaving me in just my best and only silk stockings and suspenders.

Smiling, glancing down, James ran a hand up and down my thigh, outside first and then inside, and back upwards. Suddenly realising the object of his explorations, I pushed briefly at his shoulders, but his fingers remained firmly entrenched while his mouth was on my breast again, his remaining hand on my other, and I felt a falling sensation, emitting mewing whimpers as my breasts and groin met in a series of tremors.

James raised his head and spoke softly. 'I love you, Pat,' and the rest of his words were lost in the roaring in my ears as I breathed, 'Oh, yes, oh yes, that's lovely,' and the little niggling voices rose shrilly again, and I started saying, 'but we really mustn't...' and my protest was lost, James shifting suddenly and entering me, thrusting in part of the way, first slowly and, as I began to struggle to stop him, moving into a gentle rhythm. Waves of sweet sensations washing over me, I relaxed into their depths.

I became aware of James lifting himself slightly, fumbling for his trousers and extracting a small package. Withdrawing from me, *ah, no, no, don't stop.* I looked down my body at him kneeling between my legs and saw his penis huge, erect, purple headed, disappearing into a covering sheath. Looking up and smiling, he lay gently back down onto me and into me, resuming, faster, now penetrating deeply, filling me, and for several minutes I jerked in rhythm, a burning, tearing, throbbing sensation far inside, my breasts flapping against his raised chest, my nipples rubbing, hard and erect, his eyes above me sapphires glinting in the autumn afternoon gloom, his lips compressed, then he was nuzzling my neck and I wept as I thought, *I mustn't do this but I like this, it hurts, but I like this, my God, I'm lost, lost forever...* James reared up and, arching his back, swooped down, enveloping my left nipple and aurora in his mouth, raking my nipple with his teeth. My inner being shot into the air, spasming, and I heard myself shriek briefly from afar.

Quick and urgent now and with a final groan James

speared me deepest, shuddering and collapsing slightly to my left side, his contorted face smoothing out as he turned his head towards me.

I don't know how long we lay together, hearts thudding, perspiration mingling, breaths tickling. We smiled at each other, his arm resting around my waist, my hand limp against his chest. I slowly returned to reality. James reached up, wiping the traces of mascara streaks from my tears with his fingers, cupping my face in his hand.

'I'm sorry,' he said. 'Did I hurt you?'

'A little, but it was beautiful.'

'As you are.'

I felt an astonished wonderment that he saw me so.

I sensed a shrinking inside me and James raised himself, kissing my left breast and, fumbling at his groin, dropped the sheath with a splat onto the carpet. He leaned down the bed, emitting an exclamation of concern.

'Darling, I'm sorry, I didn't realise. If I had I would've been gentler.'

I sat up and saw watery bloody streaks on the inside of my thighs. Scrambling up, my face crimson, I said, 'Oh no, my period's come early. It's not due 'til next week,' embarrassed at mentioning such an intimate matter. Absurd in view of what we'd just done.

'Perhaps it's not that,' James tried to reassure me. 'You were so passionate. So *ready*. I just didn't realise,' he repeated.

'Realise what?'

'That you were a virgin.'

I blinked, my eyes stinging a little from the mascara. 'What else did you think?' The air felt suddenly chill and I started scrambling for my clothes. 'I'm not a good time girl. I've *never* done this before. I've never met anyone like you. Fending off Bill's advances last winter was *awful*. I'd never dream of doing this with him or anyone else.'

'Bill?'

'A childhood friend who wanted me to be his girl. I

turned him down.' *What would Bill think of me if he saw me now?* I flushed crimson and fled for the bathroom where I washed myself clean as well as I could from the bath tap using one of the flannels laid out.

'Sorry, Pat, I need a pee,' James called through the door. I scrambled out, too embarrassed to meet his eye as he passed me, becoming aware of him urinating behind me, the door open. I dressed, trembling, in the bedroom, my knickers still damp, but at least the bleeding seemed to have stopped.

James emerged and I averted my eyes, then peeked back at him, fascinated by a real live specimen of the naked male body. *Now I can make sense of the pictures I've seen of Michelangelo's David*, I thought. I'd wondered how recumbent appendages could transform into the male part described in Fifth Form biology class. James caught my glance as he bent down to retrieve his clothes, his mouth quirking with amusement.

'I'll call down for some tea,' he said, shrugging on his clothes and moving to the telephone beside the bed into which he spoke briefly while I returned to the bathroom to repair my make-up.

Emerging I caught sight of a small case on the floor beside the wardrobe. James was no longer in the room and I crept to the wardrobe and, opening the door, found men's clothes hanging there and underwear and socks laid out on shelves. *This was his billet last night*, I suddenly realised, *and will be again tonight.*

I found James in the dining room beside the chaise longue clutching his jacket.

'While we're waiting there's something I want to ask you.'

'You said that before.'

'Before I was so delightfully interrupted,' he laughed.

He guided me to the chaise longue. Seating himself beside me he said, 'There was somewhere else I went yesterday afternoon that has a bearing on today.' He dipped his left hand into his jacket's side pocket and produced a small jewellery box. Suddenly Douglas' cryptic remark earlier made sense and I thought, *oh no, he's not going to, please God, no, I'm not ready for this,* and he said, 'I love you and I want to marry you, Pat. Please will you marry me. Please say yes.'

Now he had started, the words tumbled out.

'What I said about you being on the home front, and me the front line, you know anything can happen any time and I don't want to risk losing you or going myself without first enjoying life with you as my wife. I know this is probably not a good time for you as I'm sure it's not easy to walk away from a teaching job, but if you'd agree then maybe you could ask for a few days off in the circumstances. Or just leave the job. I can support you, that's not a problem. I can find somewhere for you to live close to me at Croydon and we can sort out something if I'm posted elsewhere. My leave doesn't end 'til Friday so we could fit in a coupla days' honeymoon and when this war's over I can take you anywhere you want to go for a proper one. Anywhere in the world.'

He was in full flow now and I could only look at him with widening eyes. *Teaching job? Leave the job?*

'I know,' he said, 'you're probably wondering how we can get married so quickly. I applied for a special kind of licence ahead and picked it up yesterday afternoon.' He patted his jacket.

I sat stunned and speechless.

'You're not saying anything? Can I take that as a yes?'

I started to tremble, feeling an urgent need for another cigarette.

'Oh, James, I don't know where to begin.' I swallowed.

'We get on well,' he continued, 'and we've been together for months. I feel I know you through your letters and we now know our bodies are happy together.' I blushed. 'I have never, *ever*, felt this way about anyone. The last thing I imagined when I came over here was that I would fall in love with an English girl. But I *know* you're the one for me. I've loved you from the moment I saw you at my feet and picked you up off the floor. I want to be the only one for you.'

James sat back a little, arm resting along the top of the chaise longue back, waiting for my response and, as I sat mute with mounting horror and embarrassment, added, 'We could announce our engagement today and get married on Monday. I hope your family can be there. Douglas would be my best man and Tony and Stuart would stand for me too. I checked they'll still be around. Oh, and there's your grandmother and her new husband you've told me about. And anyone else you want. It wouldn't be a big wedding, I know, and I don't want you to be too disappointed. But I can hire a restaurant, your parents wouldn't have to worry about the cost, or I'm sure we can find some catering help, maybe through the Beaver Club. Here,' he added, opening the box and holding it out towards me. A solitaire diamond winked at me, its gold ring base gleaming. Behind it, in similar pose, stood a gold band wedding ring.

'If they don't quite fit we can go back now or first thing on Monday and get them fixed.'

I thought, *if I really loved him more than anything else in the world I think I* would *give up all my hopes and ambitions, all that I've fought for and endured for, in order to be with him. But I don't exactly feel ready to do that. I like him immensely and I love being with him and he does astonishing things to my body but I've led him on, letting him make up to me. My God, WHAT HAVE I DONE? I'm only sixteen. I don't want to get married.* A vision of Janet, pregnant and married, tied to domesticity, missing out on the chance to complete her education and support herself, assailed me. *My God, I could be pregnant. No, he used something, I may be alright. My God, IT'S ALL MY FAULT. I should* never *have agreed to write to him or see him. How could I have been such a fool not to see this would happen? My mother was right.*

I said tentatively, 'James, I like you awfully and if I was ten years older I'm sure I'd say yes like a shot. But I can't say yes, not right now, I'm so, so sorry.' I drew in a shaky breath as James shot me a puzzled look and placed one hand on my arm.

'Ten years older? I don't want you ten years older. You'd be older than me!'

'I mean,' and it all came gushing out, a little incoherently. 'I want to teach, I've *always* wanted to teach for as far back as I can remember. I'm fighting my mother over this. She wants me to be a secretary and snare a rich boss, but I don't want that, I want to achieve things *my* way. So I *have* to do it, for myself, which means sticking with the sixth form, there's still nearly two years to go, of course, then there's teacher training and that's usually three years but if the war's still on they'll truncate it to two which means working through the holidays and the college I want to go to has been evacuated to Doncaster, so I'd be away tied up with that, then I want to give teaching a fair crack of the whip, for what's the point of training me if I don't justify all that my parents will have sacrificed for me to do it? So maybe if I was ten years older I'd say I'm ready for this, and maybe in ten years' time women teachers won't lose their jobs when they marry, but I can't ask you to wait that long...'

James' eyes grew ever-wider and his face grew ever more horrified as I spoke and he drew his hand away from my arm.

'Pat,' he said urgently, '*How old are you?*'

I blinked. 'Sixteen, of course.'

He stared at me, stunned, for several moments. He spoke slowly, shaking his head, as if trying to deny my revelation, 'I thought you were twenty one when we met and had your twenty second birthday in June. I thought you were a teacher at the school evacuated to Leatherhead. I must have misunderstood something you wrote or something your sister said ...'

'My *sister*?!' I exclaimed. 'I don't have a sister, I'm an only child.' Comprehension dawned. 'Do you mean my *mother?*'

Suddenly I was furious, leaping up and pacing the room. 'She *loves* it when people think we're sisters. They do it all the time. She's always looked younger than her age.' *And since thirteen I've often been mistaken for an adult,* the thought swept through me, *and that bit I've sometimes hated and at other times secretly liked and now it's tripped me up.* Aloud I said, 'So if you referred to me as her sister she wouldn't have corrected you because it's flattering for her.'

James shrugged. 'Ladies always knock years off their age. Ironic that you just have. How do I *know* you're only sixteen?' he suddenly demanded, angrily, bitterly, standing up over me, 'and not just fishing for an excuse?'

This was a side to him I hadn't seen before and felt a little afraid of it. I floundered for a moment, then remembered and, retrieving my handbag, fished out my identity card. I held it out to him, turning it over. He took it and read it several times as if in disbelief. It was my original one, and I hadn't got round to updating my later changes of addresses. I didn't have to point out my father's signature on the back, required of parents at the time the card was issued for a child under sixteen. He saw it straight away.

His face crumpled into the lines around his mouth and eyes and he slumped down onto a dining chair, one hand clutching the identity card, the other placing the open jewellery box on the table. He held my identity card out towards me and I took it back, feeling sick, trembling legs taking me to the other chair.

Leaning forward, putting his head in his hands, James said in a low voice,

'I'm a fucking cradle snatcher. Dear God, I promise you I had no idea.' He raised his head and looked at me, desolation, despair personified. 'I can't possibly expect you to marry me right *now*. I agree. Your life's ahead of you. Live it. But give me hope, Pat. I'll wait for you as long as it takes. Five years, ten years, darn it, for as long as you want. For eternity if needs be.' Now it was his turn to spring up and pace, snatching up the box, clutching it hard.

'Until I met you, flying was my whole life. I defied my father's wishes and never regretted it. All the women I've ever met only want to talk about movie stars or some such ridiculously trivial stuff, but you're fun and cultured and poised and interested in things I am. First place you took me was your "Nash Gal" and you told me about artists you like and concerts and plays you've been to and...' His voice trailed off and he stopped, looking down at the open box cradled in his hand.

A knock on the door, a discreet opening, a waiter's trolley piled with a teapot, milk jug, delicate sandwiches, cakes, accompanying crockery and cutlery, two glasses and a bottle of champagne projecting from an ice bucket like an obscene penis.

I caught the movement of the waiter hovering discreetly. This was humiliating for James and humiliating for me and I couldn't bear it any longer. Muttering 'I'm sorry, please excuse me,' I stuffed my identity card into my bag, grabbed my overcoat, the hanger spinning to the floor, and fled the room to the Ladies downstairs where I cowered behind the cubicle door, balling my fist into my mouth and repeating, *I will not cry, I will not cry.* A seismic shift had occurred, a chasm opened up that could not be bridged. Since Easter, Bill and I had danced a fandango of filial affection, saving face in front of family, maintaining a social veneer. And Bill's kissing had repelled me, not like James'. Bill had never been intimate with me, not like James. Now my innocence bubble had well and truly burst and my affectionate, friendly acquaintanceship with James that had ultimately been *safe* could not be stuck back together, not even superficially.

*He's gone to so much trouble and expense, I feel so stupid, how could I have let this happen? The Regent Palace Hotel, for God's sake. Letting him think I was a sophisticated woman in her early twenties. Secretly wanting him to think that. Idiot! How can I ever see him again? After what we've done together. I'll never forgive myself. Ever. Wait fifteen minutes until the coast is clear then go home and forget him.*

I eventually emerged and as I sidled across the entrance

foyer James detached himself from the reception clerk's desk and hurried over to me. He handed me my beret and scarf.

'I'll see you safely to your tram.'

'I'll be fine, I know London like the back of my hand.'

But James insisted, walking beside me, not touching, not speaking, then as the tram hoved into view he pulled me back, kissing me hard, passionately, desperately, there in public, in front of the bystanders, and speaking into my ear, 'Give me hope for the future, Pat. I love you. Please write.'

I nodded dumbly, my breasts sore and extended, my vagina still throbbing with his imprint. Stepping back James let me climb on board and I watched him receding, his grief stricken face growing distant, abruptly obscured by a fellow passenger and when I looked past her I could see James no more.

Experiencing many miserable nights in my life was no preparation for how I felt that Saturday night. Snippets of our conversation echoing and, like trick photography, the sight of him above me, the feel of him inside me, the sound of his melodious accent, the scent of his skin, endlessly repeating in my mind. Thoughts revolving, spinning erratically. *How could I trust a man who took me to a hotel bedroom when I was not married to him?* Granted, James asked me to marry him, and I conceded that but for my kiss in the bedroom that distracted him he would have asked me beforehand, but perhaps he planned for us to be together as husband and wife after my presumed acceptance without a nuptial blessing. Did he respect me so little? I felt let down, cheap, emotionally and physically defiled. My thoughts swung wildly in the opposite direction. It was all my fault. I led him on. I allowed him to do what he did. I should have stopped him. *I'm a good-for-nothing flibbertigibbet. I can't trust myself again. Ever.*

James's parting words still rang in my ears. Give him hope? How could I give hope to a man with such little integrity? How could I trust myself to be with him and not do the same again? I yearned to see him, to hear the soft cadences of his exotic accent, to see those crow's feet crinkle. And to feel his insistent lips on mine, his tongue exploring, my body tingling. *I feel all these things but I never once told him I love him despite his saying more than once he loves me. I'm no better than that hussy Janet who threw herself at her cousin and ended up marrying at three months pregnant.*

Weary with silent weeping, around three o'clock I sat up in bed composing a letter that echoed the one I wrote to Bill ten months earlier in such different circumstances.

*I will not deny that I feel an affection for you,* I wrote. *In some ways I realise now you have been for me a young uncle, or perhaps a cousin, figure,* I lied. *I have enjoyed your letters and your company, however brief that has proved to be, and I would be willing to remain a pen pal if you wish it. But please do not place the rest of your life on hold for my sake. I release you from any sense of commitment or obligation you may feel towards me. It would be unfair of me to give you hope. And equally it would be unfair of me to keep you committed in some vague sense for the future when you might meet someone else and want to settle down with her. It would be better for us to understand this now than for you to live in limbo.*

I didn't know what else to add, so signed off. The next morning I left early, pleading schoolwork and detoured via the Club to deliver my letter to the B pigeonhole. There was nothing for me under R.

Setting my face to the future and vowing to put the whole experience behind me and never to trust myself or any man again, I was unprepared for the letter that arrived from my mother three days later.

'Dear Pat,' wrote my mother, 'What have you done? I was sent to help with cleaning the library this morning and found your nice young man slumped in the corner looking as miserable as sin and when I enquired after him he told me there had been a terrible misunderstanding on his part and he had no idea you are only sixteen and if you'd been the twenty-one or -two he'd thought you were he would have pressed you to marry him. He told me this as I demanded

163

to know what had brought you home silent and unhappy on Saturday evening. I feared he had made a dishonest woman of you, but he assured me that was not the case.'

*Ah, so if you'd asked me that and I had assured you he hadn't, would you have believed me?*

I read on.

'He told me that he had applied to return from his leave early and was expecting to go this afternoon to North Weald to help out for a couple of weeks or so and then back to the squadron at Croydon. He was just waiting for a message to be brought up to him confirming his change of plans. He told me of his love for you and of his marriage proposal and that although you had given him no hope he was prepared to wait ten years or even longer in case you changed your mind. He showed me the rings he bought and said that he would always carry them close to his heart.'

'Pat, if you love this man and are just worried about your age, I will speak with your father about giving our permission for him to walk out with you, officially I mean, even consider marriage sooner rather than later if you were afraid of what we would say. You're the same age that I met your father and I was married at nineteen and had you at twenty and with this war on it seems young people grow up fast.'

She went on to write about other, more trivial, things and I put the letter down. *He must have received my letter before Mummy encountered him, for he told her he had no hope.*

Becky glanced up.

'Pat, are you alright?'

The dam burst and I was helpless in the torrent of grief, regret and lost innocence that poured into the valley of my despair. Handing her the letter and nodding for her to read it I rocked in my chair and dropped my head into my hands as Becky rushed to my side, hugging me and briefly perusing my mother's missive.

'Oh, Pat,' sighed Becky, 'why didn't you tell me on Sunday? You said you'd had a pleasant weekend with your parents. I thought perhaps it hadn't been pleasant, for you weren't yourself, but I had no idea you saw him and that this is what happened.'

'Sorry, so sorry,' I murmured between my fingers.

'Don't apologise, I only wish I'd known and could've helped sooner.'

Mrs Grice came running in at the commotion. 'It's all right,' Becky assured her. 'She's split with her young man and is a little upset. She'll be fine soon.'

Fussing and tutting, Mrs Grice produced cups of tea.

*I hear the English cure all ills with a cup of tea.*

My period came three days later. Perversely I wept as I tended to myself, relief mingled with grief, regret for what we had done together entwined with sorrow for what I would now never have of him.

Nothing for me under R the following weekend.

And still nothing for me under R a week later when the doorman, catching sight of me checking the pigeonhole, took me on one side. 'I'm so sorry, dearie,' he said, and I looked at him quizzically, thinking, *does* everyone *know about my rejection of James' proposal?* and I saw his head turn towards the In Memoriam board and he said, 'It was posted this morning,' and my head shrieked, *No, no, no!* and I moved towards it as if wading through treacle.

*Group Captain James Alistair Bonar. Killed in action 11th November 1940 over the North Sea by a bomb dropped from an Italian BR20 while engaging Italian enemy forces with German cover, temporarily flying with squadron 249 North Weald. Twelve known kills, also at least ten probables and damageds. A fine officer and will be sorely missed by his compatriots in the RAF and by our own squadron RCAF No.1.*

# PART TWO
# SECRETS AND LIES

*To every thing there is a season, and a time to*
*every purpose under the heaven:*
*a time to be born, and a time to die;*
*a time to plant, and a time to pluck up that which is planted;*
*a time to kill, and a time to heal;*
*a time to break down, and a time to build up;*
*a time to weep, and a time to laugh;*
*a time to mourn, and a time to dance;*
*a time to cast away stones, and a time to gather stones together;*
*a time to embrace, and a time to refrain from embracing;*
*a time to seek, and a time to lose;*
*a time to keep, and a time to cast away;*
*a time to rend, and a time to sew;*
*a time to keep silence, and a time to speak;*
*a time to love, and a time to hate;*
*a time for war, and a time for peace.*

Ecclesiastes 3:1-8 Revised Version

# 9
# Winter

Winter gripped my heart as surely as it gripped the country.

Lying awake into the nights, silent weeping, stifled sobbing, the same thoughts revolving around my head. *He'd still be alive if I'd said yes. He wouldn't have arranged a temporary transfer. He died because of me.*

Logic warring with emotion. *It was his choice. He didn't have to curtail his leave. He was unlucky but it wasn't your fault.*

Nightmare thoughts rearing up, wondering how he died, envisaging his awful last moments. *Was it a direct hit that knocked him out without his knowing, that killed him outright? Or did the bomb catch one of the tanks each side of the cockpit, dousing him in fuel and igniting, bringing searing agony to his sinewy body? His handsome, chiselled face, skin peeling back, blue eyes exploding with heat, large, firm, gentle hands agonisingly consumed. Was he still alive as the aeroplane hit the water and sank, choking, drowning, knowing that death was inevitable? Did he call out for his mother, or were his thoughts of me, who had rejected him? His body now resting at the bottom of the unforgiving sea. Had he separated from his plane or was he entombed in my namesake, the rings still resting against his unbeating heart?*

Sleeping through sheer exhaustion, clawing my way through each day, putting on a false smile and pretending all was well, I succumbed to the winter 'flu shortly before Christmas, shivering and aching as I lay in bed, Becky ministering to me with cold compresses and bowls of thin soup and watery porridge, and emptying the ancient metal chamber pot when I was too weak even to stagger to the toilet. Mrs Grice seemed to regard nursing as outside her remit. After a week or so the worst was over and I tried sitting up in bed feeling faint and exhausted. Becky propped me up with both our pillows and passed me a glass of water.

'Drink as much as you can,' she urged. 'You've got to get your strength up so you can go home for Christmas.' After a few sips I laid my head back, a tear rolling down my cheek.

'It was the cloud.'

'Cloud?'

'That went across the sun and so I decided to go in for a cup of tea. If I'd gone straight to the Nash Gal I'd never have met him and he'd still be alive.'

'Pat, you mustn't take on the guilt and regrets of the world. I know you blame yourself that he flew when he did but there was nothing else you could have done. I know how much going into teaching means to you. It wasn't your fault he thought you were older than you are.'

*Yes it is. I behaved outrageously. I kissed him like he kissed me, passionately, eagerly, lustfully. I was infatuated and I threw myself at him. I should have found excuses instead of seeing him. I should never have agreed to write. I led him on.*

Shaking my head slowly I said, 'He's dead because of me,' my tears flowing freely as Becky drew me into her arms.

'Weep for him, then. Don't bottle it up. That's what grieving is all about.'

'I k...k...killed him,' I hiccupped.

Becky held me tightly through the raging and as it subsided said, 'And now it's time to stop berating yourself. Ultimately it was the fault of those beastly Jerrys.'

'Italians,' I corrected. 'Eyeties. It was an Italian bomber.'

'They were fighting on Germany's side. Look, I'm not going to say anything crass like cheer up, but you do need to find a way to forgive yourself.'

'He said that over his mother. "The person we find hardest to forgive is ourselves".'

' "There's a time to break down and a time to build up",'

quoted Becky. ' "A time to weep and a time to laugh, a time to mourn and a time to dance". Mourn him now and the rest will happen for you when you're ready.'

'Becky, what would I do without you? Thank you for looking after me in so many different ways.'

'And one of those ways is to make sure that you eat up.' Becky, reaching for the cooling bowl of porridge and raising the spoon, cocked an eyebrow questioningly. 'Would you like me to feed you or will you feed yourself?'

With weak, trembly legs I made it home the following week, curling up in my bed and hating the festive season for I felt neither peace nor goodwill towards myself. My mother, not renowned for keeping her opinion to herself, was tact personified and I concluded that she believed James's assurance of the retention of my reputation. *Why did he tell her that he had not made a dishonest woman of me,* I wondered, coining my mother's phrase, *and not just own up in the hope that she would wade in, insisting on marriage? Was it really to protect me, or was it to protect himself?* 'I'm a fucking cradle snatcher,' he'd said, self-disgust harshening his tone. I flinched again at the indecent adjective he'd used. I was only a few months over the legal age of consent, so perhaps he was afraid of what his contemporaries would think of him. *I'll never know, but for whatever reason, I'm grateful to him for lying to my mother and allowing my family to continue to believe me virgo intacta.*

I also calculated that as Becky was my only close confidant and had read my mother's letter she, too, had no idea of the true events of the last day I was with James.

*So my secret's safe,* I concluded. *I'll never marry, no husband to ever know the truth either. And I'll not be shamed like Janet, as there's no resulting baby to proclaim my disgrace.*

On the day before Christmas Eve I was descending the stairs to the hall, having decided to test my strength by walking round to my grandmother's, when a figure appeared the other side of the frosted glass and knocked. I called, 'I'll get this,' to Mrs Haywood, the ground floor neighbour, who started to emerge from her kitchen at the rear, and I opened the door to the harassed mother from Idmiston Road, the pram parked behind her and her two older children beside her.

''Ere y'are,' she said, holding out a package. 'This come fer yer a couple weeks ago. Sorry I 'adn't got round ter passin' it on but I 'aven't bin this way 'till ter-day.'

'Why, thank you,' I said, taking it and noticing my name 'Miss P. Roberts' written in bold handwriting I'd not seen before. 'It's kind of you to come all this way.' I hesitated. 'Er, would you like to come in for some refreshment?'

'Nah, I wanner ge'ter the market ter-day, being near Christmas an' all,' she replied, ushering the children back along the short path and into the street. 'Can yer let peoples know yer's moved? I can't promise ter bring stuff over all the time.'

'Yes, yes of course,' I promised, calling 'Thank you again,' to her as she disappeared round the corner into St Matthew's Road.

I was intrigued. A few minutes investigating the package would not delay me unduly, so I tore the end open and extracted a letter. Puzzled, no address being given at the heading of the letter, I glanced down at the signature and froze.

*Douglas McKellen.*

Douglas. Tall, older, red-haired, broad Scottish accent. *'Hie there lassie.'*

Trembling, I turned and hastened up the stairs, all the way to my room at the top. *Thank God Mummy's at work and Daddy's asleep and I've no special arrangement to see Nan, I can see her this afternoon.* Closing the door to my room quietly, I tumbled the package's contents on to the bed. My letters to James. I knelt over the bed, burying my head in the letters, stifling my sobs in the bedcovers. *I must get a grip, I can't have anyone coming in and finding me like this. If Daddy wakes and hears me crying he'll investigate.* Forcing myself to calm down at this sobering realisation, I sat back on my heels and picked out Douglas' letter. It was brief.

*Dear Miss Roberts*

*Following the loss of my commanding officer, colleague and friend, a package of your letters was found among his effects. A delay occurred in returning these to you as we did not at first know your address. I thought to try to return them through the Beaver Club but I was subsequently passed a letter to forward to you which James had lodged with his own superior officer to send to you in the event of his death and which is addressed to your home address. The task of forwarding it fell to me as I was still holding your letters and other effects of his for forwarding to Canada.*

*It is not my business why you rejected his proposal of marriage leaving him broken and grief stricken. I did not ask and he did not tell me, but in honour of his memory I am doing as he wished which is to ensure that his letter is passed on to you. Of his effects I return the letters you sent him to avoid their causing his family any more grief than they are already facing.*

*Yours sincerely*
*Douglas McKellan*

Frantically I sifted through the letters and snatched out the envelope in James' handwriting addressed to the Idmiston Road address. I didn't recall telling him we had moved since the summer and now I was glad I hadn't for to have the package arrive here in my absence would have given the lie to my insistence that I had not led James on and would have brought on an interrogation by my mother I feared I would have been unable to withstand. Moving up and sitting trembling on the edge of the bed, I tore the envelope open and extracted the single sheet.

*Dear Pat*

*If you are reading this then you will have learnt that I am dead. I received your letter and this is my reply so that you will know that I do not blame you for your words in it, nor deep down do I believe them. You told me when were last together that had circumstances been different you would have married me like a shot. I understand your desire to carve yourself a career first, heaven knows that is what I have done myself despite my father's opposition. I want you to know that I still love you and I am even more sure now than ever that you are the only one I will ever truly love. Forgive me, my darling, for my insensitivity and my unthinking selfishness when we were last together. I have placed instructions with the rings for them to be sent to you if my body is recovered; meanwhile I will carry them wrapped in those instructions close to my heart. If you can bring yourself to think kindly of me, please know that as I am dead I will be content to wait for you in eternity. And meanwhile go and live your life and be happy.*

*Will all my love now and eternally*
*James*

Weeping, I read and re-read his letter several times, mouthing the words, learning them verbatim. I retrieved my package of letters from James from their hiding place behind the wardrobe, re-reading them too and trying to imprint them in my mind as much as I could. An hour passed and still I sat re-reading them, reluctant to move from the moment, yet knowing I had to act while I had the chance. Opening out my own letters, gathering all the letters together, including Douglas's bitter and angry diatribe, I hid them beneath my cardigan and crept downstairs. The fire in the living room grate had been laid by my mother before she left for the Beaver Club and I lit it, flinching as the flames burned bright, my vision of James's last moments vivid. Keeping one ear open for any hint of movement from my parents' bedroom I burned the letters one by one. Douglas' first. Then mine. Then kissing each one of James' before placing them reluctantly, sacrificially, on the pyre.

On Christmas Eve morning as I lay on my attic bed ostensibly reading, inwardly grieving, a muffled knock on the distant front door preceded Bill's deep tones ascending the stairs far below and I shot up, scrambling out of my dressing gown, grabbing clothes and throwing skirt and buttoned cardigan over my nightie, aware of my breasts hanging loose underneath.

'Anyone here?' called our immediate downstairs neighbour, Mrs Weston. 'A visitor for you.'

I descended quickly, wary of Bill's solitary appearance, our few meetings since Easter brief and shielded by the bustle of pre-arranged get-togethers.

'Thank you,' I said to the short, spreading, grey-haired Mrs Weston, panting from climbing the extra stairs. 'I'm sorry, my mother's out and my father's sleeping after his night work and didn't hear the knock.'

'All right, ducks,' she said, heaving herself back down out of view.

'Happy Christmas, Pat,' Bill said, over-brightly, I thought, from behind a large box peppered with small holes, and topped with a red ribbon tied in a bow, cradled in his arms, mewing and scrabbling sounds within. He thrust the box at me and I carried it into the living room.

Placing the box on the table, I opened the lid carefully and a little ball of mostly black with a touch of white fluff shrank into one corner, spitting and snarling.

'Oh, Bill, she's gorgeous! What an extraordinary present, thank you. Whatever gave you the idea?'

'He, actually,' said Bill, oozing smug self-satisfaction. 'My mother told me you've had a rough time of it and I thought, what better way to cheer you up than give you this little companion.'

'I can't take him to Leatherhead,' I said, doubtfully.

'Oh no, it's all been cleared with your mother. I gather she liked the idea, and my mother knows someone whose cat had kittens about six weeks ago and has been looking to offload them without putting them down.' Nodding at the kitten Bill added, 'He was the last one left. I gather he's a touch livelier than the others.'

Bill moved next to me, peering at the kitten. A spreading dampness appeared in the corner of the newspaper lining the box.

'He's supposed to be toilet trained. My mother said she'd

175

call round first with a tray and some cat litter,' Bill said, looking wildly around as if the cat's toilet would appear like magic.

'Don't worry, I know where it is. I found a bag with stuff
under the kitchen sink. Now I know what that's for. Mystery
solved.'

Setting the cat's litter tray up in a corner of the living
room and placing a saucer of milk beside it, I reached down
into the box to be greeted with tiny claws and teeth scrabbling and swiping at me.

'Oh dear, maybe he's *too* lively,' said Bill, and I hastened
to reassure him.

'Oh, no, the poor creature's probably scared, that's all.
Peggy used to hide under the table when we first got her,
I remember, but she soon came round.' Ensuring the door
was firmly shut so he couldn't escape, I set the kitten down
on the floor near the saucer and we watched as he was drawn
in and started lapping.

'I'll pop the kettle on while I'm dealing with this,' I said,
indicating the soggy box. 'Will you stop for a cuppa?'

Bill brightened at not being instantly dismissed. 'I'll take
it down to the dustbin for you,' he offered.

'No, stay here and keep an eye on him,' I ordered, sidling
out with the box.

We sat a little later companionably sipping tea, watching
the kitten explore the room.

'How've you been keeping, Bill? Enjoying sixth form?'

'Not the same without Jon but I'm chuntering along.
Doing the subjects I wanted. Keeping busy. And how about
you?'

'I'm guessing my mother told yours I had a touch of the
'flu which always leaves one feeling a bit low. Kind of you to
want to cheer me up.'

'Oh, I didn't know about the 'flu.' He took a deep breath
at my puzzled look. 'It was about your fiancé.'

I froze, the cup halfway to my mouth. *What has my mother
been saying?*

Bill plunged on. 'I'm sorry for your loss.'

*I'm sure you are. Leaves the coast clear for you to try again.*

'I've never had a fiancé. Tell me about the subjects you're doing now.' Casually I replaced the cup on the saucer.

But Bill, the real purpose of his visit revealed, would not be deflected.

'Your Canadian airman.' Accusingly. 'He asked you to marry him.'

I leapt up, furious. 'He wasn't *my* Canadian airman and his proposal came right out of the blue.'

*James nuzzling my breasts, exploring me, entering me, filling me. Forgive me for denying you.*

I snapped back to Bill. *I know how to keep secrets. Stick as close to the truth as you can to avoid being tripped up later.* Forcing myself to speak calmly and dispassionately, calculating that only Becky knew of my tryst on 15th June, and counting with my fingers for emphasis, I said,

'I met him only three times. *Once* during May half term week when I was polite to an overseas visitor and showed him the National Gallery, *once* when my mother organised us into going to one of the Beaver Club's weekly dances when I was low after Peggy died and *once* when he was on leave in early November and we walked in St James' Park and had some luncheon and then he suddenly produced rings and proposed. I don't know why he took a shine to me on such little acquaintance. Perhaps he was lonely, or maybe he even did it for a bet. I gather he was quite wealthy so he could probably afford to do that sort of thing on a whim. I might have been the last in a string of such girls.' I shrugged. 'I really don't know. I just told him I have my education to finish and a teaching career to follow and refused him politely.'

Bill slowly rose in response, wide lips pursing, eyes narrowing, head jutting forward, jealousy oozing.

'I can't believe a chap would do that sort of thing just *on a whim*. And how did he manage to arrange to meet you last month if you didn't encourage him? *If he laid a hand on you...*'

'What would you do?' I demanded, enraged again. 'Dive down to the bottom of the North Sea and biff him on his very dead nose? He was fighting for the freedom of a country not even his own, risking his life many times daily.'

I made a deliberate effort to calm down again. 'He kindly saw me home to my front door in the blackout after the dance to ensure my safety so he knew my address in West Norwood and after I moved things were still being forwarded to me from there. I hardly knew him. I certainly didn't love him. How could I, on such short acquaintance? You know I don't want to be anyone's girl. I don't want a young man. You know I want to teach. I want a *life*, Bill, not a husband.'

Bill stood silent, the kitten scrabbling at his shoelaces. Leaning down, I picked the kitten up and sat down again, stroking and tickling him, dodging his snapping teeth and claws until he relaxed a little onto my lap, emitting a gentle purring.

After several minutes of silent suppressed emotion Bill sighed, slumping back onto the seat opposite me.

'All right, all right, I'm sorry I got the wrong end of the stick. I can see now our mothers've blown it out of all proportion. Besides,' he added, cheering, 'at least it shows you've got principles. If he was wealthy you could've said yes just for his money.'

'I'm sorry there's been a misunderstanding. My mother tends to exaggerate and romanticise things that just aren't there.' *Am I now protesting too much?* I returned my attention to the kitten. 'It's sweet of you to be concerned, though. Thank you for my Christmas present. What's his name?'

'He hasn't got one yet. What will you call him?'

I considered. 'He's a bit of a scamp so I could call him Scampy.'

Bill hooted with laughter. 'That's cruel, every time you call his name he'll think fish is in the offing!'

I laughed back. The first time I could remember laughing since…

'Thank you for coming, Bill,' I said, softening. 'The 'flu'd got me really low. It's good to have you around to cheer me up.'

'Well, that was the plan. So, Scampy is it?'

I considered the kitten again. 'I'd rather *not* have a neighbour report me to the RSPCA every time I call him indoors.'

Bill chuckled. The kitten yawned and stretched, rolling over onto his back on my lap, flexing his white paws at the end of little black legs, revealing his soft white-furred stomach.

'Look at his cute little white boots,' I exclaimed. 'I'll call him Booty.'

As if responding to the name, the kitten rolled back and sat up facing Bill, who laughed and said, 'He looks as if he's all dressed up in top hat 'n tails. Like Fred Astaire. You could call him Freddie.'

The kitten turned and started climbing up my front, sinking his claws into my breasts through my cardigan, reminding me that I was indecently dressed underneath. Noticing Bill's observant glance I flushed a little and stood, gently disentangling the kitten and handing him to Bill.

'I'm calling him Booty,' I said firmly. Indicating my bare legs and slippered feet, I added, 'Look after him while I finish dressing then I'll fix us some lunch,' and retreated to my room.

Booty became my companion, my solace. Granted a respite from heavy bombing over the next few days, each night I took him in a lidded, shawl-lined box, together with the cat litter tray, up to my room, shut the door and lifted the box lid. Booty would leap out, chase imaginary mice around the room and eventually settle, purring, onto the bed where stroking him soothed and calmed us both. When I awoke in the night weeping from half-remembered dreams I would reach out to find him perhaps curled up against me, or in the box beside my bed, and feel his little warm, alive body and be comforted. Then it seemed that Mr Hitler had decreed that the Christmas festivities were over and on the following nights, disturbed by air raid sirens, I scooped him up, placing him quickly in the box, ramming on the lid and taking him down to the back garden shelter where he entertained us with his lively antics while the City of London burned around St Paul's, sky shimmering and sirens wailing.

Christmas blurred into the New Year. At New Year's Day morning drinks Reginald Whitshere told us he'd heard that about fifty people had died in a public shelter in Southwark on the first night the bombing resumed after Christmas. 'That's why I won't let Maud and Bill go to the public shelters,' Reginald said, jutting out his chin, his podgy hands resting on his knees. 'Death traps. And the Underground's no better. Look at what happened to Balham station in October. Nothing left but a crater and most of 'em drowned because of a burst water main.'

'Reginald,' murmured Maud, looking nervously in my and Bill's direction, but Reginald shrugged.

'Can't hide your head in the sand, eh, Ted,' he said, turning to my father. 'What I want to know is, why are we letting 'em through? What're our boys up there doing about it? Eh?'

*Dying, trying to save your measly self-satisfied skin*, I thought, my nightmare vision of James' last moments suddenly vivid. 'They can't do anything without night radar,' I said indignantly. 'It's not their fault they can't see anything in the dark with a blackout on the ground and being blinded by our own searchlights. They're just not being given the proper equipment for night flying.' Reginald looked at me, startled, and I realised everyone else was, too. I drew a shaky breath and, to deflect my unwitting audience from my pronouncement about night flying, of which I was supposed to know nothing, I turned to Maud and said,

'It's kind of you to be concerned about my sensitivities, Auntie Maud, but don't worry. When you've had a bomb drop in the next field and half bury you it's impossible to hide from the brutal reality of war.'

'Pat!' my mother exclaimed and I nodded apologetically

in her direction, my haste to move the conversation along overriding my consideration for *her* sensitivities.

'Don't worry, Mummy, I'm sure the basement at the Beaver Club is quite safe.'

The Beaver Club. Meeting James. *No, no don't think about it.* Of course, the more I told myself not to, the more I did and I began to look forward to returning to Leatherhead where there were fewer reminders of him and of what I had done.

'I'll miss you next week, my darling little Booty,' I told the kitten on waking the first Friday of January, 'but I'll be back every weekend and holidays and you can keep Mummy company so she won't feel so alone at night while I'm away.' Booty, of course, took no notice, burrowing into my pile of clothes on my chair and popping his head up, wearing a brassiere cup like an enormous sun hat.

'Pat,' my mother called up, ascending the stairs and stopping outside the door. 'A letter's come from your school. Can you grab Booty so I can come in?'

I retrieved Booty from the chair and my mother entered and sat down on the edge of the bed.

'The bungalow adjacent to yours has been destroyed over Christmas by a direct hit and yours has been badly damaged.'

'What? Oh, no, Mrs Grice!'

'She's apparently fine,' my mother said, scanning the letter. 'She went to her sister in Devon for Christmas and her bungalow was empty.'

'The other wasn't?'

'The letter doesn't say.'

'Oh my goodness, I only hope it was. They're an elderly couple, devoted to each other.'

The significance of the news hit me.

'So where am I going on Tuesday?'

'You're to report to the school office on Tuesday morning. It says to travel early on Tuesday and they'll meanwhile get something sorted out for you.'

The familiar churning was back, shifting sands, chasm yawning. I was suddenly weeping, clinging to my mother like a drowning man to a rope.

'I just can't bear it. It's just like this time last year. Every time I've got somewhere it's taken away.' Grief torrenting, drowning, annihilating. Knowing the school's letter was just the trigger, James' death letter before my eyes.

'Hush, hush, it's not so bad, they'll find you somewhere else,' my mother soothed, holding me close. After a while she disentangled herself and sat back, examining my face. 'You're still a bit peaky. I don't think you've fully recovered from the 'flu. I'll write to your school and say you're still ill and will be back a few days late. That'll give them time to sort something out properly then you can go to your billet the day before you start back. I'll ask them if it's possible for you and your friend Becky to stay together.'

My mother was a strange mixture, so often both childlike and childish, yet she could rise to a crisis magnificently and I opened my mouth, suddenly desperate to confide in her, to share my deepest secret, to ask her advice, to lean on the one person I should trust in all the world. A stinging, bitter soda memory surfaced along with Bill's Christmas Eve visit inspired by my mother's gossiping with Maud, and reason reasserted itself. I let the moment pass, nodding, 'Thank you,' and wiping my eyes. After my mother left I dressed slowly, drained of strength and emotion, letting Booty's antics draw me back to the present, a playful tug of war over my brassiere bringing a smile to my lips. After breakfast my mother left for the Beaver Club and my father retired for sleep.

Settling down to schoolwork, catching up on lessons I missed through the 'flu, I was interrupted after about half an hour by a frantic banging on the front door. Looking down from the window I saw Becky, hair flying and cheeks glistening, looking up at me.

'Oh my goodness,' I exclaimed, racing down and beating Mrs Haywood to the door. Nodding apologetically to her and ushering Becky up, I set out a chair into which she fell, panting and gasping,

'Oh, Pat, the most *awful* thing.'

'I know, I know,' I said soothingly. 'We got a letter this morning too. My mother's going to ask for us to be billeted together.'

Looking at me wildly, comprehension dawning, Becky burst into tears and sobbed, 'If only it was *that*.' She dropped her head onto her arms on the table. 'What am I going to *do*? I don't want to leave. Everything was going so well.'

Thoroughly alarmed, kneeling and hugging her, I said, 'Leave? Becky, what is it? What's happened?'

Becky raised a tearstained face and looked down at me.

'My mother's moving to Golders Green and is taking me with her.'

I froze. My best friend. My only real, close, understanding friend. Who kept the secret of my mid-June tryst with James, who nursed me through my 'flu, to whom I owed so much.

'You don't need to leave St. Martin's, though. Any school you went to would be evacuated and you might as well be evacuated to Leatherhead as anywhere else.'

'I feel I'm letting you down.'

'Nonsense. And anyway, I'm sure there's *something* that can be arranged.'

'No, you don't understand. It's all been arranged already. I'll be eighteen next October. My mother wants me to marry Reuben by then. She wants it sooner but I was playing for time and said not before I'm eighteen. So she doesn't see any point in me finishing sixth form. She's organised *everything*. I'm starting a clerical job next week with a contact of my aunt's. My life is *over*.'

Becky, my bubbly, humorous companion, reduced to such misery as to be almost unrecognisable.

To my unspoken question she added, 'Of course I didn't know when I saw you last weekend. We had such a lovely day in town and I thought you seemed more your old self and I was looking forward to the new term. They've stitched me up behind my back and my mother dropped the bombshell this morning. She knew I'd be upset and so she's allowed only enough time for me to organise what I'm going to pack ready for tomorrow.'

'Is it really impossible for you to stay on with your brother here?'

'I tried that. He doesn't want me here. Rachel's just announced she's expecting *another* baby and they'll need the space at home. At what's going be *their* home and their home *only*,' she added bitterly. 'I'd only be in the way. My mother and I are moving in with my aunt and her family. My mother says it will be a bit of a squeeze but only temporary because I'm getting married.'

'Aren't you both a bit young to get married? Where will you live?'

'I don't think I ever told you. Reuben's twenty-three now and he works in the family business. They own a number of grocery shops dotted around North London and Reuben's been learning the ropes and he's going to be given one of them to manage at first. There are empty rooms above. The tenants cleared off into the countryside in the autumn because of the bombing and with so many places up for letting, Reuben's father said we might as well have one of his.'

Becky put a hand on my forearm. 'I'm sorry to be talking about marriage,' she added. 'I know it's painful for you still.'

The same Becky, even in the midst of her misery thinking of others. She continued, 'Can I spend my last day with you?'

'Won't your mother be worried?'

'I don't care. I know we can keep in touch and maybe meet up in town one Sunday but I'm not stupid. You can't turn the clock back. It won't be the same.' Becky looked for the first time at the books and papers on the table. 'I'm sorry, I should go. You've got work to do.'

Gathering up the books and papers, I deposited them in

my satchel. 'Nonsense. That can wait. You're more important. What would you like to do?'

We wandered through Brixton Market and caught a 33 to
Northumberland Avenue and walked to Trafalgar Square.
Averting my eyes from Canada House sitting along the far
side and from the road beyond leading off towards Spring
Gardens, and praying that Becky didn't want to walk up the
Mall and through St James' Park, I found myself led into
the National Gallery instead and we stood for a while in the
Octagonal room where we had enjoyed the concert a year
ago. Before James. But, meandering through the echoing
halls I saw James in my mind's eye beside me. *Now look at
me*, I'd thought, *walking these galleries with this handsome airman!*

*Now look at me*, I thought, *damaged goods, guilty beyond measure. Presenting a facade of innocence, a veneer of respectability. All
lies. Responsible for sending a good man to his death.*

Becky led me out and across to St Martin-in-the-Fields
and sat beside me while I tried to pray, my devotions as
empty as the walls of the National Gallery, abandonment
and loss echoing as loudly as its halls.

*In little over fifteen months I've lost virtually everything I've had.
Nan, who understood me in ways Mummy never will, has married
and moved away. James flashed into my life and has gone forever. I
gave my virginity away for a lifetime of regrets. I've lost so many homes
in Leatherhead and London I don't feel I have a home anywhere. I've
lost Bill's easy friendship for a jumpily jealous boy I don't recognise.
And now my best and only close friend and companion is leaving me
too. Dear God, forgive what I have done and grant me a kinder 1941.*

I felt no responding revelation or spiritual succour and,
after a while, lifting my head and sitting back on to the seat,
I whispered, 'Let's go.'

# 10

# Spring

'Count your blessings' was a favourite saying of my grandmother's and as winter days slowly evolved into spring I equally
slowly learnt to do just that. I looked forward to coming home
to Booty, his mischievous escapades, boundless energy and
indiscriminate affection lifting my spirits as I mounted the
stairs each Friday evening, Booty bounding down to greet me
and scrambling up and down and around me.

Mrs Brindley was a Great War widow whose son was in
the army and she took in washing to supplement her pension.
Her home was a Lutyens-inspired cottage-style municipal
house in a deliberately rambling and countrified mini-estate
tucked behind Leatherhead High Street, with a hedge down
each side of the front garden and a white picket fence across
the front. There were even climbing roses trained onto trel-
lising either side of the front door. Mrs Brindley was a little
plump with a round, homely face above a slight double chin,
warm brown eyes etched round with laughter lines, light
greying-brown hair that was short but wayward, and her
clothes were neat without being ostentatious. Her first words
to me were, 'Welcome, my dear, make yourself at home. I've
never had a daughter, so regard yourself as the daughter of
the house. If you're feeling peckish don't hesitate to have a
good rummage in my pantry. Let me have your washing on
a Friday if you can as that's the lightest day of my week, but
if you need anything done as an emergency just let me know
and I'll fit it in. Now, let me take your coat and we'll have a
nice cup of tea, then I'll show you round.'

Enveloped by her warm greeting, gawping at the food piled high on my plate each meal and relaxing with her in front of her warm fire in the evenings after I finished my schoolwork, I found myself looking forward to the end of each day. Mrs Brindley regaled me with amusing stories of her Leatherhead childhood and of her family and friends. She seemed genuinely interested in me and my home in Brixton without being unduly inquisitive, and I found myself relaxing and blossoming in her warm kindness. She had a positive take on life that reminded me of Becky, and nothing I needed or asked for was ever too much trouble. I told her nothing of James, but shared my sadness at the change in my friendship with Bill and found her easy to talk to and thoughtful in her advice.

'Just peg away at being his friend, my dear. Ride out the storms. One day he'll meet the girl for him and he'll be grateful you kept him at the far end of your arm. You're right not to give in and go along with it. One day you'll find your own young man and you'll know *he's* the one for you. If Bill was the one for you, you'd know it by now.'

Just before half term my parents received a letter from my school listing application requirements for various post-school educational institutions, which requirements included two formal posed photographs. For the first Saturday of half term my mother, through her contacts at the Beaver Club, arranged a special deal with a young photographer who could afford to undercut his rivals. When I pointed out that the application would not need to be submitted for at least another six months, she retorted, 'Your father insists on keeping the option open for you to go to college so we might as well get them done now as Lord knows how much a photographer will charge in six months' time without this special price I've arranged.'

The photographer, seeming little older than me, had a relaxing manner and asked me to just chat to him while he tested the equipment and took a number of practice shots, and then said 'Ready,' at which point I stiffened, looking distantly beyond his right shoulder; he took just one further shot and declared the session over. *Well, no wonder he's cheap*, I thought and was astonished the following Saturday in collecting the prints to find that he had produced about thirty small shots of me in different, animated, poses on one large sheet, plus four of the last shot in a larger size. Bill, arriving to 'Catch up on the little fellow,' an excuse he'd used a couple of times when home at the weekends since the Christmas holidays, took one look at the multi-photo page and roared with laughter. I had to admit to him I found some quite comical too.

'Look at this one, catching flies or what?' he chortled. 'And what's this hand gesture meant to be? Why don't you cut them all out, put them in order and create a flip cartoon show. With a bit of lip reading we can work out what you were saying.'

'Ha, ha, very funny,' I said in mock offence.

'I must have one to give me a good laugh every day before the serious business of school begins,' Bill chuckled.

'Oh, take a couple,' I said in mock dismissal. Passing him the scissors, I excused myself to the kitchen to make tea.

After Bill had gone I examined the photograph sheet carefully. Two were missing; one I remembered as the fly catching photo; the other I eventually worked out was the small print of the larger photograph.

As the term drew on I began to think that there might be a forgiving God after all. Mrs Brindley's welcome had not proved to be a flash in the pan. She combined Mrs Fox's motherliness with Mrs Grice's staying power, and her care of me was as warm, comfortable and comforting as Mrs Briggs' and Mrs Haye's were not. At home James was never mentioned and to the few girls at school who remained from the picnic outing he'd been a throwaway in a passing conversation, irrelevant and forgotten, overridden by the horror and excitement of the capture by the Canadian soldiers.

There were occasional nights when, settling for sleep, I realised I had not thought of James once during the course of that day.

'*Back for Easter hols,*' wrote Bill on the postcard that was waiting for me on the living room mantelpiece at home following the end of term. '*Come over for tea on Saturday about 3? Just a few friends together.*'

I turned the postcard back to the picture side and smiled. Swans swam in the foreground and an elegant full span bridge soared in the background. Caversham Bridge, it said.

Somewhere around the age of eleven Bill and I were taken by Maud Whitshere to the Dulwich Picture Gallery, the first purpose-built art gallery in England, older than the Nash Gal. I stood beside Bill in front of 'Mallards on a Pond' by Marmaduke Cradock and declared disparagingly, 'Mallards are all very well, but what this painting needs is a swan!' Loving the elegant and regal bearing of swans, I took pleasure in drawing their long, curved and sweeping lines. I blamed my love of swans on seeing a performance of *Swan Lake* as a small child, perched high in the gallery on a wooden bench, squashed between my mother and grandmother, watching spellbound as the dancers glided effortlessly across the stage. After this, seeing the swans on the river when my father's Sunday morning walks took us that way gave me a special thrill. So it was little surprise that I expressed my views somewhat forcibly that hot summer's afternoon in the Dulwich Picture Gallery. An expanse of river in a painting demanded a gliding swan. Bill, taking up the challenge, led me on a search for swans in the paintings there and we came to the conclusion that the gallery's masterpieces were the poorer for the absence of swans.

Ever since, Bill took to sending me postcards, birthday cards, and other greetings cards with swans on them. It started out as a joke between us; in time I found it quite touching. Now I wondered whether this postcard was deliberately chosen with a deeper meaning. *Remember, I know you better than anyone*, it seemed to be saying. *You're my special friend and I still want you to be my girl.*

My mother bustled into the living room carrying a tray of tea and thinly spread meat paste sandwiches.

'Go and wash your hands, dear,' she admonished, nodding to me to lift the table leaf and setting the tray on the table. 'And put your case in your room, I nearly fell over it in the hall.'

I returned to find her holding the postcard, a frown on her face as she looked down at it.

Sitting down, I asked, 'Is that alright, Mummy, for me to go to Bill's on Saturday? Or do you have something planned for us?'

'Well, I *was* planning on going to see Nanny and thought you could come with me,' she said. 'I'm working at the Club the rest of the week and I said I'd cover for Sunday too.' She pressed her lips together as if to prevent her saying more.

The Club. I'd never been back. Mention of the Beaver Club still upset me but I was determined not to show it. I said brightly,

'That's not a problem for me, Mummy, I can always meet up with Bill another time.'

My mother looked up sharply. Perhaps she heard or sensed the catch in my breath. Pressing her lips in further, seemingly weighing up her thoughts, she said,

'No, you can see your grandmother another time. You go your tea party at Bill's. And Nanny can always pop in to see you here. She moved us all down to West Norwood then took herself off and married without a by-your-leave. We don't have to go running to her all the time.'

I heard the mixture of resentfulness and wistfulness in her voice and realised that she had been looking forward to having my company the one day over Easter when she wasn't working. I leaned forward and said, 'Could we afford to maybe go somewhere for lunch on Saturday? Treat ourselves to a little time together before I go to Bill's?'

Mummy brightened. 'Yes, there's a little café opened recently just past the main market area that Ethel Reid was only telling me about the other day when I bumped into her on the tram. She was wondering where the proprietor got the money from to open it.' Mummy mimicked Ethel's high-pitched and slightly quavery voice. ' "There's not enough money to go round with the war on, but he's kitted it out really nicely and even has *tablecloths and napkins*".'

'The war's given some people plenty of opportunity to make money out of it,' I said cynically. Not for nothing were bombed out houses sometimes guarded by soldiers and every street had its own spiv who could get you virtually anything, even a pound of sausages, for the right price.

'So that's settled,' said Mummy firmly. 'Now tell me how your journey went and is Mrs Brindley feeding you properly?'

Emerging from the café on Easter Saturday early afternoon, Mummy and I wandered through the market, her arm tucked in mine, stopping briefly to pick up a small bunch of closed daffodils for an extortionate price, for me to take to Maud Whitshere that afternoon. Mummy picked up some carrots for the evening meal and, 'Oh, good!' she exclaimed, swooping on a small pile of onions. 'It's so difficult to find onions being sold nowadays. I know they're not supposed to be as good for you as other vegetables, but it's poor man's goose tonight and that's just not the same without onions.' By the time we moved on from the market and reached Brixton Town Hall I realised it was nearly half past two.

'Do you mind if I part from you here?' I asked. 'I might as well go straight to Auntie Maud's early and see if I can help her.'

'You're a good girl,' said my mother approvingly. 'Give Maud my love.'

I walked slowly along Acre Lane, sticking to the north side and speeding up as I approached the buildings opposite the shop where my paternal grandfather worked. Terrifying memories of him from my childhood crowded. My stomach lurching and my heart beating faster, I kept my head averted, gazing intently into the frontages of the buildings to my right yet not seeing them as any more than a blur. Usually I approached Bill's house from the south, crossing Brixton Hill and weaving through the backstreets to a point where I only had to cross Acre Lane opposite the side road in which Bill's house was situated. Today I took a chance that my grandfather would not see me, or, if he did, he would not recognise the young lady hurrying along the other side of the road with her head tilted away. Drawing level with his shop I risked a swift glance. Although some of his wares were set out on trestles outside, the shop door was shut tight against the brisk chill wind and I realised I was holding my breath. Exhaling with relief, I left the shop behind my left shoulder and continued on until I reached Bill's house.

Knocking with the grand door knocker, the door opened, Maud greeting me with a hug and an affectionate smile.

'I'm sorry I'm a bit early,' I said, proffering the meagre handful of budding stalks, but Maud expressed as much delight as would have been evinced by an extravagant bouquet.

'How lovely to have some spring flowers in the house,' she gushed. 'Do come on in and don't worry about being early, you're like family, so there's no need for us to stand on ceremony. Take off your coat, dear, and tell me how your term has gone. Come through to the kitchen with me while I put together the finishing touches to my flourless cake.'

I followed her through after depositing my coat on the coat stand and my hat on the hat stand above.

'My goodness,' I exclaimed, surveying the table laden with plates of sandwiches, pastries and cakes. 'What a lovely looking repast. Are you expecting many people?'

'Oh, no,' Maud replied, 'Just half a dozen, but you know what appetites young people have.'

I cocked an ear, surprised that Bill had not come rushing down upon my arrival. 'Is Bill upstairs?'

'No, he's gone out to track down some soft drinks. He wants lemonade but I told him he won't find that with the war on. He'll probably have to make do with soda water,' Maud replied. 'Here, dear, would you be kind enough to put these teaspoons on the jam dishes,' passing me a couple of spoons. 'He should be back soon.'

As she spoke there was a knock on the front door.

'Oh, dear, Bill's forgotten his key again,' tutted Maud. 'Would you be kind enough to open the door for him?'

I went to the front door and, grabbing the lock handle, opened the door with a theatrical sweep, dramatically throwing my arms up high and posing with a 'Ta Daaah', a mode of greeting developed with Bill over the years. Freezing in my pose, I saw before me not a stocky grinning Bill but a tall, very tall, startled, light brown-haired young man, cornflower blue eyes raking me briefly. He recovered swiftly, sweeping his right arm in a circling, scooping motion downwards as he bowed deeply, then, reaching up, grabbing my right hand with his, bowing again to lay his mouth gently on my knuckles.

'Wha…' I started, thoroughly embarrassed by my mode of stranger greeting.

He raised his head and for the first time I understood the phrase 'twinkling eyes' I so often read in novels. His eyes positively sparkled with amusement, the skin at the sides crinkling a little while his firm, even lips quivered as he fought to imbue the occasion with some element of dignity. In that split second as I thought, *he's nice-looking and why have I never seen him before and what sort of idiot does he think I am?*, I also realised that he was not laughing at my expense, but, in returning my dramatic greeting with a theatrical one of his own, was sharing a joke with me and making me immediately feel at ease as if we were long-time friends. So, rather than retreat to a hole in the ground to swallow me up, I turned my hand in his and shook his firmly, as if my doorstep greeting was the most normal greeting in the world.

'Hello, I'm Patricia Roberts. Everyone calls me Pat,' I said.

'I know,' he answered.

I was nonplussed. 'How do you know? Am I the only girl expected at this gathering?'

'I've seen your photograph,' he said.

'Oh,' I said, feeling wrong-footed again. 'Photograph?' I repeated a little faintly. Bill's small album, like mine, included one of him and me standing with arms round each other aged about ten. *Surely I'm not recognisable from that?* I suddenly understood. *The* photograph. I just hoped it *was* the distance gazing photograph and not the fly catching one.

The young man smiled and I thought, *my God, not only is he even more handsome when he smiles, he's got dimples. He must have a string of girlfriends already.* I brought myself up short. *String of girlfriends? Already?! Whatever are you thinking?!* I inwardly shrieked. *Stop it at once!*

Sweeping a second low bow, he offered, 'Jonathan Dorringham at your service, ma'am. Everyone calls me Jon.'

The afternoon passed in a daze. I felt I was a split personality. Outwardly calm, poised, sociable and politely conversational, my pulse raced and I felt a desperate urge to run wildly around whooping loudly. Thrills coursing through me when Jon spoke, acutely aware of his proximity. Quite how he came to be sitting beside me I didn't remember. The pale mid-April sunshine illuminating a corner of the garden made everything seem bright and polished. We played charades and I found myself paired with Jon as we played in three teams of two, Bill pairing up with his cousin's friend Mary, a vivacious brunette with a ready laugh, and Bill's willowy cousin Helen, a mop of curly black hair, partnering Edward, himself tall, dark and slender, a mutual friend of Bill and Jon's from their school days. Later, as the evening shades deepened, distances in the blackout were compared and Edward gallantly offered to ensure Mary and Helen's safe return to Helen's home just off Clapham Common Southside where Mary was to stay the night.

'I'll walk you home, Pat,' said Bill.

'Brixton Water Lane?' queried Jon. 'I've an aunt lives Tulse Hill way and my mother would be pleased if I call in to check on her while I'm over in this neck of the woods. I might as well go via Water Lane, in fact it'll cut the corner off for me. If there's an air raid I can shelter for the night with my aunt's family.'

Although there had been a lull in air raids since 20th March, the threat hastened our departure.

Jon and I stepped out into the chill early spring evening, weaving our way through the back streets laughing and chatting as if we had known each other for ever. As we neared the front door I slowed, panic rising.

'How far up Tulse Hill is your aunt? Would you have time to stop for refreshment?' I asked a little breathlessly, wondering at my own daring.

'Chatsworth Way. And I'd be delighted to accept.'

I frowned. 'I don't know a Chatsworth Way at Tulse Hill. There's one at West Norwood, where we lived a few months last year...' My voice tailed off as I caught his wide grin.

'West Norwood.' Jon nodded.

'Goodness, I must have walked past her place many times last year and not known of a connection with you. What a small world.'

Jon followed me upstairs and I introduced my gallant escort to my parents. He shook their hands, exchanging pleasantries and within a few minutes conversing as if he had known them for years. I studied him surreptitiously, marvelling at social skills exceptional for a young man of barely seventeen. He even charmed Booty, casually lifting and stroking him, and allowing a forefinger to be batted and nuzzled and chased around his lap. When he rose, apologising for the interruption to their evening and indicating the twilight gloom, my mother gushed, 'You'd be most welcome to call in any time you're passing on your way to your aunt's,' and my father shook his hand firmly and said, 'Nice to meet you young man, call again.'

I took Jon downstairs and we stood a moment on the pavement, he seeming as hesitant as me to bring the evening to a close. *I can't bear to not know when I'll see him again.*

'Do you like walking?' Jon asked. 'With the recent lull in the bombing I thought I'd take the opportunity to go over to the City on Monday to see how it's surviving.'

'I've been thinking the same myself,' I lied. As the corner of his mouth twitched, I added truthfully, 'I'd be pleased to join you.'

'Shall I call for you eleven-ish?'

I nodded as he stepped back. My disappointment that he was not stepping forward to embrace me was immense. *Whatever are you thinking, you flibbertigibbet!*

With a conspiratorial smile, Jon swept me a low, theatrical bow, and, taking my hand, brushing my fingers with his lips, he turned, disappearing along the road with a wave, and it was only as I mounted the stairs that I thought, *he went back the way we came. Does he even* have *an Aunt in West Norwood?*

That night I lay awake enjoying Booty's scrabbling antics before he settled, stroking him as he stretched out on my bed. 'Well, well, little Boots. What a turn up for the books. I'm going to let you into a secret.' Whispering now, I added, 'I think I've fallen in love.' A faint echo, *'I've loved you from the moment I saw you at my feet and picked you up off the floor.'* And I suddenly and piercingly understood.

Easter Monday dawned bright and sunny. Jon and I took the tube to Tower Hill, emerging to the warmth and light like flowers opening to the dawn. He was lively and serious at the same time, full of amusing anecdotes yet ready with a moral punchline, laughingly recounting slapstick tales from his trip to France with the cadet forces in 1938, while respectfully and concernedly telling me of an older cousin trapped with the retreating forces in 1940 and now in a prisoner-of-war camp somewhere in the depths of the Sudetenland countryside. He made no demands of me, yet drew out of me memories of childhood I had thought well buried and he seemed as equally fascinated by me as I was of him.

We wandered the ruined churches, offices, warehouses and homes and sometimes Jon paused, looking down on a rubble-strewn crater, standing to respectful attention, honouring the strangers who had died there.

Two days later the bombers returned to London with a vengeance. Sirens sounded shortly before nine o'clock and my mother and I retreated to the garden shelter with our neighbours, all squashed in together. This time Booty was older and wiser than the little inquisitive and excitable kitten of Christmas time, staying in his box, jumpy over the bangs peppering the long night till shortly before dawn.

Jon cycled round to us after work late the following afternoon to check we had survived the previous night. My mother, preening at his concern, invited him to stay for supper, but he said,

'That's very kind of you but I should be going back. My mother'll worry and I don't think last night was a one-off. I think they'll be back.'

Jon was right. The remainder of my Easter holiday nights were spent in the garden shelter and I longed for a whole night in bed. As we stumbled out to the sound of the All Clear and the chill of the early mornings I found myself longing for the comfort and relative safety of my billet.

# II

# Jon

'That Jon of yours has a lot of aunts dotted around South London,' said Mummy the second Friday of May, scraping carrots for dinner. Divesting myself of my bag and jacket, I moved into the little kitchen to join her. It was my first weekend home since the Easter holidays.

'Really?' I said as casually as I could, my heart suddenly racing.

'Oh, yes, he's been calling in here regularly these past three weeks on his way to see them, or on his way back,' said Mummy, looking over her shoulder to me with a tilt to her head and amused creases around her eyes.

'He's not *my* Jon, you know,' I said, colouring under her scrutiny.

'He's very solicitous about my welfare and has had a good natter or two with your father about cricket and suchlike. But I'm not convinced *we're* the main attraction.'

Grabbing the potato peeler and busying myself at the sink, I said,

'I've had a letter from Becky. We're going to try to meet up tomorrow in town.'

'Don't change the subject,' said my mother. 'That boy's sweet on you.'

'Mummy, he's said nothing to me and, besides, I don't want a young man. I've got all my studying and then teacher training to do.'

'Of course he's said nothing to you *yet*, he's not seen you since Easter. Still, you'll have a chance to catch up this evening.'

'*What?*'

'He should be here fairly soon.'

Lighting the gas, my mother set two saucepans of water and dropped the chopped carrots into one.

Speechless, my task completed, I picked up Booty scrabbling around my feet and carried him and my case up to my room. Shutting the door, dropping the case, setting Booty on my chair and perching on the edge of the bed, I demanded, 'Now, young man, tell me what's been going on in my absence. Have you been sucking up to this Jon? Eh? Making a fuss of him and telling him all my secrets?'

Booty, meowing, stretched and leapt onto my lap.

'No? Well, I jolly well hope not!'

Jon, seated across from me at the dinner table, was charm personified. He got my father reminiscing about his naval days and my mother advising the intricacies of poor man's goose ('My uncle's a chef at the Carlton,' said Jon, 'and he's always on the lookout for something different') and when my father, leaving for work, offered to walk part way with him in the direction of his West Norwood aunt, Jon declared it a splendid idea. He turned to me.

'Tomorrow? Another walk round the City, or shall we go to a park?'

'I'm meeting my friend Becky at the Nash Gal. There's another War Artists exhibition. I saw last summer's and it was so moving I suggested to Becky we could see this year's.' Angry at Jon's arrogance in making assumptions, desperately wishing we could spend the day together.

'What time will you be back? I could call in then.'

Admiring his persistence, I suggested half past five-ish.

'What a lovely young man,' said my mother as the fading sound of Jon and my father walking and talking along the street drifted in through the open window.

Becky was waiting for me on the steps of the National Gallery the next morning and, hugging and exclaiming at how terribly long it had been since we'd seen each other, we dived inside to avoid a sudden shower. The War Artists' exhibition of 1941 had just opened, and we wandered the exhibition galleries.

I suggested that we find out about summer concerts.

'Do you remember that dreadful man swearing about Germans and Italians?' said Becky.

'I do,' I said, laughing. 'I was surprised they didn't ask him to leave.'

Deep down I doubted that we would recreate any more such schoolgirl outings after today. Already I was aware of time passing and the journeys we were making in different directions. Becky seemed much older and more serious. Without her father's radical views, her mother was leaning towards more traditional Jewish practices and Becky said, 'Reuben's family's more traditional, too. I don't mind really. I don't suppose it was *very* bad of me to have eaten pork but on the whole it's easier to conform anyway. Today's probably my last out and out rebellion.'

'Oh, Becky, the Sabbath!' I exclaimed. 'I'm so sorry, I forgot. It's good of you to meet me today.'

Becky smiled wryly. 'Well, I can't say anyone at home was too happy but I *so* wanted to see you. It's been so long since we met up.' Becky hesitated. 'The wedding plans are going ahead for the first Sunday after my eighteenth birthday. Pat, I hope you won't be very offended not to get an invitation. I've told my mother that I want you to come but she's in charge of the guest list and...'

'Becky, please don't worry about it. I wouldn't be offended. Honestly, I wish you well...'

'But the subject of weddings isn't exactly top of your agenda after last year?'

I looked around, memories echoing, and, perhaps sensing my dipping mood, Becky suggested moving off up Charing Cross Road to drop into a café for a light lunch followed by a browse in Foyles as she had a couple of books to order.

'And while we're eating you can tell me all about him.'

'Him?'

'Pat, you've got a look about you. I saw it last summer when you called in to see me after my father's funeral and now you've got it again. Who is he?'

'Just a friend of a friend.'

The friend of a friend was waiting for me when I arrived home.

'Goodness, am I late?' I exclaimed, as he hopped off the front wall. 'You've got wet. It's jolly cold sitting around. I know it's unusual for this time of year but we had overnight frost in Leatherhead last week.'

'Army cadet training soon knocked the edges off me,' said Jon. 'Besides, hanging around in the cold and wet's good practice for when I'm called up.'

'That's not for years.'

'Less than eighteen months.'

I shivered.

'Come on, let's get you into the warm and I'll say no more about it. Instead,' ushering me up the stairs ahead of him, 'd'you fancy a movie next weekend? D'you like Bob Hope? I see *The Road to Zanzibar*'s coming soon.'

I stopped halfway up the stairs, turning. 'As long as you promise you won't do what Bill did.' To Jon's quizzical look, I replied, 'Grab my hand halfway through, give yourself pins and needles and mimic a mini-earthquake trying to bring your arm back to life. And don't you dare tell him I told you,' I added hastily as Jon rocked with laughter

Jon didn't go home that night. In any other circumstances it might have been quite romantic, but Hitler unleashing one of the heaviest and most brutal nights of the London Blitz that started early and came dangerously close to us meant that we were heavily chaperoned in the garden shelter by my parents, our ground floor neighbours and Booty (Mr and Mrs Weston of the middle floor being away), with bombs and shrapnel raining down near and far, and the sky glowing eerily. A particularly loud whistle ended abruptly and, peeking out from the entrance, my father cried, 'Incendiary!' and Jon leaped across me and out in a split second, grabbing the bucket of sand on his way. My father followed, as did Mr Haywood, and thudding, banging and yelling could be heard above the distant booms. My mother wailed and threw her apron over her head, Mrs Heywood following suit, and though I detachedly thought, *how bizarre, I thought hysterical ladies only did that in novels*, my stomach was churning and my legs trembling with fear while I clutched Booty tightly as he wriggled and squirmed in terror.

Thrusting his head into the shelter's aperture and illuminating his face with a torch like a ghoul, bringing forth a wild shriek from my mother tentatively emerging from her shroud, Jon cried triumphantly, 'It's out!' and I nearly wet myself with relief. Holding the flow back with a painful effort, I slipped Booty into the box, shutting the lid firmly, and exited, pushing against Jon in my haste.

'Where're you going?'

'Where you can't go for me,' I replied, hurrying into the house, desperately feeling my way upstairs and throwing up into the basin from nervous relief while evacuating my bladder into the toilet at the same time. A distant banging on the front door below grew insistently louder and, finishing in the bathroom, splashing my face and mouth with water and feeling my way down to the hall, I opened the door. Two air raid wardens rushed past me, lights from torches bobbing. 'Where is it?' one cried. 'Back garden,' I replied and there ensued a stream of people running through the house intent on tracing the incendiary they had seen fall from the sky and eliminating it. Jon slipped through the pandemonium of the tiny back garden and caught my hand.

'Are you all right, Pat?'

'Yes, I'm fine,' but he must have felt my trembling, for he put his arm round me comfortingly and we stood just outside the back door letting the inquest as to who had seen and done what and when wash over us.

'Booty!' I exclaimed after a few moments, guiltily remembering, and we crept back into the shelter to retrieve and comfort.

The night of Jon's calming embrace proved to be the last night of the Blitz, and, as the year wore on and war raged elsewhere, Hitler reneging on his non-aggression pact with Stalin and invading the Soviet Union on 22nd June 1941, the country breathed a collective sigh of relief. I feared and equally hoped that Jon would repeat his gallant and comforting gesture as the weeks and months passed and his visits became a routine part of our lives. I didn't know what held him back, part of me appreciating the opportunity to develop a new, close, friendship uncomplicated by physical expression while another part, one I desperately endeavoured to suppress, wanting him to hold me close, explore my body and recreate exquisite, otherworldy sensations I should never have known about.

Several times that summer Bill, Jon, Edward, Mary, Helen and I got together, perhaps taking a picnic to Clapham Common where the boys played cricket and us girls chatted, or cycling further afield as the threat of bombing became a fading memory. Sometimes I caught Bill looking broodingly, calculatingly, at me, but, shifting his attention to Mary, his dreadful jokes and accompanying laughter ringing out, he would be the same old Bill and I would be sure I had imagined it. Jon gave no indication in company of any preference for me, being equally gallant towards Mary and Helen.

The summer slipped into autumn and, grieving my lost friendship, I sent Becky a wedding present. The bombing of the American ships in Pearl Harbour by the Japanese in December came as a surprise and as a relief to the British. *At last we're not alone in the war now*, I thought, guiltily aware of the cost in terms of lives but hoping that America's involvement would save more in the long run by speeding the war to an end.

1941 merged into 1942 and, with no sign of the bombing

returning, Jon and I continued our regular pilgrimages to the City of London to see what progress was being made in clearing the bomb sites. While rubble was gradually removed, the low roofless walls of many buildings remained, no money being available for site clearance and redevelopment, and, as time wore on, the ruins became picturesque, self-seeded with a variety of wild flowers and climbing plants. Articles in magazines and newspapers about the ruins' vegetation abounded and Jon and I were just two of the hordes of 'ruin-gawpers', a phrase coined by a writer at the time.

Jon sometimes invited me along with Bill, if back from Reading, Mary, Helen and other friends and cousins of his own over to his home in Kennington. The ground floor, reached by a flight of steps, contained a sitting room where a spread of dividing doors to the rear room could be opened to double the floor space and we rehearsed mini-theatricals and played charades to while away the miserable winter weekend afternoons. Bill saw Mary and Helen home safely to Clapham on such occasions, Jon offering to split the escorting duties to ensure my safe return.

One Saturday a little before Easter neither Mary nor Helen were with us and Bill insisted on accompanying me home.

'No need, Jon, for you to put yourself out. I'm going straight back to Brixton and it's no trouble to overshoot a little. Pat is, after all, my oldest friend.'

I acquiesced. Jon had never formally asked me to be his girl and for either of us to make a fuss now might reveal more than I wished Bill to know. As Bill turned to the door, Jon shrugged at me and mouthed, 'I'll write.'

Bill and I set off. A 33 was disappearing in the distance but a 16 came along soon enough and we hopped on, alighting on Brixton Hill near the junction with Water Lane. As we turned the corner I was conscious of the beech tree lying to our left at the end of the Rush Common land, and perhaps Bill was too, as he suddenly burst out with, 'What *is* it between you and Jon? Has he asked you to walk out with him? I know you see him when I'm not around. You can tell me, you know. I'm just a tad disappointed he hasn't had the decency to tell me himself.'

'Don't be ridiculous,' I scolded. 'Jon's become a friend, that's all. I don't see him all the time. We occasionally go to walk the ruins of the City of London. Lots of people do that. It's an afternoon pastime for Londoners. We don't do it *very* often anyway because I still do my Sunday morning walks with my father which is quite enough walking for one weekend.'

Bill grunted.

'He's never asked me to be his girl,' I added hotly. 'There's nothing wrong with going for a walk or to a concert with a friend.'

'If he does ask you I'll tell him about your Canadian.'

Chilled by the venom in his voice and suddenly afraid, I pulled Bill to a halt, grabbing his arm, hissing,

'There's nothing to tell. You already know that. What's the point? Only to show you're *jealous*.'

The word hung between us like a bad stench.

I tried conciliation. 'Look, Bill, you and me have stayed on in the sixth form for a reason. Because we want to better ourselves and for me that *doesn't* involve getting tied down with *anyone* before I've had a chance to do that. Besides, Jon's never given me any indication he wants me to be his girl irrespective of whether I'd agree or not. He's never even touched me beyond a helping hand over the bombed out ruins, let alone,' nodding in the direction of the beech tree, 'trying to *kiss* me.' Bill flushed angrily. *Stupid, stupid, antagonising him.* I drew in a breath.

'I'm sorry. I appreciate your concern. Please forget all about it and let's get on with life. Besides,' I added, trying to lighten the mood, 'I've heard via your mother and mine that you've been seeing a bit of Mary.'

'Nothing serious, she's just a friend.'

'Well, there you are, just like me and Jon.'

We parted at the doorstep, Bill refusing an offer to come in, indicating the gloom, and I tried to be conciliatory by suggesting we meet up the following Saturday. 'Come to *my* place,' said Bill. 'I'll get a few friends together there.'

In view of Bill's outburst I was surprised to see Jon at Bill's the next weekend. *Jon can be very charming and persuasive and terribly reasonable*, I thought. *However much Bill resents Jon liking me, Bill's definitely fallen under his spell too.* I wondered if Bill had also spoken with Jon and been reassured, as Bill seemed to have given Jon and me the benefit of the doubt, much his usual cheerful and joking self, and even waved us off as we left early that evening, Jon saying he wanted to check out the forthcoming attractions at Brixton Cinema. Proceeding along Acre Lane, Jon, as a gentleman should, walked outside, shielding me from the road and my grandfather's shop. I hadn't walked past it since the day I first met Jon, and I tried to hurry us along but Jon caught my arm, saying,

'Look, there's Madog Roberts. We'll stop and say hello.'

On the opposite side my grandfather was gathering in the shop's pavement displays in preparation for closing up for the night. Horrified, I pulled Jon back.

'My *God*, you *know* him?'

'Of course I do. My father's a Lambeth Counsellor and a local shoe repairer. He knows lots of local shopkeepers and their workers. I've met Mr Roberts a few times in recent years.' Jon stopped, looking down at me. 'Roberts. Of course, I should have realised. He's related to you?'

'He went to prison for handling stolen goods. He's only been out two or three years.'

'He only ended up there because he got pressurised by a local protection racket. My father does volunteer work with ex-prisoners. He helped Mr Roberts find this employment. Mr Roberts seems to be managing and keeping his head clear of trouble. Pat, how do you know him? What's wrong?'

Tears streaming, legs trembling, I half dragged Jon along, using him as a shield as we left the shop behind on the other side.

'He's my grandfather.'

'Pat, what's wrong with him being your grandfather? There's something up. Stop, please.'

Refusing to halt, I let go and half ran ahead, Jon striding hard to keep up with me. Veering across the road opposite the Town Hall, I turned down towards St Matthew's and Jon caught my arm and steered me to the stone bench outside the church.

'Pat, you're obviously in some distress. *Tell me.*'

Jon sat down beside me and I looked at him doubtfully. *Can I trust him?* I loved him, feeling somehow incomplete when I wasn't with him. But trust him with my deepest emotional scars?

There was only one way to find out.

'I had a happy life as a small child, just my parents and me, renting rooms in Clapham. One day, when I was four, my grandfather turned up with Uncle Barry in tow. They were homeless and jobless and moved in. The rooms were too cramped so we moved to Brixton and squashed in to a tiny mews house.

'My grandfather has a fierce temper and expected everyone to run around doing his bidding. And if you didn't, he shouted and ranted and thumped the table and threw things and if they smashed that was too bad and he would punch the wall. One day I was playing with a couple of toys and he accidentally trod on one and said I'd put it there to hurt him and he hit me and threw all my toys in the fire. I was absolutely petrified of him. Sometimes he'd have terrible shouting matches with his sons and if I'd hidden under the table where the floor length tablecloth concealed me and the arguing started, I was trapped there. I was so scared I'd wet myself and he'd smell it and haul me out from under the table and I'd get smacked for being naughty and sent to bed with bread and water. And my father stood by and did nothing to stop him or get rid of him.'

Sighing, I added, 'Don't get me wrong, Jon, I love my father dearly and as I've grown up I've realised that he was as much a victim of this bully as I was, but I've always felt let down about it. I couldn't cope and by the time I was five-and-a-half I'd become very ill with boils all over my body and my hair fell out and in the end the doctors diagnosed nervous dyspepsia. But *still* my parents did nothing. Then one day a lady turned up with a boy of about eight in tow and demanded my grandfather look after her because her husband had found out she was carrying on with my grandfather and thrown her out. And so he threw my parents and me out of the house to make room for her and the boy. It was actually a blessing for me because it gave me a chance to recover and my grandmother, that's my mother's mother, came to live with us until she got married two years ago this summer.'

I drew breath and put my hand on Jon's arm. 'Please Jon, promise me you won't tell anyone *anything* about this. Don't let my parents know I've told you. My grandfather's had other relationships. If you meet his wife, that's my father's mother, who he left destitute when my father was twelve, you must promise never to mention his name, let alone the fact that you know him. It would be too distressing for her.'

Jon put his hand over mine. 'I promise. All your secrets are safe with me. 'Secret-keeper' is my middle name. I'm so sorry, Pat, that you had such an unhappy time.'

'That's when we got Peggy, when we moved out. The doctor'd said a pet might help me and he was right.' To Jon's quizzical look, I added, 'My dog. She was loving and fun and, I forgot, you won't have known her. She died in the summer nearly two years ago.' Remembering that weekend, panicking in case I said anything more about it, I stood up. 'It's getting dark. I'm sorry I've kept you.'

'Not at all.' For a moment I thought he might put his arm

round me and was disappointed he didn't, but instead he stood and gestured for us to walk on. 'I'm privileged you've felt able to tell me about it.'

As spring turned into summer Jon encouraged me to share with him the family secrets and sorrows that had burdened my childhood. He held my hand as I wept afresh for my Uncle Barry, killed in a tragic and avoidable lift accident, plunging to his death down a lift shaft because his fellow lift engineer, leaving him to unjam the top floor door from the outside, had moved the lift down to the ground floor without warning him, contravening safety requirements.

'You've never really been able to grieve for yourself over this,' observed Jon. 'You were there when your father opened the evening paper. You were what, nine, ten? You wouldn't want to do anything to hurt your father so you never talked to anyone about how you felt. You know, you've been grieving for your father. Now it's time to grieve for yourself.'

'I shouldn't be burdening you with these things.'

'Nonsense, that's what I'm here for. You can tell me anything, you know. It seems to me that throughout your childhood you were presented with events and experiences even an *adult* would be hard put to cope with. Tell me about these things, I'm here for you. It's time you forgave yourself for the things you couldn't help. You've been carrying too many other people's burdens for too long. And I promise you my lips are sealed. I'll never reveal what you've told me to another soul.'

I told him about my half-aunt two years younger than me at my school, whom I was forbidden to acknowledge, not knowing who amongst my contemporaries knew of her relationship through my grandfather to me, afraid to get close to anyone in case family secrets became public knowledge and shamed me and my parents.

I told him of my grandmother's secret shame over her illegitimate birth and the secret of my own mother's illegitimacy.

Because I was in love with Jon I told him secrets I would never have dreamt of telling anyone else. I grew to trust him and believe in his integrity. Jon soothed my soul. But I wondered how soothing he would be if he were ever to know the truth about me. I was afraid he would ask me to be his girl and bring about my deepest secret's unveiling, yet I wanted to be his girl so desperately.

My birthday being a Monday, taking the afternoon off work Jon journeyed to Leatherhead and took me out for a special birthday tea in Gregory's tearooms. Returning me to my digs, he charmed Mrs Brindley, who said to me after he left,

'There, I told you not to give in to your friend Bill. You've found your young man in this one.'

'I've known him for over a year but he's not asked me to be his girl.'

'He's not far off, my dear. And he's worth the wait.'

Early the following month I waited excitedly for Jon's train to steam into Leatherhead Station. Revising for Higher Certificate exams was easiest at Mrs Brindley's and I hadn't seen Jon for three weeks. Having just finished the exams, this weekend was my last in Leatherhead before the Sixth Form Leavers' Assembly. Some of the girls, eighteen the previous autumn, had already joined the forces, and the Leavers' Assembly was likely to be a small affair, but I wanted to stay and say my last, formal goodbye to the teachers and the school, and to the town that had been so much of my life for the past three years.

Jon's brown-topped head sailed above the sea of passengers and, spotting me, he broke into a broad smile, my cheeks contracting in response. For a moment I thought he might clasp me to him, but he moved forward only to accept my peck on his cheek.

'Good journey?'

'Yes, thanks. You know, the route brought me past Motspur Park which I know well from my Tenison days, our playing fields were there. When this wretched war's over I'll take you there to see me playing football and cricket for the Old Tenisonians.'

*When this awful war's over I'll take you up and fly you so high even the clouds will look like dollshouses.*

*No, no, not today. I haven't thought of him in weeks. I can't bear to think of him with Jon here.*

Passing through the down platform exit and along the drive to Station Road, unnerved by the sudden memory, I observed acerbically, 'You're a great optimist. So far the Americans are over here and that's about it. The Germans still train guns on us across the channel, we're not regaining any of the ground we've lost in North Africa, the Russians are still on the back foot and we gave the Japs Singapore in February.'

Jon drew close to me, looking hurriedly around, putting one hand on my lower arm. 'Ssh, don't talk like that. You'll get us arrested for spreading alarm and despondency. Regulation 39B. People have been fined and jailed for less.'

At first I thought he was joking, but the anxious vertical creases between his eyebrows and the downward droop of his perfect, kissable lips suggested otherwise. I patted his hand with my free one.

'Don't worry, I trust you and there's no one close by.'

'All the same, be careful and don't say anything like that again, even in private. You never know who might be listening.'

*You're not my parent*, I thought resentfully. I removed my hand and released my arm from his grip and we walked silently alongside each other.

Jon sighed. 'Sorry to lecture you when I've only just arrived. It's good to see you again. Tell me about today. What's this about a War Savings Fair?'

'I don't know whether it's a special Leatherhead thing,' I said, 'or whether lots of towns have War Savings Fairs, but we're supposed to have been saving up for months and bring our savings to the fair and spend it and each stall when it's covered its costs gives the money it makes to the war effort.'

We made our way towards the Fair, held on local playing fields, skirting people lining the route from the town to the field.

'Stop here,' I said near the entrance where an enterprising local had set up a stall selling drinks. 'The weather's not been ideal recently but with the sun out we might get a bit thirsty while we wait.'

'Wait for what?'

'The parade. Ah, here it comes.'

The distant strains of a brass band growing gradually louder and the crowd swelling, I was pleased of the excuse to stand closer to Jon. Carbolic soap, engine smoke, *he must have had the train window open*, and a slightly earthy, musky smell. I leaned a little into him to allow a small child to pass in front of me. A man smell, I thought, and a memory flashed of a similar, male, smell mingling with cigarette smoke... *stop it, stop thinking of him, stop thinking at all.*

Looking over my shoulder, catching Jon smiling down at me, thinking, *put your arm round me, please, please, I can't bear this platonic friendship any longer,* the band hoving into view and the parade passing in a blur, I fought to keep my self-control. *Concentrate on what's in front of you, not behind,* I told myself sternly, then wished I hadn't as the armed forces parading past included a unit of young Canadian soldiers led by an older, firm-jawed, blue-eyed senior officer in a peaked cap topping fair, cropped hair. *Thank God he's in khaki, not air force blue,* I thought, forcing myself to remain ramrod straight, unmoving and unmoved as the Canadians passed. The parade of regular servicemen and -women was rounded off by a selection of armoured vehicles, followed by the Home Guard and other uniformed groups including guides and scouts, brownies and cubs.

As the end of the procession turned through the gate the crowd followed, and, with a 'Pat,' Jon grabbed my hand,

and, stepping back, we joined the queue for the refreshment stall.

Wandering around the various stalls, trying our luck on the hoopla and shove ha'penny, tombola and buzzer wire, stopping from time to time to admire the army gymnastics display and the heavy artillery loading and firing display (Jon assuring me they were blanks), we made our way past a mini-railway giving rides to children and meandered gradually towards the far side of the field where two enormous structures were erected, one a film set style wooden house frontage with scaffolding rising behind and the other a high square scaffolding tower.

'I'll go and grab us a couple of cheese or bacon sarnies from that stall while we're waiting,' indicated Jon. 'I'll meet you near that First Aid Post at the side there.' Smiling my understanding and thanks, I moved towards the tent. A few minutes later the fire engines and ambulances arrived and volunteers swarmed up the scaffolding tower and a few took their places behind the house frontage. The fire chief blew a whistle and firemen with ropes and ambulance men with stretchers swarmed up the scaffolding tower too, the firemen throwing down ropes and ambulance men bandaging and securing volunteers to stretchers. A rope and pulley system was set up and the first of the 'rescued' started swinging down. Jon appeared at my shoulder with a bacon roll for me. 'Sorry, rationed to half a slice of bacon each, not bad, eh?' and we munched as the volunteers were all brought safely back to earth.

'I'll get some drinks, that was a bit salty,' offered Jon. I said, 'Don't miss the rest,' and he said, 'The queues are down because everyone's watching and I can see it from a distance if I'm not back in time. You stay here, you'll have a good view,' and sped off, ducking and weaving through the crowd behind me.

After a short interval the fire chief, stepping up again, lit the base of the house front. Within seconds it was ablaze, with firemen swarming in front, setting up hoses and training the water on the fire. Ladders were brought, dramatic rescues of volunteers through windows effected. As one of the volunteers emerged and stepped on to a fireman's ladder, I felt the heat of the flames even from a distance and my vision of James' last minutes reared. Turning and stumbling, I fled through the crowd, smelling the burning and in my mind's eye seeing only his lined, exhausted, precious, so precious face melting in the heat. Towards the back of the crowd I tripped, possibly over an ankle or a bag on the ground, I didn't see the cause, but I stumbled and would have fallen if a strong arm had not caught mine and the other encircled my waist and held me close.

'Whoa there, lady, you alright?' I looked up into the face of the officer who had led his Canadian unit at the parade. The cadence was the same though his voice was grittier, the visual likeness to James artificial and as he looked down I could see his eyes were grey, not the deep blue I remembered, but it was enough.

'It's not often I have a lovely lady falling at my feet,' he joked to his men crowding round behind him. He turned back to me, still holding me tight. 'Don't look so horrified,' he smiled, 'I won't eat you.'

*James enveloping my nipple and aurora with his mouth, raking my nipple with his teeth....*

'Hey, lady,' said the officer, rearing back, his grip loosening, 'I'm darned if I'm the big bad wolf!'

'Pat, are you all right?' Looking past the officer I saw Jon shouldering through the milling soldiers. I schooled my expression, turning back to the officer who was now just steadying me with one hand under an elbow.

'Th... thank you for saving me from a nasty fall. I'm sorry. I didn't mean to seem ungracious.'

'Pleased to be of service, ma'am.'

Jon stepped up beside me, sliding a possessive arm around my waist, the officer removing his hand and nodding once to Jon and once to me. Grasping me with one arm and cradling two opened bottles in the crook of the other elbow, Jon nodded back to the officer, saying,

'Thank you, sir, for your assistance to my young lady. It's much appreciated. I'd be happy to buy you a beer, sir.'

'No need. Happy to be of service, young man. I guess you're not long for call up?'

'In the autumn, sir.'

'Good luck.'

'Thank you, sir,' said Jon, firmly propelling me away.

We walked silently toward the refreshment tent which was largely empty at that moment. Jon drew up a chair for me at a table and sat down across from me.

'What was that all about?' he asked. 'You looked petrified.'

'I was startled, that's all. I tripped and would have fallen. He assisted me. I wasn't frightened.'

Jon looked at me for a long moment. He handed me a bottle of ginger beer.

'Drink up. If there's nothing else you want to see here I'll take you to your billet. You looked like someone in shock. Anyone'd think you'd seen a ghost.'

*If you only knew.*

We made our way slowly to Mrs Brindley's, Jon's arm firmly about me. Mrs Brindley was out, at the Fair. While I disappeared to the toilet, Jon busied himself in the kitchen making a pot of tea. Emerging and placing the tray on the table, he steered me to the settee, sitting down beside me.

'Pat, why were you running when you tripped?' He'd seen it all.

Thinking rapidly. 'Seeing that display reminded me of all those blitzed buildings in London and the people who died in them,' I lied.

Nodding understandingly, swinging his arm up and round me, Jon smiled, 'You're a sensitive soul, and I love you for it.'

His first declaration of love. Prompted by my lie. Guilt washed over me.

*I must tell him now. I can't let us build our love on a lie.* But the fear of rejection at such a tender moment, a new stage in our relationship, was overwhelming. Remaining silent, I let him reach across and turn my head and he kissed me carefully, tenderly, lovingly.

I wept, assuring him I was weeping for joy, telling him I loved him, that I understood he might have said I was his young lady just to get me away from the soldiers and I wouldn't hold him to it if he didn't want it.

'Oh, I want it very much,' he said. 'More than anything else in the world. Pat, please will you be my girl?'

He kissed me tenderly again and I thought, *even his kissing is perfect*, and I didn't want him to stop, my breasts rising, my crotch dampening, my arms embracing, his arm encircling, his body pressing, my lips opening, his tongue exploring, his hand cupping my breast, his fingers kneading my nipple, my hands stealing up to the back of his head, my fingers furrowing, a memory flashing.

Knocking his hand from my breast, I pushed him away hard and scrambled to the end of the settee, as he floundered, astonishment and puzzlement in his lowered brows.

'No further,' I gasped, averting my eyes from his trousers. 'I'll kiss you and hug you but no further. We mustn't go any further.'

With a huge effort Jon brought his laboured breathing under control, standing and moving to the mantelpiece, his back to me. After a moment he straightened, turning and smiling apologetically.

'I'm sorry, Pat, I shouldn't have gone as far as I did. I promise I won't do that again. It was quite uncalled for. A chap can get a little carried away and I admire you for bringing me back to an even keel. You're a good girl, Pat, with high morals and I don't want to spoil that in you. I'll only ever do what you'll allow. If it's just kisses and hugs we'll enjoy them and I'll respect your boundaries.'

I was afraid to kiss him again in case I couldn't stop this time but, steeling myself I stood and let him kiss me again, chastely and affectionately. He embraced me with one arm, placing his other hand round the back of my head and drawing me in close, resting my head on his shoulder. We stood thus for some time and I heard a distant clock strike four.

I lifted my head to look into his eyes. 'Yes, I want to be your girl,' I said. 'More than anything else in the world.'

'I'll tell Bill,' he said.

'I'm not Bill's girl and I never have been. I turned him down. There's no need. I can write to him.'

'You're such a little innocent.' Jon's tone was indulgent. 'It's obvious he still holds out hope and hope can make a chap irrational. I'm his friend too and I owe him that at least. Promise you'll say nothing to anyone until I've told him. If he's back from Reading by next weekend I'll see him then.'

The following weekend Jon found Bill out when he called on his way over to me for the day and so left me early evening, saying, 'I'll see if Bill's there on my way back.'

About an hour later an urgent banging on the front door disturbed our supper and I ran to the window, espying the top of Bill's wayward dark brown hair. He stood back and looked up impatiently, his chest heaving, sweat glistening on his face. He beckoned, and, grabbing my bag with my keys, I dashed down the stairs, telling my parents it was Bill and I'd just be a few minutes. Ushering Mrs Haywood back, I slipped out of the front door and walked past Bill, turning right and making for the common land at the end of the road, Bill gasping hoarsely behind me,

'Liar, liar, you lied to me.' Puffing and panting in my ear as I sped up, half running. 'I believed you and you bloody lied to me. You've been carrying on for months, a year. Jon lied to me too, telling me bloody lies this evening about it only being last week you got together. You've stitched me up between you. Telling me you were just friends. Telling me you didn't want to be *anyone's* girl. You lied, *you fucking bitch*.'

Turning sharply, before I could stop myself I slapped him hard across his left check.

'How *dare* you use such language to me. How *dare* you call me that. I *didn't* lie to you. You're behaving as if I'm two-timing you, as if I owed you anything more than friendship. I *don't*.'

Suddenly afraid of what I had done and what he might do to me, I ran away from him and onto the allotment land, Bill catching me up as I drew level with the beech tree. He grabbed my arm and span me round. I yanked my arm free and backed up to the tree's trunk.

'You owe me nothing *now*,' he spat, his face contorted, 'because you don't even owe me *friendship* anymore.'

We stood in the shade of the beech tree where he kissed me two and a half years ago and I heaved dry sobs as the import of his words sank in, the ground quicksand suctioning in the schoolboy I had loved as a brother and spewing out a monster, a stranger, swearing at me, grabbing me roughly, destroying my cherished memories.

'I got my call up papers yesterday. I spent today out with my parents and I was going to come round and tell you tomorrow. I have to report to some assessment unit in Colchester on Monday. God knows where I'll be sent after that. And this is the send-off I get. A visit from Jon,' he spat the name out, 'and the best bloody news I could have hoped for,' his voice rising, 'I *don't* think.'

Bill moved towards me and I shrank back, afraid, but he stopped just short of me, growling into my face, 'Don't worry, I haven't told him about your *precious* Canadian. I wouldn't give Jon the pleasure of knowing you've turned down *two* offers before him.'

He shouldered past me and kept walking and it was only the lightness of the traffic that saved him as he walked straight across the road without looking, and I watched him go and when he was out of sight I sank, sobbing, to the ground beneath the tree where my father found me and led me home.

I grieved that summer for my loss. Bill, my companion, my mentor, my brother, my dear, dear friend. Snippets of memories, of excruciating jokes, of his head thrown back in laughter, of his boyhood pranks, of his comforting arm when I fell and grazed a knee. I grieved as I cuddled and petted Booty and was grateful in a strange way that Bill had left something from himself for me to cherish.

By the autumn, after my three letters to Bill were returned by him unopened, and I took the train to Doncaster to start at my evacuated college, I was beginning to accept that the breach would not be healed. I was also beginning to focus on Jon's call up which could be any time after late September. His call up papers eventually arrived, he wrote, on his father's birthday in early November. At Christmas after four months of agonisingly painful separation we met for as much of Jon's leave as we could.

'I just finished the assessment period,' Jon said, 'and they've assigned me to REME.'

'REME?'

'Royal Electrical and Mechanical Engineers.'

'I know what it stands for, what I mean is, why REME? I thought you were expecting to go into an infantry battalion?'

'Every cloud has a silver lining,' said Jon mysteriously.

'What does that mean? Is the reason top secret?'

'No,' laughed Jon. 'It means that breaking my foot on the last day of our cadet exercises in France in 1938 was the reason I wasn't passed medically fit for the infantry and so they've had to find somewhere else for my talents. The CO said if I wasn't allowed to walk to the battlefield I might as well drive there and learn how to maintain the vehicle I'm driving at the same time.'

I shivered. 'I don't know how you can joke about it. I know we have to keep smiling through and all that but it scares me to think that one day you'll be sent out to fight, especially after El Alamain. Now there's hope, but that means invading Europe one day.'

'It's no coincidence,' said Jon seriously, 'that the very day *my* call up papers are sent out we win our first and glorious victory of the war. The tide has turned.'

'And all because of the call up of one insignificant young man from Kennington,' I smiled. I sobered. 'I'm sorry. I just can't bear to think of you facing the enemy and maybe never coming back.' *It's happened before. Please God, don't let it happen again.*

'Well, don't think about it. Live for the moment. We don't know what lies ahead. But what I do know is that I love you and nothing's going to change that.'

*** 

The dreams about James began in the summer of 1943. Perhaps it was the long evenings, light until nearly eleven o'clock, reminding me of the summer of the Beaver Club dance. Perhaps it was missing Jon desperately, having not seen him since his Christmas leave. Perhaps it was my brain, having no physical memories of Jon beyond kissing and cuddling, playing tricks on me in my sleep.

*Where are you, Jon? I need you.* Letters from Jon had been few. They came from South Wales, telling me lightly of a Methodist church choir he joined in Swansea and the few trips he made into the city centre on leave; at some stage he was moved to Cardiff and he wrote about a Blitz damaged cathedral he visited in an area called Llandaff. Nothing of his REME training or army exercises, of course, in case the letters fell into the wrong hands. After May the letters stopped coming.

News broke of the allied assault on Sicily in July and I

thought of James. *Maybe he'd have provided air cover for the invasion if he'd still been alive.* That night I dreamt I was standing in the living room at Idmiston Road and the door opened and in walked James as I had first met him, uniformed, confident, tall, slim yet well-muscled, bright-eyed and smiling, the crow's feet crinkling. Proclaiming, 'I'm back, I told you I'd be back!' Sweeping me into his arms, kissing me, and I felt the imprint of his mouth on mine and a melting low down in my body.

I awoke suddenly, my hand pressing my mouth, my heart thudding, my lower parts wet and throbbing.

For a moment I so wanted to believe in the dream. The enormity of reality was too much to bear and I wept, stuffing the pillow into my mouth, fresh waves of grief sweeping over me.

*It's only a dream,* I told myself, *you were thinking about him last night before you went to sleep, that's all. It's not real. You sent him to his death nearly three years ago after he betrayed your trust, he's never coming back, stop thinking about him, it's not real.*

In the darkness the image of James remained vivid and I groped for my torch. Rising, grabbing my cotton dressing gown and wrapping it around me, I padded down to the kitchen. Pausing at the front door I peered past the blackout blind and saw the faint tinges of dawn in the sky. Taking a glass of water back to my room, I sat on the edge of the bed and sipped, but that only served to remind me of a large, firm hand encircling mine in the Beaver Club basement entrance. Carefully placing the glass on the bedside table, I curled up in bed and lay awake for a while feeling empty and lost until eventually sleep stole back over me.

A few nights later I dreamt of James again. This time he was the battle worn and weary James of our last meeting. Reaching out with both hands around his face and drawing his head to my breast, finding no strangeness in our mutual nakedness, stroking his head while he nuzzled and suckled, I shot upright, startled into wakefulness, finding to my shock the nipple of the same breast painfully hard and urgent.

Dreams of James haunted my nights and their memory haunted my days. We danced together as we had that night of the dance, the floor beneath me turning to the grey-green of the sea and, plunging into its watery depths, James disappeared and I was floundering, suddenly waking to a tumble of sheets and the awful inner tearing of loss and grief.

Another particular recurring dream was of him above me, entering me, his cigarette laden breath on my cheek, my body responding, deep spasms awakening me.

*Why him? Why now? Why not Jon whom I love, not a man who was a passing ship that anchored but briefly?*

By the end of August, studying frantically in Doncaster through the summer to ensure I was on track to complete the college course within the allotted time, dreading sleep with the familiar dreams only an eyelid away, I was desperate for news of Jon. Although I was writing every week, there were still no letters from him in return. Doubts and fears crowded. *Has he met someone else and can't be bothered to tell me it's all over? Has he been killed by accident in army training exercises and no one's told me?* Dismissing the latter thought on receiving a letter from his mother asking me if I had any news of him, for she hadn't heard from him either. If he was dead surely at least his mother would know.

One afternoon in early September I arrived back after my college day to find a letter in his familiar handwriting. Standing in the hall, heart thudding, I tore it open eagerly.

*Darling Pat,*

*I am sorry not to have been in touch with you for a while. This is to let you know I've recently been transferred to an army camp near Bury. It's been a busy summer and I am sorry I haven't had time to write. I hope you are keeping well. Your letters through the summer have just caught up with me. Thank you for writing so assiduously. I have enjoyed reading them. Nothing much to report here I'm afraid. We are kept on our toes and not much chance of a social life. You can write to me at Hut 20, Lowercroft Camp, Walshaw, near Bury, Lancs.*

*Chin up. We'll meet again, as the song goes.*

*Please keep writing. I look forward to the day we can be together again.*

*With all my love from your*
*Jon.*

I wept openly with relief. Elaine Morley, emerging from the kitchen on hearing my sobs, guided me in to the front room where I incoherently explained that I was weeping from joy not sorrow, and she disappeared in true English landlady style to make a celebratory cup of tea.

Later, re-reading Jon's letter, I puzzled over the sentence '*Your letters through the summer have just caught up with me.*' This was odd. I had sent them all to the same address in Cardiff. So presumably he had not been there. And not at Bury either because he said he'd recently been transferred there. But if not, where? Last Christmas he told me he was learning how to maintain army vehicles at the REME training centre in South Wales, so it seemed strange that he would suddenly disappear for the summer and not send me an address to which I could write. There was a story here that he wasn't telling me.

## 12

# Jon's Story

'Look to it and lively, Dorringham, the CO's back and he wants to see you. *Now.* At the double, at the double.'

Staff Sergeant Cooper's barked order could be heard right across the Pennines, Jon thought, as he looked to it and lively and at the double. Traversing the sloping forest of huts in the warm early September sunshine, he presented himself at Major Spencer's hut. The outer office, sparsely furnished with a desk, a chair and a low cabinet, was unoccupied. Checking his uniform, smoothing down creases and ensuring his battledress blouse was properly anchored beneath his belt, standing on one leg in turn and rubbing the front of the other's boot behind the leg to bring up the best shine, Jon knocked on the inner door.

'Come.'

Jon opened the door. *I might as well hear what I've done and get it over with.*

'Ah, Private Dorringham. Come in, come in. Sit down.'

Such familiarity from a senior officer was rare and Jon was assailed with a fear that bad news was about to be broken. He sat warily.

'I'll come straight to the point. You signed the Official Secrets Act when you joined this unit.'

Nodding, Jon went hot and cold, a wave of nausea rising. *What have I done?*

The major leaned forward, his long, angular face frowning, his voice lowering.

'What I am about to tell you and instruct you to do is not to be repeated to another living soul. Do you understand?'

'Yes, sir.'

Leaning sideways and extracting a large brown envelope from a drawer in his desk, the major opened it and removed a short sleeved white cotton jersey vest which he handed over. Jon took it and, at the major's nod, opened it out. A large square of additional similar material was sewn across the front on the inside. The stitching was complete along three sides and partially across the top an inch or so either side. The slit was secured with three tiny buttons and equally tiny button holes.

Jon looked up. Major Spencer stood, putting his finger to his lips and moving silently to the door. Suddenly wrenching it open, he looked into the outer office and, satisfied no one was attempting to listen outside, returned to his desk, sat down and spoke, his voice soft and low.

'Your parents have been watched and vetted. Your father's an ARP warden, a local Councillor and a respectable businessman. Your mother does voluntary work with the WVS. Their patriotism is without question. Nonetheless, what I am about to tell you must be hidden by you from them so successfully that they will never question any unexpected appearances you make at home.'

*Curiouser and curiouser, cried Alice.* Jon said nothing.

'You will from time to time be given an envelope to transport in person to a contact I'll give you in the War Ministry. You'll meet him at an address I'll give you immediately prior to your departure and hand the envelope to him. You'll use a phrase as a password and you will *not* hand over the papers to him without the corresponding phrase from him or his assistant. If you are not satisfied that the person you've met is the correct one, you will not hand over the papers and you will defend them to the death. You've been taught counter espionage, how to spot a tail and how to lose it, how to deal with an attacker and how to resist interrogation.'

'Yes, sir.' *This isn't just curious, it's plain bizarre.*

'The papers will be concealed in that,' the major continued, nodding at the vest. 'You'll wear it beneath your shirt. You'll travel in uniform. More suspicious if you travel in civvies. Plenty of chaps on leave in uniform. Once you get home you can change into civvies as any chap would. Any questions?'

Having learnt discretion in the army to be the better part of valour, Jon hesitated. Curiosity won.

'Why me, sir?'

The major considered the question for a moment, jutting his lower jaw. 'You showed yourself resilient and adaptable at the special training camp in Scotland and you cottoned on quickly at the AA training in Berwick. You work well with a team and you show initiative when needed. However, most crucially, unlike the rest of the privates in your unit, your home is just south of Westminster Bridge which is close to your drop off rendezvous. You'll blend in as a local chap in a way that your taffy, highland or northern colleagues won't. And you'll have somewhere to bed down without having to arrange anything unusual.'

'How do you recommend I explain my unexpected appearances, sir?'

'Tell them the unit's a primarily Monday to Friday outfit with some weekends free. The work that's done here must remain top secret and as a cover story you can say your unit's training to teach the maintenance of searchlights which can be done within regular hours. So, naturally, given the free weekends and your family being in London, you wish to visit them and your young lady there. You have a young lady from Brixton, I believe, at a Dulwich teacher training college.'

'She's been evacuated to Doncaster, sir.'

The major frowned. 'Don't know how that was missed.' He brightened. 'Find a young lady in London instead. Have every reason a young man might have for haring off home at the first opportunity. It won't be every weekend, but when required you'll travel down on a Friday afternoon and deliver the envelope. You may or may not be told to report back to the delivery address, or some other address that will be given to you, on your way back on a Sunday in time to collect any response to bring back to me.'

The major leaned forward, lowering his voice even further. 'To me personally and to no one else. If you're told to report back to collect a response on a Monday morning you will do so, even if that means you're disciplined here for returning late from leave. I shall leave you to invent an excuse for your lateness. I'll see to it in the long run your army career's not blighted, but meantime you'll take your punishment and see it as part of the war effort. You'll need to say you've applied for a travel warrant and you can tell your colleagues here that you're visiting family and a young lady. You must not do *anything* to raise suspicions here or at home as to the purpose of your journey. Careless talk costs lives. Do you understand?'

'Yes, sir.'

'Check it fits you first now, then probably best to keep it under lock and key in the bottom drawer here. You can pop it on when you come to get your orders. Report to me on Friday at thirteen hundred hours.'

'What, here, sir?

'Yes, of course you'll report to me here.'

'I meant, putting on the vest, sir?'

Major Spencer nodded impatiently and returned to the papers on his desk. Retreating to a corner of the office and divesting himself of his battledress blouse and shirt, Jon pulled the peculiar garment over his own vest to avoid the buttons rubbing his skin, moved his shoulders up and down and then removed and folded it and returned it to the brown envelope, re-dressing hurriedly.

Interrogated by his unit mates as to the reason for his unexpected summons, Jon smiled self-deprecatingly.

'A bit embarrassing, really,' he said truthfully. Showering

naked with his contemporaries was one thing, stripping down to accommodate the vest in front of the major was quite another. 'He heard I'm applying for a travel warrant to London for my next leave and wants me to call in to his tailor in Savile Row with some instructions and measurements.'

'Fookin' toffs,' sniffed Bob, hands on the hips of his stocky frame. 'Still think they fookin' own the fookin' country. Fookin' errand boy now are yer?' On each 'fookin' he jerked his dark head sideways and up.

'Watch yerrr fuckin' language, young Bob,' from Graham ironically, and, raising an auburn eyebrow to Jon, adding, 'Soo yorrull noo his inside leg measurement, Dorrris,' ending with a mocking flop of his hand at the wrist.

'Ha, ha, very funny.'

'What's this about leave?' Bertie interjected.

'I gather now we're settled in we'll be mostly working on a Monday to Friday basis so most weekends are ours. But,' Jon added hastily, 'that's only an impression I've got, it's not been confirmed yet.'

It was confirmed that afternoon, the news being given by the major himself in a post-lunch briefing, the staff sergeant first checking the perimeter of their classroom hut then standing on guard by the door. The major added,

'May I remind you all that the work you do in your special unit here is top secret. If you go out of the camp you are to tell *no one* what the unit really does. I would also remind you that even *within* the camp you do not discuss the work of your unit with the other School of Electric Lighting units operating here. They're all pukka training units for the operation of anti-aircraft and searchlight equipment in conjunction with the current Kerrison predictors. Your unit's been convened as part of the push to create a new generation of electromechanical analogue computers. There are scientists elsewhere working theoretically on the same project but you're hands-on with the actual equipment and your practical as well as intellectual contribution will be invaluable. With the information we got out of Peenemünde before it was destroyed last month we know Hitler's developing a form of robotic pilotless bomb which we anticipate will be even more difficult to bring down than their fighters and bombers. Yes?'

This to Bob who, fearing no one, had his hand up.

'I thought Peenemünde were aboot the Boche's radar, sir, not robots?'

'What I've just told you is strictly top secret. The RAF's often not even told why their target's important, just that it is. On this occasion they were told knocking out Peenemünde would destroy a radar and radio factory, to encourage the chaps in the RAF to give it their all. Which they did. Most successfully. But you need to understand that what we're dealing with in reality is a largely unchartered danger we first heard about only earlier this year. We *have* to increase the computing ability of our predictors tenfold. The speed at which the predictors currently compute is little more than when they were invented for knocking warships out a mile away travelling at only a few knots. With the most modern weapons we may only have one or two seconds' interval between receipt of the information and using the computed instruction for firing. Further, we have to be able to take variants into account and assume that whatever the Jerries throw at us will be different and new. As you know, our current predictors assume a certain constant height and a certain constant speed. What we need to develop is the ability to instantly predict the future position of a diving target. Fortunately, the Peenemünde raid is believed to have set their secret weapon programme back by six months. They'll rebuild elsewhere but that has bought us time. It's vital Jerry doesn't get wind of the work your special unit's doing here. We want them to think we're as incompetent as they thought us in the early part of the war. Oh, and watch out for pillow talk with the ATS stationed here.'

Waiting while the inevitable sniggers died down, he became serious again. 'Nearly three years ago the *Bury Echo* ran an article about us running courses training technical chaps on the operation of anti-aircraft gunnery equipment. This was a serious breach of security and although the source was tracked down and dealt with, it goes to underline the danger to the future defence of our country if *any* talk of what our special unit does here gets out. To our colleagues in the other units forming the School of Electric Lighting our unit is training to teach searchlight maintenance and that's all anyone here or at home is allowed to know. Got that?'

'Yes, *sir*,' the men chorused in unison.

On Friday after lunch instead of returning to the instruction hut, Jon veered off in the direction of the major's office into which he was shown by a lieutenant now occupying the outer office. The major fished out the brown envelope containg the vest and a large white envelope from the drawer and handed them over, observing,

'Good job you're a large sort of chap. Let's see how concealed it is when you've got it in.'

Partially stripping in the corner of the office, Jon drew the strange garment over his vest as before, shrugged his shirt and battledress blouse back on and slid the white envelope inside the pouch, re-buttoning the outer layers of clothing and smoothing the front of his battledress blouse. The major examined him from several angles and patted his front, but there was no revealing crinkling sound and, satisfied, the major stood back.

'The address is 21C Whitehall Terrace. Go to the third door along on the left and knock three times, pause and knock twice more. It'll be opened by a civil servant who'll invite you to step inside. You'll say something conversational to incorporate "The weather's a bit variable at this time of year". The other person will say, "Rain or shine it's all the same to an office worker". You'll then follow him to the person to whom you'll hand the envelope. You'll be told whether to report back on Sunday and, if so, when and where. You may have to go to an address somewhere else in the London area rather than back to that office.'

The major paused. 'Repeat that all back to me so I can be sure you've understood.'

Jon did so, and the major continued. 'If you don't get the correct response, make an excuse and leave immediately. Wait an hour and try again. It may be that the person deputed to admit you is only temporarily absent. I'm confident that provided you arrive somewhere between four and seven o'clock you'll be met by the person expecting you. If you're unable to deliver it at all, conceal it and return here tomorrow with it unopened. You'll find me at my home in Walshaw. I'm at Orchard House at the far end of Orchard Lane. Go up past the church and keep going straight, it's the last lane on your left just before you leave the village. If you're successful and you're sent back with a response, deliver that to me in person at my home also. It doesn't matter how late. If you don't present yourself at all I shall assume no response was given to you. Understood?'

'Yes, sir.'

'Good. Return the vest to me in the brown envelope at the same time, or, if there's no reply to bring me, conceal it and return it to me here on Monday morning. Well, off you go. Pick up your travel warrant from Lieutenant Sandys. Report to the guard hut for a lift into Bury.'

Jon left in a daze, convinced that a large arrow was pointing to his shirt front with *Top Secret Document Concealed Here* written along its shaft. Collecting the travel warrant from the lieutenant in the outer office and calling in to the accommodation hut for his rucksack, he made his way uphill to the southern guard hut at the bend in Lowercroft Road beside which a number of trucks and lorries were parked. Several army personnel were milling around and they gave an ironic cheer when a driver hoved into view, hurrying from the toilet block.

'Got early leave, soldier?' asked a slight, pretty brunette in ATS uniform as Jon clambered into the back of the truck behind her. 'Who's the lucky girl?'

'Going to see my parents, actually,' said Jon.

'Any chance they live in Birmingham? D'you fancy a dance tomorrow night?'

Jon, slightly shocked at the young lady's forwardness, excused himself. She turned her attention to the soldier to her right, much to Jon's relief.

The rest of the journey was uneventful, although tedious. The train meandered into Manchester, where he changed, he thought, for a fast to London, but passenger trains invariably had to give way to goods trains and troop-carrying trains and Jon was beginning to panic as the train shunted slowly into Euston a little after six-thirty. He hurried into the Underground, relieved that the system had not yet shut down for the safety of the night's intake of shelterers, and, emerging at Trafalgar Square, raced down Whitehall anxiously scanning the buildings. He found Whitehall Terrace, a narrow turning to the right, and skidded to a halt outside the correct door. It was now after seven. Dreading no response at all, he was relieved when the door opened and he gasped, 'Sorry I'm running late, the journey, you know, like the weather, is a bit variable at this time of year.'

The middle aged male secretary replied, 'Rain or shine it's all the same to an office worker,' and Jon, exhaling in relief, followed him along a corridor and into a small office. As Jon entered, the tall, thin balding man sitting behind the desk nodded, holding out a hand. Realising before he committed a social faux pas that the hand was extended for the envelope, not for a handshake, he fumbled at the top of his uniform and extracted the envelope.

Buttoning up and standing to attention he waited, while the man, slitting open the envelope, scanned the several pages and, after a few moments, looked up. 'No need to report to me on Sunday. You'll be told when to come next. A little earlier in the evening would be appreciated.'

'Yes sir, sorry sir,' Jon said, and followed the secretary to the main door.

Jon staggered along Whitehall towards Westminster, drained of energy, his only emotion relief. Seeing the Red Lion across the road, he hesitated barely a moment before diving in to the lounge bar, waiting his turn and ordering a pint of best bitter. Retreating to a corner as the pub was very full he drank deeply, the alcohol relaxing his tense muscles. *Just this one, then I'll be off.* Closing his eyes for a few moments, leaning against the wall, wondering how to explain alcohol-laden breath to his mother, he heard as if from afar a vaguely familiar female voice.

'Jon, it *is* Jon, isn't it?'

He opened his eyes to a vision in a smart dark brown skirt suit, a white blouse and a cascade of autumn colours around a neck rising to a luscious-lipped mouth, a tip-tilted nose and large brown eyes set in luminous skin beneath shoulder length straight, shiny raven black hair. A memory surfaced of a warm curvaceous body pressing against him below soft, insistent lips. Summer 1940. Reward for walking her home from a party hosted by his cousin Margery. Feeling a stirring, a hardening, *down boy, not now!*, he stooped slightly forward, exclaiming wildly,

'Stella is it? Yes, Stella, yes indeed.'

They smiled at their mutual recognition and he thought, *I never followed her up, I can't imagine why not, she's gorgeous.*

'What are you doing here?' she asked.

He raised his glass. 'Draining this.' And promptly did, which neatly avoided answering the real question. Waving the empty glass, he said, mesmerised by her eyes, 'And you?'

'I'm here with a couple of the girls from work.'

'You work around here?'

'Yes.'

'It's getting late.' He indicated the door. 'Don't get caught in the blackout. D'you still live in Tooting?'

'Got rooms in Victoria I'm sharing with the girls. Convenient for work. We sometimes have to work late.'

'Victoria's expensive.'

'Rooms to rent are ten-a-penny since half of London decamped to the countryside. Why don't you join us for another drink?'

Conscious of his uniform in a pub which seemed to consist mostly of besuited office workers and parliamentary aides, he followed her to a small table to the side in the lounge bar. Stella introduced him to Dierdre, short, a little plump, blue eyes, brown hair and a welcoming smile, and Bridget, tall, blond and thin with a gash for a mouth.

'Ladies,' said Jon, 'let me buy you all a drink.'

'I'll give you a hand,' said Stella and they joined the crush at the bar, pressed close to each other, laughing and exclaiming at the coincidence that had brought them together.

'So you're home on leave and you haven't been home yet. You *naughty* boy.' Stella wagged her finger at him. 'What *will* you tell your mother?'

'I'm very inventive,' said Jon, and she replied, 'Ah, yes, from what I recall I'd bet you can be *very* inventive!' and fortunately for Jon it was his turn to order and he turned to the barman with relief.

Returning to the table, Jon squatted on a stool and withstood a barrage of questions, saying nothing more than, 'I'm in REME and I'm training to teach searchlight maintenance.'

'Oooh, you can turn your searchlight on me anytime, soldier,' said Dierdre and the three girls screamed with laughter. Jon, supressing surprise at a Max Miller-type joke emanating from feminine lips, relaxing further with the second pint, joined in the merriment, and it was only as he threw his head back later to laugh at yet another innuendo that he caught sight of the clock behind the bar. Downing the remainder of the pint quickly he said, 'Ladies, it's nearly nine-thirty and I'm sorry I have to go. It's been a pleasure meeting you,' nodding to Dierdre and Bridget, 'and meeting you again,' to Stella, and he rose a little unsteadily, grabbing his rucksack, realising as he did so that he was ravenously hungry.

'I'll come to the door,' said Stella. She stepped outside with him, clearly reluctant to see him go.

'I'm seeing Margery tomorrow,' she said. 'I'll tell her I saw you.'

*Find a young lady in London instead.*

'Why don't you and Margery come over for tea tomorrow? I'm sure my mother won't mind. She misses the house being filled with family and friends. Everyone's off doing their bit for the war effort. She hasn't seen me since before Easter. Ask Margery if Len or Jenny's around and can come over too.' He nodded towards the pub interior. 'Your friends, too.'

Stella beamed.

'I'd be delighted. I'll pass on your invite. I'm assuming Margery knows where you live.'

'See you tomorrow. About three?' Jon hesitated and Stella stepped boldly forward, grabbing up at his head, pulling down, kissing him hard on his lips.

'See you tomorrow,' Stella said, stepping back, and he reeled away towards Westminster, resuming the walk he had commenced two hours earlier. Except in the blackout everything looked different and even with directed torchlight he stumbled several times and twice stopped to check his bearings.

Knocking on the basement door, guessing his parents would be in the cosy warmth and safety of the lowest room of the house, Jon did his best to sober up. His father's voice called out,

'Who's there?'

'Jon.'

The door was flung open wide and his mother stood, shocked and pale, the light streaming out into the night. Jon stepped up to her and quickly shut the door behind him. She threw her arms round him, which took him aback, for she had never been the most demonstrative of mothers, and he felt her trembling against him.

'Good to see you, boy,' said his father, limping forward and grabbing his hand.

'Jon!' exclaimed his mother, drawing back and sniffing, her blue eyes glinting, her greying head shaking with disapproval. 'I declare that's alcohol and perfume. What *have* you been up to?'

'A long story, Mum, and one I'd be happy to share with you over a plate of food. I haven't eaten since midday.'

Hastily reassuring his parents that no, his unexpected appearance didn't mean he'd deserted or been drummed out of the army, showing them his travel warrant to prove it, explaining that his unit were given leave at short notice and he was in such a rush to come down it didn't occur to him to telephone one of his father's shoe repair shops, that there were problems with the tube that meant he decided to walk part of the way and being thirsty dropped into a pub and who should he bump into there but an old friend of cousin Margery's and, warning that there would be a few extra for tea tomorrow, Jon piled into the remains of a cold meat pie, raw carrots and bread followed by rhubarb pie, washed down with several cups of tea.

The next afternoon the house was filled with laughter and gaiety for the first time since Christmas, Margery bringing her sister Jenny and a mutual cousin Alan, on shore leave while his ship was being repaired, and Stella bringing her two friends from the previous evening. As she was leaving, Stella said, 'Would you appreciate the odd letter from a friend while you shiver this winter in the frozen north?' and Margery added eagerly, 'Oh, yes, give us your address up there,' so Jon did so, thinking, *CO's orders!*

A letter was waiting from Pat when Jon arrived back at camp. The sight of her handwriting brought a surge of protective affection and he thought of her hourglass figure and her high cheekbones and her sparking eyes and her hand trembling coyly in his and her *innocence* compared with the sirens with whom he'd shared the weekend, and he felt a heel for encouraging Stella.

*My dearest Jon*

*Thank you so much, my love, for your letter telling me that you are safe and well. I had worried myself quite unnecessarily over the summer and even got a letter from your mother wondering if I had heard from you – at which point I realised that your lack of correspondence was not with me only and while I'm sorry you mother was so concerned I admit I did breathe a sigh of relief that your silence was not of your choosing for I know how close you are to her and you would not wish her distressed unnecessarily.*

*Pardon my rambling, I am just so thrilled to have your letter I really don't know what to do with myself.*

*My hostess, Mrs Elaine Morley, has offered accommodation for you at her father-in-law's house, which adjoins us next door, should there be a chance of your snatching even just 24 hours' leave and coming over to Doncaster. Mrs Morley senior says that even in these wartime conditions it's not a difficult journey, via Manchester and Sheffield, or via Leeds. It would certainly be a quicker journey for you than if I were at college in London! Mr Morley senior is a builder and has a telephone, his number is Doncaster 2936, so if you can get to a telephone Elaine Morley says to just let her father-in-law know when you can come and she will make all the arrangements.*

*Jon, dearest, it would be so lovely to see you again. I am sorry we couldn't coincide your leave and my college holidays over Easter and with you being incommunicado over the summer and me up here in Doncaster for much of the year I have worked out that we were last together last Christmas. I would so love to see you again before this Christmas!*

Jon put the letter down. Ironic that he was now committed to going to London for leave when Pat was so much closer. He thought the problem through and decided he could just do it depending on the time he had to report for a reply. Leave on a Friday afternoon, do the drop, take the first train to Doncaster on the Saturday morning, spend time with Pat, go back to London on Sunday morning if, and only if, he was required to collect a reply. Then take the train back up to Bury. Only slight technical hitch was the cost. He couldn't use a travel warrant to travel between London and Doncaster as that would be picked up on by the lieutenant who issued it, so it would be rather expensive funding it, but not impossible. *I can tell her I've got 24 hours' leave Saturday morning to Sunday morning. Pat's own idea.*

Jon waited impatiently for the next Friday to arrive. Presenting himself at the major's door at twelve thirty, he was nonplussed to find that the major wasn't there. The lieutenant found him dithering outside and told him the major was away for a few days and, no, had left no instructions for Jon to take a message to the major's tailor in London, neither had he left instructions for a travel warrant to be issued for Jon.

At the post-lunch session Staff Sergeant Cooper told the unit that there would be no leave that weekend and they were to report for duty as usual the next morning, 'as Mr Hitler's war don't stop on a Friday afternoon so neither does ours.' The unit members grumbled among themselves later, Bertie storming ahead to their hut, and flinging himself on his bed thumping the mattress beside him exclaiming, 'Shit,' with each thud. 'Shit, shit, shit!'

'He's got a girrul and a cheap hotel lined up for the weekend in Manchester. He met her at a dance there last Saturday while you were away.' Graham, the tall, thin, auburnhaired highland Scot, older than Jon by two or three years, seconded from the Royal Engineers, explained to Jon. 'Don't understand it myself eitherrr. Last week we're told we're a Monday to Friday outfit, now we're not. What's gooing on?'

Jon shrugged. 'That's the army for you.' Thinking, *is this because the major's away and they don't need a cover for me being away on leave?*

'Fookin' army my arse,' said Bob, flicking back the quiff of his oily black hair and speaking loudly above Bertie's continued thumping and swearing. 'There's soomat fishy gooin' on.'

'All right, Bertie, we've got the message.' This loudly from Stephen in his melodious Welsh accent. He took off his cap, running his hand through his short cropped dark hair. 'I'll have to break the news to my girl too. Had her lined up for a dance in Bury tomorrow night.'

'Oh, surely they can't make us work Saturday night.'

'Ooh yes they can,' said Graham, 'Doon't you know there's a warrr on?'

The hut door opened and banged shut behind Peter who tossed a small mail sack on the table beside the door. 'Mine's a pint for getting this.'

'Bollocks,' said Bob. 'We all take our fookin' turn to get that. No one bought *me* a pint last week.'

*My social education started with my childhood at the Elephant and Castle,* Jon thought, *but even in one of the roughest parts of London Bob's language would take some beating.* Yet when it came to compiling reams of complicated mathematical formulae Bob was second to none. How Bob came to be picked for this specialist team of high- and public-schooled boffins Jon had no idea, but it showed that the system worked, for Bob's ability to cut to the chase and pick out the one weak link was most remarkable. For all his bluster Bob had the most precise and analytical brain of them all.

Graham, moving to the table, opened the bag and proceeded to lob its contents one by one to the recipients, commenting as he did so. Eventually he picked out a pink envelope, and, sniffing and 'Ahh'ing, tossed it in Jon's direction, declaring, 'Gardenia, I swearr that's garrdenia. A voluptuous young lady I fucked through the summer of 'forty wore gardenia. Herrr mother had a stash left overrr from before the warrr. I'd recognise it anywhere.'

Jon, diving for the envelope, expected Pat's flowing writing and was nonplussed to see a rounded, more childish hand. He opened it warily, exclaiming, 'Good God,' when he saw the signature at the bottom of the fourth and last page. *Good girl*, he added silently.

''Oo is it, mate?' Bob asked, intrigued by Jon's reaction.

'Someone I was hoping to see this weekend,' Jon lied, then, remembering his hard-on in the pub, allowed a curl of his lip at the half-lie and he must have given something away in his expression for Bertie, recovering from his anguish and swinging his long legs over the edge of the bed, said, 'Ah ha, perhaps not his young lady in Doncaster?'

Bob grabbed the envelope.

'London postmark.'

Bertie repeated his question as a statement. '*Not* his young lady in Doncaster!'

'Fookin' two-timer,' Bob said, admiration tinging his tone. 'There's oos thinkin' yer's too much of a toff ter dip yer wick in one and we find yer's got two on the go at the same fookin' time. You'll be needing dooble the army condom issue at this rate.'

Putting the letter back in the envelope retrieved from Bob after a playful tussle, Jon placed it in his top pocket to read in detail later. 'Any more post for the rest, Graham?' he asked.

'Don't change the subject,' said Graham, 'You've been well and trrruly found out!'

Another three weeks passed before Jon was sent to London again. By now it was early October and Pat's letters had become increasingly frantic, while Stella's had become increasingly saucy. He left earlier than last time, skipping lunch, ears ringing to 'Get stuck in there, mate,' and 'Give her one from me,' and 'Here, catch, have my spare,' and he was in and out of Whitehall Terrace a good hour earlier than before. 'Report to me at twelve hundred hours at twenty one Camden High Road. Go round to the alley at the back and up the steps to the door. Same knock and pass-word phrases as for here. Wear civvies.'

Damn, to be sure of getting get back in time he'd have to leave Doncaster at the crack of dawn and even then it would be touch and go. He felt weary, the tension of the cloak and dagger routine draining, and he wondered if Stella would be in the Red Lion this evening. Determined to walk straight past, weakening at the last moment and arguing to himself that stopping for a pint wouldn't take much out of his evening, he was immensely disappointed that Stella wasn't there. Finding a corner to perch, nursing his dwindling pint and still debating whether to attempt a lightening visit to Doncaster, he suddenly spotted her making her way to the bar. He sidled up to her.

'Stella, it is Stella, isn't it?'

Stella turned and, shrieking, threw her arms around his neck, hugging him tight as he fought to keep the remains of the beer in the glass. He felt an instant response to her and shrank his hips back a little, not wishing to give too much away, but the tilt of her head before she pulled his head down and planted a firm kiss on his lips suggested otherwise.

'*Naughty* boy,' she said, as if she knew he liked to hear her say that to him. 'Not been home yet again, soldier?' Dierdre and Bridget, and another girl, short, dark and busty, intro-duced as Beryl, crowded round and soon he was enjoying another evening of risqué anecdotes and adoring feminine company. Their merriment attracted other comers and by the time he made his excuses the girls were surrounded by enough male hangers-on, he thought, to make his departure insignificant. Stella came to the door again.

'Thank you for your letters,' he said. 'I should have men-tioned it sooner. They've been just the ticket.' *For keeping the pretence up*, he told himself, *for following orders*.

'I'm free tomorrow.'

Decision made.

'What would you like to do?' Catching the gleam in her eye, hastily adding, 'Cinema, I mean? Trip out of London somewhere? Meet at Victoria Station and decide when we know what the weather's like? Midday? We can make the most of the day. Evenings are drawing in now, and I'd like to see you home safely.'

They caught the train to Dorking the following day, grabbing lunch in a café in the high street and enjoying the warm autumn sunshine in the park sloping up towards the North Downs.

'I'd take you to Box Hill,' said Jon, 'but it's requisitioned like any piece of open land.' He pointed out the high ridge-line beyond the main road. 'I'm determined to go there one day. I'm told you can see the South Downs thirty miles away on a good day.'

'I don't really know the area,' said Stella. 'Have you been here much before?'

Jon shook his head. 'Not Dorking. But I know Leatherhead just north of here. Pat was evacuated there and I've a pretty good idea of the lie of the land.'

'Pat.'

*Stupid, stupid, why mention her now? Because I'm feeling guilty.*

He shrugged. 'Friend of a friend.'

Stella turned to him. 'Jon, I'm not *daft*. Margery told me you've a young lady tucked away in the north. But sometimes, Jon, you just have to live in the moment. God knows that's how we survived the Blitz. Then there was the bombing we had here last January and March and again in June. Who knows when Jerry will come hunting again? Could be tomorrow. Or who knows when you'll be sent into the thick of it? We've got Sicily under our belts and we're into Italy and they said on the wireless only last week we've taken Naples. Everyone knows all these troops over here mean we'll be going for northern Europe one day.' She raised a hand, placing it on his shoulder. 'I'm not looking for a commitment from you. Just some fun in a drab, rationed, regulated life.'

When she kissed him again he kissed her back and held her close for several minutes. 'Thank you, Stella,' he said, *and you've* no idea *how your affection for me is helping the war effort.*

He forced himself to limit their physical contact to kissing, hugging and a little groping, sensing her frustration, regretting his self-control that night as he lay in bed remembering the imprint of her warm, curvy body against his, the weight of her breast against his hand.

Two weeks later he was sent to London again, the same frantic rush, the same routine except this time no reply to collect, so a chance go for Plan B. Steeling himself to carry on past the Red Lion and, racing to his father's nearest shop, he found him closing for the night.

'Just in time,' he panted. 'Dad, may I use the telephone?'

At the other end a gruff, deep Yorkshire accented voice answered and assured him he would be heartily welcome to stay the following night and that it would cheer the lass up no end to see him, in fact he would go round straight away to let her know. Jon obtained directions to the house from the station, insisting that he would appreciate the walk after the journey. 'Please tell Pat not to trouble to meet me. I don't know what time I'll arrive. I'll come straight to your house,' he added.

Arriving at Doncaster shortly before midday he saw that a train from Sheffield had just arrived beforehand and was still puffing and snorting away from one platform as he alighted from his train on another. Sauntering over the footbridge, recalling Mr Morley's directions, on descending the steps he was captured by a distant vision in dark green and soft golds, her face anxiously searching the disgorged passengers streaming towards her. *She always dresses so elegantly despite the utility garments, her clothes are always beautifully co-ordinated, she has a timeless beauty and she's mine*, he thought. Her eyes passed over him and beyond and shot back and she was hurrying towards him, tentatively holding out a hand, timorous, uncertain, vulnerable. The contrast with Stella's greeting two weeks earlier could not have been greater and he felt an almost overwhelming wave of love and lust and affection towards her and relief that he still felt the same in her presence as he remembered.

*I want to cherish her, provide for her, protect her, fuck her. Christ, she's such an innocent she probably doesn't even know what the word means.*

Relief spreading, tears glistening, she gabbled, 'It's so lovely to see you. I thought I saw everyone off the Sheffield train but I couldn't see you, I was so worried.'

'I stopped for a call of nature,' Jon lied and she flushed, embarrassed, he thought, at evincing a confession of such a personal matter, 'and I got caught up with passengers coming off the train from London.'

He bent and kissed her chastely on the cheek, and, hitching his rucksack over one shoulder, took her arm and together they turned and she led him out of the smart modern station into the Victorian centre of Doncaster.

'You must see St George's Church where we do fire-watching duties,' she said. 'It's quite magnificent.'

And it was. A mini-cathedral astonishingly recreated by the Victorians looking as authentic as its thirteenth century original. She showed him the tiny side door that led directly to the tower's spiral staircase and he looked up in horror at the height of the roof and the tiny low balustrade with a sheer drop beside which she passed in the course of her duties.

'The church burnt down in the 1850s,' said his tour guide. 'You'll never guess the architect who rebuilt it.' Jon didn't. 'Sir George Gilbert Scott,' she said as if that explained everything, and, thinking hard, Jon came up with, 'The Albert Memorial?' and, slipping her hand from his arm, she clapped excitedly like a small child.

'Doncaster has some real gems,' she said. 'I'm so thrilled I can show them to you.' Jon's travel weariness fell away as he caught her infectious mood. Turning down St George's

Gate, Pat led him to the market area where he admired the magnificent late nineteenth century Corn Exchange, then back to the High Street where, towards the end on the right, she indicted a nondescript building at ground floor level.

'This is St Gabriel's headquarters. Although we use a number of venues, we do have a few lectures here squeezed into rooms at the back. But cross over,' which they did, 'and look up,' which Jon also did, 'isn't that exquisite?' Jon thought the bold blue and gold tiled first and second floor frontage interspersed with six imperialistic ionic columns and topped by a classical, flattened, inverted V somewhat gaudy, but her enthusiasm, eyes shining, head tilted up expectantly, *again*, thought Jon, *childlike*, tempered his honesty, and he assented.

'We could get a bus from here,' said Pat, 'but there's a road I really want to show you on foot. It's on our way.' She led him to Hall Gate and stopped, looking up the gentle slope of Hall Cross Hill towards the cross itself.

'Close your eyes and I'll turn you round a couple of times, then open them and imagine you're here two hundred years ago in the heart of Georgian Doncaster,' said Pat and he did so, and because she loved the jumble of tall, elegant eighteenth century buildings rising ahead of them, Jon found that he did too.

Mr Morley senior was out when they arrived and Elaine was helping with the preparation of the evening meal. Mrs Morley senior packed them off towards her front room with a 'Eh up, my dears, make yourselves at home. I'll get you some tea and a quick bite to eat. I expect you're hungry now. How was your journey, lad?' To Jon's non-committal reply Mrs Morley added, 'I know, there's only so much the likes of you can tell the likes of us.' Pat smiled at Jon apologetically, following Mrs Morley into the kitchen and on bringing the tea tray found Jon coming back downstairs. She blushed, he thought, at the realisation of the small room he had just visited, and she ushered him into the front room and shut the door firmly, placing the tray on a small table.

Alone for a moment, Pat hesitated, seeming suddenly shy again, and, drawing her to him, wrapping his arms around her, he kissed her gently on her lips. *She's so sweet, so tasty, so delicious.* He wanted to thrust his tongue between her lips mimicking the act he *really* wanted to exercise upon her, but he was afraid of alienating her when she was at last alone and in his arms again. *Time enough for that,* he thought. *She's like a startled doe, trembling, ever ready to flee at the slightest danger.* After several moments of dislocation from his surroundings he forced himself back to the reality of the ticking mantelpiece clock and the distant kitchen clatter, but he kept his hips pressed against her, noting a slight widening of her eyes as he looked down at her. Placing a hand behind her head he drew it into his shoulder and she seemed to melt into him, and they stood silent for a while, unmoving, content.

Later, handing him a cup, seated on the settee beside him, Pat said, 'Elaine says we're eating supper together with her parents and a visitor, though in my rush to meet you I didn't catch who, probably one of Mr Morley's contacts in the building trade or some army bigwig staying in the area. Even though Elaine lives next door we often eat like this and Mr Morley likes to combine business with pleasure. It's a difficult time for them all with Harold Morley away fighting in Italy.'

Jon looked out of the window. 'We seem to be at the modern outskirts of Doncaster. Is there much countryside around here not taken over by the army where we could take a stroll before supper?'

Pat thought. 'The racecourse nearby's been requisitioned, but I'm not sure about the hinterland the other way. I'll ask Mrs Morley.'

After finishing their snack they set off eastwards, Pat pointing out the extent of the large, new estate, saying proudly, 'Mr Morley built all the houses around here just before the outbreak of war. Did you notice that his and his son's houses are a cut above the rest? He's had to put the house building business in abeyance, of course, and is busy instead with government and army contracts of various sorts.'

'I'm pleased to see you're settled into what seems a nice family. I recall you telling me about your hit and miss experience in Leatherhead.'

'That seems such a long time ago now. London seems such a long way away too. It must be difficult for you, like me, stuck in the north and not able to get back to see parents.' Pat looked up at him, eyes innocently wide, but he sensed a probing and replied, a little uneasily, 'Well, you can't have everything when there's a war on.'

Turning along the edge of the estate southwards, Pat led him to a farm track opposite, running up an incline. 'Mrs Morley says if we stick to this track and go through the farm and up towards those trees we should get a good view of Doncaster. She sometimes comes to the farm to get a few extras. But please don't tell anyone I said that,' she added hastily.

The lowering clouds threatened rain as they stopped at the treeline on the ridge above the farm buildings, picking out the top of the tall crenellated church tower in the far distance riding like a ship's funnel above the sea of roofs and treetops. Drawing Pat against himself, as much for mutual warmth as for affection, shivering, embracing and laughing aloud at the sheer pleasure of togetherness, Jon thought, *this has to be the very best moment of 1943 so far. If only I could bottle it and take it back with me.*

Although the table was laid for six, five sat down for supper and Jon wondered if the guest was not coming. However, just as Mrs Morley was carrying a bowl of steaming potatoes, Elaine following with a steaming bowl of mashed swede, the front door knocker rapped and Mr Morley bustled off to greet his guest.

Moments later he returned ushering in a tall, sandy-haired army officer carrying a peaked cap who was saying, 'It's swell of you to put me up at short notice. I hope I won't put you guys to too much trouble.'

Seated next to him, Jon felt Pat stiffen and heard her gasp. Turning his head, he saw a fleeting expression on her face of shock and horror, and something else he could not define. Grief? As he said softly, urgently, 'Pat?' her expression transformed, a huge emotional effort, into a tentative smile, a rictus, of welcome.

The newcomer, picking out with his deep blue eyes the oldest lady at the table and inclining his head towards Mrs Morley, said, 'Major Joshua Bowman at your service, ma'am,' and he held out his hand and shook hers firmly. Mrs Morley simpered and welcomed him, introducing Elaine, Pat and Jon in turn.

Mr Morley, disappearing for a moment and returning with three bottles of beers in one arm and a bottle opener in the other, asked the major,

'Beer, lad?' and, turning, offered the same to Jon, who thanked him and took one, the other being passed to the major who was settling himself at the remaining place at the table end beyond Pat.

Jon said, smiling, 'I understand you chaps like your beer ice cold. We may not have refrigeration over here but it gives you a chance to enjoy the flavour more.' To Mr Morley, 'Is this a Doncaster brew?'

'Payment in kind for work I did for Darley's at Thorne,' said Mr Morley. He turned to the major. 'That's oop north east o' here, past racecourse and keep going.' Settling himself down and diving into the laden plate appearing in front of him, he waved his fork in the direction of the major, similarly victualled, urging, 'Eat oop now, don't let it get cold, lad.' As the major duly obliged, Mr Morley added, 'Talking of t'racecourse, how're your lads settling in?'

Major Bowman gave a non-committal reply and for a few moments conversation was desultory as hunger pangs were assuaged.

Mr Morley persevered. 'Long journey, eh, lad? I'm told you're on your way to Scotland.'

The major hesitated. Jon offered, 'We understand you may be unable to tell us about military matters, sir. Have you ever been to London on leave at all?'

The major, relaxing a little, said, 'Why yes, my last billet was near a cute town called Guildford near London. D'you know that part of England?'

Jon explained Pat's Leatherhead connection and that although neither of them had been as far as Guildford, they understood it had a castle and a steep cobbled High Street.

'Sure has,' said the major. 'A month ago we marched up that High Street celebrating three years since you British won the Battle of Britain.'

Pat was picking up her glass of water as he spoke; she jerked and water spilled, and while Mrs Morley fussed with mopping it up, Mr Morley exclaimed, 'Eh, you two lads should've been in Doncaster here for our own Battle of Britain celebration last month. Quite a parade it were. It were grand.'

'So you're visiting, yourself?' asked the major of Jon.

'Yes, I'm with a REME unit in Lancashire. Nothing special,' he added self-effacingly. 'Just searchlight maintenance and learning how to teach it. First chance to pop across the Pennines to say hello.' He felt Pat stiffen again, but she said nothing, her expression schooled, her fork chasing the food around her plate.

Elaine said, 'My husband was in Sicily and he's now with the eighth army in Italy.'

The conversation moved on to the Italian campaign, the major's home city of Toronto, what he liked about England and, after some prompting, what he didn't like, the major protesting that he was sure he'd come round to warm beer and cricket before the war was over.

'I guess anyone from abroad'll get homesick from time to time, but I discovered the best antidote in London. A swell place, the only one in England to serve authentic Canadian pancakes with maple syrup. Quite a griddle room they've got there.'

'The Beaver Club,' Jon said triumphantly.

'Why, yes, d'you know it?'

'Not been there myself but Pat's mother works there.'

'You don't say!' Turning and seeming to look at Pat properly for the first time.

Pat smiled wanly, 'Yes,' leaping up with alacrity to help as Mrs Morley gathered the dishes, busying herself with fetching and carrying. Jon was alarmed at Pat's pallor and detachment from the social interaction of the evening. *She seems out of sorts. She used to be such a sociable creature. This Canadian chap really seems to have spooked her. Perhaps she's sickening for something.*

After supper Elaine offered Pat and Jon the sitting room of her house. 'I'll stop with Mum and Dad for a while. Give you and your young man a little time together.' Pat accepted with alacrity and led Jon away, visibly relaxing as they left the major to the mercy of Mr Morley and his Great War service.

'Pat, what is it?' Jon asked as they entered the house. 'You seemed upset by the major. I would've thought having the Beaver Club in common would give you something to talk to him about.'

Drawing a shaky breath, Pat stepped up to him and he pulled her into a gentle embrace.

'It's nothing really. I just wanted to be alone with you and found it a bit of a strain, that's all.'

The rest of the weekend passed too quickly for both of them. Pat saw him off at the station the following lunchtime, eyes bright with unshed tears, cheek muscles trembling from forced smiling. *She's so fragile,* he thought. *I want to wrap her up and cocoon her from the rest of the world.*

'I'll come and see you again,' he said.

Another month passed until the next trip to London, with

a reply to collect. He went to the cinema with Stella who let slip casually on meeting, 'Dierdre and Bridget are away for the weekend,' and later, reaching her digs, she invited him in for a drink. *Thank God I didn't get rid of the condoms*, he thought, to a familiar hardening. *But my vest, Christ, what if she spots the pouch?* She saw his hesitation and, misreading it, sighed. 'Don't worry, your loyalty does you credit.' Reaching up she kissed him briefly, just brushing his lips. 'See you around, soldier.'

Jon staggered home, aroused, regretting the lost moment, horrified at how close he had been to accepting, trying to recapture the wonder and awe of his love for Pat and hating the army, the war, the deception, the whole thing. If it wasn't for the war he'd be with Pat in his spare time, working his way up from office junior, eighteen months into night classes for Sanitary Inspector training, they might be engaged and he might have got further with Pat than a few chaste kisses. *Instead I might go out in a bombing raid tonight or there could be an attack on northern towns, and I might never... I'm not stupid, Stella was handing it to me on a plate. What would the chaps think if they only knew I'm not dipping my wick in either. Fucking vest.* Not daring to leave it behind in his rucksack in case his mother took it into her head to check for any loose items to add to her laundering of his uniform today, it had saved him, yet condemned him to another night of torment.

'You're seeing a lot of this Stella,' observed his mother over breakfast the next morning. Jon grunted non-committedly. 'What does your Pat make of it?'

'It's nothing to do with Pat. A chap can spend an evening with a girl without anything untoward. Pat's best friend was Bill, that's how I met her if you remember. Stella's a friend of Margery's. There's nothing in it.'

'It'll get round the family through Margery,' said his mother, ignoring his protests. 'Next I know, Rose'll be round to find out more.'

*A bevy of aunts in south London's not such a bonus after all,*

251

thought Jon. *Christ, what if Mum decides to tell Pat? I wouldn't put it past her.*

He tried a different tack, widening his eyes, drooping the edges of his mouth, trying to put on a little-boy-lost look.

'Mum, I'll confess I'm going through a bit of a rough patch and I need your help here. I'm fond of Pat but I've only seen her the once since last Christmas, and she seemed remote and detached. I'm not sure how that's going to work out and meanwhile,' turning to include his father, 'I'll admit only to you and Dad that I enjoy Stella's company and I look forward to coming home on leave as much because of her as to see you. But I feel a sense of duty to Pat and I don't want her hurt, or at least any more than is necessary. So it's really important to me to sort my priorities out first and if there's anyone to tell Pat it has to be me and no one else. Please promise you won't write to Pat and tell her anything about Stella or of me coming home on leave instead of going to see her. She thinks I've only had the one leave weekend since the summer and I want to keep it that way. *Please.*'

Receiving a promise of silence from his parents, he finished his breakfast, now leaden in his stomach, and gathered his belongings ready for his departure.

'I'll walk with you to the corner,' said his father, and, as they reached the main road, out of sight of the house, his father turned searching blue eyes on him and said, 'Your mother thinks you're playing Jack-the-Lad and is very disappointed in you. She thinks you should make up your mind. And she favours Stella. Is she right? That you're playing the field? Or is there something more to your surprise visits?'

Jon looked helplessly at his father. *If I say no, Mum's right, he'll think badly of me, but I can't tell him the truth.*

His father smiled. 'I thought so. Keep up the good work, my boy, whatever it is.' Jon tried to school his expression but must have been unable to prevent a certain amount of alarm showing, for his father said, 'Don't worry, I'll do my best to keep your mother off the scent and quiet on the Pat front.

I'll even erase my thoughts when you've gone. Just take care now, my boy,' and, reaching up and patting Jon on the back, turned and limped away.

The pale pink envelopes continued to arrive to Jon's relief and Bob continued to admire Jon's virility.

One more trip to London two weeks before Christmas, again a reply to bring back. Then all Christmas leave cancelled.

'It's like we're bloody prisoners,' said Bertie gloomily. 'We modify the specifications for the bloody computer then they have to be manufactured and tested and we twiddle our thumbs for days doing our smokescreen teaching bloody searchlight maintenance and routine AA stuff with the rest of the crew. I know what I'd rather twiddle while I'm waiting.'

Jon, alarmed at Bertie's indiscretion over the computer, slipped out of the door and made a quick circuit around the hut. No one appeared to be nearby. He slipped back.

'For fuck's sake, Jon, no one's going to be listening to us. We're not even regular army. Who's going to be interested in us?'

'You'd be surprised, Bertie. Even within the hut. After all, any one of us could be a government plant to check out whether anyone's giving away secrets.'

'Don't be so paranoid,' said Peter. 'You've been reading too many of your cloak-and-dagger books.'

Christmas Dinner in the canteen hut turned out to be quite a big party with soldiers from other units who hadn't gone away on leave joining in. The ATS girls organised a dance for the evening and, being fewer in number, were in much demand. Jon didn't feel like dancing, and sat it out, playing whist and three card brag in the corner in a foursome with Graham and two sappers from a temporarily posted Royal Engineers regiment. Bob came by with a busty brunette on his arm, saying, 'What, no girl, Jon, findin' two on the goo too knackerin' for a third, eh, mate?'

and saying to his audience, "E's a reet woon 'e is,' to Jon's embarrassment.

Jon managed another surprise trip to Doncaster the following February but all the other runs involved collecting a reply around Sunday lunchtime and he didn't dare risk missing the rendezvous. The months passed and gradually the camp's occupants were moved out southwards as part of the build up to the coming invasion of northern Europe, leaving behind Jon's unit in near solitary occupation except for brief hosting of regiments journeying south from training grounds in Scotland.

# 13

# Buzz Bombs

I got up extravagantly later than usual the morning of the first Tuesday of June, the students in my year having a reduced timetable in advance of final exams.

'I'll be popping off to the shops soon,' said Elaine. 'Is there anything you need?'

'No, but thanks,' I said, buttering toast at the dining table and eating only on my left side because of a niggly tooth. 'I'm going into the college offices later for a revision lecture so I'll get anything I need when I'm in town.'

The hall clock started whirring, a preliminary to chiming and striking eleven.

'I'll just listen to the start of the news before I go,' said Elaine, turning the dial up on the sideboard wireless. We were electrified by the announcer's words, 'This is the BBC Home Service. This is a special bulletin read by John Stagge,' followed by Mr Stagge's measured tones.

'D-Day has come.'

Elaine and I looked at each other with startled eyes.

'Early this morning the Allies began the assault on the north face of Hitler's European fortress. The first official news came just after half past nine when Supreme Headquarters of the Allied Expeditionary Force issued Communique number one. This said, "Under the command of General Eisenhower, Allied Naval Forces supported by strong air forces began landing Allied armies this morning on the northern coast of France".'

*It's actually happening!* Four years almost to the day I'd wept for the wounded, killed and captured of Dunkirk, I laid my head in my arms and wept unashamedly for the brave men at this very moment laying down their lives, for the wounded crying out in agony and for all whose lives were about to be abruptly cut short in the days ahead.

Elaine stood stunned for a few moments as the announcer moved on to a recording from a front line reporter.

'The paratroops are landing.' Gunfire sounded in the background. 'They're landing all round me as I speak. They've come in from the sea and they're fluttering down and they're just about the best thing we've seen in a good many hours. They're showering in, there's no other word for it.'

'*Harold*,' moaned Elaine and, dashing and wrenching open the back door, ran to her parents' house.

Injured in the Allied landing at Anzio, morose and bad tempered on three months' recovery leave, it was a relief to me when Harold Morley was pronounced fit in April and posted to another regiment in the south of England. No more nights disturbed by a distant drumming growing faster and faster, no more grunts and groans emanating from the next room and no more *I know exactly what you're doing and I shouldn't, I shouldn't* thoughts swimming round my head leaving me breathless and yearning. Elaine told me his parting words were, 'I'm joining t'build up for t'northern invasion. You'd've thought I've already done enough bloody invasions to last a lifetime.'

And now it was really happening and I wondered why Jon wasn't taking part. At least, as far as I knew he wasn't. His last letter from Bury ten days ago had been short and terse, but had given no hint that he was involved in the massive troop movements taking place over the past few weeks. I thought briefly of the Canadian major on his way to Scotland with his troops last autumn and I wondered if they had since been training for these beach landings. The North Sea off Scotland must have been a terribly cold practice arena in winter compared with the English Channel in summer, though the south must have been pretty chilly overnight after massive storms there yesterday and the overall forecast was not good.

Torn between the spellbinding reports on the wireless and my revision lecture, I scrambled out of the house at the last minute and was lucky to find a trolley bus at its turnaround. Arriving only a couple of minutes late, I realised I wasn't the last as there was a smaller number than usual and Nicola dashed in shortly after me. Miss Russell said, 'In view of the tremendous news this morning and the distraction it has caused, we'll wait a few more minutes. So take a break, girls, for ten minutes and we'll reconvene at twelve-fifteen.'

An excited chattering broke out, some girls weeping, others smiling, and Betty said, 'My Dad's there, he's a senior glider pilot officer. I hope he's all right,' and burst into tears and we crowded round to comfort her.

As the month unfolded and the slow, slow progress in France was reported hourly, I was relieved to receive a letter from Jon in Bury, proof that he was safe and not involved in the fighting. My niggly tooth continued to niggle and I dosed up with painkillers preparing for my final exams. The intense two year college course was nearly at an end, and I became increasingly worried that I had not secured a position for the coming September. I was looking for posts in and around London so I could be nearer home. Invited to interview in North London in mid-June I was bitterly disappointed not to be offered the post. My father was philosophical.

'You can't win 'em all. There's always something better round the corner.'

During my flying visit home, I took the opportunity to consult my dentist in Acre Lane, almost opposite the Town Hall. 'Hmm,' he said. 'It's cracked and needs a fair amount of repair. See if we can fit you in for a forty-minute session next week.' But my last exam was on the Wednesday and there were no available appointments for the Friday following, so after some humming and hawing I made the appointment for two weeks later, 28th June at 12.30pm.

My mother was delighted I would be returning soon. 'Oh, my dear,' she said, 'I read the most dreadful story in the paper today about a new kind of rocket plane that came down in Hackney yesterday and exploded and killed several people. Everyone I spoke to at the market this morning reckons it's the start of something new. It'll be lovely to have your company again after your last exam if we're going to be under the cosh again.'

'D'you think that's Hitler's secret weapon?' I speculated. 'Everyone laughed about it because they didn't think it was real, but I bet no one's laughing now. Mummy, I'm sorry, I'll have to go back to Doncaster for a final week or so after the dentist for the exam results which are being posted the first Monday in July, and I'll need to organise my trunk with my things and my artwork, but I'll do my best to get away for good as soon after that as I can.'

Booty stretched and padded over to me, rubbing around my legs and leaping up into my lap. 'And,' I continued to him, stroking and petting under his chin, 'it'll be lovely to be back sharing my room with you for good.'

Leaving London behind I discovered over the next few days that I was leaving behind the biggest threat to London since the Blitz. Even the Little Blitz retaliations in January following the British bombing of Berlin had petered out, helped by new anti-aircraft batteries in London. But this new threat was too much and hearing of the destruction of the Guards Chapel at Wellington Barracks in the middle of a service killing over one hundred people I began to feel I had no weeping left to do.

Taking the exams, my tooth still sore, desperately worried about my parents in a part of London taking the brunt of the new bombing, I was relieved to return home the day after my final exam and find everything as I had left it. I spent the next afternoon, a Friday, meandering through Brixton Market and calling in on my grandmother and Mr Torston in Strathleven Road on my way back. Thinking to pick up last minute groceries from a shop on Brixton Hill, I wove my way through backstreets and was about to enter the grocer's when I heard the distant approach from the south of a low vibrating sound, like an approaching train, growing ever louder and increasingly filling the air. Looking south east, through a gap in the opposite trees, a small aeroplane appeared briefly over distant rooftops. The low moan suddenly stopped and there was an eerie silence as the plane plunged in a steep arc and disappeared towards the far end of the opposite side road. Perhaps twelve or fifteen seconds after the droning cut out came the sound of a tremendous explosion and a column of smoke rose in the air.

'Oh my God, the people!' I ran as fast as I could, skidding across the main road and around the corner, haring down Beechdale Road, heart thudding, lungs screaming for air, and at the far end saw gaps where several buildings had stood, only side walls remaining like the spokes of a huge waterwheel, neighbouring buildings either side sliced through, opened up like a giant's dollshouse, furniture hanging precariously over the precipice. Neighbours desperately clawed at the ruins despite the smoke and flames spewing upwards, a man with an air raid warden's armband trying to take charge, crying hoarsely, 'Look out, the next one's going,' and part of a high dividing wall collapsing, blowing more dust and sparks into the air. I stopped at a little girl lying in the road. She seemed unharmed, stunned, perhaps, no blood or obvious wound. Her eyes were open, looking at me, I thought, and my college's first aid training kicked in, feeling for the pulse in her neck, then in her wrist, and frantically kneeling to check her breathing.

'It's the back blast wot's done fer 'er,' said a man crouching beside me, and he picked her body up, moving it out of the road and laying it gently down in a nearby front garden.

Joining people from nearby houses I carried on to the edge of the rubble, but the sound of the fire brigade and ambulances approaching told me there was nothing I could do that the professionals couldn't. Turning my back to the scene of devastation I saw a leg hanging over the branch of a nearby blasted, leafless, tree, and, higher up, the torso, the blood still draining, painting the side of the tree trunk dark red, the ragged remains of a frock hanging down in strips, a bizarre parody of bunting at a church fete.

I staggered and vomited onto the side of the road until my stomach was sore, scoured out, had nothing more to give. Weeping and trembling, retrieving my bag from where I had dropped it to minister to the little girl, I slunk away, ashamed at my weakness, my helplessness, my shoes crunching on the broken glass of the nearby blasted windows, as more and more people and vehicles crowded down the road.

Every time I closed my eyes that night I saw the little girl and what I surmised were the remains of her mother before me and I slept only through exhaustion.

The world gradually righting itself, by the following Wednesday I allowed the bright midday sun to warm me through as I made my way to the junction of Acre Lane by the Town Hall. My dentist's was in a Victorian building above a shop next but one down from a rest centre on the opposite corner for bombed out people. I wondered whether any of the survivors of the Beechdale Road bomb were staying there. As I climbed the stairs, the dentist popped his head round the door of his surgery at the front, saying, 'Oh, good, you're early and the person before you's not here so I can get on with it straight away.'

Taking up the dentist's offer to numb the tooth and gum, I waited about twenty minutes for the injection to take effect, passing the time chatting to the receptionist in the small rear waiting room.

'Ready now?' I followed Mr Marshall back into his

surgery and settled back, watching a desultory bird swooping outside the window facing the chair.

After a bit of prodding Mr Marshall picked up the drill and started. A moment or two later I thought the drill was developing a fault for it seemed to get gradually louder and even more growly. Mr Marshall stopped drilling but the buzzing didn't and we looked at each other in consternation. The sound arrived overhead and suddenly cut out. No words were needed. Mr Marshall threw down the drill, grabbing my arm as I hauled myself out of the seat, and we dived for the door, squeezing through together and throwing ourselves to the floor of the corridor as the V1 exploded.

The blast sounded every bit as loud as I remembered of the bomb in the Leatherhead field, the building shaking, taking the force of the blast wave as, with a high pitched instant shriek, the windows in the building shattered inwards and plaster from the ceiling rained down. The receptionist had also made for the landing serving the two rooms and was lying on the floor ahead of us crying. Trembling, I half sat up and realised Mr Marshall was mouthing something but I could hear him only faintly beyond the familiar high pitched ringing. *At least I remembered the trick with the mouth again*, I thought, as the receptionist and Mr Marshall both wiped blood trickling from their ears.

Sitting half propped against the wall, listening to the emergency services' response, I realised to my surprise that the building itself had survived. I recalled the curved trajectory of the falling pilotless plane above Beechdale Road and thought, *if it stopped overhead, its trajectory probably propelled it to a couple of buildings or so beyond us. Oh, God, not the rest centre beyond the next door church. Let it be the church*, I prayed, *and let there have been no one in the church at the time.*

Returning to the surgery to retrieve my bag I stood shocked in front of the chair. The green leather upholstery was shredded by the shards of glass from the shattered window, transparent daggers still embedded.

Mr Marshall followed me in. 'Oh my dear,' he said, as if from a distance. 'What a narrow escape. For us both.'

I turned to go, attempting to brush plaster powder off my clothes but only smearing it into the cloth.

'Come back tomorrow and I'll fix your tooth. If we're not up and running, I'll find you someone locally who can.'

Emerging from the building my worst fear was realised. The rest centre was a blasted crater, body parts strewn across the road. People were walking about dazed and shocked, blood pouring from cuts from the shattered windows. A man hurrying past said to me, 'You look as if you've seen a ghost,' and I raised my hand to my hair and it came away white with the powdered plaster, and I bent and beat out as much out as I could. My stomach churning at my narrow escape and the carnage around me, I crossed the road towards the Town Hall entrance. The Town Hall had survived but the windows were wrecked. People were flocking from the plaza in front of the cinema to help. An official of sorts stood on the Town Hall steps beckoning people in the direction of the entrance. A passer-by, blood trickling from a head wound, said to me, 'Where can I go?' 'This way,' I said, pleased to have something to do, ushering him towards the Town Hall front step, the official nodding to me to bring him in. For about fifteen or twenty minutes I helped shepherd the walking wounded to the entrance foyer where first aiders were setting up a temporary post. I said to the man in charge, 'I've done a first aid course at college, can I help?' and so stayed for a while longer helping to clean superficial wounds and bandage them, the Town Hall's own first aid supplies being raided.

As I walked home later the hopelessness overwhelmed me and the road ahead was just a blur. *Why can't they stop this? When will it ever end? How come we're three weeks into the Second Front and still they keep coming? The Germans haven't even got the decency to send men for us to fight but only these unspeakable automated weapons of destruction.*

Only when my mother, shrieking in horror at my dishevelled, plaster-smeared appearance, pointed to dried blood on my neck did I realise that I too had been cut by flying glass on the side of my head.

Returning to Doncaster two days later with a repaired tooth was a blessed relief. No buzz bombs, no terror from the skies. I felt guilty that my parents were in the thick of it. That evening I wrote a long letter to Jon, telling him the events of the past week, leaving nothing out.

*This has to be stopped*, I concluded. *What is the government doing about these things? Nothing! It's taken too long for the Allied forces to get round to the invasion. And now it's underway, when will they reach Germany and end the war? They've only just taken Caen! We are assuming victory but even if it is eventually achieved it's not going to meanwhile stop the dreadful slaughter that is right now happening before my eyes. Everyone scoffed at Hitler's secret weapon. What was the government doing to prevent it? Nothing! Where is the AA defence against these things? Nowhere! Surely we should be able to shoot these things down as they come. But all our AA guns seem to do is point vaguely in the right direction and hope for the best. Compared with conventional aeroplanes these pilotless planes are small. I know, I saw one. It may have been at a distance but I saw the planes flying in the Battle of Britain and even the smallest, the Spitfires, were very much bigger than these new strange creatures. Even so, they are big enough to see clearly in the sky and surely by now our guns should be sophisticated enough to bring them down before they reach us. I am angry, so angry that people are dying and nothing is being done about it. And I am so scared for my parents. Just when we thought the war would soon be over we are now facing a new threat.*

*I am sorry, Jon, that you are bearing the brunt of my anger and my grief. Please forgive me for burdening you. I do appreciate your contribution to the war effort as searchlights are needed to spot the ones coming over at night for our fighters to aim at even if the AA guns are useless. I thank God every night that your unit keeps you in Lancashire away from these new menaces.*

*Is there any chance I will see you again soon? I am returning to*

*London next week for good. In Bury you have been comparatively so near and yet so far. I love you and I miss you.*
  *Your*
  *Pat*

I was delighted with my exam results posted on the following Monday morning and some of the girls and I treated ourselves to lunch at Parkinson's café in the High Street, crowding into one of the round Georgian bay windows, and buying tins of precious Parkinson's butterscotch as mementos and presents. I was even more thrilled to find a letter awaiting me on my return to my billet late that afternoon from the Headmistress of Hammersmith Central School for Girls inviting me for interview for a second art teacher position which would also involve a mix of other subjects, a perfect start to a teaching career. Although the school was officially evacuated, so many girls remained in London the school needed staff to cover their London venue. I did a double take on the interview date. This coming Thursday. I dashed off a note to my parents straight away in the hope it would reach them on Wednesday morning. Tuesday was spent getting permission to finish at college a few days early, packing my trunk for collection and delivery by freight rail and sharing a farewell dinner with the Morleys. I was sad to be leaving a town and a family which had welcomed and nurtured me for two years and at the same time I was excited by the potential the future held.

On Wednesday morning I settled down for the journey, catching up on sleep and reaching London early afternoon. I picked up a train from Victoria to Brixton, walking from the station to stretch my legs from the long journey. Averting my line of sight as I passed the bombsite of the previous week, I stopped for a few quiet moments in St Matthew's Church in remembrance of the people who died in the two V1 attacks I had witnessed. I looked forward to greeting my parents and Booty, perhaps visiting my grandmother later and getting ready for tomorrow's interview. It was a warm day and I chose the longer shaded route along the Rush Common strip of land, thinking of Bill in France as I passed the beech tree beneath which he had kissed me four and a half years ago and parted from me in anger two years ago.

Turning the corner into Water Lane I thought, *that's strange, there seems to be something odd about the road ahead*. People were standing in the road near the junction with St Matthew's Road and, as I broke into a run, a cold sweat enveloping me, I saw that the entire corner and several houses beyond it along Water Lane had been completely obliterated.

'Hey, stop there, young lady,' called a warden, stepping in my way as I ducked under the rope wound round stunted trees and poles surrounding the missing houses. I couldn't even make out the line of the front boundary. Before me lay a mountainous jumble of bricks, twisted and burnt metal, singed papers fluttering and a lingering smell of burnt wood and greasy, roasted meat. Several men were carefully testing the rubble beneath their feet as they prodded the ruins with sticks.

I stood trembling, disbelieving, my mouth working but no sound coming out, my small case falling from my grasp.

'Did you know these people?' the warden asked. 'I'm afraid there've been a few casualties. We don't know if we've got all the bodies out.'

'My parents. The second house along. *I can't believe it.*'

'How old were they? We got an old couple out from that one,' he said, pointing to the place where our home had stood. 'I'm sorry, they were goners.'

'Mr and Mrs Haywood,' I said. 'The middle flat was empty when I was here last week. Did you find a black and white cat?'

The man seemed taken aback that I should be concerned about a cat.

'We haven't got anyone else out yet from this end.'

'Who can I ask?' I persisted. 'Where can I go?'

'Town Hall.'

Ignoring his suggestion, I turned and ran back along Water Lane, clutching my handbag, my head shrieking, *No, no, no!* Left onto Brixton Hill, crossing the road, diving along Lambert Street and at the end holding my sides, gasping for air, right into Strathleven Road, only a few more yards to go, launching myself at the front door of my grandmother's house and banging, desperately banging, crying, clinging to the door knocker, the door opening and my grandmother standing there dressed neatly in grey, her long greying hair scraped up into a bun and her mouth a perfect 'O' as she beheld me half bent and snivelling on the doorstep.

'Mummy and Daddy, *they're dead.*'

There, I'd said it, and I broke down completely, curling over, holding myself tight and crying out in huge, empty gasps.

My grandmother, putting her arms round me, propelled me into the sitting room, saying, 'No they're not,' me crying hysterically, 'Yes they are,' and my mother saying, 'Pat,' and embracing me and holding me tight.

I looked up through a blur of tears. She was real, her warm breath on my face, her firm hands gripping me. The relief was so immense I could not stand and my mother guided me into an armchair.

'What are you doing here, Pat? I've already sent you a letter this morning telling you about the house and that we're all right.'

'We?'

'Daddy and Booty too.'

My grandmother disappeared and a moment later returned, depositing Booty on to my lap, who meowed and purred and kneaded his paws into my leg.

'Daddy's upstairs trying to sleep,' replied my mother to my unspoken question. 'He was at work last night when the bomb landed. More to the point, what are you doing here today? How could you have known?'

'I didn't,' I gulped. 'I've got an interview tomorrow so the college released me early. I wrote to you. You should have got the letter today…'

My voice tailed off.

I became aware of old Mr Torston examining me quizzically from the armchair opposite.

'Give the child a stiff tot of something,' he said, and my grandmother found a glass and thrust a generous helping of brandy in my hand. I disliked brandy but today it was nectar. As the slow warming calm spread I remembered the sweet feeling of my first cigarette reaching to the tips of my fingers and longed for one now.

To another unspoken question my mother explained that she'd been on a late shift at the Beaver Club last night and arranged to stay on in the shelter there. 'I brought Booty round to Nanny to look after before I went in to work. With these dreadful rocket planes falling I didn't like to leave him on his own in case he was scared.'

I cuddled Booty and let the grownups fuss around me, and my father came down to see what the commotion was about and I was so reassured to see him safe that I cried again.

'Poor Mr and Mrs Haywood,' I said, and my mother nodded.

'They'd just got them out when I got back from the Club this morning. Both dead, but not too badly burnt. At least they were fairly intact.'

'Adela!' said my father warningly to my mother, and I said, 'It's all right, Daddy, you know I was at Beechdale Road and then the Town Hall one last week. How about the neighbours in the other houses?'

'I heard the young boy in the one at the far end was pulled out alive,' said my mother, 'but I don't know about the rest.'

'You'll find out soon enough,' said my grandmother.

'Where will we live?'

'You'll stay here tonight,' said Mr Torston.

'Much appreciated, of course,' said my father, 'on behalf of Adela and Pat. I'll have to go in to work as usual.'

'There'll be no trouble getting somewhere else tomorrow,' said my mother. 'Plenty rooms around to rent with more and more people getting away to the country to avoid these dreadful new sort of bombs.'

'All your lovely things,' I said to Mummy, putting my hand on her arm, tears welling again. 'All your photographs and mementos.'

My mother sat on the arm of the chair, comforting me. 'My dear, we're all alive. Be thankful for small mercies. Did you bring any clothes back in your little case?'

'My case,' I cried, my hand flying to my mouth. 'I dropped it on the ground in front of the…' I couldn't bring myself to say 'house'. *Rubble.*

'I'll go round and find it for you,' said my father, and sped off upstairs to finish getting ready to go out.

'Don't worry,' said my mother, 'we'll get extra clothes coupons and we'll manage. There's plenty of furniture going in the second-hand shops nowadays, we don't need a great deal anyway. And some of our things and most of our books Nanny agreed to look after when we moved from West Norwood as we didn't have room for everything, so they're here.'

My grandmother echoed my mother's earlier sentiment. 'Count your blessings, my dear. Plenty of people've lost loved ones. We're the lucky ones.'

'You're right,' I said, feeling guilty. Right now my trunk was on its way with everything from Doncaster, my clothes, my books, my artwork. And my father would retrieve my little case with my photo of Jon and my most precious books. Including *Great Expectations*. And my multi-photo page with the two gaps. Grieving the loss of Bill's friendship I'd nearly destroyed my links with him as I had James' letters, but subsequent regret of having retained nothing of James stayed my hand. And I still had Booty, who shifted in my lap, made himself more comfortable and in turn comforted my soul.

# 14
# Official Secrets

Staff Sergeant Cooper told the group there was an errand he needed Jon to run for him. He took Jon to the door and, checking they were out of earshot, said, 'CO wants to see you at the double, Dorringham.'

*Strange*, thought Jon, *on a Monday?*

Presenting himself at the major's hut, he was shown to the inner office door by the lieutenant who, before opening the door, rolled his pale brown eyes and executed a slicing motion with his hand across his own neck.

*What have I done?*

The major sat with a sheaf of small handwritten pages in his hand.

Jon was not invited to sit and, with mounting horror, recognised Pat's flowing handwriting on the sheets.

'One of your young ladies it seems has a mind of her own. Unfortunately for her she doesn't keep it tucked away inside her pretty little head but sees fit to put her views down on paper for all the world to read. Further, it would seem that she has previously written to you in similar vein.' The major consulted the pages and Jon could see some red underlining through the thin paper.

'I quote,' continued the major, ' "I wrote to you last week about this and I don't mind telling you again".'

He looked up, his dark eyes piercing below bushy eyebrows, narrowed with exasperation.

'Bring me *all* the letters you have received from, ah,' looking at the signature page, 'Pat. My lieutenant will accompany you to ensure you bring all of them to me.'

Jon, reeling, took Lieutenant Sandys to his hut. Peter lounged on a bed, scrambling up and standing to attention as the lieutenant preceded Jon into the hut.

'Why aren't you in the instruction hut?' barked the lieutenant.

'Dicky tummy,' Peter responded, indicating the bucket strategically placed near the head of the bed and holding his stomach. 'Both ends, I'm afraid. Sir.'

'Take that tummy to the toilet hut and stay there until I tell you to leave. And say nothing of this to *anyone*. Got that?'

With Peter gone, Jon opened his bedside locker and extracted a bundle of letters neatly tied with string. Suppressing a tidal wave of anger he handed the bundle to the lieutenant who thrust it inside his jacket. Flicking his dark head, the lieutenant led the way.

Jon stood to attention while the major skimmed each letter. Tossing the last on top of the pile, he said,

'Where's the last one? The one to which she refers?'

Jon maintained his body language and facial expression of deferential puzzlement. That peculiar training in Scotland had its uses. How to kill a man with your bare hands, how to survive in the open living off the land for days on end, evasion techniques and, most relevant now, resisting interrogation. Ironic he was now benefitting from the last against his own people. *I wouldn't mind practising the first on the major now.*

'Well?'

'The last letter, sir, is, I recall, one in which she wrote about a play that she and some of her fellow students performed in the schools where they'd done their teaching practice, sir. A little light relief, she said, from the slog of revision for the final exams.'

The major picked up the last he had read. 'Quite. Written on the eleventh of June. It is now the tenth of July. A long interval. This latest letter suggests she has written in the meantime. Are you not surprised and a little concerned to have heard nothing from her in that interval?'

'It may be disappointing, sir, but hardly surprising. She's due to finish at her college about now and has been very busy over the past few weeks preparing for and taking her final examinations. I also understand her to be busying herself with applications for suitable jobs. Sir.'

'There's nothing untoward in *this* letter. Are you *sure* you haven't received one since? What's this reference to similar sentiments in her most recent letter, then?'

Jon chose his words carefully. 'I'm sorry I have nothing to help you solve the puzzle, sir. Possibly she wrote and the letter went astray.'

The major sniffed deeply and exhaled through his long nose. 'Well, let's hope to God the letter didn't fall into the wrong hands. This sort of sentiment could land her in a lot of trouble. More to the point, her landing in trouble could prejudice our mission. Forewarned is forearmed.'

The major stacked the letters from the bundle together and stood and thrust them at Jon, passing him the string.

'If the missing letter ever comes to light bring it to me immediately. That's an order. Dismissed.'

The major sat down and drew another pile of papers in front of him.

Jon hesitated.

'Sir.'

The major looked up from the papers.

'Her latest letter. Sir.'

'The gist of it is that her house was flattened by a flying bomb and she and her family are safe and sound, including, I gather, the cat, and can be contacted at her grandmother's. Oh, and she's rescued a Jack Russell that belonged to a dead neighbour called Monty. The dog, not the neighbour. You have her grandmother's address? Your next letter to her will, of course, be read by our censors in the usual way as will all subsequent letters to and from her. Dismissed.'

Heart thudding with the effort of retraining his anger at the major's cavalier attitude to Pat's distressing news, Jon made his way back to the instruction hut, retrieving Peter from the latrines and returning him to the bunk hut on his way. 'Sorry to be a bit cloak-and-daggerish, old chap,' he answered casually to Peter's *'What the fuck was that all about?'* 'You know they carry out searches in our absence? No? Oh, well, they do, to check no one's concealing any of the stuff we do ready to hand over to enemy agents. I know, it's laughable, isn't it? They decided to check me out because they heard I've taken up smoking recently and wanted to check out my cigarette packet in case I'm using that to conceal secret formulae. Are you all right?'

By now Peter was clutching his stomach, doubled up on his bed with laughter. 'You, a secret agent for the Jerries? A cigarette packet for espionage? Ha, ha. The only thing secret about you is keeping each of your girls in the dark about the other. Ha, ha, ha. Can't wait to tell the others.'

'Don't say anything, you idiot. Lieutenant's orders, remember.'

*Thank God for cigarettes*, thought Jon, as he resumed his seat in the instruction hut. Cigarettes meant matches and lighters, which meant a concealed burning of an incendiary letter. *What on earth did she think she was doing, writing to me like that the first time, let alone a second? However much I sympathise with her distress, she was crazy to put any of it down on paper. Thank God the censors have only been checking at random, at least until now.* He longed to see her, to chastise her, to embrace her, to kiss her, to… *don't go there*, he thought, shifting in his seat.

A few days later they were given weekend leave and Jon was again in the major's office.

'In the light of your young lady's views you are forbidden see her this weekend. Don't alert anyone you know to your presence in London in case she tries to see you. Here's the address where you'll be staying. Remain there and do not go out except to collect the reply. Your food will be provided.'

The major passed him a piece of paper. It was an address in Islington. 'Memorise it now.'

He gave Jon half a moment, then put his hand out for the paper's return. 'You've been trained to avoid being followed. If you are, lose them before you reach this address. Oh, and your young lady and her family are being watched. I don't want any report that you approached her or them. Your task is to deliver these papers and return with the reply. Your usual cover remains in place as far as the rest of your team are concerned. Lie to them as to your movements this weekend as necessary. Here's your vest and envelope.'

On his return the major, instead of dismissing him on the doorstep, invited him into the hall. Ripping the envelope open, the major extracted a bundle of what looked, from Jon's angle, like photographs with a top sheet which the major scanned briefly. He looked at Jon, suppressed excitement dancing in his eyes. 'They've got one. It's on its way. Good work. Say nothing as usual. Dismissed.'

In the early hours of the following Tuesday morning Jon was awakened by a hand shaking his shoulder and a 'Ssh!' from the major. In the dim light from the stove he saw that the others were being similarly roused by Lieutenant Sandys and Staff Sergeant Cooper and being gathered together in the centre. The major whispered to them, 'Bring your notebooks. Go quietly to the guard hut and don't speak to anyone when you get there. We're officially on a searchlight and AA training exercise but I'd rather we don't make a fuss about our departure.'

Pulling on his uniform, stumbling with the others as silently as possible to the toilet block on the way, Jon reached the guard hut.

'The truck's outside and ready,' reported the staff sergeant to the major, who spoke briefly to the guards and led the group to the truck which they boarded in silence. In the gloom of the pre-dawn they looked questioningly at each other. When quizzical glares lighted on him, Jon shrugged and held his hands outwards, as if to say, 'No idea, mate.'

He wondered whether this surprise outing related to the

papers he had delivered on Sunday. Certainly the major had the same air of supressed excitement about him now. The canvas sides of the truck were brought down and fastened and the lieutenant secured the rear from the outside. The major disappeared too, presumably, thought Jon, to take his place in the front, as first one then the other door closed as quietly as a truck with doors that needed slamming could.

'Fookin' pris'ners, we're like fookin pris'ners.'

'Ssh, Bob, shut yerr gob,' hushed Graham ironically.

The truck picked up speed and further speaking was difficult above the road noise. The journey seemed interminable, the inside of the canvas quickly heating with the rising sun on its left side. Nearly four hours passed and Jon reckoned at thirty to forty miles an hour at best they would have travelled perhaps a hundred and forty miles. Somewhere in the South Midlands, he guessed. The truck drew to a halt and the rear flap was untied. Blinking in the bright sunlight the group quickly descended.

Bertie groaned. 'What's this, a field in the middle of nowhere?'

'Quiet, men,' hissed the major, rounding the rear of the truck. They looked at each other, bewildered.

'Piss stop,' announced the lieutenant, and Jon realised that he must have been the driver. *This expedition must be extraordinarily secret for no driver to have been provided with the truck and for a piss stop in the middle of nowhere.* He'd have expected to stop at one of the army camps dotted around the countryside, many unoccupied except for minimal ground staff now that the main army was fighting on the continent.

'Rations,' said the lieutenant, and he produced bottles of water and foil wrapped packs from a box under the passenger seat and these were passed round. The land was undulating, the truck hidden in a slight dip off a track shielded by a copse from the main road about half a mile distant.

'Ten minutes,' said the major.

'No toilet paper,' grumbled Peter as they made off into the

little copse. 'I promise you I am *not* going to eat my pie then dump in the tin foil and take it away with me like we were taught in Scotland. Just wipe off with leaves and bury it. Don't want anyone stinking us out when we get back in the truck.'

'You're a reet one ter talk wi' yer bucket and the runs,' said Bob.

'What *was* the point of all that training we did in Scotland?' queried Stephen.

'Waste of time,' muttered Bertie. 'We never go anywhere or do anything, just spend all day in that bloody hut.'

'Pointless, quite pointless,' agreed Graham.

*Little do you know*, thought Jon.

Finishing their dry meat pastries and quaffing water, they reassembled on the truck. The major walked to the rear and stuck his head in under the cover.

'Now listen chaps, just to remind you all that you've signed the Official Secrets Act and *everything* you see or hear today comes under its aegis. Under *no* circumstances are you to discuss anything of today with anyone, including your early start or your return. I don't want any hint from anywhere that you did anything other than a routine training exercise today. Understood?'

'Sir!'

More interminable traversing of the countryside ensued and Jon dozed as the heat rose again under the canvas.

About two and a half hours after their piss stop the truck came to a halt. There were sounds of voices, footsteps, barked orders, the truck moving slowly forward, stopping, more kerfuffle and the truck drove on a short way. It halted, reversed, stopped, the lieutenant untying the rear canvas, and the men staggered down. Ushered through a nearby small door to the rear of a large square building, Jon heard distant sounds of aircraft taking off and circling.

Inside the mini-hangar white coated figures were assembled around a long, covered object rising several feet off the ground. *Doctors?* wondered Jon. *Scientists?*

One of them hastened to greet the group, taking the major on one side and, after a hurried conversation, turned to the rest of the men.

'Welcome, gentlemen. We don't exchange names here. You're privileged to see this today. We've reassembled it from the several larger component parts we received early this morning. Part of our research is in the way we will now dismantle it completely to assist us in understanding exactly how it works and to assess its overall effectiveness. It's hoped that seeing it today will assist you in your valuable calculation work in countering its threat to our nation. You may take notes but memorise as much as you can as any notes you take will be destroyed before you leave here.'

The remaining white-coated men were grouped around the object, tarpaulins laid out beneath its base, toolboxes scattered nearby. Three very senior armed forces officers and a couple of pinstripe besuited officials also stood nearby. Their greeter stepped up and the cover came billowing down.

The creature lay on a wooden platform frame, the central planks removed to take the depth of its belly. Its tip a dolphin nose, bisected by two tiny rectangular shaped propeller-like protrusions. The nose widened sleekly to a sightless head bolted to its body by a necklace of metal rivets. A small panel, perhaps six inches by nine, lay beyond, slightly out of alignment, a screw in each corner. Its body was bisected by square-ended rectangular wings deepening in shape which narrowed sharply like a pair of horizontal elongated teardrops. Its underbelly was uneven and dented, witness to the belly flop of its premature landing.

Towards the rear of its gradually tapering body perched its snub-nosed offspring, whose single nostril flared around a metal grill like a blind deep sea creature's mouth ever ready to suck in and devour its airy sustenance, held aloft by two vertical metal struts affixed lineal to the metal body, connecting to the main craft's rear body and tail. Steadying the main craft were two tail wings, younger siblings of their larger central counterparts.

Encouraged by their host, Jon and the others walked slowly round, Jon judging the length to be equal to four men laid end to end. While far too small for an operational aircraft, it was bigger than he had expected, having imagined something more akin to a large toy plane or the RP-3 rockets built for fighter-bombers currently over German-occupied France. This was something quite beyond his imagination and he thought of Pat's description in the letter he had burnt, not at the time quite believing that she had seen such a small object from such a distance, and now he understood why and also understood the traumas she'd suffered at the hands of this creature's siblings, and he felt an overwhelming urge to pick up the sledgehammer lying across the top of one of the tool boxes and bring it down with all his might onto the creature, down, down, down again, destroying, annihilating, smashing Hitler's evil metal ambassador into tiny irretrievable pieces.

'Jon?' said Peter at his elbow and he refocused, calming his breathing, stilling the trembling in his arms.

'Unbelievable,' said Jon.

'I know what you mean. Put a window in the cockpit and it could be flown by a bunch of pygmies.'

Jon became aware of the general hubbub dying down and stood attentively as the chief scientist stepped forward with a screwdriver raised aloft and, with a magician's flourish, unscrewed the small panel just beyond the creature's neck. Peering in, they saw the cavity, denuded of its deadly cargo.

'The warhead would contain, we believe, two hundred and thirty-seven pounds of high explosive.'

Signalling to two assistants to detach the head from the body by removing the ring of iron bolts, the chief scientist waited and, when the decapitation was complete, continued.

'Here,' pointing with the long screwdriver to the inside of the nose, 'the master compass which we believe controls the course that is set. This,' pointing to the propeller-like object, 'is the counter which drives a shaft and a set number of revolutions will determine the point at which the bomb is pushed into its final dive.' He paused for further dislocation.

'Electrically fired detonators,' moving to the rear section by now also removed, 'here release flaps in the tail which causes the rear of the robot to lift up, tipping it into a dive, at which point the engine cuts out and…'

'Thank you, thank you, most instructive,' said one of the pinstripes, turning to his counterpart. 'I think my colleague and I have seen all *we* need to.'

They bustled off in the direction of the small door. The chief scientist shrugged and continued with an explanation of the working of the engine, by now removed from its perch and gradually revealing its inner structure like a body opened up on an operating table.

Jon watched the entire dissection with a sense of awe and revulsion. Here before him was the very entity their unit was working so hard to counter by calculating the most accurate prediction the electromechanical analogue computer machine could provide. What he would give for the ability to create a computing machine that computed at a thousand times, a million times the speed. These creatures of destruction were not being caught by all the interceptions attempted, Pat's letters bore witness to that. But his unit's work so far had improved the calculating machines just in time for the onslaught. Had Hitler attacked with them six months earlier the result would, without a doubt, have been very different. The time bought by the RAF's annihilation of the Peenemünde research and development centre, and its scientists along with it, in August 1943 had been crucial in delaying the V1's development and given his unit time to work on improving the accuracy of the AA guns' predictors before the V1s were eventually unleashed.

The dissection and subsequent discussions with the scientists took up much of the day. Returning to the truck, Jon offered to help with the driving, but the major said, 'This research establishment is so top secret it doesn't even appear on maps. It's not advisable for you to know where it is. But I appreciate the offer and might take you up on it after a certain point.'

A kip in the back of the truck despite its rumbling and jogging, or perhaps because of it, and Jon was ready to take over for the last leg of the journey, the lieutenant mumbling his thanks as he crawled over the tailgate onto the floor and promptly fell asleep.

'Stay on this main road north,' the major said, 'and let me know when we get to the outskirts of Manchester.'

The major also settled back in his seat and was snoring gently within a couple of miles. Jon found the driving soothing, taking him back to his early days in REME of being taught to drive and taking turns with his army mates in driving round South Wales. Such a long time ago that seemed. His thoughts meandered. Just over two years now since Pat had become his girl, and he could probably count on the fingers on one hand how many times they had been together since. Months since he'd last snatched a partial weekend in Doncaster. At least no Canadian officers to upset Pat on *that* visit. Odd thing about Pat and Canadians. First that strange incident with the Canadian at the Leatherhead Fair and then last autumn in Doncaster the Canadian major staying over on his way with his men to Scotland. She seemed so scared. She could be such fun and her spontaneity was delightful; at other times she could seem so sophisticated and cultured. Yet somewhere in the mix was that little terrified five-year-old. What was it with her strange behaviour around Canadians? She'd mixed with friends and relatives of his from the forces and never seemed troubled by them. There were a lot of Canadian soldiers in the Leatherhead area while she was at school, surely she would have been used to them. A terrible thought struck him and he jerked the wheel in his distress, for her and for himself. Banging from the rear of the cab in response to the sudden movement brought him back to his surroundings and the major stirred and muttered, 'What's up?'

'Getting a touch dark and I thought I saw something in the road but was mistaken.'

The major sat up straight. 'Anywhere near Manchester? Ah, yes, I recognise this part of the road. Carry on for the time being, we'll pick up the Bury road in a little while further up.'

After a pause the major said, 'I've had a report on your young lady. The powers that be are prepared to give her another chance. Provided she stops expressing her subversive attitude in her letters. I'll be giving you permission to visit her. You cannot of course give away anything of what we do here, but the report on your trip to London last weekend was good so I'm prepared to trust you to do or say whatever you can to ensure there are no further incidents. I'm not a fool, Dorringham, and your attempt to protect her, while foolhardy, does you credit. And that's strictly off the record.'

'Thank you sir. Will do, sir.'

'Good. We'll say no more about it. Take this next right fork. Now, tell me,' he added as Jon steered the truck across the junction, 'what did you make of today? Was there anything of use in your work?'

'Yes, sir, very interesting day, sir. I've been thinking we should expand our calculations to take into account that thing travelling at a height of less than one thousand feet, sir.'

'Really? They've been coming in mostly at around two to three thousand feet.'

'It gets its current height from the launch ramps our air force has been taking out around Calais, sir. As we advance on through France and capture the rest of their bases there, for a while they could launch from Belgium or Holland, but they'll be looking for other ways of launching these things.

Seeing the beast today, I think it would be possible to launch them from large aircraft. The aircraft might fly in low, at, say, one thousand feet, maybe as low as five hundred. So these things'll also be low enough to defeat the calculating machines and the gunnery we have at the moment. Also, they arc down rather than drop straight. We need to refine our calculations, sir, and build even more delicate machinery to take into account these kinds of miniscule adjustments, and modify our gun emplacements. Our AA gunners only have a split second from radar clocking them to the firing and they could be wildly off beam if we don't think about these matters, too, sir.'

Jon wondered for a horrible moment whether the major was a plant to see how easily he would reveal secrets, but after a short silence the major said, 'You've made good points. I'll instruct Staff Sergeant Cooper to get your unit to concentrate on improving the extra low altitude and drop calculations. How soon could your unit produce new blueprints?'

After a moment's thought, Jon said, 'With all of us on it, perhaps two to three days, sir. We'd need to test our re-calculations theoretically from several viewpoints before we can be sure enough to justify having them made up for the practical testing.'

'See what you chaps can manage in the next couple of days. I'll arrange for the prototype's manufacture to be prioritised. Your unit's hard work over the winter meant our forces took delivery of a new generation of predictors in time for the AAs protecting our invasion troops from German fighters and bombers in Europe. Your unit's also done good work bringing the predictors in line with the lower flight levels of these rocket planes from their Calais launchings. But nothing stays the same and you're right, we need to ensure prediction right down to the lowest end of the range possible. Once up and running, we can use that as a model to update the predictors serving the guns in our own sea defences.' The major paused. 'Any more thoughts or questions, Private?'

Emboldened, Jon asked, 'May I ask, sir, how the flying bomb we saw today came into our possession? Was it one that didn't explode here or in France?'

The major hesitated.

Emboldened further, Jon joked, 'If you tell me, sir, you'll have to kill me?'

The major snorted. 'Those coming over here that we don't take out in the air explode on impact as they drop from a height. We owe this one to the resistance. It was a failed launching that the resistance got to first and hid from the search party and got smuggled out. Can't tell you any more than that. Except that there'll be many over here who'll owe their lives to these brave souls but will have no idea of the sacrifices made.'

Jon nodded.

'And,' added the major, 'I didn't tell you any of that, and that's an order. Or I *will* have to kill you.'

The major had an envelope for him on Friday, and a freshly laundered vest. Exhausted from working through most of Wednesday and Thursday nights with little sleep he slept the whole journey, waking with a start to check surreptitiously that the envelope was intact and that no one was following him.

Jon caught Stella at the Red Lion. 'Please, a word,' he said, 'I can't stay long.'

Outside, she said, 'Don't worry, I know. Pat's back in London for good. Margery told me. I told you, I wasn't looking for a commitment.'

'Stella, you're a brick. I'll never forget.'

Stella's face crumpled a little. 'Trouble is, you've rather grown on me. Stupid, really, but I'll miss you, soldier.'

Jon floundering, started, 'I'm sorry, Stella, I never meant…' but Stella cut him short, reaching up and taking his head in her hands.

'One last kiss, soldier,' and he did, hugging her briefly too, letting her go and stepping back, walking away with one last wave before he did anything stupid, even more stupid than he'd done already, and threw away everything he'd built with Pat.

'Bonham Road,' said Pat's grandmother on her doorstep the next morning. 'Number twenty-two.'

Jon hared down Lambert Road and left into Bonham Road. Knocking on the door and standing back, he saw Pat's face at an upstairs window, the 'O' of her mouth, heard her distant squeal of delight and within seconds she was hurtling out of the front door and into his arms.

Ten days later the new parts for the computer arrived. The staff sergeant opened the boxes in their presence, laying out metal cogs, shafts, racks and pins on the tables, tiny round cogs like serrated silver shillings, a miniature treasure hoard in his large hands. Members of the group picked them up wonderingly. 'Now all you have to do it fit them together inside that,' said the staff sergeant, nodding to the predictor at the far end of the instruction hut. The predictor stood brooding, bovine, its belly split open awaiting reinstatement with the new parts. Two feet high and three feet deep, it was no picnic basket, as, despite the lightweight aluminium parts, fully built it weighed in at five hundred pounds.

Two days later, hauling the re-built predictor with great difficulty under cover of darkness onto the back of a lorry, as the predawn light edged blackness into grey mist, they set off across the Pennines, crowded in around it, the staff sergeant joining the major and the lieutenant in the front cab. Again, no official driver, and the major's departure speech included an exhortation to guard the predictor with their lives.

Reaching an AA battery on the windswept Yorkshire coast north east of Hull, its regular crew having been given unexpected leave, the unit hastened to erect the predictor and connect it to the anti-aircraft gun and radar equipment, plugging it in with the huge long electric leads needed to wire it to the nearest electricity supply and waiting for the appearance of the trailer aircraft. The work of the predictor began. Warned by the radar equipment and programmed to respond to the second object and not the first, a low humming out to sea, growing gradually louder, heralded the arrival of the aeroplane, a rope, invisible from this distance, trailing some way behind it a cylindrical metal object, a mock up of the one they had seen. It would have given Jon great pleasure to see a real one taken out by the AA defences.

The tow rope was loosed, the bofors gyrated round in response to the predictor's instruction, the metal cylinder turned into a nosedive and booms rang out. *Christ,* thought Jon, *I wouldn't like to be that pilot. That's bloody brave. What if the radar or predictor got it wrong and instructed the gun to fire at the aircraft itself instead of the object following?*

The men cheered as the falling cylinder exploded before it reached the sea.

'Good show chaps,' exclaimed the major. 'Now do it again.'

The testing continued intermittently during the day, depending on the supply of trailer aircraft, and on into the long light evening. After a rota'd overnight sentry duty with short sleep snatched in the primitive mud-floored AA accommodation hut adjacent to the guns, Bertie grumbling, 'Survival training in Scotland last year was more comfortable than this,' final testing of the predictor the next day confirmed the successes of the previous day at different heights between two thousand feet and five hundred feet and at different speeds between two hundred and fifty and four hundred and fifty miles an hour.

Piling into the lorry for the return journey, longing desperately for his bed in the hut at Lowercroft, Jon was surprised by their driving due south and bunking down overnight at a lightly occupied camp on the outskirts of Leicester. They parked in an isolated corner of the camp and were put on rotating guard duty in pairs over the truck to ensure that no inquisitive soul had a chance to look at the object inside. At least there was tepid water for a shower the next morning and a chance to shave. Before they left they were briefed by the major.

'We're heading for the Essex coast. Some big names from the War Office with some of their American counterparts are coming to view a demonstration of our improved predictor at oh six hundred hours tomorrow. They don't have time to travel all the way up to Hull, so the mountain,' indicating the predictor, 'has to come to Mohammed. We're using a part of the Essex coast that's currently clear of enemy action, just a few flying bombs passing over the area last month but nothing so far this month. However, be aware that while you'll be operating guns as a demonstration you might be called upon to render assistance to the regular guns there. We'll be using the golf course guns just south of the town and our demonstration shouldn't interfere with the town or the people there. I don't need to tell you this demonstration's top secret as usual.'

'I know where we are,' said Bertie triumphantly as, following their arrival, they viewed the coastline stretching in both directions from the gun post perched on the sea wall. 'That,' pointing south, 'is Clacton and that,' pointing to a distant sea of rooftops dominated to its west by a huge water tower, 'is Frinton. We used to come down on holiday in Frinton.'

'What a small world,' said Jon. 'We came to Clacton for a week in August 1938. I remember it well because I couldn't walk anywhere far with my broken foot.'

'Shame we can't take advantage of a dip,' said Peter, peering at the mass of concrete blocks and barbed wire below. 'It's so hot down south here I just want to strip off and run into the sea.'

'Come on men, stop gossiping like fishwives and get on with the unloading,' barked Staff Sergeant Cooper. 'We're on our own again like in Yorkshire and we need to get it set up before sundown.'

The remainder of the day was spent setting up the new predictor. A guard duty rota covered the night and Jon was pleased to be given the first watch with Graham whose dry wit sparred with Jon's sense of the absurd, making the time pass pleasantly. Relieved by Stephen and Bob at midnight, Jon crawled exhausted into one to the tents they had erected earlier.

The visitors arrived promptly the next morning, having set out from London in two cars in the early hours. One Jon recognised from his photograph that had adorned the AA mess hall in Berwick, General Sir Frederick Pile, a kindly uncle type with a firm jaw and laughter crinkled eyes, the General Officer Commanding in Chief AA Command.

As in Yorkshire, the target towing aircraft approached from the sea, and, as in Yorkshire, the towed flying bomb mock-up was blown up mid-air as it curved towards the water. The general expressed his delight, and the major explained that a couple more test runs had been arranged to show that the accuracy provided by the predictor was not a fluke. 'The height and speed will vary but it's nothing we can't cope with.'

The next test run was as successful as the first. They readied themselves for the last.

The plane came in very low, too low for the predictor to calculate initially and Peter hesitated for just a second to realign some of the instruments. The plane was supposed to jettison its smaller sibling over the sea but it failed to do so, and Jon watched with mounting horror as the plane passed over land to the north of the town. It curved southwestwards. The tow rope suddenly separated and the mock flying bomb was released. The radar and predictor combined to bring the gun round so that by the time it fired it was pointing across open country to the west of the town. The boom of the fired gun echoed as its projectile sped on its way. The plane flew on past the water tower and disappeared over the western horizon. As the dropping silver target passed behind the water tower a starburst of water shot into the air, cascading down and obscuring the ultimate collision of the ammunition with its intended prey.

The official observers stood stunned, disbelieving, while the major ran to the communications hut to bark orders down the telephone, the lieutenant following in his wake. Bob leapt up onto the podium, slapping Peter and Graham on the back in turn, crying, 'Greet shot! 'Ow's that fer shootin'!' and Bertie caught Jon's eye and they snorted and gasped while Stephen shook helplessly. Staff Sergeant Cooper ran up to the gun emplacement ordering, 'Down here, down here at the double.'

Peter, Graham and Bob clambered down and the six of them stood to attention while they waited for the world to fall in on them. However, the general, justifying the esteem in which he was held by his AA and searchlight troops for his constant efforts over the years to protect and defend them from criticism, stepped forward and shook hands with each of the unit members in turn, saying, 'An *excellent* demonstration. Your hard work could make all the difference in our fight against this latest menace,' and, turning to Staff Sergeant Cooper, said, 'We'll be off now, please give my compliments to Major Spencer for a good morning's work. I see he's rather occupied at present. I'm confident he'll deal with matters in his usual efficient way. Tell him I'll do my best to ensure personally that mass manufacture of the components for this latest improvement will get top priority,' and ushered his open-mouthed guests towards the waiting cars.

'Right then, you lot,' harrumphed the staff sergeant, 'let's get this contraption unplugged before it can do any more damage and onto the truck. Jump to it and lively.'

They scurried to do his bidding, glancing all the while to the west of the town, where the waterfall was now just a trickle. The major returned, his lieutenant trailing, and told them, 'Had to tell the local constabulary top secret target training, Official Secrets Act and all that, and to ensure the locals don't talk. RE regiment is sending sappers from Colchester to repair the damage *tout suite.*'

The staff sergeant meanwhile retrieved binoculars from the lorry and climbed up to the gun emplacement. 'Don't think the damage is too bad, sir,' he called. 'Looks as if we just took the top off and a chunk or two out high up. Main structure seems to be mostly holding.'

Major Spencer looked around. 'Where is everyone?'

Jon leapt into the breach. 'The general said to tell you, sir, his compliments for a good morning's work and he expected you to deal with it in your usual efficient way. And that he'll personally ensure the prioritisation of the manufacture. Sir.'

As the French launching sites were overrun by the Allies' advance in the succeeding months, the Germans switched their launchings of V1s to sites in Holland and from Heinkel 111 and Junkers 88 aircraft, targeting the east coast of England. Word came to the unit at Lowercroft of the success of the new system in defending against flying bombs coming in at various heights including those exceptionally low. On one day alone, of the ninety-six missiles launched by the Germans, sixty-eight were destroyed by anti-aircraft guns, and only four reached the Greater London area. But mingled with the thrill of success was the knowledge of the damage being wrought from early September by the new V2 rockets aimed at Britain in addition to V1s. The V2s were truly the stuff of science fiction, launched vertically and flying at over three thousand five hundred miles per hour and reaching heights of more than three hundred thousand feet. The only answer to V2s was to hope and pray that the Allies would overrun the rest of the continent and take out the launching sites as quickly as possible.

Their work done, in November the unit was disbanded. Major Spencer called Jon to his office.

'I can recommend you for a place in the army's scientific division if you want it,' he told Jon.

'Thank you, sir, but I have a career waiting for me in civvy street when the war's over,' Jon said.

'And a young lady or two,' smiled the major. 'Thank you for all your hard work here especially for the extra travelling you've done for me. And remember, the Official Secrets Act still applies after you've left here. Good luck.'

# 15

# Truth

It was still dark outside in the early morning of Tuesday 6th February 1945 when the insistent knocking on the front door beneath my room woke me. Hearing muffled voices below I sprang out of bed. Jon! The clock showed a few minutes past six. My heart thudding, grabbing my dressing gown and wrapping it around me, I sped to the top of the stairs. My mother emerged from her bedroom and I shooed her back in with a hissed, 'It's Jon, Mummy, I'll see him. Go back to bed for half an hour before Daddy gets home.'

I looked down as Jon, in full uniform, completing his apologies to our downstairs neighbour who had let him in, pocketed his torch and ascended two stairs at a time, a look of determination on his face.

'Your posting?' My voice trembled and I felt slightly sick.

Jon nodded and indicated to move into the living room. We went in, turned on the light and Monty leapt up with excitement. Grasping Monty's collar firmly and muttering, 'Sorry old chap,' Jon ejected him and shut the door firmly behind us, took me in his arms, and drew me close. Monty scrabbled at the door. I heard my mother call him softly and the scratching ceased. I was sure Jon could feel my racing heart. His right hand stroked up and down my back and his left cupped the back of my head, warm and comforting. I melted into him, and asked, my voice muffled by his shoulder,

'Where?'

'Italy.'

I drew back a little. 'Thank God. Now Italy's virtually all ours at least you'll be hundreds of miles from the Germans.'

His grip tightened, and he leaned back a little too. 'I won't lie to you, Pat,' he answered, looking down at me with concerned, apologetic eyes. 'You know not *all* of Italy's ours? That Jerry's dug in with Mussolini in the far north? It's no secret there'll be a Spring offensive. Ever since I finished in Bury in November and returned to Cardiff we've been training for this.'

'Oh, God, no! They can't send you there.' Abruptly I jerked my stiff upper lip back in place. *He doesn't need my hysterics to be the last he remembers of me.* 'Sorry. When?'

'I've got ten days' leave. I got home about midnight, bunked down, and came over to see you as soon as I decently could. Didn't bother to unpack. Sorry I'm a bit travel-stained. I have to report back by oh six hundred hours on the sixteenth when they transport us south and we sail from Southampton on the seventeenth.'

His cupped hand drew my head back and he kissed me, long and hard, with a strange new urgency, flicking his tongue between my lips, conjuring a fleeting echo of a cigarette-scented kiss in sun-warmed crisp autumnal air. I breathed in Jon's familiar, if a little sweaty, scent and returned abruptly to the present.

'Marry me, Pat,' said Jon urgently, abruptly, pulling back a little from our embrace. 'Please marry me before I embark. We could get a special licence this week and be married by Saturday and then we would have a little honeymoon together before I go. I love you and I *want* you. If I *have* to fight, I want to go and fight for my *wife*. Besides,' he added, ever practical, 'if anything happens to me you'd be entitled to a widow's pension. It's the least I can do for you.'

I stared up at him, stunned. 'I'm sorry,' he said, a self-deprecating smile hovering. 'I don't have a ring to offer you yet. Too early for the shops on the way here. But we can rectify that as soon as they're open. Get a message to your school that you're off sick and we'll get it all sorted out today.'

I pushed away from him and sat down abruptly onto the settee. *What is it about servicemen on leave wanting to get married?* A vision flashed of James leaning forward on the chaise longue, jewellery box in hand.

'I don't know what to say...' I began, and with a bound Jon was on one knee at my feet, taking my hands in his.

'Say "Yes".'

I couldn't bring myself to say anything more, afraid of hurting the earnest boy looking at me with pleading eyes and hands held around mine in supplication. *But he's not a boy any more. He's a man and he wants what men want the world over and he knows he won't get that from me unless we're married. But I don't want to be married. Not right now.* Having imagined that Jon would eventually be sent abroad and on his return we'd get engaged, maybe marrying at twenty five, I was totally unprepared. My first teaching job since only the previous September. I wasn't even twenty one yet, and he wanted us to get *married*? And I banked on calculating a wedding date to coincide with a period. Pain I could easily pretend. But my last period finished only a week ago and the risk of discovery now was too great.

The door opened abruptly and my mother, holding Monty back by the collar, popped her head round it saying, 'I'm putting the kettle on. Jon, will you have a cup... Oh!'

Jon and I were a frozen tableau save only for our heads which whipped round in my mother's direction. For once my mother was utterly speechless. Her head withdrew and she retreated with Monty. The knob turned slowly and the door settled silently back into its frame.

Jon turned back to me.

'Please say yes.'

I was grasping at straws now. 'What if we, I mean, what if I, I mean, what if...' I could hardly bring myself to say more as we had never talked about the long term future, let alone

children. Everyone lived for the moment and I had seen the
result for war widows trapped in poverty with one or more
children in tow. For goodness sake, it had happened to Janet
from school, and she might have a gold band on her finger
but I'd heard on the grapevine that the tiny widow's pension
didn't pay all the rent or feed her two children. At least Janet's parents had some means to help her. Mine didn't.

I took a deep breath. 'What if we had a child as a result
and you were….' Pulling a hand away I fluttered it helplessly
in the air.

'Killed?' said Jon, baldly. 'Well, the little chap would
have you and your parents and a whole family on my side to
help you care for him. My parents should be able to spare
something to help out. And you would have something of
me with you always.'

'But I don't want just *something* of you, I want *you*. Please, I
can't bear to speak of it anymore.'

His face brightened at my words, 'I want *you*', then fell at
the rest. He scrutinised my horrified expression.

'What d'you mean? That you just want me around when
convenient to you, but don't want to marry me? We've
known each other nearly four years and been together for
nearly three of them. You're my soulmate, the only girl I've
met I want to marry.'

I looked down at his hands, the nails neatly trimmed,
and, yes, I believed him, I didn't doubt that was true. And
I knew that he was the only one for me. I had known it the
very moment I first saw him standing on the front doorstep
at Bill's house. The echo of words spoken to me a lifetime
ago. *I know you're the one for me. I've loved you from the moment
I saw you at my feet and picked you up off the floor.* And then it
happened for me. There could never be anyone else for me
but Jon.

'I can't.'

Jon saw me look down and, hearing my response, span away
and up, moving to the mantelpiece where he held on to it as if

clinging for dear life. His head dropping, he said in a low voice, 'I should never have come. Not right now. I just *so* wanted to see you. We haven't been together for ages and who knows how long I'll be away and whether I'll even come back.'

This was a downbeat, almost melancholy side to Jon I'd not seen before. He was usually so cheerful, finding the upside of any down moment, turning negatives into positives, comforting and cajoling, practical and prosaic.

'And damn it, Pat,' he added, with an angry edge, 'what's a chap to think? Your letters are full of loving affection and you've never given me any reason to doubt your feelings. Plenty of other couples get married on leave and at least the chaps have memories to go away with to keep them going, to give them something to fight for and come back for. Can't you give *me* that?'

I heard the anguish and bitterness in his tone, and exhaustion and fear. I suddenly felt humble that he was revealing a side of himself previously hidden. He had been my rock and my mainstay and he was as human and as vulnerable as anyone.

In that moment's silence I heard the front door close and my father's greeting to my mother as he ascended the stairs. Jon heard too, and he squared his slumped shoulders and pushed himself away from the mantelpiece.

'I'll go now. I love you, Pat. I'm sorry I was wrong to think of a future with you. You can write to me if you change your mind.'

*Give me hope for the future, Pat. I love you. Please write.* And I had written and he had flown to his death with my rejection in his pocket.

*Not again, no, no, not again, not with this one I* truly *love.* My overriding emotion four and a half years earlier was guilt, but now I felt a tearing in the very depths of my being, a chasm opening beneath my feet. As Jon moved the short distance across the room and reached for the doorknob I sprang forward and grabbed at his arm.

'I'll get engaged, yes, yes, I'll get engaged, please Jon, don't go, I can't bear to have you go like this,' I babbled. 'I don't want to hurt you, I love you too and I *do* want us to be married one day when this dreadful war's over and you're back for good. But if it will help you bear things while you're away, I'll be your fiancée and we'll get engaged now and we'll have something to look forward to while we're apart.'

Jon turned slowly as I spoke, a look of incredulous hope spreading, and I thought, *what terrible power love bestows and what utter vulnerability it exposes.*

Jon's arms came round me and we were lost in each other. His tongue pushed between my teeth and I felt a familiar thrill shoot down to my groin. As we surfaced I realised my dressing gown was dislodged and Jon's hands were inside it, feeling the contours of my body through my nightdress, one hand brushing a bulleting nipple and pressing on my breast. I melted against him, feeling his hardness against my stomach and caring not even that my parents' murmurings could be heard the other side of the door, but after a moment Jon uttered a mock 'Ahem', withdrew his hands and, with a raised eyebrow, carefully drew my dressing gown around me and fastened the cord.

'I'll get dressed,' I said, smiling.

'Sorry I can't assist you now,' Jon grinned. 'I'm looking forward to the day when I can. But meanwhile I think I need a chat with your father.'

With a 'Go on with you' flap of my hand, I extricated myself from the room, sidling into mine as Jon stepped to the living room doorway and spoke to my father.

'Sir,' he said deferentially, 'might I have a word?'

'Nice to see you, my boy,' said my father a little heartily, as Monty scampered around him, and I surmised that he was *au fait* with my mother's encounter with us in the living room earlier.

My mother scurried after me.

'Well?' she demanded, shutting the door and leaning against it. 'Was it what I thought it was?'

I suddenly felt overwhelmed and burst into tears.

'I don't know why I'm crying, we're engaged and I'm very happy,' I sobbed. 'He wants us to get married while he's on leave but, Mummy, I can't and I feel I've let him down. I said I'll get engaged because I don't want to lose him. I was so afraid he would think I'd rejected him and go and get k…'

I couldn't bring myself to finish the word and my mother for once rose to the occasion magnificently, not finishing my sentence either, but holding me, guiding me on to the edge of the bed and stroking my back until the storm had subsided, Booty all the while watching from the chair, his tail swishing.

'I won't pretend I don't know what's behind this,' Mummy said. 'One day you've got to forgive yourself. You're a young lady now and not a schoolgirl, and this is different for you, I know it is. I had only one true love and that's your father, and it's the same for you with Jon. Don't be ashamed that you can't love everyone.'

I looked at my mother with grudging respect. Her prattling and carping sometimes concealed gems of wisdom.

'Jon wants me to call in sick today.'

'Tsk, nonsense,' said my mother. 'When's he going away? In a week, two weeks? Plenty of time to get you a ring.'

'In ten days,' I said. 'But you're right.'

My mother broke out the sherry for a toast, which left me feeling a little light-headed so early in the morning, and insisted on Jon staying for breakfast. An odd engagement celebration, not quite what I had fantasised, but certainly memorable.

Jon insisted on accompanying me to work, even though it meant a tram and a tube, and he left me at the school gate with a promise, 'I'll be here all spruced up when you finish. Four is it? That should still give us time to get back and consult Sanders on our way home.'

Surviving gentle ribbing from some of the girls, 'Hey, Miss, is that your soldier man we saw?', 'He's *handsome*. Can

I have him after you?', I retreated to the staffroom at break time for a kindly interrogation by Rose White, an older lady who had taken me under her wing. I was later, towards the end of the school day, most surprised to be summoned to the headmistress' office. Miss Macey got straight to the point.

'I hear your young man's on leave with a view to embarking in ten days' time for the front and that you've just got engaged today.'

I nodded, wondering where this was going.

'You are aware that your contract allows for you to take up to three family days' leave and that can be extended by the headmistress in extenuating circumstances?'

I nodded again, comprehension dawning.

'Good. So the rest of this week you will take as family leave. I will expect to see you back here next Monday. Take Friday of next week as extended family leave. Is that understood?'

'Th… thank you, Miss Macey,' I stammered.

She nodded her dismissal. 'And congratulations to your fiancé,' she added, 'and best wishes are in order to you.'

Such generosity from one whose own hopes had been brutally exterminated by the trenches of the Great War was humbling. I sped off to find the Deputy Head and the others who would cover for me in my absence and pass them an outline of the next few days' forthcoming lessons. This delayed me a little and I was relieved to see Jon, now in civvies, waiting patiently for me in the main lobby.

I explained the day's developments and he brightened. 'How kind. Let's go straight to Sanders now, they'll still be open, and could we perhaps see my parents after that? I'll make sure you get home safely later. With only the partial blackout nowadays the journey after dark'll be easier. Also, I'd like to organise some sort of special family get together, our parents and maybe some of my aunts and cousins that are in London, perhaps for Sunday lunchtime?' He saw the alarm on my face at the thought of his wider family crowding into our tiny flat. 'Don't worry, my mother's already offered to host it and we can pull back the dividing doors between the sitting room and the back room, there'll be room enough.'

At Sanders Jewellers, nestling beneath the high railway bridge in the Brixton Road, I was brought up short. In response to Jon's request for engagement rings the jeweller brought out a tray of solitaire diamonds on gold bands.

'And we have, of course, a range of wedding rings that complement them. Here,' he added and, whisking a small jewellery box from a drawer behind him, picked out an exquisite solitaire and a matching plain gold band, and placed them in the box. I stared at a flashback of such intensity that I was rooted to the spot, unable to move, unable to breath. James, beside me on the chaise longue, eager, expectant, his hand holding the opened box. *If they don't quite fit, we can go back now or first thing on Monday and get them fixed.*

'Pat?' Jon's concerned voice coming from a distance. I must have swayed, certainly I felt as if all my strength had drained from me. The jeweller hastened round, grabbing a chair and I sat, feeing foolish and a little tearful.

'I'm so sorry,' I said, 'it's been a very long and,' trying to put on a positive face, 'rather exciting day,' to the jeweller's retreating back.

Jon squatted beside me. 'We can do this another day if you're not feeling well.'

'No,' I protested. The jeweller reappeared and proffered a glass of water. I recalled the imprint of *his* large, gentle hand around mine, and, averting my eyes from the glass at the end of the jeweller's outstretched arm, caught sight of a tray of dressy rings twinkling on a high shelf beyond the line of his shoulder. Intrigued, I stood slowly up and indicated the shelf's content.

'They're pretty,' I said, a little inanely.

'Ah, my platinum collection,' he said proudly, placing the glass on the counter. 'You have to be careful with gold you know, it can clash with certain shades of stone. A ruby, for example, can look a little overdressed with gold, unless what you want, of course, is a bit of pomp and circumstance. The best stone for gold is the diamond. Now, a solitaire diamond looks lost with platinum, but the silvery effect of the platinum sets off a ruby especially perfectly, although it works well for any coloured stone. You can complement the main stone, of course, with others, including diamonds. Shall I?'

I nodded for him to bring out the tray.

Then I saw the prices. 'Oh,' I said, unthinkingly, 'they're awfully expensive, even more than the others.'

'Well, that's because they're platinum,' said the jeweller. 'A more precious metal than gold.'

Jon was watching me carefully all this while. 'Pat,' he said, 'how many years do you hope we'll be together? Forty? Fifty? More?' I blinked and calculated. His grandfather was eighty-five. I laughed and said, 'If you live as long as your grandfather we're looking at sixty-five years. At least.' *Maybe I'll be too old by then to care about James.*

'Well,' continued Jon, with his usual unassailable logic, 'assuming you wear the ring every day, that's nearly twenty four thousand days, which seems to me a pretty good return on the cost of the ring now.'

He leaned forward and put his hand on mine. 'Choose the one that you want to wear for me.'

'What about a wedding ring to match, though?'

'We can do a platinum wedding ring to match,' the jeweller reassured us. 'They tend to be narrower than the gold ones, again because of the cost.'

'Choose the ring that *you* want to wear as my fiancée now and that you'll be happy with for the rest of our lives,' Jon urged again.

And so I did. A large ruby set in platinum with tiny diamonds around, a deep red sunburst that soothed my soul. A special ring for a special love carrying no memories of the past but speaking to me only of our future together.

The next day the mild, unsettled weather continued and we decided to brave the odd shower while retracing the steps of our early courtship, walking the streets of the City of London decimated in the Blitz. We made our way to St Paul's, symbol of British resistance, and, passing truncated ruins still sprouting weeds, we speculated what might rise from the ashes of the cathedral's fallen comrades. Jon envisaged a new, sleek, modern metropolis; I argued for rebuilding in a more traditional style.

After a silent, reverential, circuit of the inside of the Cathedral we stood briefly at the top of the steps enjoying a momentary glimpse of a pale, weak February sun on the side of our faces. I closed my eyes and breathed deeply, enjoying the feel of my arm in Jon's, a moment of quiet beside the man I loved. From my left came the sound of several footsteps, the murmur of voices and, suddenly, rounding the building a male voice said, clearly and distinctly, 'And here, fellas, is the front of Saint Paul's. Let's go on down these steps first and you'll get a better view. Isn't that just swell?' And I knew from the precise, melodic cadences that he was Canadian, not American, and I opened my eyes to see four or five Canadian army officers and a couple of Canadian airmen in peaked caps standing below us to our left.

Jon must have felt me jump and freeze at the first tones of the newcomers' self-appointed guide as he turned, looking down, frowning, puzzled.

'Pat, what's the matter?'

I couldn't bear the grief, the guilt, the subterfuge, the lies any longer, and, wrenching myself free, skidding round the corner to my right, I cannoned into a pillar on the north wall and came to an abrupt halt against it, burying my head in my arms and weeping desolately. *How stupid of me to think I could have my cake and eat it. I'm going to have to tell him, I can't go on like this. I can't ask him to take soiled goods. I'll break the engagement, see if he can return the ring and get his money back.*

Jon followed me, taking me in his arms, holding me tight

as I struggled briefly, speaking softly, desperately, into my ear, 'Pat, what is it? Tell me, you can tell me, please, let me help you, please don't cry.'

'Not here, I can't tell you here.'

Jon looked round. 'Yes you can. There's no one else here. Come, sit down,' and he led me to a low workman's bench that had been left against the outside wall. Crouching in front of me as I sat and wiped my nose with my hanky, he said in a low, urgent tone, 'Pat, I'm trained to be observant. I've noticed over the years that anything to do with Canada or Canadians triggers something in you. I sense your distress and fear. There were the Canadian soldiers at the Leatherhead Fair, there was the Canadian officer in Doncaster, and now this. I know these chaps here are Canadians, you can tell from their uniforms if not the accent. I've noticed you stiffen when your mother mentions the Beaver Club. You've tried to hide it, you can school your expression but your body somehow gives it away. Pat, *did something happen to you when you were evacuated to Leatherhead?* Before I met you? I know there were a lot of Canadian soldiers stationed in Surrey since shortly after the outbreak of war, even during the Phoney War.'

Leaning forward and gripping my upper arms in his hands, he continued,

'Pat, I love you and nothing, I repeat, *nothing* that's happened to you will change how I feel about you. Was there a Canadian soldier who pressed his attentions on you in ways you didn't like and you've never felt able to tell anyone? You're not to blame for *anything* that may have happened.'

I stared at him, mute. *He thinks I've been raped by a Canadian soldier, or at least sexually assaulted, and that I'm reliving an ordeal.* I looked into his cornflower blue eyes, brimming with concern, love, affection, understanding, and I thought, *I have to tell him the truth and it won't be what he expects.* I could have said no to James and I honestly didn't think he would have forced me. He was going to first ask me to marry him. It was *that* kiss I gave him instead, my unwitting 'Come on' kiss that was our undoing. And when I was saying 'Yes, oh yes,' because I liked what he was doing, he was asking my consent to enter me and he thought I meant 'Yes, oh yes, go ahead.' And in a moment of clarity I knew I *had* heard him ask and all these years I'd been pretending to myself that it was a misunderstanding. Willing and complicit, I had wanted James and I gave him my body. It wasn't fear or pain or non-consensual sex that had caused me to cry out... And then I had rejected him and he had died because of my rejection.

'Pat, where've you gone? Come back to me.'

*I'm plain wicked. I can't lie and say I was raped by a soldier because he'd not rest until I give him a name and what if I inadvertently choose the name of a real person?* The army taught Jon how to kill. I knew him. His pride wouldn't let him just walk away.

I refocused on Jon. He shifted on his haunches.

'Canadian soldiers,' he prompted. He moved his hands down to mine and gripped them. 'Look, Pat, we're going to be married. I'm going to be your husband, your closest friend, your partner, your confidant for life. We should have no secrets between us.'

I stared at him. Beyond him, perhaps twenty yards distant, a couple of office workers, probably secretaries, walked by, intrigued by the tableau we presented. Jon saw my line of vision shift and he checked over his shoulder, waiting until they had passed. He stood up, stretching his legs and drawing me up, perhaps to hold me while I confessed all into his shoulder, and said, 'Tell me your secret, Pat, there's a good girl, you'll feel better for telling me, I know you will,' and I was suddenly very, very angry. I span from his grip and hit the pillar of the Cathedral hard, several times, as if it were his face, hissing through gritted teeth as I struck, 'Don't. Talk. To me. About. Secrets.'

I turned back to him, rubbing the heel of my smarting hand with the other. 'Your mother let the cat out of the bag.

I've been waiting for you to tell me but you haven't, you hypocrite. I'm not the only one with a secret and you, you *bastard*, have never come within a mile of admitting yours.'

Jon, floundering, managed, 'What, what are you talking about? What *has* my mother been saying?'

'It's not just what she's said, it's what she *wrote*. You remember you were out of touch with everyone the summer before last? Your mother wrote to me that summer asking if I'd heard from you. She followed it up in the September by telling me you'd been home on leave and were especially friendly with someone called Stella who'd come round for tea. She wrote to me again after our October weekend in Doncaster telling me she was pleased you'd come to see me at last because your parents had *so* enjoyed your company the weekends, *plural*, in September and October you'd been on leave *and on the Friday of that weekend too*, and she was sure she was reading *far* too much into it but you'd taken this Stella out for the day and you'd been meeting her in pubs and she thought I should at least be warned by someone with my welfare at heart.

'Except,' I finished bitterly, 'I'm sure it wasn't *my* welfare she had in mind. She's always thought me too stuck up for you. She's dropped hints about this Stella since then. She's said you took her to the cinema. God knows what else you got up to with *her* when *I* was supposed to be your girl. Your mother said it's always good for a man in the forces to have someone to laugh with and not worry about. I know she was talking about you worrying about me...'

My voice trailed off.

Jon stood stock still, his eyes narrowing, calculating, fists clenching. My heart well and truly sank through the ocean floor to the chasm beyond. *He's going to tell me it's true, that he and Stella....*

'Pat,' he said so softly I could hardly hear him. 'I'm going to have to ask you to trust me. *Really* trust me on this, because I'm bound by the Official Secrets Act. The weekends I was in London and not with you, you weren't supposed to know about. My chums on the unit and my parents had to have a reason for my trips to London. So I made out to them it was Stella. I told my parents not to tell you about Stella. I shouldn't have even told you what I've just said. I can't tell you any more because I can't chance endangering you if it ever came out that I'd told you, quite apart from the trouble I'd be in.'

'So what does this Stella have to say about any of this?'

'Stella's a friend of my cousin Margery and we were just being friendly and spending a bit of time together while I was home on leave. She told me she didn't want a commitment. I haven't seen her for *months*, not since last summer.' He hesitated as if weighing his words. 'I used Stella as a cover for something top secret to do with the war effort.'

I was incredulous.

'I've never heard such a load of twaddle in my life! What could you possibly have been doing with searchlights that was top secret?'

Jon struck the wall himself, suddenly, with his fist.

'Searchlights! Do you *really* think it was *fucking searchlights*?'

Twice before had I unwittingly goaded a man into using that word in my presence.

'You have *no idea* of the danger you were in last summer with the letters you wrote to me about the buzz bombs. I had to break all the rules by destroying the first letter; the second the censors caught and passed to my CO. You and your family were watched. You were that close,' he held finger and thumb close together, 'to arrest. And by association that could have completely scuppered the work I was doing, trying to save thousands of people. And we *did* save them, and it doesn't matter that we won't get the credit, but it *does* matter to me what happens to *us*. And all you think I did at the School of Electric Lighting was mess about with *searchlights*?'

I realised that if a fraction of what he said was true I was putting him in real danger of incriminating himself. Struggling against the tide of emotion in danger of sweeping our relationship out to sea, I drew a shaky breath.

'I'm sorry, so sorry,' I began, and Jon groaned and grasped me, pulling me tight to him, oblivious to the two workmen who, approaching and seeing us in a clinch, stopped and, perching on a low, uneven wall across the way, lit cigarettes, watching the silent movie unfolding before them.

'I swear on the lives of our unborn children that what I have told you is true,' Jon said low into my ear. 'Pat, please, please, *please* believe me. I would tell you it all if only I could. God knows how guilty I feel that you and your parents were in such danger last summer and despite our efforts we didn't stop them all coming through.'

By now I was both puzzled and alarmed. I guessed he meant the buzz bombs. How was he involved in efforts to stop them? Afraid he might say something further that would put us in jeopardy, I stopped his words by pulling his head down and kissing him hard, passionately, possessively.

Hearing the workmen's cheer behind us Jon surfaced and, glancing round, grinned wryly.

'Time to move.'

Time for me to trust him. To learn what trust really means. My life a series of broken trust. My father failing to protect me from the monster of a bullying grandfather, my mother failing to heal my childhood traumas, exacerbating them with childish behaviour of her own, my grandmother moving away. Throughout my life constantly moving from one form of accommodation to another, both with my family and evacuation. Losing the close friendship of my lifelong companion to the creeping serpent of jealousy and losing my other best friend to the vagaries of family demands. Then Jon helping me face my demons, teaching me how to trust again. So, now it was time for me to trust his explanation. And now was the time to trust him with my ultimate truth.

As we meandered south and east, arms unashamedly

around each other, Jon added, 'Pat, I promise that in thirty years' time I will tell you *everything*. By then, none of this will matter. Will you do the same for me?'

'No,' I said, 'because I'm going to tell you *my* secret now. I don't want you thinking, speculating, worrying. You can't tell me *yours* now because you're right, whatever you were doing in Bury is still in the here-and-now and I presume you signed up to it and for you to say any more will put you and maybe others in danger.' I hesitated. *Do it. Tell him. Everything.*

I stopped and drew him to the low wall of a ruined building where we perched after checking that no one was nearby. I drew his hand up and kissed his grazed knuckles. 'You're right, I *am* jumpy about anything Canadian. I'll tell you why.'

I opened my mouth to continue. And knew with absolute certainty that I couldn't tell him. Ever.

And suddenly I knew what to say. *I know how to keep secrets. Stick as close to the truth as you can to avoid being tripped up later.* And it was the truth.

'I couldn't tell you.' *You manipulating bitch. I can't believe you're doing this.* But I was. 'I was afraid to tell you because of the Official Secrets Act.'

Jon was taken aback. 'What? What's that got to do with it? Why would an assault of that nature, or the Canadian soldier involved, invoke the Official Secrets Act?'

'I know it's stupid of me not to have told you before and and it's stupid because it happened nearly five years ago. I want you to know that I was *not* attacked or harmed by a Canadian soldier in any way. I *was* very scared by a whole bunch of them on Esher Common on my sixteenth birthday through no fault of theirs.'

Speaking low, I told him about my birthday picnic, leaving nothing out, not even the desperate trips made by the girls to the rear of the oak tree, at which point his lips quivered and I caught his twinkle and by the time I finished we were both holding our sides, eyes blurring with tears of laughter, whooping and gasping as we slowly recovered.

'Oh, Pat, you're so brave,' said Jon. *No I'm not, I'm a bloody liar. I've told you A truth but it's not THE truth.* There was no going back. I would never tell him now. 'It would've been jolly frightening having soldiers firing around you. I expect they were blanks, but you weren't to know that.'

'Was the officer right? About the Official Secrets Act? I've been so afraid someone will talk and next thing I know there's a knock on the door. There were nine of us. That's a lot of girls to keep a secret. They took our details.'

Jon put his arm around me, wiping his eye with his other hand.

'Don't forget,' he said, 'there was a sense of hysteria after Dunkirk. We might say with hindsight that Hitler wasn't going to invade the next day, but he did have a jolly good try with his air force only a few weeks later, and, of course, our army needed to have fresh troops and parachutists out on exercises anticipating invasion in order to practice dealing with it if it happened. With much of Europe now recovered by the Allies and it being just a matter of months, maybe even just weeks, before the war's over, it's easy to forget how desperately alone and in danger we were then. Obviously, you didn't actually sign up to the Official Secrets Act itself, so in that sense you weren't bound by it. Yes, the officer was right to read you the riot act then, secrecy about army manoeuvres was important. But now? It still wouldn't be *wise* for you to talk to anyone else about this, and I promise you my lips are sealed, but if it comes out, it really isn't anything you need to worry about, now the *purpose* for the secrecy of the practice manoeuvres has passed.'

I made myself relax against him.

'So,' he concluded, 'd'you think you can face our Canadian cousins with equanimity in future?'

I smiled up at him. 'I'll try.'

'Come on,' he said. 'We're near the Monument. If it's

open I'll race you up the stairs and after that we'll go and find ourselves a nice hot cup of tea.'

'It won't be open,' I said. 'There's a war on.'

But it was open, an elderly balding custodian, muffled up with scarf and heavy topcoat, at the entrance, grumbling when I expressed my surprise to him, 'It's hall these Ha-mericans comin' back hon leave. The City Council fort ter make a bob or two chargin' 'em but they're not hinterested. When you gets up top hall yer sees is ruins. 'Oo wants to look at ruins, I asks yer. I 'ardly sees anyone all day. Good job the wevver's bin mild, that's all I can say. No,' he waved us up, 'I'm not chargin' our own folks. Up yer goes.'

Casting an amused glance at each other we thanked him, and ascended all three hundred and eleven steps and emerged from gloom into the blinding light. I squinted through the metal cage a little to get my bearings and found the view as breathtaking as I remembered from childhood. I stopped a moment by the doorway as Jon moved forward and on round the corner and out of sight.

*This is the nearest I've ever been to flying,* I thought.

Suddenly, in my mind's eye, James was there beside me. *When this awful war's over I'll take you up and fly you so high even the clouds will look like dollshouses.* I stood, tears welling, eyes half closed, *forgive me, James,* hovering on my lips, a calm settling within me as his voice continued, *The person we find hardest to forgive is ourselves. I'll wait for you as long as it takes. For eternity if needs be. Go and live your life and be happy.*

Forgive myself. *I will not forget you but, yes, I will forgive myself and I will live my life. Thank you. So long, James. Goodbye.*

I felt his presence within me retreat and grow dimmer and fade and I was left with the whistling of the cool high breeze and the damp of tears drying on my face.

'Pat?' Jon reappeared to my left, having completed the circuit. 'Come and see the rest. Are you all right?' This last peering a little anxiously at me.

I wiped the last of my tears away, and, diving into my bag

for a clean hanky to hurriedly dab at my make up, I smiled. 'I'm fine. The breeze just caught me as I came out and made my eyes water. It's colder up here than on the ground.'

'Ah, there's a reason for that,' said Jon the scientist, and he led me around the top of the Monument gesturing to the view while explaining thermals and heat and cold air rushing in and as we reached the doorway again I pulled him back and kissed him hard and passionately, and, wrapping my arms around him and pressing against him, held him tight, smiling up at his startled yet pleased expression, and I led him down the steps and out into the warmer air below and on into the future that was waiting for us.

# Epilogue

'She's been asking for someone called James,' the short, greying-haired, uniformed manager Maureen said, bustling along beside Emily as they made their way along the corridor leading to Pat's room. 'She was very agitated earlier, demanding to see him.'

Emily frowned, vertical tramlines between her brows deepening below a layered creation of dyed autumnal hair. 'James? I don't know anyone called James. I'll have to go through her address list. I did her Christmas cards for her only a month ago and I don't remember anyone with that name. It wasn't my father's name.'

'I wondered whether James might be a relative who has died? Perhaps some years ago? As their memories die backwards in time a lot of people with her condition tend to remember the distant past and not the more recent.'

'I know what you mean. On my last few visits she's thought my father's abroad in the army, which was before they got married, and that my grandfather's at work and my grandmother's out shopping. Maybe her memory's deteriorated further. She doesn't have a clue about me.'

They reached the threshold of the room and paused. Maureen said, 'I'll leave you with her, though you have my number to ring me if there's any help she needs. I'll be in my office or not far from there. And there's always the emergency cord if it's really needed.'

'Thank you,' said Emily, turning into the room and gently closing the door. Shrugging off her enveloping black overcoat, her curvaceous, dark-suited figure emerged. Hanging the coat behind the door, she moved to her mother's bedside. Pat lay in the bed, thin wisps of white hair like dissipating vapour trails merging with the pale pink pillowcase, parchment skin stretching over high cheekbones and curving nose, her breathing harsh and laboured. Emily sat down in the upright chair beside her and took one hand into her own. *She's cold, I'll tuck her under the covers,* she thought. The movement brought a stirring and Pat's eyes half-opened. She muttered and Emily leaned forward, catching, she thought,

'Is he back safe?'

'Who, Mummy?' she asked. 'Who's coming back?'

'The sortie. Back safe?' Struggling to raise herself a little, looking around but not focusing, adding in a low, gruff tone, '*Bloody Eyeties.*' She turned her head towards Emily. 'Didn't get him after all? Back safe?'

'The sort of what? Eyes what?'

Pat fell back, exhausted by the effort.

Emily's phone rang. She grabbed her bag from the floor and pressed to answer, moving into the bathroom as she saw who the caller was.

'Emily, what's the score?'

'Oh, Alistair, thank *God* you've called back. Why didn't you pick up earlier? They think she hasn't got long, maybe just hours.'

'*What?* For God's sake, I'm at a bloody conference. It'll take me at least four hours from here. And I'm supposed to be speaking next.'

'Where's here?'

'Manchester.'

'For heaven's sakes, I wish you'd mentioned it when I spoke to you on Sunday. Alistair, this may be your last chance to see her alive. Come straight down.'

'I've only just bloody got here after a long drive up. I'll say my bit and then I'll come. Might get there around eight.'

Emily looked at her phone. Thirteen fifty-two. Would eight be in time? She put the phone back to her ear.

'Alistair, who's James? She's been asking for someone called James.'

'How the fuck should I know? Maybe she has a secret lover.'

'*Alistair!*'

'Got to go.' Alistair sighed. 'I'm too old for this sort of thing. Roll on next year.'

'Oh, stop complaining. I'm having to work past retirement age. Just come before it's too late.'

Putting her phone back in her bag, Emily slipped back into the room. Retrieving her mother's hand she asked,

'Who's James, Mummy? Can I contact him for you?'

'Beaver Club.' Pat drew a hoarse laboured breath. 'B. He'll get it, he'll come back. Tell him sorry, so sorry.'

'Beeva Club? Bee what? Sorry about what?'

'Love him. Must tell him. I will. Marry. Then he'll come.'

Trying to raise herself again, legs working under the soft duvet, heels digging, frail hands and arms flailing, increasingly agitated.

'Mummy, please, lie back.'

Crying out, lips drawn back in a grimace of anguish.

Emily grabbed the cord and pulled. A moment later a care worker appeared, a tall, sinewy young man with short-cropped sandy hair, in a soft blue uniform. Emily recognised him from previous visits. His badge said *Marc*.

'There, there, Pat,' he soothed. He turned to Emily. 'I can call Maureen and the pharmacist. I believe you've already consented to a sedative if needed?'

'James.' Pat spoke loudly and clearly, focusing on Marc and stretching an arm, reaching out to him.

'She's taken to calling me James,' Marc said apologetically to Emily.

'You're here.' Half whispering. 'You're back.'

Moving round to the other side of the bed Marc took Pat's

hand. She beamed up at him, agitation abating, striving ceasing.

'You make a pretty good sedative,' said Emily, smiling her thanks.

Marc, perching on the edge of the armchair, leaned forward and stroked the hand he held.

'James is here,' he said.

'Safe?

'Yes.'

Pat's eyes closed and she sank back onto the pillows. Marc sat for a while until satisfied Pat was dozing again and, extricating his hand, rose and moved towards the door.

'Just let me know if she needs me again. She's such a lovely lady. She was so independent and determined to do things her own way when she first came here.'

'Yes, that just about sums her up,' smiled Emily.

'A cup of tea? I'll get one sorted for you.'

Emily pulled a small notebook from her bag and balanced it on her knee. *I must write down her last words for Alistair. I know what he's like. If she goes before he gets here he'll be devastated and jealous I was here and he wasn't.* She wrote, 'James. Sort of back. Bloody eyes didn't get him. Safe. Beeva Club. (Or is that BEVA, maybe an acronym?) Bee. Loves him. She will. Marry (?!). Come back.'

Emily read her precis through several times. It made no sense. *Mum loved Dad. So who is this James Bee? Does it matter? She's rambling. I've read people at this stage can have hallucinations with the reducing oxygen to the brain.*

A different care worker, short, dark, Filipino probably, brought a cup of tea and some biscuits.

Emily had never sat waiting for someone to die. Her father's death nearly twenty-five years earlier in a car accident, a heart attack at the wheel, had been shockingly sudden. Edgy and a little nauseous she busied herself changing the flower water and tidying tidy surfaces. Squatting beside the low bookshelf she extracted the battered cardboard photograph albums and, piling them on the small table beside the armchair on the far side of the bed, slowly went through them. She had loved looking at these when a child. *Here are the early ones of Mum and Dad together in a small back garden. Brixton. 1944. Mum's looking up at him like there's no one else in the world. You wouldn't think there was a war on. Oh, there's Monty with them in this one from 1945, Dad must have been on leave, maybe from when they got engaged. I vaguely remember Monty. I must have been only about four when he died. He would've been a very old dog.*

Emily immersed herself in her father's army service abroad and on to the honeymoon photos, Mum in smart clothes the first few days then a two-piece bathing costume she had made herself, very daring, and here were the photos of the later cramped two bedroomed terraced house in Hounslow she remembered from her own childhood. *Now where are her wedding photos? Ah, here. Dad beaming, Mum looking a little coy. I remember her once telling me she was on a period when she got married but that didn't deter Dad!*

Pat lay still, breath rasping, hands occasionally twitching.

'It's okay, Mummy, I'm here and Alistair's on his way.'

Emily had read somewhere that the last sense to go was the hearing. *How can anyone know that?* she wondered. A Monty Python-like vision of a group of market researchers canvassing corpses in a mortuary with inane questions like 'And what was the last of your senses to stop working? Was it (a) touch (b) sight (c) smell (d) hearing (e) common?' assailed her. *God, I have a sick sense of humour,* she thought, *and not sick in the way Luke means when talking with his friends.*

Luke, her eleven-year-old grandson. *Oh God, I'd better phone Malcolm and let him know.*

Emily rang her son, speaking in a low voice in the bathroom, an ear on her mother's breathing. Malcolm offered to leave work early and come over to sit with her and she hesitated, but thought, *Alistair'll be jealous. He's always resented me having a child when he hasn't. It'd better be just him and me here.*

Assuring Malcolm she was fine and would call him when she had any further news, she rang off and returned to the armchair. She searched older family photos but saw only the familiar faces of remembered friends and relatives who had gone before, including one of her mother aged about ten, arms entwined with her friend Bill. *I know Daddy met Mummy through this Bill. Maybe this James was a friend of Bill's?*

Pat became a little agitated as the afternoon wore on but this time Emily could not make out her mutterings. Supper came and she was offered her mother's meal for herself, which she accepted pragmatically. *I could be in for a long night. At least being on my own since Chris shat on me and left me for that Sharon bitch I've no one at home to worry about. Bastard!* Her mind wandered around her marriage break up and her recent move to a flat while Pat lay breathing slowly and twitching occasionally.

Around ten minutes to seven Marc returned. 'I've nearly finished my shift for the day,' he said. 'We'll be doing the handover soon. I thought I'd pop in and see Pat first.'

Sitting on the chair and leaning forward, Marc said, 'Pat, I'll say good night now.'

Pat half-snorted, drawing breath, and suddenly half-sat up, her eyes opening and moving as if reading off a sheet of paper. Enunciating as clearly as if she was addressing an art class, she said, 'Group Captain James Alistair Bonar.'

Turning her head, her eyes focusing on Marc, her hand reaching for him, a beaming smile lighting up her face, she added softly, 'You came back. For me. They didn't get you after all.'

She breathed in again and exhaled, sinking back, her turned head resting on her right shoulder, her hand falling gently like an autumn leaf. Emily sat frozen, waiting for the next laboured breath that never came. Marc leaned forward, feeling for a pulse, placing the back of his hand above Pat's mouth. 'I'll get Maureen,' he said.

Emily moved forward, placing her hand on the nearest

shoulder. 'God Bless you, Mum,' she said loudly, in case there was any residual hearing left, and, sinking back down into the armchair, gave way to tension-released weeping, where Maureen found her.

'Can I wait with my mother for my brother to arrive?' *Oh God, he's bound to want to know the rest of her last words.* Feverishly Emily scrabbled in her bag for her notebook and wrote them down verbatim.

Alistair, 'God, that *bloody* M25!' found her sitting quietly beside the dead body of their mother.

They wept, hugging each other, distant indifference transformed by mutual grief. The storm subsiding, Emily said,

'I asked them to hold back on ringing the undertaker until you got here.'

'Did she ask for me? Was she upset I wasn't here?'

'She didn't even seem to know that *I* was here.'

'Didn't she say *anything*? You mentioned something on the phone about asking for someone.'

Emily picked up the notebook and handed the opened page to him silently. Alistair read her brief notes.

'My God. *Alistair,*' he read out loud.

'I know. I've thought about little else since. Is that where she got your name from?'

Alistair looked up. 'It could be. When I was a kid I used to complain about having a name that was unusual amongst the Peters and Davids and Johns around me. She said I should be proud of it, that she chose a Scottish name because of the Clan Graham connection. I thought she meant Grandma Dorringham's Scottish paternal line which was Clan Graham. But my family history research never threw up an Alistair on the family tree to name me after.' Returning to the notebook, 'How *extraordinary.*'

Later, back at Emily's flat, Alistair googled the name on Emily's laptop and gave an exclamation that brought Emily running from the coffee maker in the kitchen.

'How *extraordinary*!' exclaimed Alistair again. 'Look, here's an airman on some obscure Canadian World War Two website with exactly the same name who died over the North Sea in November 1940. He was,' Alistair added, peering at the screen, 'a group captain. Downed by, of all things, a bomb from an *Italian* airplane.' Alistair swivelled his head round. 'I didn't know the Italians took part in bombing sorties.'

'*Sorties*,' said Emily, looking down fondly at her younger brother's thinning grey hair, his jowled face, his profile so like their mother's. She picked up her notes. 'Mum must have said *sortie*. I thought she said "sort of", but she was saying sortie.'

'And not eyes,' said Alistair, pulling the notebook back, pointing, 'but Eyeties. I remember Grandpa Roberts called the Italian prisoners of war who worked at the bakery "Eyeties".

'Perhaps she was remembering reading about this,' he deduced, returning to the screen. 'She could have just had some memory of this incident, then got it muddled with Dad, so her words about loving him could have been about Dad.'

'We'll never know,' said Emily, returning to the kitchen and bringing in two cups of coffee and a plate of hastily prepared ham sandwiches. 'Look, I need to ring Malcolm. Will you stay here tonight? If not, I might go to Malcolm's.'

'I'll put up in your spare room, if that's all right with you. Don't know if I'll sleep tonight. Want to get to the bottom of this.'

While Emily disappeared into her bedroom to ring Malcolm, Alistair typed in Beeva Club and was asked 'Do you mean Beaver Club?', tried that and got an invitation to join the most junior section of the boy scouts. But on her return he crowed triumphantly.

'Tried Beaver Club World War Two and look what I've found. The Beaver Club was set up in London in 1940. For Canadian servicemen. There are even photos of them playing billiards and chess, and here's one of a guy asleep in an armchair. Maybe Mum worked there and met the guy there.' Looking up, he added, 'I'm sure I remember Grandma Roberts talking about working at a Canadian club during the war. This must've been it.'

'I think we're in danger of making too much of this,' said Emily doubtfully. 'She was fifteen when the war broke out and would've been only sixteen when he died. This guy's a group captain. I don't know exactly where *that* is in the pecking order but I'll bet he wasn't exactly a spring chicken.'

Alistair swivelled back to the screen. 'Mum was named after a man her grandmother loved but never married. I wonder if she named me after *him*,' pointing to the screen. 'I'll see what else I can find out.'

'No, we've done enough for today. We've got a whole stack of things to do and people to tell tomorrow,' Emily insisted. 'Come on, eat up and I'll sort out the spare bed for you.'

The next few days passed in a blur of activity, organising compassionate leave, registering Pat's death, sorting her belongings at the home, arranging the funeral, and arranging to see the solicitor about Pat's Will. The day after the funeral they sat in an elegant conference room on the ground floor of a Georgian building in Guildford. Petronella Moregrave ('What a wonderfully appropriate surname for a probate solicitor,' said Alistair to Emily as they approached the building), slim, thirty-something, dark and elegant in a black suit, was welcoming and sympathetic.

'I believe you already have a copy of your mother's Will,' she said. They nodded. 'I have, of course, got the original here, and also the codicil she made when her great-grandson was born.' Ms Morgrave fished the documents out of the file, which she showed to them, adding, 'I'm not aware of your mother making any later Wills or codicils but thought I should check you've found nothing else amongst her effects?'

Emily and Alistair shook their heads in unison.

'You've brought the ID I asked for?'

They produced passports and recent utility bills. Ms Moregrave said, 'If you would be kind enough to wait here,

I'll pop out and get the certified copies done I need. Meanwhile,' she added, drawing out a package from the file and pushing it across the table before she moved towards the door, 'I have something for you to look at while I'm gone.'

The package was an A4 sized brown envelope copiously sealed with peeling sellotape and marked on the front in Pat's handwriting, '*To be kept with Mrs Patricia Adela Dorringham's Will and handed to the Executors in the event of her death. Not to be opened prior to her death.*'

Slitting the top of the envelope with his pen, Alistair drew out a wodge of typescript perhaps an inch and a half thick sewn together by a thick thread woven in and out of holes punched into the left hand margin. Attached to the front was a handwritten letter in Pat's elegant copperplate dated about two years after their father's death. Emily shuffled her chair round the table so they could read it together.

*My Dearest Alistair and Emily*

*Perhaps my mother's insistence that I learn typing has paid off as I have spent the last year or so typing up an account of my War years and your father's secret war work. The current nostalgia for the Second World War seems to concentrate on the rich and famous and there are ever more books coming out that idolise Hitler in a macabre sort of way. I want to tell you about the ordinariness of life for the people that we were and the sacrifices made for the greater good. If you choose to destroy this when you have read it you are free to do so; if you choose to publish it and make a few bob you are free to do so also. I shall leave you to choose a title. I would just ask that you do not judge but rather see me as an ordinary working class adolescent girl struggling to make sense of a world run mad by war. I know I brought you up strictly. I hope this will help you understand and forgive. Please know that I loved your father with all my heart from the moment I first set eyes on him, I love him still and will do so to my dying day.*

*And I love you too my children, I love you to bits.*

*With all my love,*

*Mummy*

Emily said, 'I wonder if Dad was her *only* love, though. I never thought to ask. She always said she met Dad in the spring of 1941. Six months after that Canadian airman's death. Do you think she loved *him*, too?'

'Well, maybe now we'll find out,' said Alistair.

Emily, drawing the typescript towards them, began to read out loud,

# *'Prologue*

*There are always days in one's life that remain forever fixed in the memory. The first day at school, the birthday when the dream of a special toy came true, the day our dog Peggy arrived, the day my father learnt of his brother Barry's death in that evening's paper.*

*I am Patricia Adela Roberts and Saturday 2nd September 1939 was the day my war began...'*

# Author's Note

Storytelling by parents and grandparents of incidents and experiences of the Second World War was something of a family pastime as I grew up, often laced with humour and irony which masked the emotional toll wrought by the events. My research into the history of such events has brought with it a reality check of the truly horrendous experience for those who lived through war and for all who continue to do so in parts of the world today. To spend many consecutive nights cowering under seemingly endless bombing and emerging to claw through another day is a tribute to the resilience and courage of the human race. I have also been deeply moved by the dangers faced and sacrifices made by the armed forces of many countries.

War changes people. In this novel I have explored examples of the effect war had in compromising standards that would probably have been maintained in peacetime, such as the opportunity for cheating the rationing system or sexual licence arising from uncertainty about the future and fears for a loved one's safe return from combat. I have woven family recollections with other inspirational sources and my own imagination to create a work of fiction. While a number of events are based on real experiences, this novel is neither a memoir nor a biography. It is the fictional story of, as Pat wrote to her children, *an ordinary working class adolescent girl struggling to make sense of a world run mad by war.*

To avoid any confusion with anyone living or dead, all names in this novel are fictional, except for the recognisable historical figures of General Sir Frederick Pile, King George VI and Myra Hess. I have however placed these historical figures in my work of fiction and as such nothing I say about them should be treated as historical fact.

For further information about the background to The Keeping of Secrets and recommended reading visit my website www.alicegraysharp.com

# Acknowledgements

In drawing together the various threads with which this novel is woven I am indebted to many people and organisations for their help, information and advice (any error or omission is wholly mine!), including (in no particular order):

Clink Street Publishing's Gareth Howard and Hayley Radford and my editor Peter Salmon for their invaluable advice and guidance

Ryan Dunleavy, Head of Media Law and Reputation Management at McMillan Williams Solicitors Limited, and his team

St Martin-in-the-Fields Old Girls' Association, especially Elaine Whiston, Marie Cross and Denise Rooke

Mrs Beverley Stanislaus, Headteacher of St Martin-in-the-Fields, for her kind permission to use the extract from the school song

Sylvia and Graham Oliver Stewards at the Leatherhead Museum (which has an excellent Second World War room) and publications of the Leatherhead and District Local History Society

Mary Douglas and David Douglas for their advice on Canadian-English and Canadian culture

Richard Bowden and the Lancashire at War website for information about Lowercroft Camp

Tony Saville (son of the original Staff Sergeant Instructor of the School of Electric Lighting)

The staff of the Bury Reference Library

Alan Piper of the Brixton Society (who tells me that the dental practice is still there)

The staff of the Doncaster Archives

John Barter and Brian Jennings of the Frinton and Walton Heritage Trust

RAF Museums at Hendon and Cosford

Andy McNab whose talk and self-help books have been inspirational

My husband for his support and historical perspective

My wider family and friends for their advice and encouragement and for their faith in me in achieving my lifelong ambition.

CPSIA information can be obtained
at www.ICGtesting.com
Printed in the USA
LVHW051714260220
648289LV00005B/818